THE DRAGON & EYE GEM AFFAIR

BOOK 1 OF STILTS AND STUBS

by

A D Rider

Shadow & Steam Press

The Dragon Eye Gem Affair
Copyright © 2024 by A D Rider
Shadow & Steam Press
www.authoradrider.com

ISBN: 978-1737199960

Cover designed by MiblArt

Acknowledgement

I wish to extend my deepest gratitude to the
incredible women who assisted with this book. They
encouraged me to write it, listened to my endless
questions, and helped keep me on track. Without
Laura, Cat, Anisa, Mary, and Brittney, you would not
be holding this book now.
Thank you!

Dear Reader

This is not your typical romance.

The female is a statuesque staff-carrying fighter. The male is a diminutive, nimble-fingered thief who can't resist a pretty bauble.

The setting is an alternate Victorian England, where steam power and magic exist side-by-side in a world inhabited by non-human races.

The romance, to paraphrase my friend, is not flowers, chocolate and champagne. It is curry shrimp, hot wings, cajun gumbo and cold beer.

So grab your slingshot, pop a pear drop in your mouth, and prepare for adventure.

This book takes place in an alternate Victorian England, so it uses British English spelling and grammar. You have been warned.

Table of Contents

1. The Bakery Confrontation......................................1
2. The Abduction Infraction..8
3. The Powdered Deliberation..................................18
4. The Briefing Vexation..29
5. The Extrication Complication..............................35
6. The Recovery Remuneration................................42
7. The Juvenile Intermission....................................50
8. The Prosperity Potential......................................59
9. The Contraption Experimentation........................68
10. The Abduction Clarification.................................78
11. The Bathhouse Visitation.....................................86
12. The Audition Obliteration....................................96
13. The Library Exploration.....................................104
14. The Burglar Interruption....................................110
15. The Identity Ambiguity......................................118
16. The Apartment Infiltration.................................127
17. The Interrogation Flagellation............................133
18. The Gemstone Capitulation................................142
19. The Madam Deception.......................................148
20. The Constabulary Contention.............................154
21. The Nobility Consultation...................................161
22. The Apprehension Revelation.............................167
23. The Prison Extradition.......................................173
24. The Alley Excitation...180
25. The Negotiation Reconsideration........................188
26. The Invitation Contemplation.............................190
27. The Manor Convocation.....................................198

28. The Dinner Interlude...208
29. The Trophies Presentation......................................216
30. The Assignment Violation.......................................222
31. The Amorous Debriefing..228
32. The Identity Exposition..238
33. The Interference Confusion.....................................245
34. The Clockwork Intervention....................................252
35. The Faroko Obstruction..257
36. The Circuit Completion..265
37. The Resolution Explanation....................................275
38. The Pheasant Revisitation......................................282
39. The Partnership Proposition...................................287
40. The Bathing Reciprocation......................................295
41. The Final Consolidation...306
    Epilogue...315
    Races...319
    Characters...320
    Gravenmore locations...323
    Terms & Slang..326
    About the Author..333

Chapter 1

The Bakery Confrontation
Or Hands Off My Buns

"**S**TOP, THIEF!"

The warning shout from the bakery's owner proved unnecessary. Calista could plainly see a pair of young skembers sprinting toward her, a cob stuffed under each arm of one, while the other clutched a cottage loaf, almost as large as himself.

She had been hired to put an end to the repeated thefts of the shop, but she hadn't expected the culprits to be children. Despite their size, they dashed across the pine floorboards, easily dodging the early afternoon customers as they made a beeline for the entrance. *Here they come.*

Whether they failed to notice the statuesque faroko female holding a staff that nearly matched her own height or believed they could slip by as she moved to block the doorway, the pair slowed not the slightest. The youth with the cobs reached her first and attempted to squeeze between Calista's leg and the doorframe. Though he barely came up to her knee, she crouched to the left and gently scooped the small figure into the crook of her arm.

The second skember, a girl no more than nine going by how undeveloped her curved horns were, went for a seemingly unblocked route where only Calista's extended boot blocked the way. Her kind were expert jumpers, their goat-like legs able to propel them effortlessly. The relatively high hurdle would be simple to clear.

Oh no you don't! Before she could make the leap, Calista's staff came in with a low swing and caught the young culprit lightly in the stomach. The force carried through, sending the cottage loaf skittering across the floor and shoving the skember under a small table. An excellent stroke, likely earning her a few runs had they been playing cricket.

"Don't let them escape!"

The third thief, a male orv with a dozen breadcakes hugged against his chest, barrelled down on the trio as the shop's owner cried out again. With their thick bodies, single-horned faces, and thuggish mannerisms, orvs ranked among the more intimidating races inhabiting Gravenmore. This young one, slightly older than his mates, matched Calista's shoulder in height and outweighed the faroko by twenty pounds. He didn't need to jump over her leg or squeeze past her, even if she was unencumbered by his companions. His bulk and velocity promised to dislodge her from her position. Suddenly, the theoretical game of cricket became a rugby match.

But Calista wasn't a random bystander. She was on a mission to thwart this bakery-robbing bunch. This was their third bread-related heist in a week, and the shop's owner, another female faroko by the name of Zusa Lolly, found herself at her wit's end. Their actions weren't only impacting profits. They were distressing her customers as well.

So as the orv bore down on Calista, she had only one shot at preventing his escape. Shifting her backside a few inches without losing her grip on the skember or her staff, she brought her long tail up in a wide arc. With practised precision, she whipped it into the youth's face, the wrought-iron end smacking his bony nose with a resounding crack. It would have earned her a penalty in either sport, but this wasn't a game. *Bullseye!*

Stunned, the orv dropped the breadcakse, sending them spinning to the ground where they bounced and wobbled a few feet before coming to rest just outside the doorway. The aspiring bread-bandit failed to land as gracefully. He teetered sideways and crashed into a wooden crate.

A plume of white powder erupted from a bag of flour sitting on it, enveloping Calista, the captured skembers, and a few customers unfortunate enough to be in the conflict's vicinity. If not for the warm breeze entering through the open door and the bright afternoon sunlight cascading through the bakery's display windows, they'd be mistaken for travellers seeking shelter from a snowstorm.

"Eek! Look at my shop! Flour everywhere!" Zusa wailed, her frilly black skirt swishing like a furious whisk as she weaved her way to the scene. After surveying the chaos — the dazed orv laying among the wreckage, the skember pinned by the staff, and the last youth trapped in Calista's arm — she fixed her gaze on the faroko she had hired. "What do you have to say for yourself?"

Calista rose smoothly as she eyed her handiwork. Pockets of flour fell from the slight folds of her brown leather corset and skin-tight pants as she straightened. A grimace crossed her face as she felt a handful slide down into her knee-high boots. *I will need to take a bath after this.* She shook her hair out, dislodging more of the powder from her dark curls and long ears, creating a brief cloud around her head. Still clutching the male skember, she raised him higher for Zusa to see. A weak smile parted her lips. "I caught your thieves."

"And nearly destroyed my shop in the process!" The older faroko's tail twitched behind her, an enraged viper ready to lash out. "By what means do you expect me to clear this up?"

Calista shifted the skember under her arm as he began squirming. "It doesn't appear too bad to me," she said, trying not to notice how bad it was. She crouched, hauled the girl out from under the table, and tucked her against her side, sending another cloud of flour puffing outward. "A little sweeping is all."

"Is it?" Zusa snapped, then softened her tone as a pair of female berkis huffed between them, their already white-coated skirts stirring up more of the powder coating the floor. "Please forgive my associate," she begged, following them to the door.

She stood a moment more, watching them disappear into the crowded street before returning inside. "And how do I regain customers put off by your antics?"

"They'll be back. Great Buns is the best bakery on Halons Road." Calista turned her attention to the remaining patrons. "Am I upsetting any of you by catching these three?"

Those closest to her, a faroko husband and wife pair holding hands as they looked over a selection of pastries and an older male berkis trying to choose a pie, directed their consideration elsewhere when she caught their eyes. Beyond them, a trio of middle-aged skembers shook their heads, then made a show of admiring a fresh tray of doughnuts. A female orv standing by a stand displaying two dozen hazelberry muffins turned her gaze away as well.

As I thought. Even when not covered in flour and holding a pair of squirming youths, Calista presented an imposing figure. Though a faroko, she stood over half a foot taller than the others of her race. The smaller, hirsute berkis only reached her hips, and the tiny, faun-like skembers were a mere third her height. The horned orv, tallest of the common races in Gravenmore, had to look up to her as well.

In addition to her abnormal stature, Calista usually wielded a wooden staff. An iron ball crowned it, making it a formidable weapon for a capable fighter. At the moment, it lay under the table, coated in flour, and her hands were full of skember.

"See?" She spun back to Zusa. "No call to worry. And now, you will have no more thefts, as soon as we take care of these urchins. No doubt their mothers will reprimand them sharply."

"I don't gotta mother," the boy in her arm mewed.

Calista crouched, setting the pair on the ground. Despite the coating of powder, she could see how threadbare and tattered their clothes were. The slabs of worn fabric tied around their feet with fraying string passed for shoes, though she doubted they provided any true protection or warmth. Even their faces appeared aged beyond their years, having seen too much suffering for ones so young. "What happened to her?"

The girl fidgeted, rubbing at the flour on her hands. "She got real sick. Then men came. Took her."

"To the hospital?" Gravenmore had only one building set aside for the ill. Fairmont Clinic sat on the river, a location allegedly chosen to provide it with a ready supply of fresh, if not wholly clean, water. Rumours suggested, however, that the waterway provided a convenient and discreet means for disposing of those who underwent treatment there. Truth or not, few dared drink from downriver.

"Horrors, I hope not," Zusa said. "That place ain't no place for sick folk. I've heard stories."

Calista shuddered. "So have I. Nasty ones." She eyed the child. "Is that where they took your mum?"

The girl's shoulder quivered, and a tear carved a path through the flour coating her cheek. "She's dead," the boy blurted in a gruff tone, which abruptly changed to a soft moan. Grief cascaded over them both, giving way to a flood of blubbering. Even the orv, now sitting up, joined in.

Sweet baby plums. Orphans. No wonder they resorted to stealing bread. "Do you have a place to stay? A guardian?"

The male sniffled, shaking his head. "Nope."

"I want them out of my store!" Seemingly unmoved by their plight, Zusa stepped outside and scanned the bustling street. At her beckon, a young berkis, little older than the youths inside, jogged up to the shop. "Fetch the coppers, boy. We've caught some troublemakers."

"Hang about." Calista stood as she reentered the building. "You can't turn them in. They're hungry, that's all."

"You heard them. They ain't got nowhere else to go."

She glared at the bakery owner. "But prison?"

The sleeves of Zusa's chestnut-coloured coat rustled as she crossed her arms. "Least in the pen, they'll get fed and looked after," she said, scowling down at the sobbing children. "And cleaned up."

Calista's eyelids narrowed until only thin slivers of her eyes were visible. "That's heartless."

"I do not believe I asked for your opinion. Unless you want to take them yourself."

Despite her protest, Calista couldn't present a more suitable option. Her own living arrangements were constrained, with no room for even one youngster. Nor did her lifestyle lend itself to raising an orphan. "I can't."

"Then you should go." Zusa dropped her pose as she reached into a slight pocket of her maroon vest. From it, she drew several coins which flashed silver and copper in the display window's sunlight. The shop owner counted a few out into her hand, then extended them to Calista. "Here is the fee we agreed upon. Minus some for the damages you caused."

Heat flushed the towering faroko's face. "That was an accident. Perhaps you should have moved your deliveries out of the doorway when expecting thieves."

"I suggest you take the money and go," came the terse response.

Calista fixed the woman with a glare but snatched the coins from her fingers and secreted them away in a pocket. She turned and crouched before the skembers and orv. Their tears had mixed with the flour on their cheeks, leaving their faces pocked with tiny lumps of dough. She wiped a dollop from the girl's chin. "Some men will be here soon to take you to a place where you'll be fed and protected. I want you to be good for them and do as they say. Alright?"

All three nodded, and the orv rubbed a finger under his nose. Calista flashed him a gentle smile, glad to see her strike hadn't caused any damage. They were a rugged people, even their children, with thick hides and hardened keratin surrounding their eyes and horn.

Poor tykes. I hope you find a safe place. Unable to do more, she retrieved her staff, stood, and moved toward the door. She stepped deliberately close to Zusa. Normally, Calista tried to put those around her at ease over height, but now she wanted to be intimidating.

And it worked. The other faroko backed away as Calista stared down at her. "Those children are to be treated with kindness. If word comes back to me that you spoke ill of them or influenced the police to handle them with anything but the utmost tenderness..." Her iron-tipped tail whipped about, smashing one of the still-intact flour sacks. A fresh plume of white powder burst forth, coating the floor and the females' boots. "You will be plagued by far worse than hungry orphans."

She adopted a fierce scowl, inhaling deeply to puff up her chest. That proved to be a mistake, as a large amount of the newly released flour came with that air, and she sneezed.

Zusa jumped at the unexpected explosion from the dominating faroko and she vigorously nodded her understanding.

I guess that works. Seeing her point made, Calista moved to the doorway, struggling to suppress a smirk. With a last glance at the youths, she hopped over the stone step into the bakery, landing deftly on the pavement. She shook herself again and tapped her staff on the ground, hoping to dislodge another layer of flour before striding confidently up the street.

This assignment was a disaster! she chided herself. *I never expected hiring myself out for jobs would have me sending children to the nick. That's got to change.*

Chapter 2

The Abduction Infraction
Or Taken By The Shadow

TRUITT NIMBLY DESCENDED the staircase of the building where he rented a flat. His black work shoes made light contact with the stone, and a rabbit's foot swung wildly from a delicate chain with each hop. The berkis was in a good mood.

Though still early in the afternoon, he was heading to the casino for another day of gambling. His attire, eclectic with a healthy dose of shoddy, suggested he hadn't been successful on any previous occasions. A faded denim jacket topped a brown shirt and tweed waistcoat, while striped trousers flowed over the shoes. Around his neck lay a tattered handkerchief, and a chestnut slouch hat hung off his head, obscuring much of his short brown hair. A single azure ring adorned his right hand.

His face presented a similarly dishevelled appearance, featuring ocean-blue eyes, a wide, flat nose, and thick lips. Despite his rough appearance, he boasted a clean-shaven visage, hinting at his youthfulness of no more than thirty years.

It worked for him. While not classically handsome, he had a charismatic presence and graceful movements, smooth and assured.

He could be considered tall for a male berkis, measuring a few inches above three feet in height. Soft hair covered most of his body, which, despite the baggy clothes, was surprisingly fit.

Upon reaching the sidewalk, he stepped toward a patch of mud near the stairs and smeared some on his face. He wiped the extra on his jacket, then ran dirty fingers through his hair. Satisfied with the results, he continued down the walkway toward his destination.

The Right Hand Casino had seen better days.

More precisely, the section of town known as the Ward had seen better days, and the Right Hand happened to be a part of it.

Like most cities in Leverhelm, the rise of modernisation had caused an explosion of growth in the larger urban areas. Towns such as Cinderbury shrunk as their citizens fled to the metropolises. Newly built factories needed workers and provided a powerful draw to those wanting a better life.

But for most, their dreams weren't met. Working in the mechanical monstrosities, which constantly belched smoke and filth, proved hard and paid a pittance, leaving those eager migrants broken in spirit and body.

The higher-ups of Gravenmore, unwilling to spend much money on their workforce, developed cheap housing around the factories. These soon became overcrowded, taxing the basic water and waste removal systems built for them. Worse, many living there grew ill from the factory byproducts or sicknesses that ripped through the dense population, causing the mortality rate to spike.

The gentlefolk who made their livings by more sanitary means in the Mids and Sunside tried to distance themselves from those in the slums. The ones who could afford it moved toward the west side, putting several blocks and streets between themselves and those they considered objectionable. Folks who were unable or unwilling to move remained, acting as a living barrier between the haves and the have-nots. With less money flowing through, the neighbourhood also declined, though not as severely as the Rookery — a term used throughout Leverhelm for the overcrowded, poorest areas that resembled the nesting patterns of rooks.

So, after decades of neglect, the Right Hand Casino stood as a melancholy shadow of its former self. The walls retained their rich green wallpaper and decorative panelling, lavishly decorated carpeting still covered the floor, and the ornate crystal chandeliers still hung from the patterned ceiling. But the wallpaper was peeling, the panelling chipped, the carpets thinning and fading, the chandeliers tinted yellow, and the ceiling coated in a layer of grime. The aroma of stale upholstery, body odour, and alcohol permeated the air.

The furniture fared little better. Card tables had long since lost their shine, and the green felt covering their tops had faded to a muted, almost melancholic hue, worn thin in spots. The cushioned booths now sagged, their covers threadbare and torn. Every intricate wooden chair wobbled, its joints pulling apart from years of neglect.

Other items had been sold off in the past to pay bills, like the roulette table, which once dominated a wall, and a wide hanging mirror on the opposite side.

Only the short bar in the rear showed any attempts at repair, with its polished brass railings and a pile of bricks supporting one end.

Despite its condition, the Right Hand remained a popular establishment in the Ward, and today was no exception. Over thirty patrons occupied a dozen tables, most immersed in various card games.

At a single table sat three individuals, their attention fixed on the spread of cards in their hands. It was a common position, and they could be found like this at most times of the day. Before each lay a meagre pile of pebbles, buttons, and rusted bolts, no doubt fallen from a bit of machinery and gathered up from the dirt. A few of the small rocks formed a growing heap in the centre.

Truitt approached the group, casually tossing his hat to the back of a tall chair. He climbed the rungs onto the padded seat, then settled in, feet dangling, palms on the table.

The trio said nothing, too intent on their game for a greeting. After a few minutes, two folded, placing their cards on the felt, while the third, a female faroko, smugly revealed her hand, then slid the collection of pebbles from the centre to her own pile.

Once the cards were collected, she shuffled the deck and dealt to the four of them. Only then did they break their silence. "Your tokens are as intangible as the Grey Shadow 'imself," mumbled the male skember to Truitt's right as he peeled the pile before him off the table, shielding their values from the other players. "Your lordship cannot be betting air."

Truitt chuckled, slipping a hand into his trouser pocket and pulling out a small collection of assorted items, which he deposited on the surface beside him. Rather than carrying around actual coins, the circle of gamblers used the bits of rubbish to represent their funds. "I do not understand why you listen to that tommy-rot," he said, picking up his cards and scowling at the assortment of suits held between his fingers.

"Here now, Truitt. You don't think there's a Grey Shadow?" the female faroko across from him challenged. She was a palette of blacks, browns, and golds. An array of trinkets decorated the fur lining circling the deep neck of her charcoal blouse. A coal-coloured under-bust corset with gold trim, fastened by iron latches, cinched her narrow waist. Short bloomers extended a handspan below that, then became stockings supported by garters. Her feet were clad in worn but stylish shoes with charcoal toes and chestnut uppers with laces.

She adorned the ensemble with an ornate side pouch, a brass pendant around her neck, and a maroon felt top hat featuring lensless goggles and additional baubles on the rim. The last rested on a bed of wavy, raven-hued curls. Beneath were equally black eyes, offset by angular cheeks, a slightly bulbous nose, and thick crimson lips. A pair of thin gloves sat on the table beside her.

Truitt raised his gaze to meet hers. "I believe he — if it is a he, and as of yet there is no confirmation of that fact — is quite real, my dear Faye. But tales of his exploits would not be out of place in the pages of Hot Air, along with reports of demons bathing in the river and stories of airborne, man-eating mules terrorising the Rookery."

"The locals believe it well enough. After he nicked that lady's gold amulet a fortnight ago and that fancy paintin' last week, the bobbies be advisin' folks to lock up their valuable bits and bobbins, in case the Shadow comes callin'." She scooped a pair of pebbles from her pile and delicately placed them into the middle group.

"Then we have not one whit to worry about. Unless this phantom has a taste for old cards." He raised his selection slightly, being careful not to reveal them to the others.

"The Duke will catch him, I bet." Faye shifted in her seat, setting a few baubles on her hat wiggling. "The Shadow cannot hide in Gravenmore."

"I hold the opinion that the Duke will fail to apprehend the thief. His toffness has been in pursuit of the Grey Shadow for years. Our city will not enhance his competency."

"Meanwhile, 'e takes up residency in the Sunside," added the older male skember as he tossed two pebbles into the pot. He wore brown woollen trousers even sorrier looking than Truitt's with a matching jacket that should have had him sweating in the spring afternoon air. The worn waistcoat covered a shirt once white but now looked as if it had been used to clean a chimney. That was highly unlikely, however, as its owner rarely did anything other than hold up a hand of poker. His boots were the same colour as the clay caked on them. A small black cane rested against the table.

A scraggly beard covered his chin, while a whitening moustache that drooped at the ends sat beneath a sharp nose and squinty eyes. His horns were worn smooth in several places, with spots chipped from some unknown abuse. His chair stood the tallest of the four, specifically designed for the stature of his kind.

"Nothin' wrong with that, Raffles," Faye chided. "I hear he is a true buck."

A chuckle escaped Truitt's lips. "You're barking at a knot. He's as likely to walk in these doors and tip the velvet with you as our chum Hugh here is to recite a soliloquy."

The fourth member of their group, a young male orv in an olive-coloured shirt, brown pants, and suspenders, grinned at the comparison. "Innit?"

Faye's mouth curled into a pout. "He'd be more of a gentleman than you!"

"Of that, I have no doubt," the berkis agreed.

The older skember lowered his cards as he fixed his gaze on Truitt. "Why do you not believe the tales of the Grey Shadow?"

He let out a slight sigh, as if his reasons were obvious. "Because they stretch the very fabric of belief. A ghost-like figure, only a smidge visible at times as a wisp of soot, entering houses of the well-to-do and nicking their pretties, whom not a soul is able to capture?" A set of pebbles made their way from his pile to the centre. "No man is that proficient a thief and no spectre would have a need for baubles."

"What 'bout the orange?" Faye pushed, leaning on the table.

"Bless me! How could I have forgotten the orange?" Truitt cried out, slapping a hand to his chest. "A mortal or ethereal who leaves behind a selection of fruit after each burglary?" He dropped his arm and with it, his mocking tone. "When such items are a rarity, how can a thief not only afford one but have the audacity to leave it?"

"Mebbe 'e feels bad about stealing," Raffles suggested.

The berkis erupted in hearty laughter. "So the oranges are meant to be a sort of compensation? If that is the case, then I applaud our Mr Shadow for his droll sense of humour. Now, who's turn is it?"

"Hugh's." Faye nodded toward the orv. "And I think he's 'bout to fold."

All eyes turned to him. Hugh stared at his cards, nervously scratching his scalp and dislodging the bowler sitting atop it. He caught it before it slid off, tapped it back into place, and swallowed hard. After a moment, he scowled, shook his head, and dropped his cards face down on the table.

"Whee!" Faye squealed, wiggling in her seat again and sending her baubles into a frenzy. "I was right. Let's see..." After studying her cards, she pulled two buttons from her collection and added them to the pot. "Raise."

Raffles considered his own hands, then tossed in a matching bid. "'Ow about the dragon?"

Truitt's eyebrows went up. "Kettlebelly? What about him?" He sent two more buttons in without glancing at his hand.

"You think 'e's flummadiddle, too?"

The berkis let out a low whistle. "It would be foolish to think anything of a dragon except how to avoid falling into its path. My attitude toward him might change if he starts popping into homes to pilfer their paintings or depositing melon-sized oranges about the countryside. Faye?"

The female's face drooped as she lowered her cards to the table. "I've gotta fold. All this talk of shadows and giant fruit makes me lose my 'centration."

"More like you're pining for that Duke." Raffles glanced at his pile. "I'm short one button. Can I use pebbles?"

"Only if you have a dozen," Truitt told him.

The skember counted them out, silently forming the numbers with his lips. "I've nine."

"And is that more or less than a dozen?"

"It's more, isn't it?" Faye interjected.

"How much is a dozen?"

"Twelve." Her face screwed up as she tried to run the figures in her head. Her hat trinkets remained still, as if not wishing to distract her from the delicate deliberations. "So, more than nine?"

"It is indeed. But since I have no intention of sitting here while Raffles scours the street for more..." Truitt brought a hairy hand up to his worn waistcoat and yanked a button from it with a single tug. He dropped it into the pile, a strand of thread still hanging from one hole. "Now you have enough."

Raffles tossed in the other and stared at Truitt, awaiting his turn. For the first time in a few rounds, the berkis looked at his cards. He rearranged a few, considered them a little longer, then finally lay them on the table, face down. "I'm out."

Faye let out a cackle as Raffles revealed his own hand, two pairs of threes and nine, before pulling the pile of pebbles and buttons toward him. "What a surprise!"

Truitt shrugged off the insinuation as he gathered the deck together. "Another round?

"I bet Raffles could out-steal the Shadow."

Raffles clicked his tongue at the female's comment. "Too kind. Now that reminds me..." Stiff fingers fished into his trouser pocket and pulled out a worn copper ring. He held it up between his forefinger and thumb to let the others see before tossing it onto the table. "Lifted it off a gentleman the other evening. Masterful bit of pick-pocketing."

Truitt eyed the jewellery. Scuffs and scratches marred its surface, rendering it of almost no value except as scrap. "And was this poor soul drunk at the time?"

Raffles maintained his smile. "Possibly."

"And awake?"

The grin widened. "I admit 'e might 'ave been a bit on the soused side. Didn't mean it was easy."

"No," Truitt agreed with a head shake and tone that said he did not believe him while remaining polite. "Certainly not. But not something your Shadow would pursue."

"He's going for the Dragon Eye Gem, I bet," Faye exclaimed. "That would be a prize. I hear it's the size of a melon and lights up the night better than any lamp!"

"Another fiction. There ain't no such item. It is likely some fragment of glass a huckster claimed was dragon in origin. Don't be so gullible."

The faroko jabbed a finger toward him. "Then why else would the Shadow be in Gravenmore, hmm?"

Truitt cut the deck, shifting the top pile to the bottom. "Possibly for our fine selection of meat pies."

"Certainly not for the gambling. Deal, boy!" Raffles grumbled, tucking the stolen ring away. "Besides, you said 'e ain't real."

Truitt nodded, shuffled the cards, and began dealing them to the others. "It is not that I don't believe there has been a series of thefts in the cities of Leverhelm. But to attribute them to a single individual with seemingly supernatural skilfulness is courting folly."

Faye tapped the brim of her hat. "But you believe in Kettlebelly?"

"Dragons are nothing new or mysterious. Just a nuisance."

"'E's destroyed several buildings, eaten a flock of cows, and defecated upon the slums of Tinkerhelm," Raffles reminded him.

"Herd," Truitt said as he finished the deal.

"'Erd what?"

"The proper term is 'herd of cows', not flock. And had he consumed that many bovines, he most likely could not control where he relieved himself. Which also happens to prove he's real."

"Then why is Gravenmore on alert for the Grey Shadow and not massive faeces drops?" Faye pressed, ignoring her cards.

"I would assume because no reward has been offered for collecting copious amounts of dung," Truitt responded. "The pompatic Duke Patrick Cameron has been upping his compensation for the capture of his burglar since he arrived here a month ago. Money is an alluring pipe song to those whose hearing is poor."

The female's head bobbed, sending her baubles wiggling. "I hear the latest amount is five hundred pounds! What would you do with that kind of money?"

"Nothing, as it will never be paid out."

"Killjoy," she pouted, picking her cards and arranging them between her fingers. "A girl can dream, can't she?"

"By all means." Truitt nodded toward the silent Hugh to begin the ante. "Dreams are the truest reminders of what you don't have. But any of us collecting that reward is as likely as the Grey Shadow waltzing through the entrance of this establishment and stealing *me* away."

As if in answer to his challenge, the main doors flew open as two nasty-looking orvs stomped in. They were similarly dressed, with shabby trousers and frayed waistcoats, though one wore a bowler and the other a lengthy navy blue frock coat. Each had a spiked whip hanging from its belt, while the one with the hat held a huge burlap sack.

They scanned the casino, eyeing each guest as if searching for someone specific. When their scrutiny fell upon Truitt's table, the pair stormed across the room, shoving aside any chairs, tables, and patrons in their path.

Despite their bulk, the orvs moved swiftly. The gambling companions barely had time to realise the intruders were coming before one grabbed Truitt by the neck and yanked him from his chair, sending his cards to the floor. The other pulled the sack open, and he was dropped unceremoniously in.

Then the bag full of Truitt was slung over a burly shoulder while its contents kicked and yelled. His gambling partners, too stunned by the brazen attack, simply looked on from their seats, their own cards still clenched in their hands.

With the object of their intrusion secured, the orvs dashed to the entrance, shoving aside any who tried to stop them. Once through the doors, they took off down the street, with Truitt shouting and thrashing about wildly.

Inside the Right Hand, Kate, a female faroko and one of the drink servers, rushed to the group's table as the other patrons started to retrieve their chairs and rearrange their tables. "What just happened?"

Faye finally put her cards down. "The Grey Shadow just stole Truitt!"

Chapter 3

The Powdered Deliberation
Or Don't Bring Your Work Home

L IKE MANY CITIES, Gravenmore was home to people of all economic classes. They inhabited largely segregated communities with little overlap. The poor rarely mingled with the better off, and they never interacted with the rich, at least not without the threat of imprisonment.

The western part of the city housed the affluent, including nobles, business owners, government facilities, and financial buildings. This section, commonly known as the Sunside, implied a bright and prosperous lifestyle for its residents. Far from the riverside factories, the air remained moderately clear, and the streets were reputed to be so clean that they gleamed.

The sprawling roadways east of the Sunside belonged to the middle class, full of fancy shops and working men who hadn't quite reached the upper echelons of society and income. One could walk the avenues in the Mids with little fear of harm coming to their person. The second largest district of Gravemore housed the Great Buns bakery, along with the pub where Calista lived, just a few blocks over.

Majestic townhouses and grand storefronts lined the way, adorned with intricate details and decorative motifs, each trying to outdo the others. A few boasted ornate, wrought-iron balconies extending from the second and third stories. Brick and stone made up most of them, but a few had timber facades.

Small stones, long since worn down and hardened in place, paved the streets, while cobblestones, smooth and uneven, comprised the narrow sidewalks lining it. Both lay coated in a layer of grime from the factories on the east end, which no amount of scrubbing by the street cleaners could remove.

The occasional deposit of dung dotted the roadway, a constant reminder of the Mids' lower status. As the primary means of propulsion for carriages transporting citizens and carts carrying goods, horses were a common sight. Their rhythmic clip-clop of hooves contributed to the mix of voices that gave the city its ambience.

Gas lamps stood sentinel, unlit in the bright daylight, waiting for their moment to shine at dusk. The smell of coal and wood smoke from chimneys here and on the outskirts wafted through the crowds of people.

Despite racial differences, most pedestrians adorned themselves in similar styles of clothing. Females typically wore lengthy skirts and corsets, many with their long hair tied up in a bun. In the case of the hairless orvs, they sported a fancy hat with a wide brim and a flower or other ornamentation. The men, regardless of the warm weather, donned bowler hats and finely tailored suits, complete with high collars, refined waistcoats, and jackets.

A few, less-well-off individuals dressed in shabbier variations, though they carried themselves with the same poise, refusing to admit their slighter income. Polite folks didn't discuss such topics.

They weren't above gawking, however, and Calista did her best to ignore the stares levelled at her by her fellow pedestrians as she crossed to the opposite sidewalk, her boots thunking on the stone street. Though she had made Gravemore her home for more than a decade, her abnormal height still set her as a regular target of curiosity. The layer of whiteness coating her didn't help.

They live in such an elegant part of the city, but I'm the object of their attention. Maybe I'd be less noticeable if I had the figure of a building.

The staff didn't help, as it stood out in stark contrast to the smaller canes wielded by the gentlemen passing by. Not being an armament any lady would use, it brought her nearly the same amount of notice as her stature.

But Calista Temira never considered herself a member of that gentle class. Her physique matched, even surpassed the standard in other ways than height. No one observing her shoulder-length curly black hair, high cheekbones, deep brown eyes, and red lips would attribute her to any other group than female. The figure under her flour-covered clothes fit perfectly with the ideal set by the sand-filled timekeeping instrument so many women strove to match.

Nearly perfectly. In her mind, her nose was too large compared to the rest of her face, her hips jutted outward more than she liked, and the elongated ears extending up through her dark tresses lacked the smooth roundness she admired in other faroko.

So let them stare, she thought as an orv couple strode by. *I don't hide anymore.*

The man dressed like most males in the Mids, with a high-collared white shirt and fitted trousers tucked into leather boots adorned with brass buckles. A tailored waistcoat, held closed by a dozen ornate buttons, and a silk cravat with a red and gold design completed the ensemble. A simple silver-topped cane dangled loosely from his right hand.

The woman interlocking her arm with his wore a feminine version of the outfit. A deep blue corset snugly hugged her puffy, cream-coloured shirt to the abdomen and bosom. Her layered crimson skirt, puffed out unnaturally by some hidden framework, flowed to her ankles. The shin-high boots she sported gleamed from under the cotton folds as she walked, revealing tiny brass trinkets sewn into the tops. The current fashion in women's footwear aimed to draw a man's eye, giving a suggestive hint of what lay in store when her attire came off. No female wearing such items would, of course, admit to seeking such attention. A bit of rebellion against societal expectations.

Both orvs gave her a passing glance, then returned their eyes to the sidewalk ahead. Calista caught the disapproving look of the woman. She had no doubt noticed that, under the flour, the faroko's outfit aligned more closely in style with her husband's than her own. Such a breach of etiquette called for a certain degree of criticism, and had she not been so imposing a figure, the woman would have made that known.

It wasn't as if Calista hadn't tried. Growing up in the town of Cinderbury, she had pursued normal feminine pursuits. She spent her youngest years learning proper manners and the useful skills of cooking, washing, and cleaning so that one day, she might be an adequate housewife to a gentleman. Her training rarely extended beyond that singular goal, although she received enough of an education to read and write. For a time, her future looked promising.

Then puberty hit her like an out-of-control steam-powered train with a mad engineer. Within a few years, she had outgrown not only her fellow adolescents but most adults in her town, including her parents. But her height wasn't the only thing which blossomed. Seemingly overnight, she had transformed from a scrawny, flat-chested girl into a curvaceous young woman.

That's when the trouble began. Her metamorphosis might have been viewed with elation had she been older. However, for a youth surrounded by her peers who were only beginning their changes, she stood out like a rusty cog. Daily she endured the stares, laughs, and mockery from the other children.

Adults didn't treat her much differently. She had learned early on how the women around her envied her figure. The men also desired it, but in an entirely different and unwholesome manner. Coupled with her abnormal height, she became Cinderbury's freak. The oddball.

Calista had attempted to hide her differences. Oversized, baggy clothes dominated her wardrobe, though all were tailormade. The cost of these grew too great for her parents, however, and she had to rely on existing adult items altered to her shape. This contributed to her perceived bizarreness, as these modifications were often poorly executed, leaving her with arms that were too long, dresses that were too short, or shirts which were too tight across the chest. She had to master new breathing techniques to wear the last.

Now, she wore what she liked, with a few exceptions. She still needed her clothes altered or custom-crafted, but they were designed to fit her body, not hide it.

A faint whirring sound drew her gaze to the sky. She shielded her eyes from the sun and spotted an airship — a wooden and iron behemoth drifting lazily above Gravenmore, thrust forward by a pair of huge metal propellers.

She watched it float out of view, then returned her attention to the street. Only a few others had shown any curiosity in the sight. They weren't common, but most citizens had already grown accustomed to their passing. *I hope I never become that jaded.*

The airships never stopped in Gravemore. Despite the city's size, it couldn't capture the interest of those rich enough to hire such an elaborate means of travel.

A shout brought her gaze to a young faroko boy on the corner, standing by a pile of printed material and waving a few sheets of it in the air. "Newspapers! Get yer newspapers here! The Grey Shadow strikes again! Read about it now!"

Calista's long ears perked up, and she scooted closer. The moniker "The Grey Shadow" belonged to a high-end thief who had plagued the people of the Leverhelm region of the Imperialist Kingdom of Prettanika for years. He moved from one city to another, plundering the valuable artwork and jewels, then moving on. Gravenmore had become his hunting ground a few months ago. Since then, any shopkeeper, banker, and gentleman or lady with the slightest shiny trinket had been seeing the nefarious figure in every shaded corner.

It went beyond being just an ominous nickname to stir the imagination. The thief, whoever he was, possessed the ability to travel almost entirely unseen. According to the few witnesses who caught sight of him, he resembled a mere shimmer of smoke. But the strangest part evolved not around his appearance, or lack thereof, but of what he left behind.

At the scene of every theft, large or small, sat a single orange.

No one had yet been able to deduce why this master burglar chose to announce his handiwork in this fashion. Was he taunting the police with the bold choice of fruit? Was it a statement on society? Did stealing such valuable pieces make him hungry for citrus?

Calista didn't care about his reasons. What she did know was it brought an uptick in her number of protection jobs. Zusa hadn't been the only individual concerned about her merchandise going missing. Since the Grey Shadow had arrived in Gravenmore and made his presence known, she had taken assignments to guard more than just baked goods. The tasks included protecting an ornate vase, a painting of a lady floating in a stream, a consignment of spinach ice cream, and a gentleman's beagle while he travelled out of town. She enjoyed the last one, as it gave her a few days to spend with a playful puppy.

She considered purchasing a copy of the newspaper, then decided against it. *I don't need to hear more about the Grey Shadow. From the reports, he's only ever stolen lavishly expensive items, which rules out everywhere except the Sunside. The chances of my having a run-in with him are as slim as a skember in a corset!*

Moving on, Calista passed a few street vendors peddling goods from small carts like lamp wicks, ginger cakes, and sheep trotters. The last one made her nauseous, but she flashed the youthful female berkis selling them a smile, anyway.

She finally reached her destination. The red brick pub stood on the corner of Foxglove Land and Ironclad Road. An inviting arched entrance, flanked by sturdy wooden double doors, served as the main point of entry. Decorative moulding climbed each side, then flowed outward to border the walls. Into these were set large, multi-paned windows with ornamental sills and lintels. Above them, faded grey canvas awnings extended from the upper floor, providing shelter from both the sun and rain to those passing by.

Over the entrance, a brass signboard swung gently from iron chains, displaying the pub's name in elegant, cursive letters. The Happy Swallow. Above the words had been etched a stylised bird, meant to represent the titular joyful warbler.

I doubt anyone in this city has ever seen a sparrow. One wouldn't survive long in this pollution. There had been a nest of them near her house in Cinderbury, and she thought it a cheerful name for the pub. Fortunately, the owner took her up on the suggestion.

She pushed open the doors and stepped through to the interior. The inside of the taproom lay in a perpetual state of dimness, despite the bright sunshine outside. Little of its warm light could penetrate the tinted front windows. A haze of tobacco and oil smoke hung over the room, with the lamps constantly kept low.

Smoothed wooden benches, straight-back chairs, and small circular tables filled the space, with a handful strategically arranged near an unlit fireplace. A glass-covered candle and an enormous clock, its gears and cogs ceaselessly ticking and whirring as it tracked every passing hour, minute, and second, adorned the intricately carved mantel.

Pictures of refined gentlemen, interspersed with small mirrors and various signs advertising the foods and drinks available, filled the wall spaces between lamps.

Cushioned booths cosied up against panelled walls, and a variety of patterned rugs decorated the hardwood floors. Darkly stained wooden beams traversed the ceiling, imparting a rustic ambience to the room.

The bar itself boasted thick, dark, polished wood, with rounded sides curving inward, offering space for two dozen four-legged stools sitting before it. A trio of taps sat in the middle of the bartop, while bottles of liquor lined the shelves on the wall behind it. Twin doors stood at each end, and above all of it hung a brass replica of the window logo.

Despite the early hour, a handful of patrons littered the pub. It never failed to depress Calista how the working class of Gravenmore relied upon the consumption of alcohol to bolster themselves through the day. Though proper to have an occasional glass among company, indulging in it multiple times when alone showed a lack of moral fibre and strength of character. She expected it with the eminently poor, whose lives were so wretched one would want to wash the reality away with a bottle of ale. But not those in the Mids at ten in the morning.

"And the mighty warrior returns from the hunt," came a voice from the bar. "Hmmm. It appears the jungle is experiencing a blizzard."

Behind the counter, on a specially made shelf, stood a male skember dressed in an oversized open waistcoat, a tan-chequered shirt, and baggy trousers tucked into snug maroon boots, resplendent with multiple silver buttons and buckles. His full, curved horns, forming a tight spiral on both sides of his head, along with their faded grey hue, indicated he had reached middle age.

"You might say that. Armend, the job wasn't as it seemed." She spanned the distance between them in a few long strides. "May I sit?"

"And cover my stool in... what is that?" He waved a tiny hand at her frosted curls.

"Flour. Freshly delivered this morning." Calista leaned the staff against the bar, dislodging only a few flecks of the white powder, and slid onto the seat, smearing a trail along her backside.

"I trust this doesn't indicate that you'll be bringing your work home henceforth."

She raised an eyebrow. "I doubt I'll be working there again. Change that. I refuse to work there again. Make a note in your ledger: accept no more assignments from Miss Zusa Lolly of the Great Buns bakery."

"Hmmm." Armend scratched his hairless chin. "That has an ominous tone to it. What happened?"

Calista exhaled. "She requested I capture the individuals pilfering her shop. However, she failed to clarify they were children."

He bobbed his head in understanding. "Rather an important detail."

"I thought so. I only learned this when a trio of them were racing toward the door, their arms full of bread goods, with me in the way."

Armend leaned against the bartop. The shelf rose three feet and extended most of the length of the counter, providing a convenient space for the owner and bartender of the Happy Swallow to interact with patrons. "And you stopped them?"

"That *was* the assignment. A pair of skembers I caught easily enough. I had to stun the young orv with my tail." She flicked it now, bringing its end up to eye level. Deft fingers flipped a tiny latch and the iron orb split open. Once removed, she set it down between them. "I know I trained to use the flail in that manner, but it didn't feel right doing it to a child."

"Was it harmed?"

"Briefly stunned, but they are tough. The crying came later. All three were orphans, only stealing because they were starving. The skembers' mother is dead, and likely the orv's is as well." She took in a deep breath and let it out slowly. "I felt terrible, but what could I do? I'm in no position to look after one child, and certainly not a trio."

"Hmmm. What became of them?"

That drew a frown. "Zusa called the coppers. There was nowhere else for them."

Armend tapped the polished counter lightly, his fingertips tracing the smooth surface as he pondered his thoughts. "Perhaps the orphanage can take them in," he offered. "They could be safe there."

But Calista shook her head. "That would be worse than the pen. Too many children go missing from Etheridge to consider it an alternative, safe or otherwise."

"If you believe the stories," he said in a tone which made it clear he didn't. "'Rumours are the currency of gossips and the ignorant.'"

"You and your quotes." She jabbed at him playfully, which he easily dodged. "Rumours are also your trade. How else do you gather what's needed doing?"

"Ah, that is different," Armend answered, holding up a single finger. "My web of informants, as it were, seek only the more pertinent of new items and deliver them to me with no additional bias."

"Like the job you gave me last month? Spirits of the supernatural kind were reported to be haunting a tailor's shop on Belstein Avenue with a five-pound reward for whoever caught it. Not only did the owner offer no such compensation, the ghost turned out to be merely a grey cat who'd got a length of lace tangled around its neck."

He lowered his arm and shrugged. "Well, you cannot expect every job to be thoroughly vetted. You did catch something."

"Oh yes. The feline in question was so grateful for my freeing it from its frilly entanglement that it tried to take a chunk of my finger." She held up her left hand, revealing a faint outline of a set of cat-sized teeth on her third digit. "You can still see the scar."

"Then perhaps you should count yourself lucky today's undertaking only resulted in your taking on the appearance of a ghost." He looked her over again. While the most concentrated patches of flour had fallen off, a coating of white remained over most of her front and down her right side. "You are fortunate no one mistook you for a Baubas."

Calista clicked her tongue. "That hardly seems likely. They are said to be male, with red eyes. And dark, not white. And can only be seen by children. Other than that, I bear a remarkable resemblance," she finished with a tone of sarcasm, which prompted another sigh. "No, I merely ensured those youths will be sent to prison. That makes me worse than any malevolent spirit. They were starving!"

"If you hadn't taken the assignment, you would be starving too."

"If I take more assignments like this one, I still might." She straightened, picked the few coins out of her pocket, and dropped them on the counter beside the flail. "The miser docked me for the flour damage."

Armend poked at them, idly counting up their value. "Hmmm. Certainly less than promised. Perhaps I should forgo collecting my percentage."

"No. Take it all. I can't look at it." Calista shook her head again and leaned forward. "Armend, what do I do? I have been taking on these jobs for years, and I like to believe I have done some good. But the last few assignments make me question if maybe I am putting money over morality."

He nodded. "Those in the most need seldom have the currency to seek help."

"Is that another quote?"

"Merely common sense. To secure enough income for survival, you must find those who can provide it."

"Survive?" Her voice took on a playful tone. "Are you suggesting you might toss me out if I can't earn you enough?"

"And lose my favourite protector? I would not have this place if it wasn't for your intervention. As long as I own the Happy Swallow, you will have a home. I owe you that much."

"Thank you." She rose, leaned towards him, and bestowed a gentle kiss upon his cheek. "I am not sure who owes who, but I am grateful for your friendship."

"Yeah, yeah," he chided, reddening. "Now go take a bath before you powder up my pub any further. When you return, I should have a new assignment for you."

A grin split her face. "Try to make this one not involving bakeries. Or flour." She grabbed her staff and started for the entrance. After a few steps, however, she returned and snatched her flail along with a coin off the counter. "For the bath," she explained, then tucked both items away and strode out the door.

Chapter 4

The Briefing Vexation
Or Someone Request A Rescue?

C ALISTA STARED AT the faded letters on the building's front window. The Right Hand. This was definitely the location of her next client. *Why would anyone be kidnapped from here?*

Dressed in her freshly laundered clothes and thoroughly defloured by a bath, she had returned to the Happy Swallow to accept a new assignment. When Armend had pulled out his stuffed ledger, she requested he find a job that would be of definite aid to someone. After a quick search, he'd found an appeal to rescue an individual forcibly taken from a gambling establishment. It sounded suspicious, but was there a greater way to be of service than to physically remove another from danger? So she accepted.

The scene of the abduction being located in the Ward came as a surprise to her. If it had been one of the better-offs in the Mids, or the best-offs of the Sunside, then a kidnapper could request a ransom. But who would pay for the return of a Ward resident?

Except my client, it seems. There must be a good reason. So she had hiked the several blocks to the edge of the Ward, then asked for directions from there. That part of Gravenmore held some familiarity for her. She had visited most parts of the city while performing her tasks, though most of the time, the paying jobs came from the western sections.

The dim light inside prevented her from making out much more than the thick velvet curtains framing the windows. The outer facade of brick displayed chipped and broken areas in too many places to count. Above the doorway, a pole with hanging chains protruded a few feet, the last remnants of the casino's sign.

Well, you aren't helping anyone standing out here gawking. She pushed open the door and stepped inside, then rested the staff while her eyes adjusted to the lesser illumination. Something about gambling necessitated a shadowy atmosphere.

Two dozen tables, some small for cosy pastimes, others large for spectators, sat around the room. Chairs and stools of varying sizes and heights circled them, catering to a wide range of patrons. The place, half-full, had most of its clients engaging in card games. A pair of faroko seated in a corner were casting dice and calling out numbers. Even as she watched them, one rolled a winning number, slapping the table with a cheer while his companion groaned.

Nobody looks too concerned about a customer being grabbed. Instead of guessing which person she intended to meet, she crossed to the bar and waved to draw a server's attention. Kate saw it and stepped up to greet her. "What might I get for you?" she asked with a smile, showing only the slightest surprise at her height.

"Pardon me. I am looking for a gentleman by the name of Raffles. Would you know where I could find him?"

Her expression morphed into a scowl. "Aye. That's him." She gestured toward a table near the back. "The scruffy skember with the cane. But I wouldn't be calling him a gentleman."

That does not sound good. "I appreciate it." She gripped her staff and strolled to where Kate had pointed. The trio seated there were focused on a game of cards. One chair stood empty except for a slouch hat on the seat. They didn't notice her approach until she spoke. "Are you Raffles?"

Faye and Hugh glanced up at the newcomer, but Raffles remained fixated on his hand. "You a bluebottle?"

Calista blinked. "No. I am here — "

"A bumbailiff?"

Her tail twitched in agitation. "No. I — "

"Sky pilot?"

"I've never even been aboard an airship," she answered.

"Not them. A devil-dodger. A pulpit-pusher. A — " He finally turned his head to her, then had to readjust it upward. "Odds bodkins! You're a neck stretcher. Are you on stilts?"

Calista let out an exasperated sigh. "I'm here about the request for a rescue. Is your associate still missing?"

Raffles's gaze returned to the table. "Truitt? Well, this is 'is place when we play cards." He gave a slight nod to the chair with the hat. "It may 'ave escaped your attention, but we is playing cards now. You might 'ave also failed to notice the seat is currently empty. 'Is 'at is 'ere, 'owever."

She felt her cheeks flush as Faye snickered. *Sweet batty pearls! The waitress was right!* Her lips tight, she bent over until her face aligned with the skember's, though hers measured three times larger. "What you may not have considered is the complete lack of willing participants to retrieve your gambling buddy. Look around. All you have is me." She dropped her voice as she moved in closer, leaving less than a handspan between them. The smell of stale ale and body odour hit her nose, and she swallowed the urge to wretch. "So if you wish to continue your mockery and ignore my proposal for aid, I will leave you and your companions to handle matters on your own."

Raffles's smile faded only slightly. "You take the egg. Perhaps you are bricky enough to retrieve our lordship."

Calista's eyebrows shot up as she stood. "He is a lord?"

The trio laughed, even Hugh. "Naw," Faye explained, laying her cards on the table. "We tease him that occasionally he sounds like a toff. Course, he ain't. One of their lot wouldn't be here with us."

Raffles's head bobbed. "So the reward for 'is return is one shilling, payable upon completion."

"That isn't much against the life of a friend," Calista noted.

"We are acquaintances, not friends. Truitt is fortunate there is any interest in 'is abduction at all. But 'e owes me a sum of money, and I wish to collect."

Lovely! "Do you know who took him?"

"Well, first we thought it was that Grey Shadow, the one that's been swipin' folkses stuff." Faye wiggled in her chair.

Her baubles are bouncing all over! "Is that likely?"

"Upon further reflection, we realised not." Raffles shifted a few cards in his hand. "Nothing valuable about Truitt."

"Then who?"

"A pair of orv scoundrels!" Faye said. "Blustered in here with not so much as a by your leave, latched onto his arms, and stuffed him in a sack."

"Dreadful business," Raffles chimed in. "We barely recovered 'is cards and were forced to play the rest of the 'and without 'im."

Your concern is touching! "Did you know these orvs?"

"We are gentle folk. We don't cohort with ruffians."

"And you've never seen them in here? Maybe Truitt owed money, and they came to collect." She spoke the last while keeping her eyes fixed on Raffles.

But if he understood her insinuation, he ignored it. "'Is lordship only enters into contests of the cards with us."

"Then perhaps at another establishment?"

"Naw," Faye said. "The Right Hand is his only means of entertainment."

That's just sad. "And I assume you do not know where they might have taken him?"

Raffles snorted. "Would we need your services if we did?"

Calista's tail twitched as she stared at him. "You have not provided me with much information to work with."

Faye shrugged, causing the trinkets on her blouse to tinkle. "That's all we've got."

The skember looked up at her again. "If the task is too difficult for you — "

"I will locate your friend and return him here," Calista said before he could finish. *If I'm truly intent on helping others more, what better way than rescuing a kidnapped victim?*

"Unless he's passed," Faye suggested.

"True." Raffles resumed inspecting his hand. "If 'e's snuffed it, don't bring 'im 'ere."

Calista's mouth dropped open. *Who are these people?* "Do you believe that is a likely outcome?"

He shrugged, rearranging his card. "Could be."

Calista had no response to that, and when Raffles began tapping his fingers on the table, she guessed he was done with the conversation. Hugh continued staring at his, and she wondered if he had been doing so the entire time. When she caught Faye's eye, her fellow faroko gave her a little wave.

"I'll be off, then." No reply. *What an odd lot.* Calista shook her head again and headed back out into the street. With no apparent motive or leads, the task looked almost hopeless. She had one advantage, however. A pair of orvs carrying a sack large enough to hold a person would likely be noticed. *I doubt that the berkis went quietly. So, ask around if anyone witnessed a kidnapping, and hope this isn't a natural occurrence!*

It wasn't, she learned. After asking a few vendors and street urchins, she followed the trail to a handful of abandoned houses in a section even more dilapidated than the one she had left. The Rookery began a few blocks further east, so if these buildings were deserted, they should have been reclaimed by those in the overcrowded area. Yet they stayed vacant, at least to the living.

Brilliant. They brought him to the Bedevilled. I hope the rumours are just rumours! With night rapidly approaching, lamplighters would be making their rounds, but the nearby gas lamps remained dark. *Maybe they don't come here anymore. This would be an ideal place to bring your captive.*

The five houses, all detached from each other by slim alleys, had been abandoned six years before. Something, or someone, had taken them over, driving out the original occupants and keeping them off limits to anything to move back in. Rumours spoke of slamming doors at all hours, furious scratching, as if a trapped individual was trying to escape, and eerie laughter that terrified all who heard. People considered it cursed by a devil, and the name stuck.

Calista perceived nothing suspicious now as she cautiously approached the group. Even if the stories were merely the products of spooked imaginations, she did not know how the orvs were armed or their intent toward her or their captive. Best to keep her presence quiet.

After a few minutes of investigation, she spotted a flickering light coming from the rear of the second residence and moved closer. None of the tales had spoken of anything like that. *That must be them.* No way existed to see into the building from the street, though. She would have to use the main entrance.

Just walk into a haunted house containing hostile orvs through the front door, she chided herself. Of course, it was a bad idea. Still, she found herself creeping closer.

Perhaps stopping orphans from stealing isn't so terrible a job.

Chapter 5

The Extrication Complication
Or We've Been Robbed!

C ALISTA CAT-FOOTED UP the stone steps leading into the house, hugging her staff to her side. The weather-beaten door stood wide open, allowing her to step through into a small anteroom. Splintered wood, dirt, and animal droppings marred the tiled floor and rain had rendered the cross-patterned wallpaper streaked and puffy. It smelled of mildew and smoke. A plump rat skittered past her with a muted squeak as it ran into the street.

Rats. That's a good sign, isn't it? Rats wouldn't stay in haunted houses. Following the voices, she slid silently up to the second door, which stood similarly ajar. But as she prepared to step through, a low moan reached her ears, sending a shiver through her body. *What do rats know about it?*

The sounds of talking didn't stop or acknowledge the sound, and she chided herself. *There is nothing to fear. Whoever is in there isn't bothered, so why am I?* She straightened, tightened her grip on her staff, and peered inside.

Across from her, thirty feet away, stood a doorway into what she assumed to be the kitchen. A flickering light, presumably a lantern, cast shadows of two largish individuals involved in a discussion against the papered wall. She still couldn't understand what they were saying, but as her eyes continued her surveillance, that no longer mattered.

Most of the partition between the main hallway and living room had collapsed or been smashed through, allowing her to easily spot a figure on a chair in the centre. He was a berkis, dressed in shabby clothes with his chin resting against his chest.

That has to be Truitt! All I have to do is get in there and grab him! But as she inched closer, she noticed a thick rope wrapped around him several times, holding him in place. A handkerchief circled his head, serving as a gag. She might have to carry him and the chair out together.

Being careful not to step on any of the loose debris littering the floor, lest she alert the pair in the kitchen, Calista manoeuvred soundlessly through the remains of the wall to the captive and knelt beside him. She saw no wounds on his face as she set her staff down, but that didn't mean he was well. Gingerly, she touched his hand.

A muffled gasp escaped his mouth around the cloth and his head snapped up. Calista lay a finger on her lips as her attention went to the kitchen. Their murmuring continued, and no one appeared in the doorway. *Not yet.*

"You Truitt?" she hissed, and he nodded in the affirmative. "I was hired to find you. Are you hurt?" He gave a slight head shake. "Good. I'm going to get you out of here." She moved to study the ropes binding him. They were interwoven with the rods of the chair. Her original plan had been to haul him out over her shoulder, a task she figured would be simple enough for anything except an orv. The wooden construct complicated that. *I doubt I can carry him, it, and my staff without making noise.*

After a glance at the surrounding rubble, she spotted a jagged piece of metal. She plucked it up carefully and raised it to show Truitt. "Keep quiet." He nodded in understanding. It took a minute of working it back and forth on the knot for the rope to fray. Another minute, and the cord pulled away. She quickly unwound the rest of it from around him.

He shook out his hands and yanked the handkerchief down from his mouth. "At last!" he proclaimed loudly.

Calista hissed at him, but it was too late. The lamp light in the other room began advancing toward them as the mumbling got louder. "Run!"

She reached a hand behind and shoved him forward off the chair when he didn't move. He stood up briefly, then tumbled to the ground. "My legs!"

He's been sitting too long! Her eyes shifted to the kitchen where two orvs were emerging, one donning a bowler and the leading ruffian wearing a frock coat and carrying the lamp. *I can't carry him and outrun them! I'll have to give him time to recover.* She wrapped her fingers around the staff, then in a single smooth motion, she stood and tossed it to her right hand in a move she hoped looked intimidating.

But the pair continued advancing. Whips, known as *slashers*, were clearly visible hanging off their hips. "And just who might you be?" demanded the lamp wielder.

Calista stepped away from Truitt as he tried to stand, only to stumble again. The two orvs didn't seem to notice him, though, as they were too focused on her. Maybe she could bluff their way out of it. "Good evening, gentlemen," she greeted loudly. "My estate agent asked me to scout this section of Gravenmore for possible properties to purchase." She tapped the floor with her staff. "Am I to assume you are the proprietors of this establishment?"

"Are the whatsie?" demanded the second, stepping out from behind his companion and moving toward the outer hallway.

"She is asking if we own this dump, Maurice," the other answered, not letting his gaze fall from Calista.

"Oh." Maurice paused. "Do we?"

The first started to answer, then stopped, his mouth half open. "I don't rightly know."

Calista couldn't see Truitt in her peripheral vision and hoped he'd escaped. "Then perhaps you will direct me to your employer, so I may discuss the matter with him."

"I'm supposing we might be the owners," the lamp holder said, still considering the problem. "There ain't no one else here."

"No there ain't," Maurice agreed, glad to have something he was sure of. "'Ceptin' a few rats."

"And the berkis we nabbed. That's him over..." The first waved the lantern to the left of Calista, where the chair stood. In the flickering light, he could see it was now devoid of their captive. "We've been robbed!"

"We has!"

And we've been rumbled. Time to leg it! Calista took a step toward the broken wall, plastering a smile on her face. "It sounds as if you gentlemen are engaged in delicate affairs." She moved again, trying hard to make it look like she wasn't about to flee, which proved very difficult when that was precisely what she planned. "Perhaps I can call on you at a later date."

But they no longer cared about who owned the house. "Ya know what, Bertram?" Maurice started advancing on the tall faroko. "I think this church bell has nicked our berkis chum."

"Why would she go and do that?" The other waved the lamp high, scanning the room for the missing captive.

"Gentlemen," Calista began, shifting toward the door again. "I assure you..."

"You gibfaced meaters! Ptow!"

A pebble flew from the same location as the voice behind her and struck Maurice in the face. He didn't flinch as it bounced off his tough hide. "Who said that?"

"The chum you grabbed with your filthy mitts and dragged to this cesspool, you pigeon-livered flapdoodles! Ptow!" Another pebble hurtled past, this time striking Maurice's eye. "And I was winning!"

Calista cursed, realising it had to be Truitt. "You're supposed to be gone. I was stalling them while you skedaddled."

The berkis came forward enough so she could see him. "Not until I teach these unlicked cubs some manners!" He brought up a slingshot, pulled back the elastic, and released a third stone, which hit Maurice in the stomach. It bounced off, but Truitt shouted "Ptow!" anyway. Apparently, he added his own sound effects.

With a roar, Maurice grabbed his slasher and started lumbering toward Truitt as he sent another pebble flying. This one missed as Maurice raised his whip. The berkis's eyes grew wide as the leather weapon drew back. Too late, he stumbled backwards as it lashed forward, its deadly iron hooked tip diving for his face.

It struck Calista's staff instead. Before Maurice realised what had happened, the female twisted the rod and pulled it aside, yanking the whip from his fingers. Continuing the motion, she whirled two large steps toward him and rapped the orv sharply on the skull with the wooden end.

Hands to his head, he stumbled away as his companion laughed. "Maurice, you great foozler! Trounced by a trollop!" His mirth changed to anger when a pebble smacked his nose.

"Mind your tongue, hornbrain, or you're next!" Truitt had recovered and was back in taunting mode.

Which isn't what we need! Calista scowled at him. "Stop! You're making it worse."

"Aww. I fear nothing from these kneebiters. They haven't got the...look out!"

Maurice had regained his footing and lunged for Calista. Thanks to Truitt's warning, she managed to sidestep in time, and the orv hurtled past. She swung her staff after him, letting the handle of the slasher strike the back of his head. He yelped and tumbled into the dirt.

Truitt whooped, but the female scowled at him again. "Run!" she shouted, then turned to see Bertram's whip lashing at her. She dodged, but it nicked the sleeve of her upper arm, creating a tear in the white fabric. Not stopping to examine the damage or allow the orv to get another hit on her, which would undoubtedly inflict more harm, she continued her dodge, converting it into a spin. As her legs brought her closer to Bertram, she re-gripped her staff at a lower point and extended her reach to close the distance. The orv yelped as the steel ball smashed his knuckles, driving the weapon from his hand.

Calista pulled the staff back, pausing to consider her next move. Bertram shook his damaged fingers, the lamp in his other hand bouncing with the movement. He didn't seem eager to pick up the slasher again. Perhaps the ruffians were subdued enough for them to leave.

"He's getting up!" Truitt yelled. "Watch — "

This time, his warning came too late, and a growling mass of angry Maurice slammed her backward several feet. Fortunately, he'd struck her with the rock-solid skull and not his horn, or she would have been gored. She landed hard against the remains of a wooden post, the charred end protruding up through the rubble. A foot further and it would have impaled her. Releasing a growl of her own, she snatched up her staff and swung as the orv launched at her again. Wood met thigh and he yelped and rolled to the side.

It halted him for only a moment. She jumped to her feet as Bertram recovered his whip and brought it up to lash her. Standing just within range, she needed to only move back a short distance to avoid it.

Instead, she leapt at him, tucking her body into a roll and coming up on the inside of the whip's strike. But as she started to stand, he swung the slasher around and this time she stood too close to dodge.

A pebble smashed the glass of the lantern. Bertram hurled it aside with a yell and dropped his whip. Oil splattered over the wood and debris, catching fire a second later as the burning wick struck it.

Calista saw the burst and scrambled to her feet, staff held ready for another attack. But the flames had sent Bertram into panic mode. "Look! Fire! Fire!" He kicked a pile of rubble at it, which only caused it to flare brighter.

The faroko barrelled past him in Truitt's direction, who remained staring at where his pebble had gone. "Smashing shot, that was!" he beamed. "Did you — whoa!"

The rest of his question got lost as Calista grabbed him around the stomach, hoisted him off the ground, and continued running toward the front door. Truitt squirmed, but she ignored him as she glanced back to check if they were being pursued. Bertram and Maurice, the latter limping on his left leg, were hoofing it out through the kitchen though, no longer concerned with their captive and his rescuer.

Certain they were safe, Calista ran out the door, Truitt in her arms.

Chapter 6

The Recovery Remuneration
Or A Frog In The Fog

T
HE PAIR FLED the building, Calista running with Truitt squirming against her, as the fire spread to engulf it. Only when they reached the safety of a dark corner three houses down the street did she stop and lower the incensed berkis to the ground.

They watched the blaze grow, orange flames shooting from the windows and licking the sides. Black smoke poured out and plumed upwards, causing their eyes to sting even from the distance. If not stopped, the fire could consume the entire section of buildings, and then move onto the rest of the city.

"I hope those orvs escaped unharmed," Calista said, unwinding Maurice's whip from her staff and tossing it into a scraggly bush by the house.

"If not, they had it coming to them."

She looked down at him. His head barely topped her waist, but she could see him focused on the flames. "Do you truly feel that way?"

Truitt hesitated before answering. "No. I..." He turned to look up at her. Despite seeing her fight and being carried by her out of the fire, he hadn't realised the impressiveness of her height. It was unmistakable now, especially standing next to her, with his eyes level with her tightly packed groyne. He could hardly see her face over her full chest.

Calista recognised the stare. "Go ahead. Say it. I've heard it all. Clock tower. Lady long legs. High pockets. Sun blocker. Toothpick. Your friend calls me Stilts."

He shook his head and lowered his gaze, only to get an eyeful of her crotch again. He redirected his attention to the blaze. "I - I didn't need rescuing."

"I am certain you didn't," she said with a smile.

The sound of a clanging bell approaching meant the scene would soon be crawling with firemen. Gravenmore had one of the most efficient fire brigades in Leverhelm, or so she had heard, though she had never seen them in action. This probably wasn't a good time for it, either. "Come on. We don't want to be caught here."

He didn't answer, but followed as she turned away from the disaster he caused. They plodded through the bleak section of town. The gas lamps here were lit, illuminating the nearly empty streets. A gang of children sprinted past them, heading to see the blaze. More people were milling about, chattering among themselves about the alarm.

Calista's mind raced with questions. What should have been a straightforward assignment had taken an unexpected turn, like the morning's job, but in a much more destructive way. She had rescued the victim, which was good. But in the process, she had also fought his abductors and set a building on fire. Not so good. She wanted answers. "Who were they?"

"I don't know." Despite his earlier bluster, Truitt had gone strangely silent.

"Why did they grab you?"

"I don't know."

Calista exhaled. "What do you know?"

"That I didn't need rescuing," he snapped. "I could have handled them."

"With a slingshot?"

"Yes."

He's either highly skilled or addled. "What happens if you run out of pebbles?"

"Can't happen," he chuckled, holding up the shooter. "Enchanted. Never runs out."

Calista looked down at the weapon. Even fully extended, his arm didn't quite reach the bottom of her chest. "Magic," she said, though it showed no visible evidence it possessed such power.

"You don't approve?" The slingshot returned to his pocket.

"I'd rather depend on my own abilities."

He looked up at her. "Not all of us are the size of lamp posts with massive staffs."

"The way you challenged them, I'd say your staff is plenty massive," she responded, meeting his gaze. "Or your thinker is on the small side."

Truitt turned his eyes back to the street. "That is something you must figure out for yourself."

"That is not something I need to know." Ahead of them, curious gawkers, awakened by the noise, crowded the way. No one, however, paid any overt attention to the pair, except a few who were startled by Calista's height. The bell had ceased clanging, suggesting the fire had been brought under control, so they walked on in silence.

She still didn't have answers, though. *Why would someone grab him? He doesn't seem dangerous. What is he caught up in? Besides gambling.* "Your skember friend in the Right Hand seemed concerned for your safety."

Truitt chuckled again. "I am certain ol' Raffles had only my best interest in mind. Was it he who sent you looking for me?"

"He hired me, yes."

"Hired, eh? That doesn't sound like something the skinflint would do. I wonder what his concern is in my matters."

More questions. "He mentioned you owed him a sum of money."

"There's the culprit. A truly generous nature has Raffles. Be sure to count whatever he's paying you. Twice. Then take stock of any valuables upon your personage to ensure they have not mysteriously absconded."

"You sound as if you don't trust him," she observed.

"I have had the pleasure of that chuckaboo's company for a considerable number of years. I trust him to be utterly untrustable." After a pause, he added, "Which appears contradictory, and I admit it might be, but I have not a better way to explain it."

Sounds like pure affection between them. "Perhaps. But he did have me rescue you. That must account for at least a positive tally in your ledger."

"Harumph! I did not require assistance in obtaining my freedom. The means of my escape would have presented themselves to me eventually, and I would have employed their usage."

Calista let out a laugh. "I find that difficult to believe, considering you refused to take the opportunity I provided. We could have fled without the fight and fire."

"And not avenge my capture?" He came to an abrupt halt beneath a street lamp. "My body belongs not to the fowl, so call me not chicken-hearted or pigeon-livered!"

She stopped too and turned to him. "Hang about. I never questioned your spirit, just your sense. You weren't alone in that collie shangie. I was hired to recover you, not endanger my future commissions defending your scrawny backside."

Truitt brought a hand to his chest. "I was defending my honour."

"*I* was defending your life." She tapped her staff against the pavement to punctuate her argument. They glared at each other for several seconds before she threw up her hand. "Once I return you to your friend, I can collect my fee and we can see the backs of each other."

"Then let me aid us both in that endeavour." He pointed ahead and resumed walking. "My house is a mere stroll away on this street. I will take my leave now, and with the errand complete, you are free to request your payment from our mutual acquaintance. Tell him he shall have the balance of what I owe him in the morning."

Calista shook her head but followed. "You must come with me. He'll want proof I rescued you. I doubt he will accept my word alone."

"That is not my concern. But I see no reason for him to call your honesty into question."

"You said he isn't to be trusted."

"He isn't. However, your virtue will counter his lack of the same, and the transaction shall be a fair one." Truitt paused, then added, "In theory."

Was that a compliment? "What makes you think I'm virtuous?"

Truitt shrugged. "Would a dishonest individual attempt to not only liberate a fellow but also exchange blows with his captors?"

"I am getting paid to do this."

That made him pause. "Is that what truly matters?"

How did we end up in a discussion of morality? Was it only the money? She needed it, but is that why she began taking the assignments Armend found for her? She liked to think she did it to help others. The image of the previous day's attempted theft in the bakery flashed in front of her. Who was she truly helping there? Would she have taken the job if not for the reward? Probably not. But perhaps she could have chosen a task that matched the virtue suggested by this berkis. "It isn't. But — "

"Then when you return and Raffles declines to fulfil his part of the agreement, you will still be content in the knowledge you helped another." He hopped up the stairs of a sad-looking house of flats before turning to address her. "Now that is settled, I will go. It has been a trying day. I would thank you for your assistance, but as we agreed, it is the satisfaction of the work which is the most rewarding. I would not wish to sully that with gratitude." He twisted the knob and ducked inside, pulling the door closed behind him.

Calista stared at where he had been, feeling the heat rise in her cheeks. *Did he just manipulate me into not accepting payment?*

The door re-opened a few inches and Truitt's face appeared in the crack. "Besides, I didn't need rescuing," he told her, then disappeared again.

Why, that.. Fist clenched, she took a step toward the building, only to stop herself. *Remember your training. Fenton says anger makes you lose focus. But that berkis is so aggravating!*

She drew in a lungful of air. As she released it slowly, she looked at the sky. It was late, and Truitt had been correct in one regard. It had been a trying day. After orienting herself, she made her way to the Right Hand, which she believed sat only a few streets over. Despite what she said, she did need the money and hoped Raffles had not taken his leave.

That the casino was open at the late hour came as no surprise to her. Like the drinkers at the Happy Swallow, gamblers always found an excuse to engage in their activities, regardless of the hour. Upon stepping inside, she discovered it was even busier than before. Still, she located the trio at the same table. As far as she could tell, they hadn't moved from the spot all day. They were involved in a card game like before, too, although the number of buttons, bolts, and pebbles in each pile differed.

When they saw her approach, Faye placed her cards face down on the table and Raffles tucked his against his chest. Hugh glanced at her, then resumed staring at his hand.

"Lookity who it is!" the skember intoned. "The missy with her 'ead in the clouds! Come to collect, eh?"

Calista nodded. "I have. Your friend is safe at home."

"Why not bring 'is lordship 'ere? The scene of the crime, so to speak."

"He refused to return with me. But he said to tell you he will pay you what he owes tomorrow."

Raffles clicked his tongue. "That promise's as useless as a frog in the fog if 'e's still captive. You might be spinning tales."

Calista felt her face warming again. "And I told him he needed to come here, that you wouldn't accept my claim. He hoped you would believe me by virtue of my virtue."

"Always the optimist, our Truitt is," Faye piped in.

"That what you call it?" The faroko couldn't keep the ire from her voice, and Faye visibly retreated. "After I freed him and tried to defend him while he escaped, he started pelting our adversaries with pebbles and insults. I barely got him out of there with his hairy arse intact."

Raffles guffawed. "That'll be Truitt, alrighty. I believe you." He reached into his pocket and extracted a single coin. "One shilling, as promised. Don't spend it all at once!" He laughed again at his own joke.

Calista glanced at the other two as she took it from his fingers. Faye wore a grin. Hugh remained stoically focused on what he held. "You don't seem to be overly concerned about his welfare. Have you tried to aid his return in any fashion, or are cards your singular focus?"

The older skember looked up at her, and his eyes softened. "Truitt's continued drawing of air, 'owever foul, is a blessing to us all. We sent you, Stilts, to assure that 'appened. Suggesting we is 'eartless cuts deep. You wound me."

"What else was there to do?" Faye chimed in. "Run about the streets, knockin' on doors. 'Pardon me, miss. Sorry to disturb you, but I hoped you might have seen me chum. He was enjoyin' some entertainments of the bettin' kind when two ruffians jammed him in a sack and hightailed it.' We stayed here in case he came back, but I've had the morbs all day. So's Hugh."

"That's the mutton he had for lunch," Raffles corrected. "Told 'im to go easy." When the orv's face reddened, he laughed again. "Our lad Truitt 'as a talent for getting into scrapes in a blink, then getting 'isself out just as quick. It is a wonder. So when 'e gets nabbed in the middle of a game, we figures it's another of 'is adventures. No need to fuss, as 'e'll come back in 'is own time."

Unbelievable! "If that's true, why send me? Surely not to finish the hand," Calista asked.

"Not for that. Though I was winning."

"He said the same."

The trio chuckled. "Not likely," Raffles told her. "When it comes to affairs of the table, our lordship's luck is beggar poor."

"Makes you wanna weep," Faye added.

Calista found herself understanding Truitt's comments about not trusting Raffles and guessed that extended to the other two. "But you keep taking his money?"

"Who are we to deprive 'im of 'is fun?" The skember's tone was almost mocking.

It didn't sit well with Calista. "I see. And how much does he owe you?"

"Today? Eighteen pence. That sounds right."

"That's all? You spent a far greater amount to collect that paltry sum."

Raffles shrugged. "It's the principle of the matter. Truitt's no skilamalink. 'E'll pay up when 'e can. But we would be doing 'im a disservice if 'e was allowed to cultivate bad 'abits."

"We's helpin' him, we is," Faye chimed in with a nod, setting the trinkets on her hat bobbing.

I can't believe them. I thought Truitt rude for not returning with me, but with friends like this, I don't blame him. "You've got a real heart of gold."

Raffles nodded. "It's a burden. Now, seeing you've been paid and our chum's been liberated, perhaps you could push off. I've got a game to win." He pulled his cards away from his chest and began considering them again.

Calista couldn't resist the temptation. She glanced at his set of numbers and suits. "Not with that hand, you aren't." He glared up at her, and she returned a smile. *Try to win now!*

She flourished the coin before slipping it into her pocket. The job done, she gripped her staff, spun on her heel, and strode out the door of the casino. *I'm glad that assignment is over. I'll never have to interact with any of them again.*

Chapter 7

The Juvenile Intermission
Or Got Any Sweets?

T RUITT WAITED SEVERAL minutes in the apartment house front hall before opening the door again. The female had gone! He crept down the steps, peering about in case she had stuck around after all, but he found no sign of her.

Alone. Finally! he thought, straightening his jacket. The kidnapping had taken him by surprise, but apart from having to sit, tied up and gagged, for hours, he remained not much worse for the wear. Hungry, tired, and in need of a bath, but he could take care of those needs soon.

With a last look around, he started down the street. The smell of smoke and the curious chatter of a few residents still milling about filled the air. He ignored both as he crossed to the sidewalk, then rounded the corner, heading west.

"Hiya, Mr Truitt. Ya going to the casino?"

He turned to the voice and saw a young orv female shuffling toward him. The skirt of her lavender dress displayed significant fraying, while the corset enveloping her torso appeared disproportionately large for her age. In contrast to the feminine clothes, a worn aviator's cap topped her head, its flaps dangling down past her shoulders. Her horned nose hadn't yet developed a sharpened tip, giving her the appearance of perpetually trying to smell something repugnant. While only eight years old, she stood several inches taller than him.

"Good evening, Lavinia," he greeted, stopping for her to catch up. "No, I have taken too many gambles this night. It is time I return home."

"Ya mind the company?"

After the day's events, Truitt found himself craving the presence of a friend. "I would be tickled for your companionship."

The girl's face lit up. "Chirky! Ya hear the bells?"

He continued walking with her beside him. "Is that what they were? I thought the opera had come to the Ward."

She giggled. "Naw. There was a fire in the Bedevilled."

Truitt tensed. It was a bad section of the city where no one should visit by choice. He hadn't been given one, and didn't like the idea of her being there. "Did you observe it yourself?"

"No!" Her eyes widened in astonishment at the suggestion. "I never go there. Wicked things live there."

"Quite right," he told her, relieved she had the sense to avoid it. "You stay far away from it. And perhaps the fire took care of whatever is there."

"Mebbe." She went quiet as she considered the next question. "Got any sweets?"

Truitt grinned. *That didn't take long.* "It is entirely possible there is one in my pouch. Shall we look?"

Lavinia's face lit up again. "Oh, yes!"

They stopped while he pulled a purse from a waistcoat pocket. Made from coal-black silk, it measured no more than three inches in length. He lifted it so the girl could see it clearly in the lamplight. "Behold how it is empty." He pinched it flat. Lavinia grinned in anticipation, her body spinning slightly back and forth. She had seen the show before and knew what was coming.

"But when I reach inside..." Truitt tugged the drawstrings open, extended two fingers within, and pulled out a pink and yellow hard candy. "We find a treat!"

He placed it in her hand, and she popped it in her mouth eagerly. "Mmmm. I love that trick."

"I'm glad," he said, closing the pouch and tucking it away. "How's your mum?"

"Alright."

They resumed walking. "Still working at the chemist?"

"Yeah."

The pair remained quiet for a time, the orv girl's shyness reasserting itself. Truitt appreciated that she felt comfortable talking with him. She had a group of friends she normally hung around with, and the berkis knew all of them. He often gave them candies and, when he could, a bit of money. He was fondest of Lavinia, and she seemed to reciprocate the feelings.

As they approached a line of street vendors, still promoting their goods despite the hour, he noticed her eyeing a few of the food carts. It reminded him of his own hunger. "Have you eaten today?" he asked her. She shook her head. "Neither have I. Would you kindly join me in sampling some of these wares?"

Her eyebrows went up, but she feigned disinterest and gave an exaggerated sigh. "If ya insist." She could only hold the expression a moment longer before a grin split her face again.

Truitt guided her under the small, tin-roofed canopy of one. The sturdy wood and metal cart perched on large, iron-rimmed wooden wheels, which allowed it to be moved to various sections of the city. Though faded and chipped, a mix of red and green paint adorned its sides, along with a hand-painted sign. Atop the simple wagon lay an assortment of delicacies, kept heated by a coal brazier underneath. Behind the mobile stand, an older berkis sporting a flat cap stood on a stool. "Good evening, sir," the seller greeted. "What can I get for you and the lass?"

The pair looked over the selection, Truitt with an experienced eye, Lavinia with barely contained longing. "What do you think of these?" Her eyes doubled in size. Taking that as affirmation, he turned to the berkis as he pulled out his pouch again. "I would like six of your finest meat pies, with three wrapped for later, a fourth wrapped separately, and the final two here, so my companion and I may enjoy them now."

Lavinia shook with excitement, and he struggled to keep his smile from her. "Oh, and kindly package up some trotters," he told the vendor. "Two sheep, two pig." The berkis nodded as Truitt looked at the girl. "Because it's Tuesday."

Truitt pulled some coins from the seemingly empty pouch and passed them over. The seller handed a pair of meat pies to him, and he, in turn, gave one to Lavinia. The warm pastries were a tad dry, but nicely flaky around the beef and potato insides, with just a hint of rosemary.

Truitt had not realised the extent of his hunger and wolfed down the food eagerly. He felt a twinge of embarrassment until he saw Lavinia already stuffing the last of hers into her mouth. She caught his eye and grinned, a few crumbs falling from her lips.

They collected the rest from the vendor — three bundles in paraffin paper — and continued on. Truitt bore the single pie he planned to have later and Lavinia carried the remainder. Her arms were larger and stronger than his, and he doubted he could have pried them away from her if he tried.

Lavinia's father had died a few years ago from an unknown illness, and though she and her mother weren't strictly poor, he knew they didn't always get as much food as he thought they should. Enough conversations with the girl told him they needed aid, as did many in the Ward and the Rookery.

The pair chatted idly as they continued through the night streets. The earlier alarm had brought the restful residents of the city out of their homes. *Nothing like someone's suffering to get people excited,* Truitt thought as he watched them huddled together in gossiping groups under lamps and in business doorways. *No doubt by tomorrow they'll blame this on the Shadow or Kettlebelly. Or whatever lives in the Bedevilled.*

He knew the truth, though. Or part of it. The fire started from a pebble shot, not a supernatural means, but he didn't care to make that fact public knowledge. The authorities of Gravenmore considered arson a grave crime, and he had other plans for his time that couldn't be carried out behind bars. Or dead.

No distinct delineation existed between the Ward and the Mids, but most living in either of those understood where one section left off and the other began, and the pair were approaching it now.

"This is where we should part, my young friend. The hour is late, and your mum will be worried about you.

"I know." She stared across Woodcock Way, which acted as an artificial border. "Why do ya come here if ya live there?"

The question didn't surprise Truitt. It's one he'd asked himself many times. "Would you want to live there?"

A smile crossed her face. "Oh, yes!"

Naturally, you would. You only see the surface. "Well, it's full of sniffies who stand around all day nattering about the weather and pleasantries. 'Tippy-ho. Isn't it sunny? What-hey! Yes, it is. Golly-gee, will it be sunny tomorrow? Bumbly-rumbly, it could be!' That is why I come here. Who wants that?"

Lavinia giggled. "Not me!"

"Me neither! And the meat pies are better here." He held up his single-wrapped pastry, then placed it under his arm. "Now, you make sure you share them with your mum, as well as the trotters! Don't go gobbling them all yourself."

Lavinia giggled again. "I won't. Bye, Mr Truitt."

"Wait." The pouch appeared in his hand. "I think there is one more candy in here." He tugged it open and pulled out a single sweet, which he handed to her. She smiled and popped it into her mouth immediately. "And this is for your mum." From the same seemingly empty bag, he extracted a large coin. "Because it's Tuesday."

Lavinia's eyes brightened as he reached up and carefully placed it in her pocket. "Now go! And keep clear of the Bedevilled."

"I will. Thanks!"

Truitt watched her sprint back toward the inner streets of the Ward. *Sweet chavy. Now, home!* He tucked the pouch away and took the pie from under his arm.

His flat lay just a few blocks northwest from the edge of the Mids, and within ten minutes, the stairs leading up to its front door stood before him. From the outside, it resembled an average townhouse. But when the city had expanded, many single-family houses were converted into multiple flats. This one appeared to be in better condition than the house he tricked Calista with.

Truitt hopped up the steps and withdrew a slight brass key from the multi-pocketed waistcoat. After jiggling it in the lock, he opened the door and stepped inside. In what had originally been the reception hall, a double flight of stairs led to the upper storeys. They were a combination of deep and narrow short steps, the standard in buildings open to all races. Skembers and berkis used the thin while the others skipped them and utilised just the larger ones.

Truitt climbed to the second of three levels and, with a smaller key, unlocked the only door there. He stepped inside and relocked it before returning the bit of metal to its pocket. *Finally home!*

Illumination from the street brightened the room sufficiently for him to ignite an oil lamp on a low table. With the matchbox from there, he lit a second in the corridor ahead of him, then did the same for the lamps in a chamber off the left of that.

While more extravagant than most domiciles in the Ward, he considered the flat modestly comfortable. In his bedroom, simple lined moulding framed white-flower patterned maroon wallpaper. Tan ceilings offset the rich, cherry hardwood floors. A few paintings dotted the walls above a chest of drawers and a dressing table. On the opposite wall, a pinwheel-adorned coverlet with matching pillows decorated a low, queen-sized bed.

Truitt circled it, lit another lamp on a nightstand, and crossed through a doorway there to the lavatory. With the room illuminated, he turned his attention to the water heater.

The oblong cast-iron construction stood nearly as tall as the berkis. A relatively new invention, it could be found in a few businesses where hot water was essential, the homes of the rich living in the Sunside, and, oddly, in the flat of this individual.

Truitt turned the valve of a copper pipe leading into it. He listened to the gurgling liquid flowing, filling the many coils of piping within. When the echo nearly vanished, he closed it off and opened a pair of doors at the base. From a bucket beside it, he scooped in two small loads of coals. Once they were lit, he shut the chamber and walked back into the bedroom.

Bath is in the works. Now to change. From a tall, rosewood wardrobe in the corner, he retrieved a dressing gown and tossed it on the bed. He reached for his head but found only hair. *My hat! Damn and blast! It must still be in the Right Hand.*

After spilling the contents of his pockets onto the dressing table, he proceeded to take off his jacket, waistcoat, and shirt, folding each garment meticulously on a chair. Next, he peeled off his shoes, socks, and trousers. He came to the cloth around his neck and scowled. *Those devils gagged me with my own handkerchief! I will thrash them properly if we cross paths again!*

He tugged it off and deposited it on the pile of clothes, then donned the robe, pulling the belt tight about his waist. *I must find out who they were first. And why they targeted me.* A gurgle from his stomach drew his attention. *But before I embark on any endeavours, I must eat.*

After he polished off the other meat pie, Truitt returned to the lavatory. By fiddling with a few valves, he released cold water directly from the city supply and piping hot water from the heater into a copper bathtub. After some experimentation, it soon reached the right temperature for a soothing bath.

The berkis hung his robe on a hook, dropped his drawers, and eased himself into the tub. A sigh escaped his lips as he reclined against the metal, his body immersed. For a few minutes, he let the heat soothe his muscles. The orvs hadn't been gentle, but their kind wasn't known for grace. If you wanted a tough job handled, you'd hire one of the thick-skinned individuals. Just make sure what you needed done didn't involve something fragile. Anything less sturdy than a cast-iron ball was likely to be damaged.

Truitt was much more vulnerable than that. He winced as his fingers rubbed a sore area on his arm. *I dare say I'm fortunate to escape their hospitality with only superficial wounds. But what was their intent?*

By the time they reached the abandoned house, he had worn himself out with his protest. When they tied him to a chair, he resumed his shouting, resulting in the gagging. For a few hours, he struggled against the bonds, but they were too tight, and he finally gave up and nodded off.

When he woke, it had grown dark. Despite having his back to the orvs, he could hear them arguing in the kitchen. They didn't sound happy. Truitt got the impression they were waiting for someone, but most of what they said had been muffled. He'd made out the words 'boss' a few times, along with 'tonight', and guessed the one who ordered his abduction would arrive that evening, but who or why he didn't know.

Then she showed up. He pictured the woman who had saved him. *No, she didn't rescue me. She merely facilitated my escape.* She had been ungodly tall. As a berkis, he typically had to look up to most of the population, but she stood out in a class all her own. *Legs as long as my whole body! And her coker-nuts looked juicy, from what I could see. I'd need a stepping stool to examine them properly.* Under the water, his hand shifted closer to his crotch. *Or I could just climb her, one luscious inch at a time. But first, trot down her petticoat lane.* He touched his stiffening staff, remembering her comment about it.

Stop it! Truitt sat up abruptly, retracting his hand. *Distractions like this will ruin my plan. I have to remain focused. Anyway, I'll never see her again.* He snatched a washcloth from a short shelf. *It is most likely I have only a few days to do it.* The soaked cloth moved to his face, and he scrubbed it in earnest. Away came a layer of soot from the fire. Then the dirt he smeared on that morning. *I studied the layout last evening. I know how I'm getting in.*

He ran a wet hand through his thick, black hair. *Tomorrow night, I steal the Dragon Eye Gem.*

Chapter 8

The Prosperity Potential
Or That Sum Could Buy This Pub

FRUSTRATED AND TIRED, Calista returned to the Happy Swallow a few hours before midnight. Not prepared to face a pub full of people or answer Armend's inevitable questions about the night's assignment, she used the back entrance.

The room Armend set aside for her exuded simple elegance. A single ornate rug covered a third of the floor and the wallpaper had a muted floral pattern darkened from years of smoke. The furnishings were basic: a double bed with a striped bedspread and twin pillows, a cushioned high-backed chair, a tall wardrobe in a corner, and two small tables. On one sat a long-necked lamp, which added to the illumination from the streetlights outside a heavily curtained window.

On the way back from the Right Hand, she had picked up a bit of hard cheese and a ham sandwich from a street vendor. They lasted her the return trip, but her hunger had returned.

As a child, her appetite had been slight, and her mother regularly scolded her for not eating more. When her growth spurt began, so did her cravings. By the age of sixteen, she consumed more in one meal than her parents did in a day. When she arrived in Gravenmore, her needs eased off, but she still found herself hungry more often than she liked.

There is probably something to eat in the kitchen. But that would mean dealing with more people. Ugh! Instead, she snatched up a bag beside her bed and pulled out a pear drop. It wasn't filling, but it might ease her cravings. She popped it into her mouth and began stripping for sleep, starting with her boots.

I suppose I can now say I visited the Bedevilled and suffered no ill effects. I guess the stories aren't true. Those orvs no doubt figured it would be a secure place to hide their victim. No one would be stupid enough to investigate. Except me, of course. And for a single, lousy shilling.

She dropped her corset onto the bed and began unbuttoning her shirt. *That skember was a bigger miser than Zusa this morning. What was his name? Raffles. Parting with a solitary coin for the return of a friend, only because he owes him money. I wonder what would have happened if Truitt hadn't lost to him.*

Once she removed her blouse and folded it neatly beside her corset, she started on her pants, first emptying the few coins and flail from their pockets and setting them on the dresser. *And that Truitt! I'm not sure which one is worse. The tight-arse or the supercilious coot. It wasn't a rescue, my tail! You were tied to a bloody chair, you great fopdoodle! Then you can't even show appreciation for my efforts!*

Calista tugged her pants off and lay them on the bed before crossing to a small closet and pulling out a nightgown. *And he definitely did not save my life. I wouldn't have been there if not for him getting himself caught.* She pulled the item over her head, threading her arms through the sleeves. It remained a few inches too short, and the sleeves billowed, but it fit well enough. The gown had been made for a female orv, shorter and thicker than her own form.

But what did they want him for? She crossed back to her nightstand and popped another pear drop onto her tongue, taking a moment to savour its sweetness. *He professed ignorance, but he must have some idea.* Abductions were not a common occurrence in Gravenmore, as far as she knew. Not that every crime that happened got reported to the general population. *For all I know, kidnappings occur all the time in the Ward, and this Truitt was just the victim for the night.*

Calista pulled down the spread and sheets of her bed and sat on the edge. *That isn't likely though, or we would have heard many more requests for rescues. Or maybe there were, and I didn't ask Armend for them.*

With a sigh, she lay down, resting her head on a plush pillow as she tugged the bedding over her. *Even if there are, I'm not asking for that again. There is no point in helping people at the risk of my sanity or my hide.*

She reached out and extinguished the lamp. The light from the street illuminated her room in a soft glow, and she let herself relax to the muffled sounds from the pub below. Before long, thoughts of arrogant berkis, greedy skember, and hostile orvs were replaced by the gentle embrace of sleep.

Calista awoke hungry a few hours after sunrise the next morning and reached for another candy. It was her last piece, and she moved it slowly to her mouth in an attempt to prolong the enjoyment. *I should have purchased more yesterday when I had the chance. Maybe I can get more this evening.*

She dressed quickly. Despite what she told herself the night before, she still wished to help people in a more meaningful way, but didn't see how she could do that if her last assignment was any indicator of what that entailed.

Once fully clothed, she reached for her staff, then paused. *Breakfast first. I shouldn't need to fight anyone downstairs. Unless they are blocking the food!*

Her hand ran along the smooth railing as she descended the stairs, flat-heeled boots padding against the oak steps. The bottom level stood empty except for Armend wiping down tables, cleaning up after last night's customers.

His head raised when he heard her and prepared to speak when she held up a finger. "Not yet. I need food."

"As I was about to say," he said, pointing toward the rear wall, "there are a few mutton pies in the back. Probably cold now."

Calista smiled. "That'll do. Thank you." She reached the bottom, stepped behind the bar, and pushed through the first swinging door. What had been an office area for the previous hotel had been converted into a bare-bones kitchen.

Near the doorway stood a tall ice box with multiple doors leading to internal cooling chambers. Several copper and iron pots hung above a range cooker sitting on the far end. Between the dual appliances lay a long counter next to a deep sink. Above that sat a wide shelf. A handful of varying-sized step ladders were set at various positions to allow Armend to access all sections. A second door led to a basement.

A trim orv busied himself emptying the ashes from the range into a metal bucket. Silas was Armend's assistant and cook, though the Happy Swallow did little actual cooking. In the evening hours, a few vendors regularly set up their stands outside the pub, allowing a small selection of food to be made available to the patrons, such as the two mutton pies perched on the counter. Silas used the cooker to warm any purchases and, on occasion, make a pot of rich stew.

Calista grabbed a plate from the shelf and wiped it off with a cloth before approaching the pies. Too hungry to search for other utensils, she snatched up the wide spoon beside them and began carving out a section, scooping the pastry and its innards onto the dish. Several chunks fell aside in her enthusiasm, which she eagerly plucked up and dropped on top of the growing pile.

When she felt she had enough, Calista took the plate and sat on one of the taller step stools. She'd shovelled three spoonfuls of the pastry into her mouth before realising her opportunity. "Silas, I have a question," she said after a large swallow. Her eyes widened as the pastry tickled her throat. *This is good pie!*

The orv straightened, brushing blackened hands against his apron. "Yes, Ma'am?" They had known each other for several years, ever since Armend hired him on, yet he always addressed her in the most formal of manners. She had long ago given up on dissuading the practice.

"Why would an orv kidnap someone?"

"That is highly specific," Silas responded, scratching his forehead with the back of his wrist, being careful not to smear ashes on himself, his clothes, or the spectacles perched on his horned nose. "Perhaps a better question would be 'why would anyone kidnap another'."

"Because my situation deals specifically with orvs." *And because I can't imagine a skember or berkis attempting to carry someone off.* Her people would not, of course, ever engage in any such activities, though she wouldn't admit that bias, even to herself.

"My kind does not have a greater proclivity toward abduction than others, Ma'am. You will have to ask the perpetrators directly."

"I can't. They all ran off."

Understanding registered on his face. "Ah. Your assignment last night, I believe?"

"Yes. Armend tell you?" Calista took another gulp of pie. *So delicious!*

Silas nodded. "He said you were seeking to lend your services to those in need. 'Lend' being the operative word if they could not pay."

"Not anymore," Calista began, around a mouthful of meat. She shrugged in embarrassment, swallowed, then continued. "I've learned my lesson. From now on, I want high-paying assignments that don't involve ungrateful victims."

"In Gravenmore?"

"I know," she laughed. "Dream the impossible dream. Thanks, Silas."

She hopped to her feet, gave him a final wave with her spoon, and shoved through the door into the main room, pie in hand. After moving around to the front of the bar, she plopped down onto a stool and took another mouthful.

Armend finished arranging the tables and pushed a rolling step platform back to its position in a corner. He needed to move it from table to table for cleaning them, sometimes shifting it a few times for the larger seating areas. Calista had asked him once why he didn't let her or Silas wipe them down instead, considering it obviously entailed a lot more work for him. But he insisted he relished the physical activity, and it wasn't significantly more challenging.

It also served as a pleasant reminder that this pub belonged to *him*, and he could take care of the tables if he wanted to.

"Remember what I said yesterday? About wanting to make helping people a priority over money?" Calista watched him cross to the bar and took another spoonful as he climbed to the shelf there.

"I recall a conversation in that vein."

"Well, you may forget it now," she told him, emphasising her decision with a spoon jab in his direction. "I want an assignment where I can get paid for standing around. No more rescuing unappreciative abductees for selfish clients."

A chuckle escaped Armend's lips as he leaned against the counter. "Last night's task went that well, eh?"

"The skember who made the request was deliberately unhelpful in details on how to find his friend. I tracked the missing berkis down myself to, of all the places I wouldn't want to go, the Bedevilled."

"I am guessing, then, you played some part in the fire there."

Calista paused, her utensil mid-scoop. "That was an accident. Mostly." She wiggled in her seat. "Instead of fleeing to safety when I freed him, the ratbag assaulted his captors with a slingshot. Pebbles against a pair of orvs!"

The skember scratched his chin. "Sounds rather bricky. Were they armed?"

"Fully! With slashers. That's why I had to step in. With my staff."

"And the fire?"

"One had a lamp. When he tried to whip me, Truitt smashed it with a stone. The distraction helped me get out of range, but splattered oil and flame to the floor. Fwoom." Bits of mutton went flying as she mimed the flames igniting with both hands. "The place erupted, and we ran. I carried him away. The orvs escaped in the other direction."

"Quite an adventure," Armend noted, casually removing a bit of pie from his horn and setting it on the bar top. "So this Truitt saved your life."

"I beg your pardon? I freed his scrawny little arse. Yet, he didn't express gratitude, claiming he didn't require any rescue."

"And now you are giving up on helping others this way? Because of one unlicked cub? Is this the same faroko who trains with Master Lightfoot?"

"It isn't like that," she protested. *Is it?* "Maybe it is. At the moment, I need a simple job that doesn't involve people."

Armend gave her a toothy smile. "Spoken like a true altruist. Fortunately, I found an assignment you might enjoy. I wasn't sure you would want it, after — "

Calista groaned. "Yes, I know. I'm a jobber knot. Just tell me what it is."

"A mere guarding assignment. Overnight. No orphans or berkis involved. Hopefully."

But she recognised his tone. He used it whenever the task sounded too good to be true, but he wanted her to take it anyway. Armend consistently had her best interests in mind, but that didn't mean she always agreed with what he thought those were. "What are you leaving out? What am I guarding, and from whom?"

"Oh, a little something called the Dragon Eye Gem."

The faroko dropped the spoon with a clatter to the wood bar top. Her jaw similarly fell, but with far less sound. *He must be joking.* She studied the bartender for any sign of deceit, but found none. "It's rude to poke fun at me after the night I had."

Armend's grin widened. "There is no deception on my part. That is the request."

"That means I would be protecting it from — "

"The Grey Shadow himself," he finished with a bob of his head. "Or anyone attempting to mimic his success."

Her eyes bulged as she leaned forward. "But is it possible? The Shadow is rumoured to be just that. A shadow. How do you defend against that?"

Armend shrugged. "A lamp?"

Calista frowned. "I am being serious! What kind of job is that?"

"A generous one. Fifty pounds a night."

She stared at him, her tail twitching behind her. "Fifty pounds!" she hissed, then took a deep breath. "That sum could pay for a house."

"That sum could buy this pub."

"And all I have to do is guard the gem? For how long?"

"Not specified. Could be weeks until the Shadow moves on or is caught."

Calista's body deflated as she sat back and retrieved her spoon. "Sounds like a dream assignment. I'm sure it has already been snatched up. For that reward, every would-be defender from the Rookery to the Sunside will be offering their services."

Armend tapped the counter. "That is why Lady Aishwarya is holding auditions for suitable applicants this afternoon. And the number who show up for that will be limited. This request came through discreet channels."

"You mean Esmerelda?"

The skember collected offers and requests from across Gravenmore by means of a wide-reaching network of youths, adult gossips, and specialised 'listeners'. Those in the last group ingratiated themselves into particular parts of the city and walks of life. Once they were accepted into those groups, they used a mix of persuasion and charm to entice information from those around them. Esmerelda, an older berkis and trusted listener working the Sunside, occasionally fed Armend particularly profitable opportunities. "The very same."

Calista tapped the nearly empty plate with her spoon. *With only a few vying for the position, I should have a fair shot. If I don't get it, I just look for another assignment. But if I do...* "Then I'm in. What time do I need to be at this lady's house?"

"I will send word that you are interested. You must be there at four." Armend reached for a pen and paper from under the counter. "Amberlux Manor. I'll give you the address."

"Then I find myself with several hours to idle away," she said as he scribbled down the location. "It allows me the opportunity to engage in some training."

"Leave time for a bath and change of clothes after. You will be visiting one of the warmest toffs of the Sunside."

Calista clicked her tongue. "I know! This won't be my first visit to the Sunside. I can be proper when it's required."

"I hope so," he said, the smile returning to his face. "One would be unable to determine that from watching you eat."

She scooped up another spoon's worth of pie. "Well, I don't need to impress you, do I?"

Armend chuckled and grabbed a worn rag from under the bar. The bartop remained immaculate, save for the crumbs Calista had spilt, which he meticulously wiped into a pile. "Suppose not. But one day, you may find a man to whom manners are all important."

"And lives in a manor house. And dines on oysters and pheasant." She smiled as she cleared her utensil. "If we are imagining my future fantasy husband, please dream larger than proper etiquette."

"If you complete this job, perhaps you will have all those without the gentleman." He watched her begin to wipe her greasy lips across her sleeve, then reconsider and grab the bit of cloth from his fingers. With an exaggerated flourish, she dabbed it against her mouth. He groaned. "Except manners."

"I cannot tell which is the most fanciful of those ideas. Perhaps we will learn after I finish this assignment." She dropped the rag on her empty plate and hopped off the stool. "And who knows? This might be what I need to turn my luck around."

Chapter 9

The Contraption Experimentation
Or There Goes My Blouse!

O NCE SHE FINISHED her breakfast of leftovers, Calista retrieved the staff from her room and left the pub for training.

The Harden Up Gymnasium lay just two streets over on Copper Coin Avenue. A plain building, it didn't possess particular ugliness, yet its bleak exterior sharply contrasted with the fancy storefronts buttressing it. An oak sign hung on the outer wall with the name of the gym painted in simple black letters.

Twelve years ago, Gravenmore's government had decided that citizens should seek physical exertion. Healthy body, healthy mind, and all that, so it had funded a few gymnasiums to be established around the city. They had not mandated that people attend, though, so the new constructions remained empty.

When she arrived in Gravenmore and learned her size could be of value, she sought the nearest gym, hoping to improve her strength. She had met Fenton Lightfoot then, and he offered to teach her to fight. Through his training, she had refined the technique she had adopted out of necessity as a teen into a smooth, efficient rhythm.

He had also suggested the staff as a non-lethal alternative to guns and knives. It would suit her reach and strength, giving her an edge over most opponents.

There had been little equipment to work with then, but soon after, another government decision installed exercise machines in the gymnasiums. In this one, a skember named Peg Pumper arrived to handle their maintenance and instruct on the use of the contraptions.

Calista entered and glanced around. As it often happened, the gym sat vacant. Most days, only those two, the trainer and the mechanician, occupied the space. Three, when she came for training, but she didn't always have the opportunity, like yesterday.

The facilities stood in sharp contrast to the bathhouse. That establishment of relaxation exuded elegance and refinement, with all the amenities to relax someone. The Harden Up Gymnasium, however, had a bare-bones brick interior, with drab walls and unfinished floors. Calista never knew if that was intentional to keep a person focused on their exercise or merely a product of being a government-run institution.

On the left side of the room stood an older male berkis wearing a simple suit of a crimson shirt, white baggy trousers, and an odd leather vest with a high collar. Short black hair topped a clean-shaven face. As she stepped in, he lifted his head to greet her. "Good morning, Little One. Have you come for your training?" It was an affectionate name he had adopted toward her, despite the faroko's height being a few feet taller than his own. He was one of the few people whose nickname for her did not imply she was some freak of nature.

How does he do that? Upon each visit to the gym, Calista found him in this position, as if expecting her arrival. "I have, Fenton. If you have the time."

He made a show of looking around the room. Only the two of them were there, with even Peg absent. "Well, as you can see, we are quite busy this morning. So many citizens wishing to improve their physical well-being. But I believe we might find a space for you," he told her, barely suppressing a grin.

She nodded in return. "That would be appreciated. Thank you."

"Not at all."

They flock to the pubs and casinos at all hours, but cannot spare a moment for exercise. "Has anyone been in at all this week?" Calista asked.

"Oh yes. Only yesterday, a pleasant berkis couple stepped through those doors." Fenton tilted his head. "Granted, it was a mistake. They were looking for the bank. Still, it was nice to see fresh faces. And the day before, after you left, an orv gentleman entered this establishment."

"For callisthenics?"

"To deliver a package for Miss Pumper. Some part or tool she had ordered. She seemed quite pleased to receive it."

"If it was something mechanical, I'm certain she was." She swung her staff up into both hands. "Well, I am here now, so you can honestly say you had a person here to use the gymnasium properly."

"Indeed." Fenton gestured toward an area of the floor, separate from the machines, where a large square of thickly packed hay lay. "What would you like to focus on today?"

Calista rubbed her neck. "Something that will help me work off some frustration. Yesterday was not a good day for me."

"I am genuinely sorry to hear that. What occurred? An unpleasant task?"

"Two of them. The first had been stopping orphans from stealing bread. The second had me rescuing a berkis who had been abducted by orvs."

"Did your skills assist in these?"

"Yes, in both. It was the ungrateful attitude of those I helped that has frustrated me."

Fenton gave an understanding nod. "Appreciation is an uncommon commodity. Most never fully acknowledge their good fortune or the kindness of others."

"I've learned that. But I have a chance tonight to end the need for these assignments." She paused, remembering her possible new task. "Do you know any move I could use against the Grey Shadow?"

Fenton blinked, the only physical indication of his surprise. "That is quite the odd request. If he is merely a person like us, then you should be well suited to deal with him."

"And if he isn't?"

"You must consult someone versed in the occult for that."

Wonderful. "Thank you." She returned her gaze to the gymnasium equipment as a female skember emerged from a doorway in the rear. Recognising the mechanician, she waved.

"Good morning! How are you today? Any aches? Are you feeling tense? Stressed?" Peg bounced toward them, wearing a heavy tool belt around her waist. From it hung multiple wrenches, a hammer, two pairs of pliers, and a mallet. They collided as she walked, producing a constant jingling with every step. To hold them all up, leather suspenders hooked over her shoulders and ivory-coloured shirt, attaching to her black trousers on the front and back. Atop her head of dark, tight curls, between her horns, perched a flat cap and a set of tinted goggles.

While Fenton's still nature mirrored an elm, Peg's mimicked that of an aspen in a storm. She seemed to be always in motion, like the machines she worked on.

"Hi, Peg. I am well. No stress. I — " Calista paused as Fenton fiercely shook his head behind the skember. *I guess he wants me to play along.* "Now that you mention it, I am feeling a tad tense."

Pat clapped her hands. "Wonderful! Wonderful! I mean, sorry to hear that. But I have exactly the solution to all your problems."

Calista eyed her. "You have a way for me to defend against the Grey Shadow?"

"What? Oh, no, no, no!" She gestured toward the collection of devices. "But I have a machine which will ease your tired muscles. Might even help you lose weight!"

"Are you suggesting I need to?" Her tone made it clear that any answer in the affirmative would have dire consequences.

Peg frantically waved her hands. "Oh, no, no, no. That was merely one of the proposed benefits of the new device. Come! Come! This way." She beckoned for her to follow as she bounced over to the contraptions.

Calista looked at Fenton for help, but he just grinned. *Here we go again*, she sighed and followed the mechanician.

They stopped at a simple-looking apparatus. A five-foot-tall pole, topped by a pulley, sat at one end of a long board. A thick cord around the pulley connected to a horizontal pendulum device at the bottom and another pulley attached to a sling at the top. At the opposite end, a short iron framework extended upward from the board.

Peg ran her hand up the pole. "This arrived a few days ago. You wrap those rubber straps of the sling around the tense muscles, and the device pulls back and forth rapidly to vibrate them. Easy, right?"

Calista looked over the machine. It didn't appear particularly problematic, but Peg's devices rarely did. "That's all it does?"

"What? What do you mean? That's what it's built to do." Peg patted the pole. "I admit, the design is simple, but I am positive it is suitable for its purpose."

"I was referring to some of the other times you've 'helped' me with these contraptions. That one," — Calista pointed to a rack with a system of pulleys attached to it — "nearly dislocated my shoulder. And that one," — the finger moved to indicate a rounded hunk of wood stuck on a pole with a saddle on top — "had my crotch sore for a week, without the pleasurable activity that should precede such a malady."

"Bolts! These devices merely require a few adjustments. Take this one. I call it the *Vibrator*."

"That should be the name of the one that rattled my fancy bits. What title have you given that?"

"I had called it the *Back Avenue Shaker*. But after your complaints, I shall re-dub it the *Saddle Sore*." Peg looked up at her with a pained expression.

Calista softened her tone. "I was not complaining. I merely wish to know what condition my various extremities will be in following this experiment."

Peg's face brightened. "Oh, this will be more of a demonstration."

"Then you've tried it before?"

"Not as such. But I've envisioned how it will proceed in my head."

"That's an experiment, then." Calista sighed and stepped up to the device. "Well, let's get on with it. You said put this strap over my shoulders?"

"If that is where you are the most stressed, yes." Peg watched as the faroko moved behind the iron barrier and looped the harness around her torso, resting it atop her shoulder blades. "As I was saying before, the machine pulls back and forth on those attachments. It normally does this using a pendulum system, as you see there. But for today's demonstration, we will hook it up to Madeline." Peg motioned to the berkis. "Mr Lightfoot, if you could be so kind."

Madeline was what she called her portable steam engine. Considerably more compact than those used in the factories, it perched on a wheeled base, allowing the skember to move it around the gymnasium easily. Above a tray of burning coals sat an elongated iron chamber. A tube extended from it into a smaller metal cylinder, and from that emerged a lengthy brass piston. The wheel it drove had been removed and left leaning against one of the other devices.

Fenton helped her roll Madeline to the front of the Vibrator. Peg lined the piston up with the pendulum on the machine, then pulled a length of cord from her pocket and wrapped it around both. "This'll hold them together." Her agile hands tied the ends into a thick knot. "I've kept the flames on low, but now that we are ready... " She retrieved an iron poker from a small hook near the cylinder and jabbed at the coals underneath. Once satisfied, she replaced it and looked at a gauge attached to the boiler tank. "We need only wait for it to build up a head of steam. So what's causing you so much stress?"

"Our friend was telling me about a strange assignment she undertook this previous night," Fenton offered, watching the flame from the coal grow. "A rescue and battle."

"More of a skirmish than a battle," Calista remarked, downplaying the danger despite her narrow escape from injury. "A pair of orvs had abducted a berkis from the Right Hand, and I was hired to retrieve him."

Peg snorted. "Hmph. Probably owed them money. Nasty place. I have an uncle who gambles. He's always broke and miserable."

It couldn't be. "He isn't named Raffles by any chance, is he?"

"No. Jeremiah. Who's this Raffles?"

"The gambler paying to have the berkis, Truitt, rescued, on the grounds he owes him from a game."

"I knew someone must owe someone money!" Peg glanced at the gauge. "Pressure still building."

"I found him, Truitt, held captive in the Bedevilled by the orvs and released him," Calista continued. "But instead of running, he attacked them with a slingshot."

Fenton's lips spread into a smile as he nodded. "I know a few of my kind who enjoy that weapon. I am fairly skilled with it myself, but I doubt I would attempt to fight such foes with it. Were they armed?"

"With slashers. I relieved one orv of his, but the other nearly struck me."

"It appears one did." Fenton raised a finger toward her shoulder. "Or did you get that tear from someone else?"

"What tear?" Calista felt her sleeve where her trainer indicated. "Bloody! He must have snagged me. I didn't notice. Hang it all! Now I will need to have it repaired.

"Almost ready!" Peg looked up from the instrument. "You didn't, by any chance, have an opportunity to employ the modifications I made on your staff, did you?"

"Afraid not. I used the staff, but mostly to block slashers. On yesterday morning's job, I used the flail. Brought down a young orv who was stealing bread."

Peg ran a hand over her horn. "Maybe your stress is from dealing with all these orvs. Have you consulted an astrologist recently? There may be something in the stars." She checked the gauge. "Flipping the machine on!" Her fingers went to a valve on the pipe extending from the boiler.

"I don't really believe in — Yikes!" The steam motor burst into action, abruptly yanking the right side of Calista forward. Just as quickly, the pulley holding the sling shifted, and it pulled the left side. The motion repeated. Right. Left. Right. Left. Rapid tug after rapid tug, jarring her whole body with vibrations.

"Tuurrnn...iiittt...oofff!" She struggled to get the words out through chattering teeth as her head bounced back and forth. "Nnooww!"

The entire Vibrator contraption shook wildly, as well as the engine, living up to its ill-chosen name, as the skember scrambled for the steam motor's pressure valve. Her fingers brushed the knob, accidentally turning it higher. Pressurised water vapour surged even more swiftly to the piston.

The contraption, engine, and Calista began bouncing around. The Vibrator started hopping off the gymnasium wood floor and striking it hard when it landed, taking the trapped faroko with it. The steam motor, rolling on its wheeled platform, tagged along.

"Shut it down!" Fenton shouted.

"Don't you think I'm trying!" Peg cried back. Each time she reached for the dial, the trio of power, device, and victim leapt away several inches.

Meanwhile, Calista tried to pull the sling off herself, but the two ends moved too swiftly. Nor could she move past the barrier. Her body remained in constant motion, every limb flailing, every muscle worked to the point of breaking.

Finally, almost on instinct, she brought her arms together and ducked at the waist. Most resistance gone, the sling flew forward. But the strain had frayed one end, leaving a sharp edge exposed. That snagged the side of her shirt, ripping the fabric apart and pulling it off her.

Free of the machine, she backed away. Calista watched it hopping around through blurred eyes. Every muscle screamed. Her jaw had clenched shut to keep her teeth from chattering. She barely kept herself from tossing up the mutton pie.

Unable to reach the dial, Peg finally grabbed the fire stoker and swung it at that coal tray. It dislodged enough of the embers to hopefully reduce the steam, but that would still take time. Fortunately, apart from the three of them, the gym stood empty, and they were able to stay out of range of the manic device as it slowly lost energy.

Calista's senses similarly returned to normal. Her mind abruptly realised the white fabric dangling from the sling comprised the remains of her shirt, leaving her standing topless. She hastily crossed her arms to cover her exposed chest. Her corset remained intact, but it only covered her belly. "That thing of yours tore off my blouse!"

Peg hopped about in agitation. "I'm so, so, so sorry. That wasn't the intent, I assure you!"

"Intent or not, it did it!"

"But you are unhurt, aren't you?"

"No! I ache everywhere! My teeth hurt. Sweet baffled pillows! I'm topless! My arms nearly fell off. My neck feels like it's been trod on by horses, and my back has turned to rubber." Calista rolled her shoulders and winced. "About the only part of me not screaming in pain is my muff. I think it's laughing at the rest of my body."

Peg clapped her hands. "Then that is good! My machine works!"

"Works! Look at it!" She pointed to the device. It continued pushing and pulling away, but no longer hopping across the room. Instead, it wiped the floor with her shirt. "That monstrosity is a menace!"

"Now, now," Peg chided. "It merely needs some adjustments. I am positive that with the correct setting — "

"You could rip all my clothes off next time?" Calista barked. "Snap my neck clean off? This is the last time I allow you to use me for one of your experiments!"

Fenton stepped forward, extending his hand toward her. "Come, Little One. Let us find something for you to cover yourself with. Miss Pumper will handle the device."

But Calista teared up as she stared at the white fabric being dragged across the floor, back and forth. "That was my favourite blouse."

Peg followed her gaze. The Vibrator seemed to be tidying up in the aftermath of the mess it had caused. "I will purchase a new one for you," she promised. "As compensation."

Calista wiped her eyes. "You can't. That was custom-made. Most of my clothes are."

The mechanician grinned. "Clangers! I will have another crafted for you, even better than this one!"

Fenton reached up, placing his hand on Calista's thigh. "There are some towels in that cupboard. Take a few of those to cover yourself until you can return home. I am afraid this puts an end to any training for today."

She allowed herself to be guided away. "Fenton, it would be a miracle if I could even raise my staff." They continued toward a wardrobe in the corner. When they were out of earshot of Peg, she leaned down, careful to keep herself covered. "Why did you motion for me not to turn her down? All this could have been avoided."

"I shook my head so you would *not* let her experiment on you," he explained.

Ugh! "Then why did you not stop us?"

"And miss seeing what happened? We need some excitement around here." They arrived at the cupboard and he opened the door so she wouldn't risk exposing herself.

So I'm entertainment now. Grand. She plucked out a pair of large grey towels. Like most things in Gravenmore, they came in multiple sizes, with smaller linens perched on lower shelves. *I only hope I can get back to the pub without providing anyone else with a show.*

Chapter 10

The Abduction Clarification
Or Welcome Back, Sinner

AROUND MID-MORNING, TRUITT entered the Right Hand. He wore a similar outfit to the day before, but had forgone the neck handkerchief. If the same ruffians who grabbed him returned, he wanted that particular advantage removed.

Dirt from the street smeared his cheeks and chin. He had applied it carefully outside his flat. After last night's bath, he felt too clean to pass off as a Ward resident.

The casino didn't appear any different from yesterday. He couldn't be sure the orvs hadn't damaged it during his capture, but there appeared to be no lasting harm. The general run-down condition of the place made it difficult to tell, though.

No one seemed overtly concerned by his abduction or his return. A few regulars nodded at him as he strolled through the collection of tables to the one near the rear he and his gambling companions usually occupied. *Glad I didn't upset anyone's betting.*

He saw his hat hanging off the back of his chair as he approached. That, at least, had been spared the trip in the sack. He would have hated seeing it crushed.

Faye spotted him first from their table. "Truitt! You're safe!"

"Course 'e is." Raffles switched a few cards around in his hand. "I never doubted it. 'Is lordship always gets out of trouble."

Truitt stood beside the table, the top of it level with his neck, as he stared up at the skember in his high seat. "That's why you sent the woman?"

Raffles met his gaze. "Stilts? I sent 'er to collect the money you owed me. I knew you didn't need 'elp."

"Quite right." Truitt climbed into his own chair. It wasn't as tall as Raffles's, but it gave the berkis enough of a boost to use the table normally. As scaling up proved more convenient than scaling down, furniture designed for public spaces primarily catered to the larger-sized races. "Thank you for your concern, Faye," he told the female across from him as he settled in. "And for taking care of my hat."

She tapped the brim of her topper and grinned. "Hugh was worried, too. Weren't ya?"

Surprised at being addressed, the orv snapped his head up from his cards. Upon realising the nature of the question, he nodded, then resumed studying his hand.

"Then I thank you as well, Hugh," Truitt told him.

Faye shifted in her chair. When he offered nothing else, she dropped her cards and leaned across the table, her knick-knacks knocking about. "So... spill! What they want?"

He had known they would need an explanation and had spent the morning coming up with one that sounded harmless. It wouldn't benefit his plan if they began asking too much about his activities. The four of them rarely spoke about their lives outside the Right Hand, which suited them most of the time. He couldn't let this become an exception. "Oh, they were members of some church and wished to discuss my mortal soul."

"That'd be a brief talk," Raffles quipped.

Truitt ignored the jab. "I insisted my mortal soul was just fine and not requiring their assistance."

"They not like you gamblin', I bet," Faye said, but didn't return to her cards. "But why the sack?"

He shrugged, honestly not knowing the answer. They could have hauled him away bodily with little effort. Did they want his identity kept hidden? "Perhaps part of their ceremony. Kidnapping for the Lord."

That seemed to satisfy her, as she sat back with a chuckle. "Someone picked the wrong sinner. There ain't no savin' your hide. But why they have you so long?"

How much do they know? "What did the woman tell you?"

"After she freed you, you pebbled them."

"I did. They had me tied up as they tried to exsor... excit... tried to remove my bad bits." He sat up straight, a hurt expression crossing his face. "And the female did not free me. She merely aided in my vengeance."

"So why not come back and tell us yerself?" Faye pressed him.

Because I wasn't prepared to answer these questions. "I am doing so now, aren't I?"

"What I don't understand," Raffles drawled, "Is why, with all the adventure, you still 'aven't coughed up what's due."

"A thousand pardons. I held the delusion my welfare ranked as your top concern." Truitt pulled out a shilling and several pennies he had set aside and handed them to the skember. "There is the balance of my debt."

Raffles quickly counted the currency in his palm. "Your welfare is a concern. Not tops, though. I feared for the safety of these little coins. It must 'ave been an ordeal for them."

"I consoled them throughout and am certain they will recover."

"Chuffed to hear it," Raffles replied, tucking the winnings into his own pocket.

Truitt watched them disappear. "Do not put them away so soon. I intend to win them back today."

That earned snickers from all around the group, even Hugh, eliciting a rare, "Not likely."

A mix of curiosity and disappointment prompted one of Truitt's eyebrows into an arch. "My safe return is not worthy of two words, but mocking my skills at cards is? Perhaps I should have stayed with the church beadles. They at least showed concern for my well-being."

"Hey now!" Faye slapped the table, a thought abruptly materialising under her hat. "What if they come back for you? Or try to take one of us?"

Excellent question, and one which I have no answer for. "Allow it not to vex your thoughts. I gave them a thrashing and told them never to enter my presence henceforth, nor to disrupt the company of my associates." A lie, but it might console them.

"Then we need not worry," Raffles concluded amicably. "Are we playing or not?"

A female voice shattered the possibility. "Truitt! You're back!" Kate, the faroko server, strode toward the table. All the companions turned to look at her, even Hugh. Their table usually fell under her jurisdiction, so they had become quite familiar with each other over the years they had been patronising the Right Hand. She wore the same outfit as the other cocktail waitresses — a short black dress safeguarded by a white apron, an ebony corset atop a low-cut ivory blouse, coal stockings, and heeled tan boots.

"So I'm told," came the indifferent response.

"Are you hurt? What did they want?"

"I am well, thank you." He tried not to stare at her, but he found himself idly comparing her to last night's encounter. While taller than him, Kate stood at least a half foot shorter than the woman who aided him. *Get her out of your head!*

"They wanted to save his soul, but he told them he ain't got one," Faye blurted out, happy to repeat the joke and the news. Taking the role of the group's gossip, she considered it her duty to share any and all information she had gleaned from those around her.

"Oh, I am sure that's not true," Kate countered. "We all have souls. Even Raffles here, though you would never know it."

"That is an optimistic view," Truitt told her. Raffles either didn't notice the backhanded compliment or didn't care, as he remained fixated on his cards.

But her words got the other faroko's attention. "You really think I gots one?" Faye asked in a disbelieving tone.

"Without a doubt, Faye. You have a kind one. You were worried for Truitt's safety."

The female latched onto that explanation as absolute confirmation. "I was!" She slapped the table again. "I told you I was! So was Hugh."

"I know. Hugh's soul is quite beautiful." Kate turned her focus on the orv. He'd been staring at her since she arrived, an action he normally reserved for his cards or a dish of Yorkshire pudding. When she caught his eye, though, he ducked his head and blushed.

Faye snickered. "Too bad he don't talk much."

The waitress dropped her gaze as well. "I'm sure he speaks when he has something important to say."

"Apparently, that includes mocking my gambling abilities." Truitt was glad to get the topic onto anything but himself.

"You do lose a lot. I mean, a lot!" Faye leaned back in her chair, the card game forgotten in the conversation. "If you had the same luck in gettin' out of trouble, you'd be lyin' in a gutter somewhere now."

The suggestion was in poor taste, and Kate did her best to dispel it. "Well, I am glad Truitt was not stolen by the Grey Shadow."

The berkis looked around the table, then at the server. "Was that the assumption?"

Faye gave a curt nod. "You did invoke that possibility before you got nabbed."

"Our lordship doesn't believe in the Shadow," Raffles said, finally joining the conversation.

"That is a blatant misrepresentation," Truitt protested. "I merely don't accept the tales of his exploits."

"The Duke wouldn't lie, and he would know!" Faye leaned into the table again, throwing her folded arms onto it and sending her pile of tokens sprawling. "I hear he's a true buck."

"I have too! Tall. Handsome." Kate lowered her voice and gave Faye a wink. "A wizard with his tail."

"Fiddlesticks," Truitt grumbled. "How could anyone ascertain his degree of attraction if they've only seen his smokey form?"

"Not the Shadow," Faye chided him with a sigh. "The Duke!"

"Where are we?" Raffles said, looking around the casino at the other patrons, his lips curled in a sneer. "Did I enter a lady's crocheting circle this morning?"

"Not enough gambling?" Truitt asked, though the answer showed plainly on his face.

"Not enough gambling! This establishment is still one that specialises in that pastime, is it not?"

"Shut your sauce-box," Kate growled at him. "I came for your drinks orders. The usuals, all around?" She looked at each for confirmation.

"Perhaps mine could be on the house, considering my harrowing ordeal." Truitt adopted what he hoped was a pitiful expression.

"Sounds to me like you got your nut knocked. You've gone delusional."

He exhaled. "Only in believing that it mattered." He hadn't expected to get a free drink. As long as they were fussing over his absence, though, he felt it couldn't hurt to ask.

"Aww. You matter." Kate stepped closer to him. "I'm glad you weren't stolen. Or caught in the blaze last night."

"There was a fire?" He looked up at her, feigning ignorance, casually observing that she had arranged her chestnut hair into a bun. *She had curly black tresses and soft eyes. Stop it!* "I had not been apprised."

"Yup. And by all accounts, it was in the Bedevilled."

Faye pounced on the news. "I heard that! And that the thing there started it."

There's the first accusation, Truitt thought. *Dragon next?*

"The girls and I think it was Kettlebelly!" Kate told her, referring to the other waitresses. "He visits our fair city at last!"

Two down.

"Perhaps it was the Shadow," Raffles suggested. "If we are sacrificing our game for this topic, then let's cover all bases."

Faye tilted her head toward him. "Why would he burn a building?"

"Why would a dragon?" the skember countered. "All I knows is we're 'sposed to be playing cards!"

"I best be getting back to work. Your friend here is mad as hops." Kate glowered at Raffles, then directed a smile at the other three, winking at Hugh, before sauntering to the bar.

Truitt frowned at Raffles. "That was rude."

"Rude is preventing those that come to gamble from gambling," came the reply. "Who's turn was it?"

"I don't recall. Let's restart." Faye dropped her cards on the table, face up. With a grin, she leaned across the rosewood surface and directed her attention to Truitt. "So. What happened to her?"

"Who?"

The faroko's smile broadened to the point where it seemed poised to engulf her entire visage. "The long-legged lady in the gas-pipes. I wouldn't wear pants that tight."

"You don't wear pants at all," Truitt observed.

"And if I did, I wouldn't wear those."

"Course not." Raffles took her cards, adding them to his own. "Much too long for you."

Faye scrunched her face. "That's not — forget it."

"I parted her company when I reached my flat. What became of her then, I do not know," Truitt answered. That part was true. "Nor do I care." That was not.

The pout from Faye showed she didn't like that answer. "That's not a nice way to speak about the woman what rescued you."

"She did not — " He bit off the retort, instead grabbing Hugh's cards and the deck Raffles had been sorting. "I came here to gamble."

"Didn't we all?" the skember retorted.

Truitt shuffled a few times. *Why did Faye have to mention her again? She's gone, and good riddance. I don't need some female whose face I can barely see.* He then remembered what blocked it as he began to deal. *Those kettledrums. Maybe if she bent over in those tight pants, I —*

"Is that card mine or not?"

Faye's question brought him out of the daydream. "What?"

"You stopped dealin'." Her face lit up with a wide smile again. "You got that bit o' raspberry on your mind, haven't you?" She leaned forward eagerly, watching his reaction.

Truitt realised his hand was stretched out toward her, but frozen in the air with a single card in his fingers. He quickly dropped it in front of her and continued dealing. Despite his efforts, he could feel his cheeks flushing. "Dagnabit! I had merely lost count of how many cards I'd dealt. Where was I?"

"Before mine? One."

His face further reddened as he finished up the deal. Another memory from the previous night came to the surface, one of being pressed against the woman's body as she carried him away from the house. He couldn't focus on his hand. *I have to know.* "Just as a matter of information, how did you find her?"

Raffles shrugged as he considered his own array. "I made it known we had someone who needed rescuing. She found us."

Faye pounced. "You *are* thinkin' 'bout her!"

Truitt's head drew back. "Fiddlesticks. My attention is on the game. And, for the last time, she didn't rescue me!"

"Course she didn't." She tried to suppress a giggle as she glanced at Hugh. The orv stared at his cards, but a grin nearly matching hers split his face.

I knew she would be a distraction, and she's not even here. I must put her out of my mind. Tonight, I steal the gem. "Bugger it. Come on. Let's play."

Chapter 11

The Bathhouse Visitation
Or Time To Get Wet

A FTER THE INCIDENT in the gymnasium, Calista had made it back to the pub with only a dozen shocked stares and a single, loud gasp. Towels were not, apparently, the height of fashion, even if worn only on the upper torso. Despite her earlier protests, she barely noticed the looks she got. That had been her life for too many years to have one more factor make much of a difference.

Once back in her room, she donned a fresh shirt. The red colour and ruffles didn't match her corset, but that wasn't important. She only needed it to reach her destination, where she would change into more formal clothes. Though she hadn't taken part in any training, the ordeal with the machine had worked her up enough to feel the need for another washing.

Get Wet Bathhouse stood only two streets away, on Copperpipe Road, and ranked among Calista's favourite locations in the city. Despite the frustration and heartache of the past few jobs, there was a spring in her step as she strode along the cobblestones. Her staff tapped the stone beneath her in rhythm with her feet. Baths always lifted her spirits.

There it is! She waited until a carriage passed before crossing the street. It rattled by with the soothing clip-clop of the horse's shoes against the pavement. Other cities were rumoured to be experimenting with steam-powered vehicles, the goal to one day replace the older buggies with their dung-producing methods of propulsion. Calista hoped that technology would never come to Gravenmore. She enjoyed seeing the animals around the city.

The grey brick building sat between a tobacconist on the left and a barber shop on the right. A gentleman could have his hair trimmed, soak for an hour, then restock his pipe supplies with no need to travel more than a few dozen feet between them.

She had, on occasion, visited both establishments, much to the dismay of their clientele. *Just A Cigar* had a variety of cigars which Armend enjoyed and requested she purchase a box at times when the pub kept him too busy. *I wonder if they have any pear drops in stock! I must remember to stop in after I've soaked.*

The trips to *Keep It Trim* were rare, as she preferred a long hairstyle, but not the length fashionable for the ladies of Gravenmore as markers of status, modesty, and affluence. Calista had none of those.

With a bounce, she topped the single step and pushed through the wood and glass door to the opulent interior. Burgundy wallpaper, embossed with circles of varying sizes, covered the walls from their knee-high baseboards to cream-coloured moulding edging the ceiling. Ornately framed paintings depicting bucolic scenes of the countryside further decorated the room. A pair of wide gilded mirrors set on opposite sides, with the left one sitting above the mantle of a stone fireplace.

Lavishly padded chairs and sofas, some flush with the walls, others jutting out into the space, provided seating for the bathhouse's patrons awaiting an opening or merely wishing to relax in the comforting atmosphere. Short, intricately carved end tables, on which were perched a selection of spirits in decanters with matching glasses or a recent newspaper, accompanied most of them. A few men were partaking of the refreshments while they reclined, deliberately ignoring eye contact with her, though they couldn't help but do a double take at her unnatural height. While open to all, the bathhouse generally catered to a male-oriented clientele. The presence of a female put them off, as most preferred the privacy of their own homes to wash, but the gentlemen were too polite to remark on it. Instead, they chose to punish her by not acknowledging her at all, which suited Calista just fine.

Still, she gave them a flirty wave, wiggling her fingers seductively. A young orv spotted the action and quickly turned away, but not before a blush spread over his face.

Blue and gold tiles formed a series of patterns on the floor, which Calista always imagined could be found in the homes of the eastern continents. She'd spent hours tracing them with her eyes on previous visits.

No lanterns or chandeliers hung from the olive-green ceiling, but fancy brass oil lamps were fixed to the walls at regular intervals. These were currently unlit, as enough natural light came in through the dual picture windows to illuminate the sitting room.

Calista had seen the insides of a few rich houses in the course of her assignments over the years, yet the sight of these lavish layouts always caught her breath, as it did today.

"Madam?"

The baritone question brought her attention back to the task. "I've come for a bath, Mr Chambers," she told the formally dressed berkis standing at the ready near a pair of oak double doors across from the entrance.

Cream-coloured trousers were tucked into fine, knee-high ebony boots that literally gleamed from polish. His spotless white dress shirt had a tall collar, ruffled like a lady's skirt. Over it, he wore a midnight black waistcoat with a matching jacket. Calista thought the entire ensemble looked uncomfortable, but the attendant carried it with such dignity that she felt certain he never protested.

Mattigan Chambers himself appeared nearly as immaculate as his suit. The normally scruffy hair associated with his race had been oiled, combed, and parted down the middle. His chin and upper lips were devoid of facial growth, although he had thick sideburns extending down in front of his ears. These were similarly groomed.

"It is the sort of thing one does in this establishment," he told her in a deep monotone. If intended as sarcasm, Calista could detect no trace of it in his voice. She never could. "Would you like your usual suite?"

"I would."

Mattigan straightened his coat — a completely useless action as it conformed perfectly to his body with not a wrinkle. "Follow me."

With a click of his heels, he turned to the double doors and pushed the left one open. She sauntered after as he led her into a hallway extending to the left and right. A duplicate set of doors stood ten feet ahead. Calista knew the communal baths were through there, likely filled with semi-naked men discussing business and politics. She'd never used them herself, as she didn't want to cause that much of an uproar in her second favourite establishment.

Mattigan ignored them, instead pivoting on his heel and heading right. The lamps in the hallway were lit, casting a tinted glow over the walls and floor. She followed him around the corner, turning left into a similar hall, with more lamps on the right wall and four doors on the left, set at regular intervals. Each had a brass number in the centre, starting with five. He led her to the end and opened the door to room eight. Formed from pearl and copper, its handle had a length of thin rope attached to its tip, dangling just a few inches from the floor. This allowed the shorter skember to gain access without assistance.

"Thank you, Mr Chambers." Calista fished a coin from her pocket and placed it in his outstretched hand. *If I get this assignment, I'll have enough money to take a bath every hour! Maybe I'll never have to leave the tub!*

The berkis gave a nearly imperceptible nod. "I hope you enjoy your time in our establishment, Madam." He clicked his heels again, then retreated sombrely back down the hall.

Once he turned the corner, she entered and closed the door, setting her staff against the wall next to it. While not as fancy as the lobby, this one still had a touch of elegance.

At the room's centre, a sizeable cast-iron bathtub rested on small ornate feet. One end featured a metal octopus, its arms spreading around the edge of the tub. A short stand, holding a few bottles and washcloths, stood beside it. Twin carved wooden chairs with brass-covered armrests sat against the wall. A pile of towels lay on one for when she finished. On the far side hung two lit oil lamps with a mirror between them.

Beneath those, a pair of copper pipes emerged from the decoratively papered barrier and extended to the bathtub, where they joined the octopus. Two tentacles, one on each side, with valves attached, extended around the edge a few inches, then opened into the basin. She fiddled with each, releasing hot and cold water until she found the temperature she liked. Satisfied, she dropped the rubber stopper into the plug.

As the tub filled, Calista stripped, delicately folding her clothes and placing them on a chair, then setting her boots beside it. When the water had nearly reached the rim, she adjusted the valves to stop the flow.

She stepped gingerly into the bath, letting the liquid creep up her toes, then her foot, ankle, and shins, gradually warming each section of her body. Gripping the sides, she lowered herself slowly into the tub until her posterior sat on the bottom, the water halfway up her chest. She needed to cross her legs, as they were too long for the vessel.

The faroko tried to relax, but her mind continued to replay the fight at the Bedevilled. There shouldn't have been one. It had been a recovery job, not a combat assignment. *If that stupid berkis kept quiet, or at least ran when I told him, we could have escaped with little resistance. Instead, I nearly got whipped, and we set the neighbourhood on fire. I still don't know if he's bricky or a foozler.*

She noticed how he looked at her once they were clear of the blaze. It hadn't been fear, insecurity, or discomfort. He hadn't mocked her, as his casino friend did. *He was excited, like Peg getting a new machine.*

He appeared more confident in his evaluation of his prospects with her than most. Her towering stature and formidable physique intimidated most potential partners. *Or maybe the ordeal addled his brain.*

The first time she realised how her body influenced others proved to be a painful experience. She had been involved in a few romantic relationships since moving to Gravenmore, but what she remembered took place in Cinderbury.

From the small table, she grabbed a washcloth, immersed it, then began applying it to her hands and neck. His name was Victor, and he was the first boy to see her nude. It was the summer she turned fifteen.

As she got older, the bullying had only become worse. The same youngsters who lashed out at her strangeness grew into insecure juveniles. Females saw her as a threat. Males viewed her as a challenge. When either became emboldened enough through the cajoling of their friends, tensions erupted into violence.

Fighting the oversized female was not a decision guided by rational thought, of course. With the average skember, berkis, faroko, and orv standing only as tall as her thighs, hips, mouth, and nose, respectively, it often became more a test of her restraint to not accidentally hurt them.

Her mother had explained after each of these many altercations the usual platitudes to soothe young people's fears, such as they only misbehaved because they were jealous and her differences made her special. But Calista only ever wanted to fit in, so her words only reinforced that she never would.

Since there seemed no way to end the aggression, Calista's mother pulled her from the small town school where most of the interactions took place. Not wishing her daughter to grow up ignorant, she asked their neighbour's son, a skember only a year older than Calista, to tutor her.

The pair had grown up playing together, although their friendship had become strained between them. It had not been easy for the lad to watch his friend go from a scrawny girl to a mature-looking woman many times bigger than him. With Victor visiting regularly again to catch her up with what she missed in school, it felt as if the years had been rewound to their childhood companionship.

But they weren't children anymore. The point was brought home rather abruptly one day when Victor entered the residency for another lesson. His knocks went unheard, both Calista's parents having been out at the time and she busying herself in her bedroom. Thinking nothing wrong, he moved through the few rooms to hers.

Finding the door slightly ajar — a fortunate happenstance, as the faroko house lacked the usual adjustments made for the smaller races — he placed a tiny hand on it and pushed it wide.

The sight took his breath away.

Calista giggled, imagining again how she must have looked. After a recent growth spurt — the third in the last half year — she found herself with a very limited selection of clothes that would still fit. They were sprawled upon her bed as she surveyed them, stark naked, her tail swinging casually back and forth like clockwork.

She'd heard a gasp and whirled around to find Victor standing in the doorway, eyes wide, staring at her with a mix of shock and desire. Embarrassed herself, she had sprinted to close the door, not thinking of how it must look to her tiny friend — a giant nude female, descending upon him. Whether it was her size or his overwhelming arousal, she didn't know, but he fled with a single shouted 'Eep' and bolted from the house.

He returned a few days later in his best suit, making sure to knock loudly until Calista's father answered the door. She had seen him approaching through the living room window and felt too timid to greet him herself.

As he stepped inside, she could see him visibly shaking and believed him angry at her. He wouldn't look at her, though, keeping eye contact with her parents. He informed them stiffly, struggling to keep his voice steady, of his deep regret, but he could no longer tutor their daughter. Calista hadn't waited for him to give a reason as she ran to her room and threw herself on her bed in a wash of tears. Her last remaining friend had given up on her, too.

In the tub, Calista wiped the washcloth across her face, absorbing a tear that escaped in her melancholy remembrance. A frown quickly replaced the pout, and she leaned back, placing her head alongside the octopus's body and extending her legs out. They dripped water onto the floor, which was instantly absorbed by the cotton mat placed below for that very purpose.

After that, she had moped around her parents' house for two years, rarely going out or speaking with anyone. Who was there left to talk to? Her hometown, where she had been born and raised, had essentially rejected her for not fitting in with its expectations. So when she grew old enough, Calista said a tearful goodbye to her family, flicked a final obscene gesture at the town, and boarded the train in hopes of finding a more accepting part of the world.

And for what? Her fingers stirred the surface of the water, creating ripples and swirls to match her memories. *I've been here ten years, but I'm still scraping by with petty jobs for the well-to-do. Armend was right, I need them to survive. But when is just surviving not enough?*

Her mind went to the bakery incident. She kept seeing the orphans' faces. *Sending them to gaol was wrong. But what could I do? I barely have a place to live myself.*

After first arriving in Gravenmore, she found work in a few shops, but they never lasted. Her body still possessed the clumsiness of youth, causing her to knock over one too many displays or drop one too many orders. Her employers, always apologetic as they dismissed her, further explained she proved too much of a distraction to patrons. They paid more attention to the oversized and voluptuous young woman than the goods they came in search of.

That changed when one day, she witnessed a male faroko being mugged by a gang of youths. Without thinking, she had stepped in, driving them away. Sadly, the man ran off too, too stunned by the sight of his saviour, but she realised she could use her height and fighting skills to help people as well as earn an income. She also learned she liked the feeling of using her 'gifts' to aid others.

After that, she began hiring herself as a mix of bodyguard and protector. She had little experience apart from her only having to protect herself, but her presence alone often dissuaded any wrongdoing.

Nice, isn't it? The oddball being sought out for being an oddball.

It led to her biggest break, though, when she met Armend. He had won a hotel in a game of cards, but the owners chose to renege on their agreement. They hired Calista to use her talents to intimidate the skember so he wouldn't attempt to claim ownership. But after they spoke, she and he formed a friendship, and rather than prevent him from collecting his prize, she helped ensure the others lived up to their end of the deal.

Armend had the structure converted into a drinking house, with most of the upstairs turned into private rooms for patrons. The Plump Pillows Hotel became the Happy Swallow Pub. He kept a few quarters as they were and designated one for Calista, asking her to remain close, in case the former owners ever tried to take their establishment back by force. At least, that was the excuse he used for continuing to let her stay free of charge.

To help her further, he began seeking information on odd jobs she could hire herself out for. He had underestimated the citizenry's needs, though, and soon it expanded into a side business, where he provided the same service for others, taking a percentage of their payment as a fee. He kept the best assignments for Calista, however.

And I'm sick of it. The only ones I seem to aid are those who can afford it. Those orphans needed help more than that harridan Zusa. But I sold them out for a few coins! She slapped the water in anger, accidentally splashing a handful onto the floor and starting a wave which bounced around the tub. *Then when I try to change and help someone in dire trouble, my own life is put in danger. For a miserly client and an ungrateful recipient. I need this next assignment to go well!*

Calista drew in a deep breath and let it out slowly. *He was dashing, though. And it's been a long time since I've put my hands on a man like that.* She giggled, then sighed. *It's for the best that I never lay eyes on him again. I have to concentrate on the job, not annoying distractions, no matter how handsome.*

With that decided, she held her breath and ducked her head underwater to wash her face and curls. It was time to enjoy her well-earned bath. With luck, by morning, she would have enough money to retire from the tasks, at least for a while.

As she immersed herself in the soothing waters, she allowed herself to momentarily forget about childhood heartbreaks, orphans, and stubborn berkis.

Chapter 12

The Audition Obliteration
Or Bush On Fire

CALISTA STRODE ALONG the sidewalk of the Sunside district, staff in hand and dressed in a fresh set of clothes. It was nearly four o'clock, and she needed to be at the address Armend had given her by the hour.

After the bath, and wearing her new outfit — a black dress with a white skirt, crimson corset, the red blouse, stockings, and thigh-high leather boots — she got a bite of food for a late lunch from a vendor. Once she had dropped off her other clothes at the pub and picked up the address, she headed out.

Unfortunately, though she had been to the Sunside a few times, she didn't know it nearly as well as she thought and found herself lost among the crowd of affluent pedestrians.

It wasn't an entirely bad position to be in. The streets here were cleaner, or at least not as decorated by trash and manure. The shopfronts seemed crisper, as if the soot which coated the city was regularly cleaned from the sills and glass. Even the street vendors appeared better dressed, their carts less ragged, their wares fresher.

And the people! Nearly every gentleman wore a polished top hat, with most carrying a matching cane and a watch tucked into a waistcoat pocket. The women were equally dignified, each wearing a headpiece more elegant and outrageous than the next. The few without an adornment had their hair done into tight buns or coils, a few curls hanging down loosely and brushing their ears.

Calista, with no hat and whose curly tresses lay about her shoulders unbound, found herself out of place. While her dress was finer than her normal attire, she felt like one of the scrape-alongs from the Rookery compared to the fashionable women she saw. *No matter how much I try, I could never match their poise.*

Eventually, with the help of a kindly skember gentleman who gave her directions despite being unable to stop staring at her hips far above him, she found the correct route. It led her beyond the boundaries of tightly packed townhouses into an area of mansions, each delineated by lofty gated walls and embraced by verdant lawns, vibrant gardens, and scattered shade trees.

Calista reached the address and entered the grounds through an open gateway of wrought iron. Metal bars, bent and shaped, formed curling patterns, with an ornate top forming tight spirals and triads. Pointed finials topped the rest of the fencing around the property, signalling that trespassers were wholly unwelcome.

She followed the cobblestone path to the sprawling house. Amberlux Manor, boasting bright yellow walls and stark white trim, embodied Calista's vision of how all buildings should appear in the Sunside. One could easily believe it sat at the centre of the city, its brilliance only dimming the farther one travelled from it. Rhododendron bushes circled it, and a stately elm grew on the east side, giving shade to the beaming construction.

Calista picked up her pace when she spotted a group of individuals already standing before a columned porch. On the raised platform stood an older female faroko in a patterned blue dress, her greying hair bound into a ball on her head. Her scowling gaze snapped to Calista, who instantly lowered her own and slumped as she hurriedly joined the line. *Looks like I'm the last here. Great way to start the auditions.*

The woman shifted her glare back to the others. "It appears everyone has arrived. Finally. You are standing before Amberlux Manor. I am Lady Aishwarya Aetherborne, wife of Lord Aetherborne. Refer to me as 'Madam' or 'Your Ladyship.' Maintain proper etiquette in my presence. Rudeness will not be accepted." She paused, as if waiting for a protest to her rules. When no one peeped, she nodded sharply. "Shall we begin? I have a list of those who have confirmed interest in this undertaking. Please make yourselves known when I say your name. Mr Tinker and Miss Kipps?"

A finely attired male orv, with a slasher at his side, lifted his chin. However, it was the female berkis beside him, dressed in an ensemble akin to Calista's street clothes but distinguished by twin guns holstered at her hips, who spoke. "That's us." Her gravelly voice reminded Calista of one of Peg's machines in motion.

Lady Aetherborne glanced at the pair, then returned her attention to the list. "Mr Ambrose?"

"Present," responded a slender male faroko with rumpled black pants and dressed in a cream-coloured shirt and dark trousers held up by leather suspenders. A long device that appeared to be a gun with several metal and glass attachments hung from his shoulder by a thick strap. "And please allow me to say, it is an honour to have this opportunity to serve you, esteemed lady." His nostrils flared as he spoke, giving Calista the impression of a mouse seeking cheese.

"You have," Lady Aetherborne replied brusquely, having no time for idle flattery. "Mr Hedgecock, Mr Hedgecock, and Mr Hedgecock?"

"We're here." One of three roughly attired skembers stepped forward. Scratches and scuffs marred his horns, and a miniature sword hung at his side. "I am Barnaby. These are my brothers, Brisco and Buford. And if *I* may say, you don't want none of these gollumpuses." He jerked a thumb at the other applicants. "We'll do the job just fine." His siblings bobbed their heads in agreement.

Lady Aetherborne glowered at him like a school headmistress who just caught a boy smuggling a lizard into class. "You may not. That decision rests solely with me." Her expression managed to get even more menacing as she looked at Calista. "I presume you are Miss Temira."

She nodded. "I am. You may call me Calista."

"I will not." Lady Aetherborne raised her voice for all to hear. "You, all of you, are here to perform a single duty. Guard the Dragon Eye Gem during the night, from late evening until sunrise. My staff are capable of watching over it during the day."

"If I might, and begging your pardon if my question appears impertinent," Ambrose, the faroko with the gun, began, "but what prevents your personnel from safeguarding the jewel themselves during the darkened hours?"

Barnaby, apparently the mouth of the skember trio, chuckled. "Sounds like someone here is none too keen on the job. My brothers and I will gladly take his place."

"Not at all. I was merely placing a respectful inquiry into the nature of the affair."

"My staff sleeps at night," Lady Aetherborne interjected. "As do I, though not soundly, with this Grey Shadow scoundrel in the city. That is who you will be facing. The Dragon Eye Gem is unique. Priceless. I have no doubt that the rascal will attempt its theft. Until he leaves Gravenmore or is captured, it shall stay under constant guard."

"Why not keep the gem in a bank, under lock and key?" Miss Kipps, the female berkis, asked.

Lady Aetherborne straightened. "The gem has been in my family for generations and shall remain there. I'll not entrust such a valuable item to any government institution."

But you will place it under the care of total strangers you hire from the streets, Calista thought. *She's desperate.*

Miss Kipps's orv partner shyly raised a hand.

"Yes, Mr Tinker?" Lady Aetherborne prompted.

"If this Shadow person fails to make an appearance, do we still get compensated?" he asked.

"Naturally. The task is to guard the gem, not capture a thief. Now, if there are no more questions," she paused, waiting for any other interruptions. "The auditions may begin."

Mr Ambrose raised his hand, too. "If you will allow, another inquiry?"

The older woman's shoulders sagged. "Yes, Mr Ambrose?"

"Would it perhaps not be more advantageous to employ all of us, so that our combined services might ensure complete protection?"

"You truly don't think you can do the job." Barnaby stroked the hilt of his sword. "Then step aside and let the professionals handle this."

"In this instance, I am inclined to agree with the gentleman," Lady Aetherborne added. "Your questions imply a degree of doubt in your abilities. Are you certain you wish to undertake this task?"

Mr Ambrose smiled and shook his head. "I humbly beg your pardon if my inquiries offer a semblance of apprehension. I am a scientist, you see, and it is my professional nature to obtain all the information I can. In this instance, all facts regarding the situation so that I may be best prepared to handle any eventuality."

"This ain't no place for a scientist," Barnaby sneered.

"I disagree. I find it a nearly perfect opportunity to put to use my newest invention." He gripped his weapon and lifted it for the others to see. Apart from the glass tubes, coils of wire, and other metal adornments, it had the semblance of a normal firearm, albeit a long one. "It is a converted blunderbuss, with my own modifications of an electric battery at its core. My adjustments provide a more stable flow, allowing for a blast of plasma, which is both powerful yet harmless." He paused, then added, "Well, mostly harmless. Allow me to demonstrate." Without waiting for permission, he brought the butt of the gun to his shoulder and flicked a few brass switches. The device began to hum like a dozen bumblebees.

For the first time, Lady Aetherborne's expression changed to something other than scorn. "Mr Ambrose, I believe we should — "

The glass container atop the weapon filled with crackling streaks of light dancing around inside. The chorus of bees became a hive. Mr Ambrose swung the gun to find a suitable target and brought it to aim at an innocent rhododendron bush. He closed one eye as he peered down a piece of cut iron which acted as sight and pulled the trigger. Bluish lightning crackled from the barrel, forming an arc from the blunderbuss to the shrub. Leaves and purple flowers sizzled as electricity seared them, filling the air with noise and black smoke. It lasted only a few seconds before the plasma dissipated, leaving the charred remains of the plant brown and smouldering.

This proved too much for the elderly faroko. "Mr Ambrose!" she yelled, her body trembling with anger. "Your actions are utterly distressing! Please refrain from destroying any further vegetation."

Mr Ambrose flicked the switches on his weapon before lowering it to his chest. The buzzing faded. Despite her admonishment, he wore a satisfied grin. "I beg your forgiveness, Lady Aetherborne. But you must agree, that was a most impressive presentation."

"And one which disqualifies you from this position. I will not have you setting fire to my furnishings. You might burn down the entire house with that contraption. Who is next?" Lady Aetherborne turned her focus to the orv and berkis pair. "What are you proposing to use in defence of my property?"

Miss Kipps held up a soothing hand. "Nothing so violent, I assure you, madam. Merely a slasher and a few firearms. Two flintlock pistols and a pepper-box. Nothing that will burn bushes or furniture." She swivelled her hip to display the holstered gun.

But Lady Aetherborne wasn't convinced. "Unacceptable. You shall not be thrashing whips about in my house. And unless those guns shoot only flower petals, they will also not be discharged inside my home. I am trying to mitigate a theft, not promote damage." She looked at the skembers. "Pray, tell me you have different armaments."

Barnaby's face split into a grin which Calista guessed he meant to be ingratiating but which made her uneasy. The trio had a sinister air, but she couldn't see anything particularly frightening about them. "We do. None of these barkers or slashers. Just reliable, old-fashioned pokers and chivs." With a flourish, he drew his sword and held it out to catch the afternoon sun. "Clean, precise, and quiet. We'll slice that Shadow into a dozen little shadows."

"And in doing so, get blood on my floors." Lady Aetherborne placed a hand to her chest, as if the notion itself caused her pain. "Although my staff is skilled, I doubt they could scrub that up properly. You and your brothers are also disqualified."

The skember lowered the sword. "Don't be so hasty. We will be extra careful to let not one drop of bodily fluids escape his stinking corpse."

"That is quite enough, thank you, Mr Hedgecock."

"How about me and my brothers just use our fists? Rough him up a bit."

"I said that is enough! Please restrain yourself." She stared at Barnaby until he grudgingly sheathed his blade. With a sigh that seemed to deflate her whole body, Lady Aetherborne shifted her attention to Calista. "And what means of destruction do you intend to unleash on my premises?"

"None, Your Ladyship. I have only my staff." She nodded toward the wood in her hand.

"Does it shoot anything or whip about?"

"No, madam."

"Does it splatter blood across the room?"

"I said we would be careful," Barnaby protested, still not ready to give up on the job.

Not unless I use the modifications Peg added. "Not normally. As you can see, it's a piece of wood." Calista raised it slightly, subconsciously noting that it, like her, stood taller than everyone else present. She knew that while it was, as she said, a piece of wood, in trained hands, it could be quite dangerous. Its innocuous appearance was one reason Fenton had suggested she master it, and she gave a silent thank you to her trainer for his foresight.

It seemed enough to convince Lady Aetherborne, who looked it up and down from her perch on the porch. Having disqualified the other applicants, she had little choice anyway. "Hmmm. Very well. The job is yours." She stood straight to address the others. "The rest of you may go. Thank you for your inquiry."

Chapter 13

The Library Exploration
Or You Are Reading What?

C ALISTA FELT HER heart leap. *I made it! Once this assignment is completed, I'll have enough money to retire. Perhaps I'll have the funds to find a house in the Sunside. It would be difficult saying goodbye to Armend, though. And Silas. But they would understand. This could be my big chance, my —*

"Miss Temira, will you be joining me or not?"

Lady Aetherborne's agitated prompt brought Calista back to the present. "Coming!" She glanced at the other applicants as they disbanded quietly. Miss Kipps and Mr Tinker sauntered toward the gate, not seeming to be terribly upset by the outcome. Mr Ambrose didn't either, instead making his way to the rhododendron bush he'd toasted and inspecting it closely.

Only the Hedgecock brothers appeared genuinely irritated over not being chosen. Buford and Brisco muttered between themselves, while Barnaby glared after the older faroko as she turned toward the house. When he caught Calista looking at him, his expression grew even darker, and she felt the sudden need to sprint up the stairs.

"Young people these days. Always have their heads in the cloud rather than their feet on the ground," Lady Aetherborne told her as they came to the door. "I trust you will be capable of maintaining your focus throughout the night."

Calm down. She's right. I have to stay grounded. "I will."

Lady Aetherborne led her into the house, and Calista found herself staring at the luxurious interior. Though they were only in the parlour, she recognised how rich the owners of the gem truly were. Elaborately patterned wallpaper and decorative moulding flowed into plush, ornamental carpeting. A grand marble fireplace adorned by a carved mantelpiece, with a large mirror above it and decorated with vases and carvings, sat against the far wall. Plushly cushioned chairs and sofas, along with fancy, polished tables, rounded out the chamber. *This room alone must be worth more than fifty pounds!*

They didn't linger. She followed Lady Aetherborne as she shuffled through a doorway into an even grander space. Servants in dark clothes and aprons fell away before the pair as they moved from one section to another. Calista caught sight of a portrait of a distinguished gentleman above a grand fireplace, beside what she presumed depicted a younger Aishwarya. "Where is Mr Aetherborne?"

"In Brassmont." The woman of the house didn't even look at her guest as she continued, her skirt rustling with each step. "On business. He is expected to return by the end of the week. This way."

After they entered a lavish dining hall, she suddenly halted, her dress flowing forward with the motion before settling around her legs again. Her tail, which had remained strangely still throughout their march, came to life, sweeping the air behind her head. "Beatrice!" she bellowed, producing a volume Calista wouldn't have thought her capable of.

A female berkis dressed in a maid's outfit hastily rounded the corner, her short legs pumping to meet her mistress's needs. "Yes, ma'am?" she asked when she stood a few feet in front of them, her eyes on the floor.

Lady Aetherborne waved idly toward Calista. "This is Miss Temira. She will be spending the nights here for the foreseeable future in the study, keeping watch over the gem. I wish you to provide her with a simple supper each night after I have dined. Nothing fancy, mind you, as she is here to work, not in-dulge in the privileges of a life she is not suited for. Under-stood?"

Beatrice gave a single glance at the towering faroko, then returned her gaze to the floor. "Yes, ma'am."

"You may go."

Calista watched her curtsy and retreat from the room. Lady Aetherborne's slight recalled the thoughts she had on her walk to the house. Instead of embarrassment, however, it caused her anger. *Not suited for? What does she mean by that? I'm no Lady, but she likely only got that title by joining giblets with some wealthy man.*

She kept her tongue in her mouth, though, as they pro-ceeded to an elegant staircase which carried them to the sec-ond floor. The pair passed a few more rooms and servants be-fore entering a large room that unmistakably served as the li-brary. While furnished similarly to the parlour, it also con-tained a few chairs in the corner, a stepping stool for reaching higher shelves, and a few expensive-looking vases decorating the sections without books. A small statuette of a winged cherub perched alone on a tall pedestal. Two windows on the opposite wall overlooked the backyard, and a single doorway led to another chamber on the left. The scent of aged leather book bindings mingled with the fragrance of wood polish on the shelves they rested upon.

In the centre of the library stood an ornate round table, a few feet in diameter. Upon it sat a white case, half a foot in length on every side. It appeared to be made of some hard ma-terial, perhaps ivory, although Calista had never seen this much of the precious substance.

"Here is what you will be protecting." Lady Aetherborne crossed the plush carpeting to the box, placed aged fingers on its lid, and lifted it open on its brass hinges. Inside, Calista saw a round gem, no more than two inches in diameter, nestled in a bed of velvet. It shone with a rich emerald hue in the light from the window. Its sides appeared to be in perpetual motion, shifting multiple times with every slight change she made in her own position. She let out an involuntary gasp.

For the first time since she'd met her, Lady Aetherborne allowed herself a satisfied smile. "That is the usual response, followed by a barrage of questions."

Her words barely registered with Calista, so focused was her attention on the jewel. "It is spectacular. I don't understand the colour, though. I've heard some stories which claim it is green, as I see it now. But others say it is deep red."

"It is both. In the light of day, it shines green. In lamplight, however, it will appear red. That is just one of the qualities which sets it apart from other jewels. It is also the cause of its current peril." As if suddenly remembering to be cross, the elderly faroko closed the box and turned to Calista. "You are to remain here tonight. Through that doorway is the study where Beatrice will deliver your meal. You may have use of these two rooms, but no more. Once Beatrice leaves you, the doors will be locked. This ensures no one attempts to steal the gem from inside the house."

And prevents me from roaming the rest of the mansion. Fine with me. "I understand."

Lady Aetherborne looked her over again, as if only now noticing her height. "Is there anything else you require?"

Calista's face reddened. "Only to use the water closet. If I am to be locked in here all night, I had best pay a visit to Mrs Jones."

After she had eaten — a 'simple' dinner of cold ham slices, a few slabs of bread, yellowish cheese she had never tasted before, raspberry jam, and lukewarm tea — Calista explored. She might be confined to only two rooms, but in this mansion, that constituted quite an expansive environment. The library stood three times the size of her room in the Happy Swallow, and the study was easily larger than the main floor of the pub. For the abnormally tall faroko, it felt as if she finally had space to move about indoors.

She tested a few of the stuffed chairs but hesitated to take a seat. Since she had entered the house, she'd been acutely aware of how expensive everything must be. *If I damage a single chair or vase, I'll likely not live long enough to pay for it.* Calista had eaten her dinner seated on a section of the floor not covered in carpeting, and even then, she had feared scuffing the hardwood.

Now she walked along the walls of books, hands clasped behind her back, examining the various titles. She knew how to read, though she rarely had the need to. When she first arrived in Gravenmore, she had written to her parents every month to update them on her progress in the 'big city'. She had also taken a few trips home, only to find nothing had changed. The folks of Cinderbury still viewed her as a freak, and after a few more incidents there, she decided to never return. She continued the letters to her mother and father for several more months, but they were a painful reminder of her life as an outcast. As her situation in the urban setting improved, she eventually stopped them as well.

None of the titles on the thick spines sounded familiar to her. Not that she thought they would. The only book she remembered from her childhood was "The Adventures of Thomas and Gerald", a collection of stories about a humorous cat and mouse pair. *Wouldn't that be something if there is a copy of it here?*

Intrigued by the notion, Calista spent an hour scanning the selection of works for the children's tome, not actually expecting to find it, but having nothing else to do. She stumbled across a few she thought sounded out of place in the house of an affluent lord. *Exploring the Garden of Venus. Arbor Vitae and The Agony of Bliss. Buttering Your Buns. Sounds as if Lady Aetherborne or her husband are not always so proper.*

When the sun set, she lit a few of the gas lamps lining the walls. Bored now of the books, she cast about for something else to hold her interest. In the dimming light, she traced the patterns of the carpeting with her eyes, like she enjoyed doing at the Get Wet Bathhouse. She soon tired of that as well, though, and turned her attention to the study. There, she finally overcame her fear of damaging the furniture and plopped down into a spoon-back chair with scrolled arms and black velvet cushions. *If I am to do this every night, I will have to find some way to entertain myself. This is duller than ditchwater.*

After a while, she drifted off into a gentle slumber, but a scrabbling at the study window brought her instantly awake. Too far from the street for the light from there to penetrate the darkness, and with no lamps lit in the smaller room, she struggled to make out the movement at the aperture's lock. Still, she could tell someone was there, attempting to gain entry. *Finally, some action!*

Trepidation dampened her enthusiasm, though. She didn't know how to handle the Grey Shadow, and for a moment, she wished she had Mr Ambrose's weapon rather than the shaft of wood by her side.

She heard the soft click of the latch. The window was unlocked, and a second later, the undeniable sound of it sliding open reached her ears. *Ready or not, I have to act.*

In a single, smooth motion, Calista rose, snatched up her staff from where it leaned against the chair, and crossed to the window. A shift in shadows told her a figure was coming through. Remembering Fenton's training, she planted herself before them, her legs spread apart, her weapon held before her.

She took a deep breath in a vain attempt to calm her thumping heart. *It's happening. The Shadow is here.*

Chapter 14

The Burglar Interruption
Or Let's Not Get Carried Away

ASCERTAINING THE WHEREABOUTS of the Dragon Eye Gem proved to be an easy task. One could always gain information by exchanging money with the right hands. Casing the house hadn't been an arduous venture, either. Truitt had posed as a wealthy gentleman to walk near the grounds and the only person who seemed to notice his activity had been a beggar, probably hoping for a handout.

He'd climbed over the iron fence with relative ease, minding the pointed finials topping it. The room being on the second floor, with only a few windows giving access, proved a more difficult challenge. If the agile berkis hadn't entered a dozen houses before by climbing the various ledges and carvings, he may not have made it. But experience allowed him to reach the study window, and from there, he needed only to jimmy the latch with the proper tool, which he, of course, possessed.

Clutching to the siding, his fingers finding purchase in the cracks, he slid the sash up. Once there was enough room to fit his slight body through, he slipped one leg in, eased his torso through, then brought in the other as he silently dropped to the ground.

He paused a moment in the gloom, straining to hear if anyone heard him enter. Satisfied he remained undetected, Truitt stood slowly and turned around. To his surprise, the berkis thief found himself facing a wall of fabric. *I forgot about the curtains.* He reached out to shove the black and white cloth aside, sliding his fingers deep into the folds.

His astonishment intensified when an enormous hand swung in and seized his wrist. "Watch where you're putting that," scolded a feminine voice from above.

Truitt lifted his head with a deliberate and unhurried motion, uncertain of the identity of the individual standing before him. In the dim light, his eyes traced up Calista's dress to the straining corset. Just past its twin bulges, he could see a face looking down at him, but couldn't make out the details in the shadow. He yanked his hand from her grasp and adopted his politest tone. "I beg your pardon, madam. I seem to have entered the wrong domicile. Please forgive my intrusion. With your permission, I will take my leave." Without waiting for a reply, he turned toward the windowsill, which stood level with his chin.

But Calista squatted and reached for his shoulder. "Not so quick." Her fingers barely brushed his shirt when the berkis abruptly swung back, shoving her in the chest. Surprised by the unexpected grope and thrown off balance by the push, she toppled backwards. She landed hard on her arse as her legs kicked out and her staff fell soundlessly onto the plush carpeting.

Truitt lunged for the open window, hooking one arm over the ledge and gripping the outer lip. But before he could pull himself through, Calista leapt to her feet and grabbed his ankle. With little effort, she yanked him from the aperture, leaving him dangling upside down, his face level with her hips.

The faroko stepped into the dim light streaming through the doorway as she lifted him higher. Truitt enjoyed a leisurely inspection of her body, at least the parts out of reach the previous time. The crimson corset, bulging pleasantly. The breathtaking cleavage. The powerful but graceful neck. The familiar face, albeit inverted.

"It is you!" Calista blurted out, having reached the same realisation.

Truitt groaned. *Why did it have to be her?* "Likewise. With those pleasantries completed, you may return me to the window so I can take my leave."

But the amazon was not that accommodating. "Not yet. Did you come here to steal the gem?"

He feigned a look of indifference, an impressive feat, given his current position. "I have not the faintest notion of what you are referring to."

Her eyebrow shot up, but rather than answer, she crossed through the library, still dangling the intruder upside down and six feet above the ground, to the ivory box. With her free hand, she flicked the box open, revealing the Dragon Eye Gem inside. It shone a deep red in the lamplight.

Truitt gawked. Though he learned as much as he could about the jewel through rumours and the newspapers, it couldn't compare to the breathtaking beauty in person. "Oh, that one."

Calista clicked her tongue. "As if there is any other." She closed the box and carried him to a small table against the wall, casually swinging him back and forth, disorientating the berkis. Finally, she flipped him upright and set him on the wooden surface. Even with the elevation, he needed to crane his neck to see her face. "I can't let you take that," she told him, keeping one hand on his shoulder to steady him until the blood that had rushed to his brain resumed its normal flow. "I have been assigned to guard it from thieves. Like you."

Truitt shook his head, as much to clear it as to indicate his disagreement. "My dear lady, you misapprehend my purpose. I, too, have been employed to watch over the precious jewel."

"Really? In all-black attire? And is that oil on your face?" She brought a finger up to touch the dark smears, but he pulled back, and she relented. "Alright. Tell me by whom."

He knew the name. Or had known. It hadn't seemed an important detail. "The noblewoman who resides in this dwelling."

Calista leaned in closer, using her size to intimidate him, as she had done so to Zusa. "Tell me her name."

Truitt nervously ran his fingers through his scraggly hair. It was working. He sensed the heat radiating from her body, and he fought off the urge to place a curious hand against her chest. Instead, he did his best to meet her eyes, a handspan above his own. "Come now. It reflects poorly on your professionalism if you do not know the moniker of your patron."

She grinned down at him. "Oh, I know it just fine. It is your story which is in doubt."

I need another bluff! "I confess. Her name momentarily escapes me."

"Then why don't we go discuss our mutual assignment with her, so you may be reacquainted?" The towering female brought her hands up towards his hip, seemingly ready to snatch him from the table and carry him to Lady Aetherborne.

Dratted bit o' raspberry! He hastily raised a hand in protest and took a step back. "We must not interrupt the mistress during this late hour. I propose instead I take my leave now, let you continue on with your evening, and once the sun is again brightening the sky, I will pop around and give her a report of tonight's happenings." He lowered his voice in a conspiratorial manner and tapped the side of his nose. "Do not fret. I will not mention your inexperience in these matters."

"That's most kind of you, but I genuinely can't let you go. Lady Aishwarya Aetherborne will be furious if she learns I set a thief free."

Confound it! Truitt straightened. He was running out of excuses. "Well done. Well done, indeed. You passed the test."

Calista folded her arms, a sceptical gaze narrowing upon him. "What test?"

Under her scrutiny, Truitt's throat parched, and he faltered. He lowered his eyes as he searched for an answer, but that left him staring into her decolletage. The sight of the seductive line only further scattered his thoughts, and he forced himself to look up again. "Why, the one to verify your loyalty. Lady Ash... Aishwi... She hired me to assess your worthiness.

The nobles are always seeking those they can trust for further employment in their establishments." Truitt put on his most endearing smile. "And my dear, you have proven yourself to be most worthy."

She nodded, seeming to accept his lie. "And I suppose my rescuing you yesterday was also part of this test?"

"Assuredly! You see, the mistress and I are very close. Like this." He held up two fingers and flexed them, trying to get them to cross. They wouldn't. Fearing his comparison was failing, he dropped his hand. "Like a pair of aces in a deck."

Calista's eyes narrowed again. "A moment ago, you could not even recall her name. No, no, let me guess. That was also part of the test."

"You are a clever lass. Precisely. All part of the test."

"And your chums in the Right Hand? They are all in on it, too?"

A bead of sweat ran down his forehead. *Drat! I forgot she met them!* "Oh, aye. Them too."

The faroko stared at him. "My! You draw the long bow. I am impressed by your attention to detail. And you truly believe Lady Aetherborne will praise my work?"

He let out a breath, his body easing for a moment. "Un-doubtedly!"

"Why put it off until morning? Let's go see her now." She lifted him off the table and tucked him against her side, like a mother carrying a child.

Truitt gasped as he suddenly found himself pressed against her supple figure. *She possesses immense strength!* "Wait!"

Calista paused, her face close to his. For the first time, they were eye to eye. "Problem?"

The berkis squirmed under her gaze and in her grip as her powerful hand clutched his buttocks tightly. Even if he pulled free, a four-foot drop to the floor awaited him. He'd fallen further than that before, but it wasn't an activity he enjoyed. His hands posed another issue as he struggled to decide where to place them. One found its way to her shoulder for stability, but the other had to hang by his side. Any alternative positions, however pleasant, were bound to elicit a protest. He sighed. *The jig is up.* "You have won this round, madam. I am not under your mistress's employment. And I beseech you not to awaken her now. For my sake and her own, as I was sincere in my concern for the lateness of the hour."

"Then why are you here?"

Truitt considered his next lie. *Appeal to her vanity?* "Would you accept that I came to keep you company?"

"You didn't seem that eager for my company when I was saving your backside." She squeezed said posterior to match her words. "Try again."

He jumped in her hand, not completely disliking the feeling. It was the first time he found himself so easily dominated by a woman, leaving him uncertain about the emotions he should be experiencing. Despite this confusion, he recognised the urgent need for an escape plan. The current situation differed wholly from the way he envisioned his heist unfolding. "Alright!" he snapped. "I endeavoured this evening to catch a glimpse of the famous jewel. I've heard tell it has the power to mesmerise all those who gaze upon its wonder."

"You could have requested an audience for that." She squeezed a second time.

He trembled. For a moment, he considered feeding her another falsehood just to experience the rump clutch again, but he had run out of lies. It didn't seem as if she would believe him, anyway. There remained a way to achieve his goal, though. "Very well. I confess, I came to pinch the gem. But you have shown me the error of my ways, and I am committed to renouncing my avaricious nature. Release me, and I will take myself forthwith to the nearest nunnery."

"Don't you mean *monastery*?"

Truitt tutted. "Dear lady, I said I would cease stealing. Let me maintain some enjoyment, however."

"You should have been out tot-hunting tonight, then," Calista told him. "Give me your word."

You're barking at a knot, missy. "You want a promise? I am surprised and touched by your concern over my amorous congress, but such matters should not be of interest to angelics, such as yourself."

She jostled him as a reminder of his position. "Give me your word you won't try to steal the gem."

Truitt made an exaggerated expression of understanding. "Ah, that matter. As you wish. I swear by your beautiful brown eyes not to try to steal the gem."

Calista blushed a little at the unexpected compliment. "Now, was that so hard?" She carried him to the study window and set him down on the floor. "And I am living up to my end of the agreement. You are free to go."

Truitt stared up past her prominent chest to the face gazing back down at him. A hollow sensation lingered in his stomach, already missing her embrace. A lower part of his anatomy experienced a stronger reaction., which he concealed with a bow. "You are far too generous to my humble personage. I will, indeed, make my retreat." As he straightened, a bang sounded in the other room. Both looked to the doorway. "You seem to have another concern to attend."

Calista glanced back at him, then rushed to the entrance. No visible evidence indicated an intruder. She turned to the window, but Truitt had gone. With that problem at least solved, she hurried about the library, searching for any sign of movement. The figurine of the cherub lay on its side. It couldn't have fallen over without help.

She tried the doors. Locked. The only other means of entry were the windows, but they were still closed and secured as well.

Shifting into a panic, she passed her eyes over the room again, then crossed back to the study and did the same. She checked behind the chairs, under a sofa, and even glanced into the fireplace. Nothing. Finally, she returned to the window Truitt used, slid it shut, and switched the latch to a locked position.

Another noise drew her attention to the library. A breeze of cool night air brushed her cheeks as she sprinted through the doorway. One window stood open! Hadn't she checked them all?

Dread took hold of her body. If the Shadow had come, then he wouldn't have left without his prize. She walked toward the ivory box as if she were in a dream, knowing what she would find but unable to stop herself from the discovery.

A flick of her wrist opened the box, and the nightmare became reality. After all her plans, the audition, the derision by Lady Aetherborne, and the hours of boredom, she had failed.

The Dragon Eye Gem was gone!

Chapter 15

The Identity Ambiguity
Or He Ain't No Saint

NEEDLESS TO SAY, Lady Aetherborne was livid in the morning.

"This is unacceptable!" She didn't quite yell the phrase. That would have been improper. Instead, she raised her voice just loud enough so those within the surrounding rooms and the floor below could be alerted to her anger. "It was your task to guard the gem! Where has it gone?"

Calista accepted the admonishment as she stood, head bowed contritely, staff in hand, before the older woman. She had anticipated it with dread and felt almost relieved when it finally came to fruition. "I apologise wholeheartedly, Lady Aetherborne. I kept watch the whole night, but never saw who took it."

It wasn't an entirely accurate account. It left out the few hours she slept in the study chair, along with the appearance of Truitt. But he had given her his word he would not steal it, and for reasons unknown to her, she refused to accept he had broken his vow. Even if he did, she hadn't witnessed him take the gem, so that, at least, remained truthful.

The apology was not well received. "The Grey Shadow's reputation is that he *isn't* seen, which is precisely why I requested those with some expertise." Lady Aetherborne waved an angry finger at the imposing faroko, too enraged to be daunted by her size. "Instead, it seems I hired an amateur who could not handle a simple assignment."

Simple? You expected me to take on the most infamous thief in Leverhelm! But Calista kept the retort to herself. The truth stood that she *had* failed and needed to make it right.

During the long, painful hours until sunrise, Calista found ample opportunity to review the night's encounter. Despite that, she had no explanation for what occurred. Truitt had arrived through the study window to steal it, yet she had been with him the entire time. He could not have caused the figurine to fall in the other room, which meant someone else must have been in the library. However, when she checked, all the windows and doors were still secure.

From the stories, she guessed only the Grey Shadow could have entered and left so effortlessly. That led her to three possible explanations. First, Truitt was the Grey Shadow. This notion she found the least likely. While he confessed he intended to steal the gem, Calista couldn't believe the master thief who had eluded both the law and the Duke pursuing him for so many years would be that easily captured. She had merely stood by the window and grabbed him.

The second possibility suggested Truitt might be aiding the Shadow. His entry into the study served as a distraction while the true burglar absconded with the jewel. Calista found this to be the most plausible explanation. The Grey Shadow's having an apprentice could certainly go a long way to explaining the claims of his numerous capers.

Third, Truitt's presence might have merely been a coincidence, however extraordinary. But that meant two different thieves would be attempting a heist of the same item at the same time. Calista found that likelihood too big a haddock to swallow.

No matter which proved true, she only had one course of action: find Truitt and learn what happened. She raised her head to meet the woman's glare. "I think I know how to recover the gem."

Lady Aetherborne's tail whipped about, barely missing Beatrice, who stood behind her. "How in blazes would you possess that knowledge? You said you saw no one last night. Was that a deceit?"

Calista dipped her gaze again. "No, madam. I honestly did not see the gem being taken. But I might be able to recover it."

The elderly faroko straightened and shook herself. "And how may I be certain you are not the very individual who has stolen the jewel? It is conceivable that such a nefarious objective was your pursuit since the outset."

"Search me." Calista's fingers moved to her corset and began undoing the busk. "Verify it is not upon my person."

"Cease this activity at once! I will not have you flaunting your unclothed attributes in my house like some dollymop." Lady Aetherborne glared up at her until she stopped. "You are granted until mid-afternoon to restore the gem to this household. If not, I will have the constabulary take you into custody. Am I understood?"

"Yes, Lady Aetherborne." Calista curtsied, dipping as low as she could. "You are most generous. I promise to return as soon as I can." Not waiting for a reply, she ducked around mistress and servant and headed toward the staircase. "I'll see my way out." Grabbing up her dress, she bolted down the stairs, taking them two at a time, before Lady Aetherborne changed her mind.

Only when she had passed through the ornate gate and travelled halfway down the street did she slow herself. *Gaol! She is threatening to put me in gaol if I don't recover the gem! I must track down Truitt. Again.*

Calista made her way through the streets of the Sunside as quickly as she could without appearing rude. This trip, she refrained from admiring the polished storefronts or marvelling at the fashion of pedestrians. She simply didn't have the time or the desire. Yesterday, she daydreamed of taking up residency here. Now, the inside of a cell seemed a more likely future if she failed to find the gem and the berkis who swiped it.

It must be him. It has to be him. I can't afford it not to be. Her staff tapped against the pavement as she marched, keeping time with her frantic footsteps and even more frantic mind. *I was a fool for trusting him. I should have turned him over to Lady Aetherborne the moment he entered.*

Why didn't she? As Calista hurried through the streets, weaving around gawking pedestrians, she considered the question. She owed him nothing. Indeed, it was he who owed her a debt for rescuing him from the orv ruffians the night before, whether he acknowledged it or not.

Nor did she have a reason to trust him. He was rude, manipulative, and stubborn. Add to that the fact he lied to her multiple times about his intent and you had a recipe for a most onerous individual. The only time he seemed to be straight with her was when she squeezed his backside.

Gracious, that was satisfying! He was completely under my power. I could have done anything I wanted with him. Calista's heart quickened for another reason than her rapid pace along the sidewalk. *Do I want to do something with him? He's handsome enough. Blue eyes. Round cheeks.*

It barely registered with her when she crossed the imaginary border into the Mids. *He's also half my height. I would need to drop to my knees just to look him in the eye. Would that be so bad?*

Calista stopped to get her bearings. She'd been walking almost completely without concern for direction and found herself further north than she intended. After spotting the sign on a building giving the street name, she reoriented herself and resumed marching southeast.

Why am I thinking of him like this? He's a nuisance, and now my freedom is at risk because I protected his. Next time his fuzzy rump is in my hands, it will receive a firm whacking.

Once she crossed Woodcock Way, her ire had dulled, only to be replaced by hunger. As the sun crept lazily up the horizon, her stomach rumbled, having not been fed since last evening. She chided herself for being too worked up and missing the vendors in the better parts of the city. Instead, she would need to satisfy herself with samples of what the Ward offered. She avoided the trotters and jellied eels. As popular as they were, they made her queasy. She also steered clear of any broxy, as the meat frequently came from diseased animals. She settled on ginger beer and a few raspberry tarts, unabashedly devouring the pastries before washing them down with the sweet liquid.

Finally sated, she continued through the Ward to where she had parted with Truitt two days before. While not as bad as some of the nearby buildings, the townhouse appeared sorely neglected. Bluish-grey paint peeled from the siding, and a few of the bottom windows were boarded up.

Seeing the dilapidated dwelling made her question her mission. *If I had to live this way, I'd most likely take to stealing as well. It's like the orphans. If I turned him in, he'd be sitting in gaol too now. Do I have the right to condemn him to prison?* A profound sense of guilt came over her, and rather than barging into the building in search of the deceitful berkis, she took a seat on the stone steps, setting her staff beside her. *I can't send someone else to that fate, even if he is the Grey Shadow. So what if that harlot loses a jewel?*

She drove a clenched fist into her leg. *I get sent to prison if I don't return it. It isn't a matter of what Lady Aetherborne deserves. It boils down to either him possessing the gem or me regaining my freedom. I haven't disclosed his identity to her, and there's no need for me to do so.*

"Hiya Miss. You lost?"

Calista lifted her head. A juvenile female orv, she guessed no older than ten, wearing a lavender dress and an old aviator's cap, stood a few feet away. In her contemplation, the faroko failed to hear her approach. *You're getting too distracted!* "Good morning, young lass. I am not lost. More confused about what I should do."

Lavinia's expression grew serious. "I understand."

Her answer surprised the faroko. "You do? Have you been confused before?"

The girl nodded enthusiastically. "Oh, yes. Sometimes, I wonder whether I should speak to strangers or not. My mother says no, but my friend says that a stranger is just a friend you ain't met yet."

"Your friend sounds wise. But you should be careful who you speak to. Not everyone is amicable."

"What's that word?" Lavinia's face screwed up as she tried to repeat it. "Am-ca-bull?"

"Amicable," Calista corrected. "It means 'friendly'."

"Then why not say friendly?"

I can't argue with that logic. "You are right. I was just being silly."

"Yes," Lavinia agreed helpfully. "I also wonder how I can help my mum. But then I talk to my friend, and he helps me help her. We get pies and trotters and candy."

She is lucky someone is looking out for her. There should be more people like that. "Does this saintly friend have a name?"

"What's that word? Sane-tee?"

"Saintly. It means good. Yes, I know. I was being silly again."

Lavinia drew her hands behind her and began idly swaying her body left and right. "Oh. Mr Truitt is very good. You would like him."

Calista's jaw dropped open. *It can't be!* "Who did you say?"

"Mr Truitt. Do you know him?"

"Male berkis? Chestnut hair, blue eyes. Dresses ratty. Always grumpy."

Lavinia stopped twirling and nodded again. "Hmm-mm. But he's not grumpy. He's the nicest man I know."

It must be a different person. But what is the likelihood he has a twin with a more favourable disposition and the same name? Only one way to find out. "I've met him. He lives here, right?"

The girl giggled. "No, silly. Mr Truitt lives in the Mids. But he doesn't like it there. He comes here to get away from there."

Can't be the same berkis. Calista searched her mind for a means to identify him better. There was his weapon, and Raffles claimed the hat on his chair had been his. "Does your Mr Truitt own a slingshot and a brown slouch hat?"

"Yup! And a magic pouch! That's where he gets his money and candy."

Everything matched, except for the pouch. But she did remember seeing a black bag on his waist which could correspond to the description. "Then you and I have the same friend. Would you happen to know where Mr Truitt currently resides?"

Lavinia's face lit up at the prospect. "Chirky! I've only been there twice, but I can show you! Come on!" She waved a beckoning hand.

I hope he is the same. The physical seems to line up, but unless he's got a wholly different personality tucked in his trousers somewhere, I don't see how he could be. If she is wrong, I can always come back here. That decided, Calista grabbed her staff, stood, and hopped down from the stairs.

The girl's eyes nearly popped from her head at the height of the woman and her weapon. "Are you a giantess?"

Her innocent reaction touched Calista. She seemed to be in awe rather than disgusted. "Depends. Would that be a good thing or a bad thing?"

The grin returned to Lavinia's face. "Oh, a good thing!"

Finally! "Then yes, I am. My name is Calista."

"I'm Lavinia."

The faroko gave her an exaggerated bow. "It is a pleasure to meet you, Lavinia. Will you guide me?"

With the girl in the lead, the two headed back toward the Mids, following almost the same route Calista had come by less than an hour before. Despite Lavinia's initial friendly greeting and discussion, she soon grew quiet.

Meanwhile, Calista tried to reconcile her own experience with the thief and the orv's description. She needed to know more. "Why did you say Mr Truitt doesn't enjoy living in the Mids?"

Lavinia glanced up at her. While not as short as a berkis, she still only stood eye level with the faroko's belly. "He said it's full of sniffies natting about the weather."

That sounds more like the ratbag. "I live there, as well as my friends. We don't behave that way."

"Mebbe that's why he likes you."

Oh, I am certain he does not like me. He definitely won't when I catch up to him. "Why doesn't he leave, then?"

Lavinia tugged at the strap of her cap. "Dunno." Her eyes grew wide as a thought occurred to her. "Mebbe he's being forced to. Mebbe he's being punished!"

To think I actually felt sorry for him! "Oh, he will be."

"I hope not." The girl abruptly stopped and a profound sigh escaped her lips. "I like cake."

The change in topic surprised Calista. She looked down to find Lavinia staring at a vendor selling sponge cakes. The imagery reminded her of the orphans stealing bread. She had wanted to make a difference and failed. She wouldn't fail again. "Cake is good. Would you join me for some?"

Lavinia nodded. "If ya insist."

A few minutes later, the pair resumed their course, with both females munching happily on the soft delicacy. The smacking of lips and licking of fingers were the only sounds they made for several blocks. When they reached Woodcock Way, however, Lavinia halted.

Sensing her trepidation, Calista crouched beside the girl. "Whatever Mr Truitt told you, the people of the Mids aren't much different from those in the Ward. It might surprise you to know they were once the same."

Lavinia began her swaying again. "That's silly," she said with the absolute certainty only a child could muster.

"It is. But it is also true. But you don't need to continue if you are afraid."

"Am not!" The girl ceased her nervous spin. "I just didn't want *you* to be scared."

Calista held back her smile. "Thank you. Shall we go, then?"

With a huff, Lavinia looked up and down the street before heading across, the faroko on her heels. They headed northward and west for ten minutes before she stopped before a townhouse. It looked little different from those around it, but she lifted her face to her giantess friend. "Here it is. This is where Mr Truitt lives. First floor."

This building appeared in much better condition than the one they left in the Ward. *He definitely isn't poor. I couldn't afford a place like this on what I earn.* "Have you ever been inside?" Calista asked, crouching again.

"Zounds, no! Mr Truitt offered to show me once, but that wouldn't be proper. I'm from the Ward! I don't belong in no fancy houses."

Her protest surprised the faroko. "Now *you* are being silly. It's just a building."

"No ma'am, it ain't. Don't make me go up in it!"

"Very well. But how do you know his flat is on the first floor?"

"He told me," Lavinia explained. "He said the top is too close to heaven, and the bottom is too close to hell. He figures he falls somewhere in the middle, so... first floor."

Then I will get the gem back now. She tugged the girl's shoulder. "Thanks for bringing me here. I wouldn't have found it without you."

"You going in?"

"I am. Mr Truitt and I need to have a serious talk." *And more if he doesn't fess up.* "Can you return to the Ward on your own?"

"Course. You give him my greeting, alright?"

"I will." Calista paused, sensing from the girl's stare at her dress that she wanted something more. "Was there anything else?"

"Yes," came the reply as she began swaying again. "Do you have any candy?"

Chapter 16

The Apartment Infiltration
Or Unhappy To See You

C ALISTA HAD NO sweets to offer the girl, but instead handed her a few pennies she had tucked away in her dress. Once they said goodbyes, with Lavinia promising to head straight back to the Ward, Calista climbed the stone steps to the townhouse entrance.

The door wasn't locked, and she quickly stepped inside. She then bounded up the staircase there, following Lavinia's instructions, to the first floor, where she saw another door.

It bore no sign or plaque, no indication of the residency's occupants. She raised a hand to knock, then decided to enter unannounced. *If he doesn't want to be found, he isn't about to respond to a visitor.*

The door featured dual handles, with the first situated three and a half feet above the floor and the smaller second positioned around eighteen inches from the ground. Their mechanisms were linked, so turning one also moved the other. Both possessed identical locks, which she discovered were secured.

A mechanism within the wooden barrier controlled a bar inserted into a hole in the floor, holding it in place. Rather than try to break the knobs, she gave the door a rough shove. The bottom frame snapped, allowing her to push her way inside.

Calista found herself in a short hallway, with rooms off to the left and right and a corridor almost directly before her. She wandered in, wondering if perhaps she got the wrong apartment, when she heard humming from ahead. The faroko advanced cautiously toward a partially closed door, where a faint light spilt out from the edges. After setting her staff against the wall, she slipped in.

The lavish bedroom surprised her. While not as opulent as Lady Aetherborne's abode, its owner obviously lived a comfortable life. Despite the lateness of the morning, heavy curtains were drawn closed to block out the sunlight hitting the windows. A single lamp perched on a nightstand provided the room with just enough additional illumination to keep the atmosphere cosy. Beyond it lay an open door through which the humming floated through.

This cannot be right. Truitt is a scruffy rascal who tried to guilt me out of payment for rescuing him. Why would he pretend to be a pauper when he lives like this? Lavinia must have been mistaken. This can't be his residence.

She began to retreat from of the room when Truitt, clad in only a dressing gown, slippers, and the single ring on his left hand, walked in through the far doorway. His face was scrubbed and his hair slicked back. A yelp escaped his mouth when he saw her, and he quickly drew the robe tighter. Calista grinned as he composed himself and addressed her. "You've got the wrong house."

"Wrong house for what?" the faroko asked innocently. *He certainly looks better washed up!*

"For whatever it is you are being paid to do. I have no jobs for you. So if you would please see yourself out... wait, how did you get in?"

Calista nodded toward the entryway. "I used the front door. That is the usual way to enter an establishment."

Truitt's expression darkened. "It was locked."

"So was the window last night."

The berkis shrugged, his face becoming indifferent. "Then kindly retrace your ill-chosen path and exit this establishment. My bed and I have set aside this time for our nightly reunion, and it is a private affair."

Calista pointed to the covered window. Despite the curtains, rays of sunlight shone through around the edges. "It's mid-morning."

"I confess our appointment has been delayed, due to an unforeseen... detainment."

"You seem to get detained a lot."

Truitt shrugged again. "It is an all too common likelihood in my practice."

"And what *is* your practice?" Calista stepped into the room, making a show of looking around. The maroon wallpaper and hardwood floors. The raunchy paintings hanging above the furniture. The decorated queen-sized bed. "What matter of occupation allows you to possess not one, but two households?"

He bristled at seeing her enter further, but kept his voice level. "The dwellings on Bucklebarrow Road street are not my home. If you must know, and may have already guessed, that place is a facade. A cover. Part of my other persona."

"I did guess that. And I have to say, you clean up nicely." She ran her eyes up and down his body, not attempting to hide her interest. It wasn't every day she found herself alone in a barely-clad man's bedroom.

"Well, I ... thank you." His aloof attitude, shaken by her attention and words, faltered. "As do you. The dress flatters your..." His voice trailed off, seemingly unsure how to finish the appraisal.

That's thrown him off. I wonder what he's really thinking. Let's see. She bent over, intending to place her palms on the bed. It sat lower than she expected, however, serving someone of his size, and she abruptly displayed a greater amount of lush cleavage than she intended. If not for her training keeping her limber, she might have fallen over completely. "My what?" she asked, hoping he didn't notice her miscalculation. "I missed the rest of your compliment."

Truitt squirmed, his gaze firmly locked on her hanging chest. "Your...your...eyes. It brings out the grey in a most flattering manner."

"My eyes are brown," she chuckled. "Are you sure it's my eyes you are admiring?"

Calista struggled not to laugh as his face blushed a vibrant shade of pink. As gracefully as she could, the statuesque female turned her body, sitting sideways on the edge of the bed. It stood a few inches over a foot tall, requiring her to greatly fold her knees. Even seated, the top of her head easily cleared his. Truitt wasn't focusing on her height, though. "Is this better?" she asked, waving a hand to draw his attention.

It worked, and he grudgingly brought his eyes to meet hers. "No. I mean, yes." He shook a fist and pointed to the exit. "However, it would be best if you were to leave through my doors and allow me my sleep. I retreated when you told me to. It would seem a reciprocal reaction is in order."

She wagged a finger at him. "Ah, but you didn't. The gem wasn't in its place this morning, and only you and I were in that room last night."

"Then I hope you see the error of your ways and return it promptly. I will not think ill of your character."

"*I* don't have it. But since its owner doesn't know about your little visit, she has drawn the same conclusion. Which means..." She rose and turned toward him, hands on her hips. "That my job from last night is incomplete. I cannot leave here without that gem to clear my name."

The berkis waved aside the veiled accusation. "Alas, as I told you, I obeyed your orders. So you will have to look elsewhere for your jewel. It is not on these premises."

His smooth response troubled the woman. Was she wrong? "You *must* have it. If you don't, then where else could it be?"

"Search me."

Calista had made a similar proposal to Lady Aetherborne. She looked him over again, admiring how the robe hung off his frame. From when she gripped him last night, she knew he was in fine physical form, despite his seemingly opulent lifestyle. He was small but fit. *I did plan to get my hands on him.* "I should take you up on that offer." She started to move around the bed. "There isn't much to go over, but I'm sure I can find something in all that hair." She stopped, blushing at her own words. *Where did that come from?*

Truitt pulled his robe tighter, then seemed to reconsider, letting the belt fall loose. "If that is what it takes to convince you of my innocence, then consider this body yours, on loan, for the duration of your investigation." He slid onto the coverlet, lying sideways, one hand propping up his head while the other adjusted the cloth to drape seductively.

Calista stared. *I didn't think he would take it seriously. What do I do now? Does he really want this? Do I want this?* Unsure how to respond, she continued around the bed.

"Hold a moment. If this is to be a proper...examination, then I feel it only fair and equitable that I am afforded the same freedom to pursue my own inquiries."

Calista stopped again. "I don't understand."

"Strip." It was an order, not a request. "Twice now, our paths have intertwined, raising questions I wish answered. Also, it would be an act of barbarism to sully that fine dress."

The faroko giggled. *He acts the gentleman while asking me to get nude. But if this is necessary to clear my name...* She bent over, holding back her hair, as she began untying her boots. "This will take a moment."

He watched her from the bed, his eyes shifting from her body to the footwear. "There is no need for haste. Brittney & Ashe?"

Naturally, he wants me to undress slowly! Has he done this before with other women? "Martinez," she told him in answer to where she purchased her boots. "Brittney & Ashe is too expensive on my income." She slipped the right one off and began with the left.

"Pity."

Does he have a thing for boots? Good. If he doesn't give me the gem, I'll shove him in one. Calista removed the second, set it beside the bed with the first, and slowly slid her stockings down her long legs, letting him ogle her thighs. "You still haven't told me what you do to afford this place." Calista stood, her fingers setting to work on the busk holding her corset tight. "Clothes from upscale shops. Enchanted weapons."

"I have a rich uncle." Truitt feigned indifference, but didn't take his eyes off the woman. His hungry stare suggested this wasn't a common occurrence for him. "Is this part of the interrogation?"

She tossed the corset onto a pillow at the head of the bed. "Just making conversation while unfastening my clothes. You are the one who insisted I remove them."

Truitt reached his free hand down and adjusted the robe, pulling more fabric to the front. "If that is the purpose, then enlighten me to what you do."

"I'm doing it." She saw a smirk appear on his face. "Not *this*. I hire my services to those in need. Like when I rescued you two days ago."

The berkis frowned. "That was not a rescue. That was merely..."

Calista unbuttoned her dress and pulled it over her head, her curls bouncing free of the fabric. Below them, her breasts performed a more mesmerising celebration of their own as she shoved her drawers to the floor. Towering over the bed, completely naked, she left him speechless. "Yes?" She tossed the last items of clothing onto the corset. Her tail swayed leisurely back and forth behind her, performing its own seductive dance. "What were you saying?"

Chapter 17

The Interrogation Flagellation
Or Talk To The Cheek

TRUITT'S EYES WIDENED at the sight, threatening to permanently disfigure his face. His jaw alternated between open and shut, as if he wanted to speak, to make some commentary on the vision, but his brain couldn't find the words.

Calista knew the feelings she aroused in him and decided to turn up the heat. After the incident with Victor, it had taken her a long time to accept that her body wasn't something to be ashamed of. Now, she relished the berkis's reaction.

She stepped forward, feigning an innocent expression as she bent to put her hands on the bed again. Her breasts swung hypnotically as she began crawling across the pink coverlet. "Can't speak? This won't be much of an interrogation if you are unable to form words."

Somehow, Truitt's eyes widened further as she approached. "My power of speech is not impaired. I merely...whoa!"

Calista grabbed his ankle and yanked him toward her. Friction held his robe back, revealing a bare stomach, hairy thighs, and a healthy member, fully erect. It wobbled with the movement, and it was her turn to gawk. "Sweet bulging plugtails! Looks like I've found a hidden treasure already. How have you kept that tucked away?"

"That is not part of this inquiry!" Truitt spluttered as he tried to untangle himself from the robe. He only succeeded in causing the stiff member to sway more violently.

She yanked him down further until he lay completely under her torso. Her face stared down at his, her drooping black tresses reaching for his cheeks. His arms were freed, but she quickly pinned his wrists to the bed above his head. "Oh, I'm afraid it is. You did not propose any restrictions on our arrangement, and since I've already met your requirements, you cannot renegotiate now."

"I disagree! I think — "

A devilish idea crossed Calista's mind, and she arched her back, dropping her breasts onto his face and quieting his protest. He began shouting, but the twin orbs, each bigger than his head, muffled the sound. The vibrations rippled through her flesh, sending a shiver down her stomach to her groyne. She had been intimate with other men before, mostly farokos like herself, and while her larger form and strength outmatched them, she had allowed them to control their lovemaking. Experience taught her that male self-esteem could be easily wounded. The berkis beneath her, however, seemed to possess the ego the size of an airship, and she wanted it bruised. *I can't believe how effortlessly I'm dominating him! He's so little!* His full erection brushed her belly, eliciting a giggle. "What's that? I can hear you, but I cannot quite understand it." She stayed there several more seconds, then pushed herself up. Her grin widened as she stared down at him, gasping for breath. "Could you repeat that?"

Truitt tried to yank his arms free, but her grip remained strong. "Now see here! This is most unfair! I demand..."

The breasts dropped back into place, his features becoming swallowed in the weighty soft flesh. "Nope! Still can't hear you!" she snickered. When she came to retrieve the gem, she never imagined she would be smothering her target in this manner. It wasn't an activity anyone would be likely to envision topping their day.

Then something smacked her arse, hard. Startled, she immediately lifted herself off him and moved her hands to the bed for a more solid base as she twisted her head around in search of the culprit. Free, Truitt quickly wiggled down the mattress, slipping under her rear. On the other side, he jumped to his feet and met her eyes. Not believing what she saw, Calista looked down but found him gone. "What the deuce?"

"Aha!" he shouted triumphantly from behind her backside. "You aren't the only one with tricks!" He drew back his hand and smacked her right arse cheek. The sound of the slap echoed around the room. "That is for breaking into my abode. You should know better than to invade a gentleman's privacy." Another swing struck her buttock again. "This is for accusing me of pilfering. You impugn my word and my honour."

Calista seemed little bothered by the assault on her back avenue, however, as she reached for the robe and pulled it to her. She came for one reason, and a few spanks would not deter her. A quick examination revealed the gem to not be among its folds, though. "We have not yet agreed that you are innocent," she called to him. "That is what I'm trying to determine."

Another blow sounded as his hand made contact again. While fleshy, her years of training with Fenton had given her buns of polished brass. The hits hurt his hands more than her rump. "That's for repeating the slander! If you continue this line of claims, your ability to rest your ample behind will be hindered for a considerable period."

"Are you saying I have an oversized posterior?" Apparently, her breasts had failed to lessen his conceit.

"Proclaiming it is unnecessary. One need to only observe it."

Calista looked over her shoulder. He was definitely enjoying the situation, as his engorged virility slapped against her leg each time he swung. She needed to rely on that touch, as all she could spot of him was his upper torso rising above the curve of her arse. "Well, I'm observing someone in need of a spanking themselves."

"Ha! I'd like to see — Ouch!" The faroko's tail had sprung to life and swatted him in the rear. "What was that for?"

He's lucky I'm not wearing the flail! "You really don't know? Look around. You lead a lavish lifestyle when you aren't playing cards, but you ruin *my* job by stealing a gem I'm guarding. And if you touch my arse again, I will stuff you in a sack and squash you into marmalade!"

Truitt blinked and appeared properly chastised as his hand dropped to his side. "Continue."

She nodded toward the artwork on the wall. "Well, you've got all these luxuries — the clothes, furniture, art — so I don't understand why you would want something so trivial as the gem. Doesn't seem to suit your taste."

"And what do you presume my taste is?"

"Given our current positions," — Calista wiggled her posterior — "I would say rather lascivious. And your paintings! That one with the lady and the octopus would make a dollymop blush. I'm certain the action of those three skembers and a horse in the corner painting is morally as well as anatomically incorrect. And what is that woman supposed to be doing?" She gestured her head toward a picture of a female berkis shown only from the top of her shoulders and upward. She appeared to be lying on some kind of fabric, with her face contorted into a mix of pain and ecstasy.

Truitt straightened and thrust out his chest. The action caused another thump against Calista's leg. "That, I will have you know, is the famous *Moaning Elisa*, painted by Leonard Avinchi. Or a copy of it, at least. The original was nicked a few years ago from Brassmont by the Grey Shadow."

Him again! "He definitely gets around. Are you aspiring to be like him?" she asked, turning her head back toward him.

Truitt scowled. "Bah! That pompous arse. What kind of thief is foolish enough to leave an orange behind every caper, alerting the world to who the perpetrator was?"

"A bold one, certainly," Calista answered. "One who doesn't get caught. Maybe you can learn from him."

"Ooh! The insolence!" His hand resumed its attacks with a quick slap. "I'm going to make sure you can't rest your backside for a week." Another strike.

"I don't think so." Without warning, she shoved her arse backwards as she pushed off from the bed. Her buttocks slammed him to the mattress before settling onto his chest, leaving everything from his waist down exposed between her legs. "That's better," she announced, sitting with the berkis pinned beneath her. She had taken a similar position with previous lovers, but only briefly, as again, they always wished to be the dominant role. *He has no choice, though. And we aren't lovers. Not yet. Don't even think that!*

"Get off! You're squashing me!"

"I did warn you. Now you have the opportunity to become real cosy with my backside as we continue our discussion." Her attention was drawn to his stiff member tickling her pubic hair. She flicked it with her finger and felt his body tremble beneath her. She smiled. "Answer my questions or else."

"Or else?" The joyful bravado his voice had adopted during the spanking gave way to a softer, slightly higher-pitched tone.

"Or else I snap your third leg like a wishbone." She flicked it again, sending it bobbing about like a broken piston in a steam engine. "Understand?"

His body shuddered again, his hairy torso tickling her nether region. "Y-Yes! I'll tell you what you want to know!"

"Good." Calista wiggled her rear, feeling her buttocks settle around his chest and stomach. *I wonder how loud he'd yell if I squeezed.* "For starters, tell me proper. How can you afford such a lavish flat?"

"I said already. I have a rich uncle."

"And I'm supposed to believe that? He just dotes on his favourite nephew from the love in his heart?"

"Hardly." The berkis squirmed, trying to work himself out from underneath the huge faroko, but only got himself further wedged between her cheeks. "He covers my modest expenses to please my parents."

His wiggling caused her heart to race, and she nearly missed his explanation. "That's it?" When he did not answer, Calista ran a finger down his shaft. It resembled a pork sausage she might get from a food vendor. *I wonder what it tastes like. Stop it!* "Truly?"

"And to keep me from my occupation!" he blurted. "That's the truth."

Keep him from his occupation? The only thing she'd seen him do was play cards. And attempt to nab the gem. "And that would be stealing?"

His chest deflated. "Guessed it in one."

Finally getting somewhere! "So you admit you stole the gem."

"What importance is it to you?"

"That noblewoman thinks I stole it. She might have me arrested if I don't produce it."

"So? Without the object, they cannot tie you to its disappearance. At worst, they take you into their custody for a short time until the item resurfaces. They nab the true culprit, or you go to trial, at which point, without sufficient evidence to convict you, you will be released on your recog... regoni... they let you go." He squirmed in vain, rubbing his hairy chest between her legs and almost eliciting a squeal from his captor. "Now please, release me. As pleasant as your arse cheeks are to spank, I feel they have worn out their welcome."

"Cheek."

"Pardon me? I was being polite."

"No. Cheek, as in singular." Calista pointed to her left buttock, drawing in a sharp breath at seeing how it dwarfed his head. *Could he still speak if I sat back? Stop it!* "You only ever spanked one side. You owe the other an apology for your neglect."

"Surely, you are in jest."

"Am I?" She wiggled again, grinding his body into the bed. *I want to smother him!* A few drops of her juices escaped, slicking up his stomach, showing he was not alone in his arousal. As an added aggravation, her tail dipped down and brushed its end along his forehead and nose.

"Alright! Tarnation! I apologise for not rendering equal attention to both sides of your arse!" His expression twisted, trying to knock the furry tip off.

"Not to me. To her." She flexed her left buttock, causing it to jiggle pleasingly a few inches from his face.

His eyes goggled. "Do that again." She did, with a laugh. "My dear lady, you have an unnatural, dare I say, divine, control over the more abundant portions of your personage."

"I am glad you approve," Calista said, pleased with the compliment. It wasn't often someone praised her posterior manipulation. *Sounds like he isn't wholly against this situation.* "Now, apologise."

Truitt cleared his throat, then raised his voice. "Oh, magnificent and blessed buttock, I offer you my deepest and most sincere offering of remorse for not turning your plump and shiny flesh the darkest shade of crimson. If it ever falls upon my good fortune to be in such a position once more, I promise to light you up like a bread oven."

Gracious, he's smooth! Almost. "Bread oven?"

He tried to shrug, but found himself too tightly clamped beneath her. "An allusion to hot buns. Too subtle?"

She laughed and slapped his truncheon, causing him to shout. *Oops!* "You alright back there?"

"Everything's tickety-boo," he answered through clenched teeth. "My sleeping time is often interrupted by the need for me to apologise to abundantly fleshy orbs."

"From how well you did, I'd believe that. But now I feel the other side might be envious."

"Then it must remain in that state. I am *not* indulging it with a peace offering. It should be satisfied with the whacking I gave it."

"Perhaps. But you need practice in spanking."

"I will concede to that. It is not one of my commonly used skills."

What to do now? He seems to genuinely not have the gem. But then who does? Calista's tail twitched back and forth, idly swishing over Truitt's face. *Could I have missed someone else in the house last night? Could the Shadow have come after all? I didn't spot any fruit in the gem's place in the morning, though. Perhaps another thief?*

Truitt coughed again. "Pardon?"

She looked down at her pinned quarry, twisting her neck to face him. "What?"

"I do not wish to interrupt your contemplation, but if you are satisfied with my answers, could you see yourself to detaching your nether region from my chest? Numbness has taken my left arm, and I am fearful at least one of my ribs has been shattered."

"Oh! I forgot. Hold on..." She began to rise, then abruptly plopped down again. Her thighs and buttocks slid back into their intimate clutch of his torso. "You've got it nice here, yet you present yourself as a shabbaroon. Why do you put on the show? And don't sell me no dog. I want the truth."

"Is it not obvious?" he grunted. "You've been around those toplofters. All sniffy and putting on airs. The parties. The nights at the opera. Makes my insides want to crawl up the chimney and spew all over their tea and crumpets."

"You pretend you aren't one, so you can gamble and drink with the locals?"

Even trapped under her, the berkis managed to bristle. "It is not an affectation I'm taking. I'm not one of those uppity snots."

"You companions think you are. And from where I'm sitting, you sure look like one." *And feel like. Are all rich folks this comfortable as cushions?* She turned her attention to his member, which had started to go limp. Her plush posterior in his face couldn't sustain it indefinitely. "Figuratively speaking. I've never seen a nobleman's truncheon before, so wouldn't know. Are they all so...robust?" She wrapped her fingers around it, pleased it filled her oversized hand. *It's almost as big as his ego!*

A sharp pain in the base of her tail ended the enjoyment as Truitt's teeth clamped down on it. She jumped in surprise, lifting off him while tightening her grip on his member. Her momentum pulled him forward several inches before she plopped down, grinding her muff into his face. Just as quickly, she pushed herself up again, yanking him completely out from under her.

But the stimulation drove him over the edge. He gushed almost straight up, with some of his pearly shower hitting the ceiling before splashing onto the wall.

Calista's laughter echoed through the room, a wild and unrestrained outburst that filled the air while he lay there stunned. "Oh, my giddy aunt!" She continued giggling as she finally released his stiff sinew, now rapidly deflating, and fell to her side, landing on the bed's pillows.

Chapter 18

The Gemstone Capitulation
Or What's Under That Robe?

TRUITT STARED AT the wall, trying to work out what happened, while Calista lay on his bed laughing. She accused him of being a noble, so he bit her tail. After that, everything blurred together. She had yanked him out by his member, which might have hurt if he hadn't been so well-endowed. He touched his face, remembering the moist and scratchy feel of her muff on it a few moments ago. There was also the release both contacts had caused, as he gazed at the spot on the wallpaper.

After a moment, her mirth quieted, and he turned his head to see she had fallen asleep. Realising he was free, Truitt carefully shifted himself sideways to the edge of the bed, trying his best not to jostle her awake. He needn't have worried. *She's been up all night. Well, so have I.*

Once standing, he stepped gingerly to the chest of drawers a few feet away. Acutely aware of his nudity, he glanced back toward where he lost his robe. It lay in the grip of the huge female, who had pulled the garment close to cuddle in her sleep.

This complicates matters. His eyes traced over her body. While stunning when she first disrobed, now slumbering peacefully on his bed, he found her nearly irresistible. *She is a rather attractive complication, but one I still must deal with. She has uncovered not only my alternative life but my little hobby. If I don't silence her, she will ruin all my plans.*

He watched her shift, then pull his robe down to her chest. *Not my dressing gown! I'll have to get another.* Truitt took a tentative step toward the ornate wardrobe near the window when the floor creaked loudly. He quickly stepped back. She shifted her legs on the bed, rubbing them against each other. *Dratted. Now I will have to remain starkers. I suppose, given her deficiency of attire, that is an equitable trade.*

She moved again, this time shoving the robe between her thighs, abruptly reminding Truitt how she had easily overpowered him earlier. How much larger she stood than him. How she could probably snap him in half without trying. His eyes looked down at his stirring member. "Think twice," he hissed. "She threatened to snap you, too." This didn't dissuade his staff, though. It almost seemed to spur the eager organ on. *Do I enjoy being dominated?*

He shook his head. *Don't get distracted. She's already set the cat among the rats. If I fail to put an end to her meddling, my little hobby will be a mere happy, prosperous memory.* He watched her turn over to face the wall, leaving the twin orbs of her posterior exposed. His eyes traced the smooth curve of her back down to the lush cheeks, which seemed to taunt him. Or were they inviting him to a second round? *Maybe I should retain her presence a tad longer, to ensure her cooperation.* He took a step toward the bed, but the resulting creak made him retreat. *Distractions!*

Truitt whirled around angrily and reached for the bureau. The man winced as he opened the top drawer, his movements painstakingly slow and deliberate, fearful she might hear the slight scraping of wood on wood. When the gap grew wide enough, he slipped his hand in and pulled out his pouch. With delicate motions, he tugged the strings holding it closed and squeezed two fingers inside. A second later, he extracted the Dragon Eye Gem.

A grin split his face as he stared at the treasure. *What a sight!* In the dark the night before, after he snuck past Calista and nabbed the jewel, he hadn't got a chance to see it fully.

Now, in the dim glow of his apartment's low lamp, the precious stone sparkled, splitting the light into dozens of tiny triangular red shafts that bounced off the bureau. He turned it slightly, entranced by the shifting patterns it produced.

"And you said you didn't steal it."

Truitt jumped, nearly dropping the jewel. He clutched it against his chest and whirled around. "You're awake! I mean, good, you are awake." The hand moved to behind his back as he adopted a gruff voice. "Now remove yourself from my premises immediately. I have had enough of your slander today."

Calista rose into a sitting position, her legs spread. In a display of modesty, she dropped his robe over her crotch. "First, you show me what you've got in your hand," she ordered, her tail twitching irritably.

"I do not take orders from you. I should have evicted you the moment you darkened my doorway."

"Probably." The female scooted forward on the bed. Truitt instinctively tried to back up, but the wooden furniture behind him prevented it. "But you didn't. So I'll ask this one more time. What do you have in your hand?"

Truitt's face flushed. "Nothing. It's none of your concern."

"On the contrary, I think it is entirely my concern. I think it is my entire reason for darkening your door." Calista scooted to the edge, curls and breasts bouncing with the movement. Her legs remained spread as her feet hit the floor, leaving her knees the same height as his waist. "Must we conduct another interrogation? Have you recovered from the first?" She glanced at his member, pointing strong and proudly toward her covered crotch. "Oh my. It looks like you have."

Truitt reached forward to cover the erection, then switched his hand with the other when he remembered the jewel. But his stiff sinew stood too large to be hidden so easily, and he only succeeded in sending it bobbing.

Calista smirked and offered him the robe she had been using to conceal her crotch, leaving herself exposed. "Need this?"

Truitt nodded and took it from her, his face reddening. The scent of her juices still stained the cloth. He brought the dressing gown to his chest, letting it flow down over his throbbing member. Rather than hide the appendage, the fabric emphasised its size, forming an odd tent between himself and Calista, who giggled. "I think that made it worse."

He stared at the jutting garment, hoping it would ease off. But his gaze wandered past the cloth to the woman's legs, then her thighs. His eyes continued tracing her body until they caught sight of her bare madge. When they first met, he wondered what it would be like to explore the deep patch of wiry hair and the protected flower within. Now it lay just a few feet before him, beckoning.

No! He snapped his gaze up. His view changed to the twin, ruby-tipped globes hanging before him. They smothered him less than an hour ago, and he felt the desire to bury his head in them again.

A twitch in his groyne reminded him of his attempts to lessen his arousal, not double it, and he brought his stare up to Calista's face. She beamed, no doubt flattered by his attention to her multiple assets.

He closed his eyes. If he couldn't see her, he couldn't be seduced by her. Right? "Just go, I implore you."

"You know I can't," she intoned. "If I don't return with that gem, I'll be blamed for stealing it."

"And as I explained earlier," he said, his eyelids raising, "the authorities will be unable to hold you for longer than a fortnight."

"A fortnight?" Her voice rose in frustration. "You're addled if you think I am living in a copper's cage for two weeks on your account."

"But you reckon that would be a pleasant time for me, is that it?"

Her tone softened again. "Not in the slightest. I am not planning to rat you out. Although after you lied to me, I should! You are the reason I'm in this mess, and you must get me out of it."

"I disagree. It is you who got me into this cockup." Truitt winced at his choice of words, realising how true the slip of a tongue was. *I'd like to slip my tongue...* "If you had refrained from taking up the position of guardian, I would have been able to retrieve the gem unhindered, and we would both be happy."

Calista clapped her hands. "So you admit to stealing it!"

"Absolutely, I stole it." He whipped his hand out from behind his back and opened his palm to show her. "Look! This is a masterpiece of craftsmanship. Such beauty should never be locked away."

But her stare remained fixed on him. "And you lied to me. You promised...no...you gave your *word* that wouldn't steal it."

"I said I would not *try* to steal it. And I didn't try. I succeeded, as you see." He snatched his fingers back from her when she reached for the jewel.

Calista glared. "You don't know right now how close I am to repaying you for that earlier spanking! "

"You wouldn't!"

"I would! You, face down, over my knee. My hand, tanning your fuzzy little arse!"

Truitt's eyes grew wide as his cock twitched at the suggestion. "But you don't understand its importance. I *need* the Dragon Eye Gem."

"I am sure you do. But I need it more."

If I give the jewel to her, my plans are ruined. But if I don't, I will be sending an innocent woman to gaol. He glanced at the wall. The dollop of mettle still clung to the maroon wallpaper. *Well, maybe not so innocent, but she never intended to get involved. Besides, I can always steal it a second time.* "You swear not to reveal my part in this?"

"I swear. All I will do is return it, then we can both be free of this. You won't have to see me ever again."

Truitt's shoulders sagged, but he held the gem out once more. She smiled softly and extended her hand under his. He released it hesitantly, his fingers gently brushing hers. A jolt of excitement went through his body, and his erection, which had begun sagging, sprang to life. "Seeing you again wouldn't be so bad."

Calista closed her fingers around the jewel. "Thank you, Truitt."

He didn't answer, as his head drooped. She leaned forward a few inches, then stopped and stood. Her crotch lay in front of him, but he no longer cared. *All that planning. Ruined! And for what? A woman.*

She extended her arm and ruffled his hair. The action snapped him out of his melancholy and he swatted her hand. "Stop that."

Truitt watched her walk to the side of the bed and pick up her dress. "Don't be so glum." She tugged the garment on over her head, then reached for her drawers. "I'm sure you will find something else to not steal."

If only it were that easy! His truncheon relaxed at last as she slipped on the underwear, corset, and stockings. "I do have a favour to ask," he said as she grabbed her boots.

"Don't worry. I won't reveal your secret quarters." Calista slid her leg into one boot and bent to tie it up.

"No, not that." He pulled his robe on. "Well, yes, don't do that."

The faroko looked up, revealing a deep cavern of cleavage again. "Then what?"

Truitt tugged his gown tighter. "Help me clean the wall. The white clashes with the rest of the decor."

Chapter 19

The Madam Deception
Or No Reward For You

CALISTA SKIPPED DOWN the stairs of the town-house, slipped through the door, and jumped the half-dozen steps to the sidewalk below. Her staff struck the stone with a resounding crack, startling the pedestrians around her.

She didn't care. *I have the gem! All I need to do is return it to Lady Aetherborne, and I can put all of this behind me. No gaol! No suspicion!* She doubted the jewel's owner would reward her for its recovery, and she knew she would not be hired on for another night. But that no longer mattered. She would find other assignments, other ways to earn what she needed to survive. What mattered most was she was free!

The sun's position high in the sky told her it was just after noon. Having to return the gem by mid-afternoon meant she had plenty of time to cross the Sunside again.

Still, she set off in earnest. While she did not need to rush, the quicker she put the whole affair behind her, the better.

So I was right. Truitt did steal it. I don't know how, and I don't care. Does that mean he's the Shadow, though? I didn't see him grab the gem, same as no one has witnessed the Shadow committing his thefts. And Lady Aetherborne seemed convinced the Shadow would be who I encountered.

Calista paused as she waited for a horse and carriage, driven by a tall orv, to pass before she crossed the street. *He does live a double life, pretending to be downtrodden when he's not. That could be a form of disguise if anyone ever caught sight of him. Maybe he has money from selling off what he steals! That story about his uncle sounds like codswallop to me. He even admitted one of the paintings he had was stolen!*

But what about Lavinia? By her accounts, he is practically a saint, helping her and her mother. That doesn't match with what I've heard of the Grey Shadow. Duke Cameron claims he is ruthless and dangerous. Would such an individual aid a child?

And then there is the travel. The Shadow has moved from city to city, stealing what he can from one, and fleeing to another to avoid being captured. Truitt seems rather entrenched here, with the flat, his gambling companions at the Right Hand, and his friendship with the locals.

She recalled Raffles's ill manners. He had wanted the berkis recovered, but not, it seemed, out of concern for his safety or even caring what happened to him. *But what if that is part of the cover? What if he has similar living quarters in other cities, with other companions and associates? What if his pattern of thievery is so complex that he has established personas in every city? That would certainly explain why he is never caught and the double life. He merely blends into an existing false identity.*

An image appeared in her head of Truitt, draped in a dark cape and hood, sneaking about in the darkest sectors of the city, breaking into buildings and running off with their valuables, which he then took to his secret lair. *The whole idea is ridiculous. This is the same berkis who allowed himself to be captured by a couple of thugs. Hardly a criminal mastermind.*

But he has the courage. Or at least the delusion of his own capabilities. What if his strike against those orvs wasn't foolish, but because he possessed the skills to successfully handle them? What if the pair were hired by the Duke to capture the Shadow, and she helped him escape?

It barely registered with Calista that she had crossed into the Sunside. *No. That doesn't make sense either. The Duke undoubtedly has the support of the police. If he suspected Truitt* was the Shadow, he would have had him arrested, not kidnapped. So why did they abduct him? *If it were for money, like Peg suggested, then maybe they knew about his double life and hoped to ransom him. But to whom? Certainly not Raffles and the others. They probably had only a few pounds between them, and were most likely unaware of Truitt's sizeable wealth.*

She shook her head so furiously that a passing orv gentleman veered an extra few feet around her. *If he is just a thief, which he finally admitted to, and not tied to the Grey Shadow in the least, then why all the deceit? And why did he say he needed the gem? Not want. Need. He would never be able to sell it, not once reports of its theft spread through Gravenmore.*

There are too many questions and not enough answers. Those aren't likely to be coming from Truitt. I had to literally pin him down and threaten him with castration before he would speak truthfully, and I still can't trust what he said. Nearly every conversation had been a series of excuses and lies. If I want to learn what is really happening, I'll have to sit on him again.

She replayed the earlier interrogation in her mind. The method of stripping down to their Adam and Eve's togs was not any technique of information gathering she had considered before, but both seemed to accept it without question. *I enjoyed it! And despite his protests, he obviously liked it as well. Our needing to clean the wall confirms that!* She had done the actual removal of the glob from the wallpaper, as it sat far too high for him to reach. *And his playfulness! When he escaped me the first time, he could have run. But like the confrontation with the orvs, he stuck around to fight back, although what we were doing couldn't be described as fighting. So, brave on the battlefield, brave in the bedroom?*

Admit it. Despite his deceitfulness, stubbornness, and arrogance, he is attractive and intriguing. And he seems attracted to me, or at least certain parts of me.

He is also to blame for a fair amount of my recent misery! I should have rendered his hairy arse numb before I left, as payment.

Calista continued going over the last two days until she came to Amberlux Manor. *Almost done!* She strode through the open iron gate and headed up the cobblestone path, too focused on reaching the house and returning the gem to notice the four-wheeled horse-drawn carriage a short distance from the entrance. If she had, she would have seen the words 'Police Patrol' on its side, painted in white block letters.

Ignorant of the situation, she marched up to the front door and rapped it with the ornate knocker hanging from its centre. *Come on. Let's get this taken care of,* she thought impatiently.

A moment later, the door swung inward, revealing Beatrice staring up at her. "Yes, ma'am?"

Calista beamed pleasantly. "Good afternoon, Beatrice. It's me, Miss Temira, from this morning."

"I can see that, ma'am."

"I've returned with the Dragon Eye Gem, as I promised your mistress. Are you going to let me inside?" She leaned in, attempting to catch sight of Lady Aetherborne.

Rather than answer, the berkis stood aside and gestured for Calista to enter. Once she had stepped over the threshold, Beatrice closed the door and held up a hand. "Wait here," she ordered, before walking unhurriedly from the room.

Calista stared around the parlour. After a minute, she began pacing, tapping the staff gently on the carpeted floor. Her tail swished irritably, nervous energy flowing from it into the rest of her body. *What is taking so long? I guessed she would be waiting for me. Doesn't she want her jewel back?*

Another minute passed before Lady Aetherborne entered, Beatrice on her heels. She wore a relaxed expression, nothing like the fury of the morning or the arrogance of the night before.

Calista noticed the change and halted her pacing. "I - I've recovered your gem." She fumbled in the pocket of her dress, unnerved by the elderly woman's calmness. Once she wrapped her fingers around the item, she drew it forth it held it out as proof. "See? I said I could retrieve it."

Lady Aetherborne's face brightened only slightly as she stepped forward and took the jewel from Calista's hand. "And who had it?" she demanded, fixing her with a stare. "The individual must be brought to justice."

"Does that matter? You have what was taken." *Why does she keep looking at me like that?* "I understand you will not, in all likelihood, wish me to stand guard over it another night, given the results of the last time. So, I'll just go now. No need to show me the way." She took a step back from mistress and maid.

But Lady Aetherborne followed. "You cannot leave until you have revealed from where and from whom you rescued this. There is a reward out for *him*, you know."

Hang it all! "I apologise, Your Ladyship, but I cannot tell you that. I promised." Calista gripped her staff tighter and took another step toward the door.

"Pity." The elderly woman tucked the gem into her dress, then she and Beatrice moved away from their guest. "Sergeant!"

The shout startled Calista. Fear washed over her as a muscular orv male dressed in a dark blue uniform and a tall, rounded hat appeared in the doorway. *Bloody! She called the coppers!*

As he started for her, a hand going to his waist where a flintlock pocket pistol rested in a holster, she bolted for the door. In seconds, her hands gripped the handle, and she yanked it open. Standing before her were two more police officers, a faroko and a skember, each with their weapons drawn and aimed at her.

Calista knew she couldn't escape them. Taking on ruffians in a deserted house was one thing, but fighting three armed policemen was a whole other kettle of fish. Fear morphed to anger, and she spun to face the room and the pair of females off to the side. "You promised me I had until mid-afternoon! I returned your precious gem!"

"Returning it is not enough. It should never have been stolen. If I let you go free, you might return and steal it again."

Firm hands gripped Calista's wrist, and a band of metal clicked around one as Lady Aetherborne spoke. "Even if you aren't the thief, you know who is, and that person may come back. So until you confess your crime or the real criminal is caught, you will enjoy the company of the constabulary."

Chapter 20

The Constabulary Contention
Or You Are A Jobber Knot

T HE RIDE TO the police station was one of the most miserable experiences of Calista's life.

Added to her humiliation and fear that came with being slapped in handcuffs and arrested, her journey unfolded in the company of the three officers who had caught her. She sat in the back of the carriage, sandwiched between the male faroko and his skember partner. Though taking her into custody caused them no great strain — she knew fighting them would have been more dangerous than she liked — the stink rolling off them suggested neither had bathed in days, if not weeks.

Across from them sat the orv sergeant. The scattering of wrinkles lining his face, along with the lightening of his grey horn, showed his greater age than the other two. Much older. He kept a watchful eye on Calista the whole ride, but other than that seemed bored with the entire proceedings.

His subordinates, in comparison, were positively giddy.

"We caught the Shadow, we did. Isn't that a fine day's work!" The male faroko on her right slapped his knee. "Mind you, I wasn't expecting he'd be a hen."

"We don't know she is the Shadow," his skember companion on her left reminded him. "We've only got that old haybag's word on it."

The faroko picked at his ear with his pinkie. "She could be, though, couldn't she?" he said, examining the glob of wax he had removed.

"Lewis, how many Shadow sightings have we had this week?"

"Well, let's see." His partner began ticking off the reports on his fingers. "There was the tobacconist who thought the Shadow had been sucking his cigars. Then the seamstress who assured us the Shadow was rumpling her skirts. Also, that butcher who feared the Shadow was touching his loins. And don't forget the baker claiming the Shadow was grabbing her buns. Does the haberdashery's baubles count? If so, then at least five."

"And this makes six. So what suggests this sighting is more likely to be true?"

Lewis rubbed his nose as he considered the question put to him. After a bit, he found a response. "It's the only time we caught someone, Percival."

"Not so. There was the cat."

"We never caught the cat, remember? It tore off before we could nab it."

"Alright then. She is the first," the skember, Percival, admitted.

Lewis turned his head to appraise her, his eyes lingering on her cleavage. "She is certainly the most attractive. The jammiest bits of jams. I wouldn't mind her grabbing my jewels."

"Steady on," the orv grunted.

Percival nodded in acknowledgement. "Sorry, Sergeant."

"Sorry," Lewis added.

Calista appreciated their superior stepping in but seethed at the faroko's lewd suggestion. *If I had my staff, I would do something very different with your jewels.* It had been confiscated, however, along with the few coins and the flail she had tucked away. They currently sat beside the orv, out of reach. Even with the weapon, it would be too difficult to wield while wearing handcuffs. And they still possessed their pistols.

"Perhaps we should ask her if she's the Grey Shadow," Lewis suggested after a few minutes of silence.

Percival peered at him. Given their positions and size differences, his gaze traversed Calista's filled corset. More of a gentleman than his counterpart, though, he didn't stare. "To what end? You think she'd tell us if she were?"

"Perhaps," Lewis said. "Let's give it a try!"

"Proceed, then."

The sergeant remained quiet but kept watch over the trio.

"Alright." Lewis shuffled in his seat, trying to turn to more directly face the female beside him. "Miss, are you the infamous and illustrious Grey Shadow who's been stealing folks' stuff?"

"No," Calista told him bluntly. "I am Calista Temira."

Percival shrugged. "What did I tell you?"

But Lewis remained unsatisfied. "Doesn't that prove she is? Denial is proof and all that?"

"Then what if she admitted it? Would that prove she ain't it?"

Lewis rubbed his nose again. "I suppose it would."

Percival made a face, apparently used to the faroko's lack of higher thinking capabilities. "Lewis, you are an absolute jobber knot."

"Am not."

"You denying it?"

"Undoubtedly."

A smug smile crossed Percival's lips. "Must be true then."

It took a moment for Lewis to realise he'd been tricked. "Shut your pie hole!"

The broad-shouldered orv shifted, then fixed each of them with a stern glare. Despite his age, he still easily commanded their respect. "Steady on, you two. Keep it up, and I'll have your weapons."

"Sorry, Sergeant," Percival said again.

Lewis turned forward in his seat. "Sorry."

Everyone grew quiet. Calista found their behaviour confusing. They seemed menacing enough when they arrested her, wielding pistols and handcuffs. Once in the carriage, which she berated herself for having missed, they acted like a couple of brats under the watch of a weary parent. *Lavinia is more mature than this pair.*

That they weren't more enthused over having supposedly captured the most notorious criminal in years made sense, given how many wild mongoose chases they had already been on. Her being a female, no doubt, also quelled their belief that they had finally nabbed the Grey Shadow.

But from all her encounters with law enforcement — of which there had been precious few, thankfully — as well as general discussion among the population, they were seldom armed with anything more dangerous than a truncheon. "Since when do the police carry guns?"

Lewis tapped the weapon at his side and sneered. "Since we've got a deadly robber on the loose in our city. Never thought it would be a bobtail."

Lady Aetherborne must have informed them about my staff. The old bag truly wants me punished. "I am *not* a bobtail," Calista told them. "Or the Shadow. I returned the gem, remember?"

The sergeant drew in a deep breath. "We will discover the truth. If you are innocent, then you have nothing to fear." He glanced out the window as the carriage rocked to a stop. "We have arrived. Bring her."

The other officers stood. Lewis grabbed her arm and tried to yank her to her feet while the orv collected her belongings. She remained seated, however. No one would accuse Calista of being overweight, but she was tall, solidly built, and not about to let the scrawny faroko who insulted her multiple times while leering at her body manhandle her.

Lewis tugged again, but she didn't budge. Percival, though, seemed to understand her actions and grinned. Only when he asked her politely did she consent to being led from the vehicle.

The pair escorted her — Lewis gripping an arm, Percival grasping a fistful of her dress — toward the police station. Formerly a bank, it had been converted for law enforcement when the original occupants moved to more fortified facilities. The security of the population's wealth ranked higher than dealing with its criminals.

The heads in Brassmont had decided a few decades be-fore there should be an organised police force in each city, rather than merely a constable with a few chosen individu-als. Ironstaff Station in Gravenmore still consisted of little more than a few dozen men under a single chief, so despite being more formal and better equipped, much of the popula-tion, such as Lady Aetherborne, continued to refer to them as a constabulary.

When they reached the doors to the station — thick oak and brass constructions with multiple locks — the sergeant took hold of Calista's arm and led her inside. The change in es-cort puzzled her until she saw the clusters of uniformed men turn and applaud. *Looks as if word got around they were head-ing off to arrest the Shadow. I bet I know who told them that.* It wasn't a difficult guess. The same officer who remained so quiet on the ride now beamed with pride, waving to his fellow officers and gesturing toward her. *Why do I feel like the turkey who's been brought home for the Christmas meal?*

When the excitement died down, the sergeant, who she learned from the various calls of congratulations was named Reginald, led her to the rear of the building. They passed two doors, each at least as sturdy as the main one, and into what might have been a section for safes and storage boxes. It had been converted into a series of gaol cells, complete with solid walls, thick doors, and thicker locks. Twin oil lamps at each end of the hallway provided the only other illumination for the area.

As far as she could tell from the open cells, they were all empty. Reginald brought her to one nearer the middle of the room, though she couldn't fathom why. They all had the same desolate appearance.

"In you go, miss." He must have noticed the sadness on her face, as he laid a hand on her shoulder. "I know they look bad, but you won't be staying long."

A bubble of hope rose in her chest. "Then you believe I'm innocent."

"You misunderstand my meaning. See all these empty cells? No one stays long in here. If you're innocent, then you'll be free soon enough. And if you ain't, well, let's just say we won't make you suffer."

Calista's fear sprang up again, but not entirely for herself. Zusa had the trio of orphans she stopped arrested, and they would undoubtedly have ended up here. They were absolutely guilty. She'd caught them stealing, with witnesses. According to Reginald, they were likely already dead. She wanted to scream, cry, do something! First, she had to know. "A few days ago, three children came here. A boy and girl skember, and a young male orv."

"Yes. So?"

"Can you tell me what happened to them?"

"They were brought in for stealing bread. Caught in the act, no doubt about it." He saw the sadness return to her face. "I see what you're thinking. After we learned they were orphaned, they were sent to Etheridge. Don't worry about them. You've got your own problems now."

He led her gently into the cell. Dull red bricks comprised the back wall, part of the original structure, while thick, unpainted timbers made up the three remaining walls. Two long, ragged wooden cots with stained canvas stood against them, one on each side. A copper bucket sat in the far corner, the only other thing in the small room. There were no windows, save for a square opening, set into the upper section of the door. The stench of mould and piss nearly forced Calista to wretch, and she'd only occupied the prison for a few seconds.

"Like I said, you won't be here long. A few days, tops." Reginald drew a tiny key from his pocket and removed the handcuffs. "If you be needing anything, don't ask, as this is all you'll be getting. One of the boys will come around this evening with your dinner." He retreated into the hallway and slammed the door shut. "I advise you not to eat it all at once," the sergeant called through the opening. "As you only get one meal in here."

Calista dropped onto a cot as she rubbed her wrists where the binds had dug into her skin. She glanced around the cell again, not daring to believe she was here, hoping it was all just some horrible dream. All was dark, except for the window in the door and the singular square of light it cast on the floor. Morbid thoughts filled her head. Nothing had prepared her for this reality. The playful banter with Truitt. The informative conversation with Lavinia. Gone. *Were they even real?*

She knew in the back of her mind they were, but in that moment, it didn't matter. Reginald had said days. She doubted she could stand being in that horrible place for more than a night.

Despondent and exhausted, she stretched out on the cot. Her feet dangled off the end by several inches, so she bent her legs and hugged them tight. The embrace gave her a little comfort. *Please. Someone, anyone, help me!* She slammed her eyes shut to prevent herself from crying, but the tears flowed nonetheless as she drifted into a troubled slumber.

Chapter 21

The Nobility Consultation
Or I'm Just A Girl

A FEW HOURS passed. At almost four o'clock, the sound of a door clanging open startled Calista from her sleep. Heavy footsteps in the outer corridor, at least two individuals, approached. She looked up when they stopped outside her cell. In the tiny window set into the metal barrier, a pair of silhouettes appeared and bobbed. A key jiggled in the lock, and the door swung inward.

Realising it was likely someone important coming to take her away, she hastily stood up. *I must make them understand I am innocent!*

In walked a handsome faroko man in a plush suit of charcoal trousers and a wine-coloured long-tailed jacket of crushed velvet, similar to Calista's own corset. The shiny black shoes adorning his feet tapped loudly against the stone floor with each step. He clutched a matching cane in his left hand.

Though clad from his gleaming toes to his tall, decorative collar, one could sense a well-toned body underneath. His face appeared no less refined, with short, perfectly styled blonde hair, clean-shaven high cheekbones flowing into a firm, equally smooth jaw, strong lips, and an aquiline nose.

But his most striking features were the pair of piercing coal-black eyes which scrutinised Calista now. She felt supremely uncomfortable as he looked her up and down, and bowed her head. As she stood a few inches taller, it had the opposite effect, making her appear to be looking down at him.

The gentleman — for she had no doubt he was, dressed in that manner — showed only a flicker of surprise at seeing the cell's occupant. "Please forgive my intrusion." He spoke with a deep, resonant timbre that resonated like a well-oiled machine. "The officer must be in error. I was seeking the individual who stole a precious gem."

"That's her," she heard Sergeant Hightower assure him from the other side of the door.

"You are in the right place," Calista added, lifting her gaze only a little. "That is me."

The man tapped his chin with the grip of his cane. "Interesting. I wasn't expecting... well..." He looked her over again.

"Someone this tall?"

"A female," he corrected gently, pointing to the bench. "Please, sit."

Calista lowered herself to it while the gentleman took a seat on the opposite side, tucking his tail behind his back and setting the cane between his spread feet, his hands resting on its handle. Made of brass, it took the shape of a bird's head and beak, with azure jewels for the eyes. "Let us start with introductions," he said. "I am Duke Patrick Cameron. You might have heard my name."

Calista's heart pounded in her chest. *A duke! And not just any duke. The Duke! The one after the Grey Shadow. Why would he be here, talking to me?* Then the reality struck. *Sweet bouncy puppies! He believes I am the Shadow.* "I have, but I'm not him!" she exclaimed. "I swear!"

The Duke chuckled, a low rattle in his throat which she somehow found soothing. "I know you are not the Grey Shadow. I realised that the moment I saw you. But I would still like your name."

"Calista. Calista Temira, your grace."

"Pleased to meet you, Miss Temira."

Her heart raced faster, and her left foot joined in, tapping at the same beat. *If he knows I'm not, then why is he here? And why does he have to keep staring at me with those eyes? Say something! Anything!* "Thank you."

The man laughed again. "I have never received that response before."

"What? Oh. I mean, me too. Pleased to meet you, that is." Her knee began shaking at this point, the stress from her heart and foot meeting in the middle and setting the joint vibrating. "It's just. I don't understand — "

"Why I'm here?" he finished for her.

"Yes."

He nodded in understanding, as a professor might before lecturing a student. "As you've no doubt heard, I have been pursuing the Grey Shadow for many years. Whenever he moves to a new city, I follow. I have put all the resources at my disposal into hunting him down and seeing him tried for his crimes. But the villain continues to thwart my efforts." His smile lessened at the confession. "I still understand so little about him after all this time. What he is called, beyond the descriptive moniker? Even that is in doubt, as I believe his appearance is more silver in colour. Is he faroko, skember, berkis, orv, or something wholly different? How does his countenance appear when not in shadow form? What device allows him to commit these thefts almost thoroughly undetected?"

"And why he leaves an orange each time," Calista added, then cringed at her own interruption.

Duke Cameron tensed at her addition, as if that point annoyed him in particular. "That too. But there are a few aspects of him I have been able to glean. He has a taste for fine art, jewellery, and rare items. He is clever and patient." The man paused as he leaned forward a few degrees. Light from the little window bounced off a silver bracelet on his left wrist, creating a brief flash, as if to emphasise his words. "He is also ruthless and dangerous, letting no one stand in the way of what he wants."

The last sentence chilled Calista, and her frantic limbs calmed. "And you do not think I am clever enough to be him? You have only just met me."

He straightened his posture. "Explain to me why you are here."

Calista let out a long breath. "Lady Aishwarya hired me to guard the Dragon Eye Gem. She was concerned about the increase in thefts. I spent the night, but come morning, the gem was gone. I recovered it for her, but she assumed it must be I who stole it. And here I am."

"Does that not answer your question?"

Her nose crinkled as she considered her description. "You think the real Grey Shadow wouldn't have been caught?"

"I think the real Grey Shadow would not have returned the gem."

"Oh." *That's a relief! But Truitt didn't get caught, even after I tried to stop him. And he was ready to let me take the fall for the crime, rather than turn the gem over. That doesn't quite rule him out.* "But you must have known the matters of my case before you entered. So why did you only know once you saw me?"

For the first time since his arrival, the Duke's expression turned dark, his eyes narrow. "His crimes are not only those of larceny. I said the Grey Shadow is ruthless and dangerous because he has killed before and I fear he may again."

Calista's hand clapped over her mouth. "What happened?" she asked through her fingers.

"A while back, no more than five years, I am certain, I was in pursuit of the Grey Shadow in Eisenhaven. He had been careless, and the smoky appearance he gets his name from was spotted more than once. The complexities of these robberies suggested he had an accomplice. I had that notion confirmed when, after a particularly large heist, we, the local police and myself, discovered a woman's body at the scene. Her neck had been snapped.

"That was his last theft in the city. A week later, we learned of another robbery in Ravenedge with his signature calling card. We concluded the woman had been the accomplice, and she had either gone against his wishes or simply no longer been useful. She had been a faroko, like you, perhaps a few years younger. Her name, we discovered, was Persephone."

Calista felt her stomach drop. *And I planned on confronting him if he showed!*

The Duke leaned forward again, but his expression relaxed. "Despite your presence, the gem was stolen last night. You retrieved it, which means you saw who took it. I believe you know who the Grey Shadow is. Furthermore, if you are not outright aiding him, you at the least are covering for him. All that you need to do to be free of these conditions is name him. Then the true criminal can be apprehended and his reign finally brought to an end."

Just tell him Truitt did it! The truth! It was that simple. She didn't owe him anything. He owed her. Twice now. And if he was the Shadow and murdered that young woman, he deserved whatever the Duke planned for him.

But the Duke's tale didn't match the berkis she met. Yes, he lied to her about stealing the gem. He lied to the others about his financial state. Indeed, she struggled to think of any truth he had told her when not under direct threat. But what about the rest? Why did he give her the gem when he could have let her take the fall? And why did the orvs grab him? *Still too many questions!* "I appreciate your concern, truly, but I cannot tell you the name of the Grey Shadow, as I do not know who he is."

The man sighed in resignation and sat back. "I commend and admire your loyalty. I only doubt your sense in this. Are you sure this is the path you want to pursue?"

Calista frowned. *Truitt said I would be out before too long, as they can't prove I did anything wrong.* "I've told you what I can."

"Then I wish you luck." He rose from the seat, taking his cane once more into his grip, before addressing her. The bird's eyes on its tip stared at her, as if silently passing judgement. "You have only a brief time to reconsider revealing his identity, as your trial is set for three days from now. In Brassmont. Because you retrieved the gem and know who stole it, you will be tried as an accomplice. The police believe it is the work of the Grey Shadow, and since that villain is wanted for murder, punishment for aiding him is stiff. If you are fortunate, it might just result in your hanging. A quick death."

Calista's panic rose again. "But he said nothing would happen to me!"

"As I told you, the Grey Shadow is a liar who uses people. I hope you do not become another victim." He pounded on the door with his fist, and the metal barrier opened a few feet. Without a glance at her, Duke Patrick Cameron marched from her cell, the door slamming behind him. She was alone again.

More confused than before, she tried to reconcile what the man had told her about the Grey Shadow with what she knew of Truitt. He *had* given her the gem to return, and the Duke had said the true Shadow wouldn't do that. Yet he demanded she reveal his identity, as if Truitt were the Shadow. Did he know something more he wasn't telling her?

His final words named the Shadow as a liar who used people. Truitt was undoubtedly dishonest, even making her believe she wouldn't be in trouble on the off chance they suspected her. Was he setting her up the entire time to take the fall for his crimes?

Does it matter now? I could have given up his name. Let them put him in gaol instead of me. Let him face responsibility for his crime. So why didn't I?

The question plagued her for a while longer until she collapsed back onto the cot. She had hoped for help, but got only the Duke. Had she missed her chance to free herself?

I don't need help, she told herself as sleep overtook her again. *I need a miracle!*

Chapter 22

The Apprehension Revelation
Or No Hanging Around

T RUITT STROLLED INTO the Right Hand much later than usual. His escapades with the gem during the night, then his more stimulating meeting again with Calista, had left him thoroughly spent. He finally managed to get a few hours of fitful sleep before dragging himself back to the gambling house.

His presence wasn't required for their game. Raffles and the others would continue playing whether he participated or not, as his abduction showed. He suspected that if the city fell under siege from the dragon Kettlebelly himself, the greedy skember would still be contemplating his hand as Gravenmore burned down around him.

No, Truitt's time spent at cards served a much more personal purpose. He hadn't lied when he explained to Lavinia his reasons for visiting the Ward. Truth be told, he disliked what he viewed as the upper crust of society.

He was one of them.

Born into the Hobert family of southern Brassmont, he grew up among the partially-wealthy, the wealthy, to which his clan belonged, and the extremely-wealthy. He attended all their parties, took part in the sports — cricket being the worst, in his mind — listened to all their discussions of politics, finances, and philosophy, and endured endless small talk and niceties that bound high society together.

And he found it all infinitely dull.

He discovered excitement in theft, though. Not for money, as being a Hobert ensured he possessed plenty of that. Nor was it malicious. He bore those he stole from no ill will.

It was the challenge of planning the heist. Calculating the timing. The rush of secrecy. The flush of success. It was the doing of something which went entirely against expectations. Why would a rich man steal?

He also found it fun. When he would swipe an object of value, no matter how small, from one of the families, he enjoyed watching those involved go through the stages of distrust. First, they would question those around them to determine whether any of them had seen the item. When that proved futile, they would suspect someone took it by accident, and their inquiries would grow more insistent. Finally, they would proclaim loudly they had been robbed.

Truitt found endless joy in watching the supposedly well-mannered friends and family turn on each other at even a hint of betrayal. Once he'd had his entertainment, he would replace the object in question, sometimes in its proper place, other times in a completely improbable location.

While it started as a game, that lesson of falseness stayed with him into his adult life. It served as another reason for playing with the trio at the Right Hand. There existed no pretence of friendship there. No chance of betrayal.

As Truitt approached their common table in the casino, he spotted the three engaged in a round of cards, their seemingly eternal position. Hugh, the terse orv, topped by a bowler the berkis had never seen him without, fixated on his hand. Faye, the gossiping faroko with her assorted trinkets. Raffles, the oldest among them, whose only concern in life seemed to be the next deal.

"Lookie who finally saw fit to join us," the skember called out, glancing only momentarily away from his cards. "'Is Lordship must 'ave 'ad important affairs of state to attend before 'is presence could be made."

Truitt never scolded Raffles for the title he'd given him. It acted as an unsubtle reminder of the life he'd left behind. Mostly. "As a matter of fact, I did," he said, removing his hat and hooking it over the back of his chair.

Faye lowered her cards with a smirk. "I bet he's the one what stole it?"

The berkis froze halfway into his seat. "What am I supposed to have pilfered? Raffles's manners? I must inform you, his were absent when I met him." He swung himself into place and lay his palms on the table.

"The Dragon Eye Gem!" she proclaimed, adding a flourish with her hands. "Rumour is, someone nicked it last night from the Sunside."

Truitt raised an eyebrow, feigning surprise. "Did they now? Perhaps you should ask our resident filcher here about his activities during the evening hours."

Raffles grinned at the compliment. "Naw. Twern't me. I 'ave no need of baubles."

"Even a bauble as exquisite as that one is purported to be?" Truitt pressed.

"Not even that one. I'm more a connoisseur of fine metals. 'Specially those stamped with the Queen's visage."

Of course, the berkis knew he wasn't the one who stole it. When they first met, Truitt learned Raffles possessed an interest in pick-pocketing, mainly to procure a few extra coins for gambling. He encouraged the skember to give it a try, in part because he recognised in him the same desire for the challenge. It also helped direct any discussion of larceny away from himself. "Do your rumours say who the gentlemen in blue believe is the culprit?"

"They know. They have them in custody right now." Faye leaned into the table. "The Grey Shadow hisself. Or rather, herself."

So the hoary dowager had her arrested even when she returned the gem. You just can't trust people these days. The girl will be fine, though. "That is an interesting turn. And here I was, believing it would be the dragon."

"What would Kettlebelly want with that sort of thing?" Raffles asked. His fingers swapped the places of two cards he held, as if changing their order would reveal a better hand.

"Have you never read the old stories? Dragons are notorious treasure hoarders. They used to build up heaps of gold, silver, and anything else of value."

Faye slouched in her seat. "We ain't as well learned as you, is we? Next, you'll say the gem is his actual eye."

"That would be far too outlandish a claim, even for me," Truitt assured her. "I am sure the two, jewel and lizard, are wholly unrelated."

"Lucky for Kettlebelly. The Shadow is to be tried in three days for multiple thefts and murder."

The berkis froze again. "Murder? Are they certain they have arrested the right individual?"

"They say the Duke wants to be making an example of 'em. Take 'em to Brassmont in the morning, put them before ole Judge Holloway."

Truitt shuddered. He knew who she meant. Judge Obadiah 'Hanging' Holloway carried the reputation as the harshest magistrate in all of Gravenmore. During his youth, fear of facing him played a crucial role in the decision to abandon the capital for good. *If she goes before him, he might sentence her to the noose even if she is innocent!* "I must take my leave again." He hopped down and snatched up his hat.

Faye stared at him. "Where are you off to now?"

"Those affairs of state you alluded to before. I realise they still need my attention." *And my help!* "You will no doubt carry on without me. This will likely not be completed until tomorrow."

"Waste of money," Raffles grumphed. "Should 'ave let those orvs keep you. With you coming and going, we wouldn't 'ave noticed the difference."

"I'll be back again to lose more money to you. Do not fret." With a nod to the others, Truitt nimbly exited the establishment and turned in the direction of the Mids.

He stalked through the streets, keeping his pace steady yet not too fast to draw attention. He mastered the skill early on, when he needed to vanish in a crowd. The urgency of his current task brought everything about that time rushing back.

As he grew into a young man, his skills at thievery improved. He began practising outside the safety of his family. Pick-pocketing. Nicking items from vendors. It came too easily to him, and he longed for more. The same thrill he got as a boy.

So he did as he had then. Targeted the wealthy. Those with the most expensive treasures and the most elaborate security. Utilising his place among the gentry, he could ferret out the most promising marks.

This new form of theft proved more challenging, though, leading to him getting caught many times. Due to his family's position in high society, he received leniency and remained unreported. But when he didn't stop, he became an embarrassment. Finally, when he came of age, his father allotted him a sizeable chunk of money and threw him out of their house.

For Truitt, it couldn't have come soon enough. He had an occupation now, of sorts, and the liberty to exercise it without the constraints of his family. But best of all, he enjoyed the freedom from the falseness of it all.

So he set himself up in a luxurious flat, bought himself fine clothes, and continued on as before. Despite his dislike for the people, he had only ever known the extravagant lifestyle and resumed it once on his own.

It went well for several months. During the day, he passed himself off as just another rich aristocrat. At night, he stole as he pleased. He narrowly avoided being caught on multiple occasions, always somehow managing to escape in the nick of time.

Then reality came crashing in. While his family's money had a source, his was finite, and close to running out. Two choices were open to him. Return home and beg his parents to accept him back into the fold, or begin selling what he stole.

There really was no option. Truitt had no intention of ever returning to the life he had fled, so he began seeking buyers for his ill-got gains. That's when he saw how those without money truly lived. It both fascinated and terrified the young man, and he found himself purchasing second-hand clothes with little remaining funds to walk among the less fortunate.

He blended in too well, though. One night, while trying to fence a gold necklace he'd stolen from a wealthy home, he was arrested and taken into custody. Fear of incarceration, or worse, overcame him, and after a few hours, he managed to convince the chief officer to contact his family.

His parents were required to make the trip themselves to positively identify him. The shame of collecting their son from gaol was too much, and once back in their manor, they confronted him. They knew of his continued life of crime and had begged their friends to let him escape if they stole from them. That would stop, though. They cut him off financially, never to get another penny from them. Furthermore, they ordered him to leave Brassmont. They didn't care where he went, but if they caught him stealing in the capital city again, he would be turned over to the authorities without question.

The news struck Truitt hard. Not for the loss of the money. He told himself he would find a way to support himself. Nor did the disowning and banishment particularly hurt. He had found another existence, outside the snobbery of the posh life.

What stung was the realisation that he wasn't nearly as good a thief as he thought. That he had been allowed to escape cut his pride deeply. He vowed that night he would become the greatest burglar in Leverhelm, if not all of Prettanika.

He wasn't that yet. But tonight, Truitt needed to be something more. To put aside his selfishness and vanity. To do more for someone than merely give handouts.

Up the stairs of the townhouse in seconds, he slipped inside and bound up to the first floor, energised by the excitement of his new challenge.

Tonight, I have a damsel in distress to rescue.

Chapter 23

The Prison Extradition
Or May I Pick Your Lock

UNAWARE OF THE memories she had stirred in the berkis, or even what hour lay beyond her cell, Calista drifted between fitful bouts of sleep and passages of despair.

What had happened? The night before, she'd been on the brink of wealth. A simple job with a reward greater than any sum she ever witnessed. With it came the offer of a life among the wealthy, or at least not among the poor. No more taking jobs that benefitted the wrong people. No more taking any of them. Unless *she* wanted to.

And now? All alone in a stinking gaol cell for a crime she did not commit, to be sentenced and executed in a few days if they didn't catch the real Grey Shadow before then. Considering the thief had eluded capture for years, she doubted he would abruptly become incompetent in time to save her.

The whole situation was madder than a box of frogs. She knew she could escape all of it — the trial, the sentencing, the execution — if she only revealed the identity of the true culprit. She didn't owe the berkis anything. Nearly every bad occurrence for her in the past few days could be tied to him. He should be sitting here in the dark, contemplating his life choices instead of her.

But then, so shouldn't the orphans. They had done no differently than him, save they were caught. Did they deserve to be sent here?

She shifted to an upright position and ran a hand through her hair. *They had no choice, though. Truitt did.* She saw he lived quite comfortably and certainly didn't have to resort to theft to survive. Despite his claim, she couldn't imagine an instance in which he would actually *need* the Dragon Eye Gem.

Was that the moral line she wanted to walk? Stealing is justified when the need is great? So if every poor soul in the Rookery began robbing those on the Sunside, would they be justified? Who makes that decision?

Not me. But does that mean I have to die for him? For a man I barely know? Maybe it is an unfair punishment, but a greater injustice is having an innocent person pay the price.

Unless Truitt *is* the Grey Shadow. If so, that blackguard has done far more than swipe a few valuable items. Patrick sounded convinced I worked for him, and Lady Celeste seemed certain the Shadow would attempt to steal the gem.

If he is the Shadow, he certainly doesn't deserve my protection and should be executed! But how am I to know the difference?

A trio of knocks on the base of the door startled her. A moment later, a voice hissed, "One with the magnificent posterior. Are you in there?"

Magnificent posterior? "Truitt. Is that you?"

"Keep it down, hen! The detail might have slipped your attention, but you're sitting in a copper's shanty."

"I am well aware of my situation, thank you. Can you get me out?"

"That's why I'm here. Needed to confirm this was the right cell first. Sit tight."

"Little else I can do at the moment."

A faint clinking sound, as of tapping and scraping metal, came from higher up the door. *He must be picking the lock!* Despite his command, she slipped to the entrance and placed a palm against the wood. *But should I trust him?*

After a few seconds more, a solid click signalled his success. The door swung inwardly slightly, and she tugged it open the rest of the way. Before her, metal probes gripped in his hands, stood the berkis. Dressed all in black like the night before, he grinned up at her. "Simplicity itself."

Calista dropped to her knees and threw her arms around him. After a brief, crushing hug, she pulled away. "Thank you!" she whispered.

Truitt stared into her eyes for a moment before tugging his waistcoat straight. "Just so," he told her in a low tone. "Now hush and stay near."

She followed him closely as they passed through the door into the prison hallway, then through another into the larger station. It stood eerily quiet, nothing like the raucous greeting she got upon her arrival. Calista might have believed the building empty, if not for Truitt creeping along in the dark, barely making a sound. She tried to match his stealth, but even with the teachings of Fenton, she felt like a drunk at a tea party.

As they approached the corner, he flattened himself against the wall and motioned for her to do the same. She crouched behind him as he peered around the edge, then rapidly retreated.

"We're in luck," he whispered to her. "He's still asleep."

"Who?" she asked, matching his volume.

"The gentleman in blue on guard. Leaning back in his chair, snoring away. That great stick of yours is there, too."

My staff! Calista stood and leaned forward to see past the corner, her knees pressing into the berkis's spine. He was right. A portly orv officer snoozed, his seat tipped on two legs against the wall. Her flail and selection of coins they confiscated from her person when they brought her in lay on a small table a few feet from him. The polished length of wood rested against it.

"We have to retrieve it," she whispered, withdrawing into a squat.

"Absolutely out of the question. It's too risky. We need to ascertain an inconspicuous route from these premises."

"How did you get in?"

"Through there." He pointed toward a window set high into the wall, on the opposite side of the hall with the sleeping guard. It swung inward and remained slightly open from when he had slipped inside. "Easy for my size. You, however, are far too big."

"Hey! I didn't hear you complaining when they were in your face this morning."

"As I recall, it was because I was being smothered."

"So we just find another way out. Is there a back door to this place?"

"If there was, do you not think I would have used that instead of risking the window?"

"Alright. The front door it is. With my things. You are the reason I am in here, remember. I am not losing my weapons because I refused to turn you in."

"So be it. But that ends any chance we might have had in exiting this establishment unnoticed. You must be prepared to run. Are you able to?"

The question surprised Calista. "Of course I can. I'm not a cripple."

"I meant, did they hurt you at all?"

She felt a twinge of surprise. Did he truly care about her? "I am unhurt. Though my posterior is smarting a tad from the spanking it got earlier."

Despite the low light, she thought his face reddened. "Do you recall the layout?" he asked.

"Some. Around the corner, then straight ahead, will take you into the main entry hall, where the officers have their desks. At the far end of that are the doors to the street."

Truitt frowned. "How many are on duty?"

"I don't know." Even the time eluded her. Beyond the window lay darkness, but whether that indicated late evening or early morning, she couldn't tell. The cries of the watch patrol, who walked the streets calling out the hours, could not penetrate the walls of the station.

"Hopefully not many, then. That's why I came at this hour. What is the lighting type?"

Again, his question puzzled her. "What?"

"What kind of lighting is there in the hall? Lamps? Candles?"

"I - I'm not sure. I wasn't paying attention as I was being led through dozens of officers to a gaol cell. There were more pressing matters."

He shook his head disapprovingly. "First rule of being a thief is always be aware of your surroundings."

"I'm not a thief!" she hissed.

"These blokes think you are. Best play the part."

Calista's face scrunched in frustration. "Only because of you."

"And I am fixing that now," he acknowledged with a nod. "When I tell you, grab your stuff quick as you can, then race around and out the doors. Pray they aren't locked."

"What about you?"

"Just you focus on getting out. I can handle myself."

He began moving toward the corner again when Calista pulled him back and forced him against the wall. "I wasn't doubting your ability," she scolded. "I was worried."

"Well, don't," he told her, returning her stare.

"I will if I want to. You can't stop me." On impulse, she wrapped her fingers around the top of his shirt, tugged him forward, and assaulted his lips with hers.

She felt his body tense, but didn't release him. After a moment, he gripped her shoulders and returned the kiss with a vengeance.

Her mouth and tongue were much larger than his, but his passion more than made up for it. They stayed like that for several blissful seconds, neither fully understanding why it was happening while not wanting it to end. Her free hand reached for his pants as she remembered him nude. *He came for me! He deserves a reward, doesn't he? I know I deserve something for my troubles!*

But she pulled away, breaking off the kiss and releasing him as the realisation of where they were struck her. A copper's shanty was not the proper place for what she wanted. Instead, she caught his eye again. "Told you," she said in a voice much huskier than she intended.

Truitt touched his lip, visibly surprised. "You did. Ready?"

She nodded. "Ready."

"Go!"

The berkis's left hand twitched in a slight gesture as he leapt forward, Calista on his heels. As they rounded the corner, the back legs of the chair holding the officer suddenly shifted, sending its occupant tumbling to the floor.

Calista rushed past the prone man and snatched up her staff and flail, leaving the coins. She twirled away, glad to be free of the cell and in possession of her weapons again.

But she wasn't safe yet. On Truitt's instructions, she rounded the next corner into the long hall. Three coppers occupied desks behind the counters, two of them engaged in a game of cards. Another pair stood at the far end, chatting. Beyond them lay the doors to the outside.

The sound of the falling chair and its occupant's curses drew their gazes in her direction. She had no option but to increase her speed as she ran for the entrance. *I may have to fight my way out. I hope none of them have guns!*

She saw no sign of Truitt. He told her not to worry about him, but that didn't sit well with her. She considered going back for him when she heard a loud crash, the unmistakable sound of breaking glass. The area behind her grew darker. *That must be him, taking out the lights! That's why he asked!*

Finally understanding his plan, she sped forward even faster. The officers were shouting now, with the two in the outer hall drawing their batons. The other three raced to join them, but the barriers were a holdover from the bank and not designed for easy access.

Smash! The lamp she just passed winked violently out, accompanied by a shout. "Ptow!"

Her skirt billowed with each stride. Calista was not accustomed to running in a dress and certainly not fighting in one, but she had no choice. She shoved the flail into a pocket hidden in the folds as the lantern she approached shattered. Each strike from Truitt's slingshot diminished the interior brightness until only the area between her and the entrance remained illuminated.

The two ahead of her spread, one on each side of her path. "Ptow!" Behind them, another oil lamp exploded, its fluid, glass, and ceramic remains splattering against the wall. With only a single light source remaining, the pair of officers became silhouettes before Calista.

It was enough. She brought her staff up before her, gripped tightly in both hands. Fortunately, the coppers blocking her way were a faroko and an orv. Her manoeuvre would be more dangerous to those of the smaller races. These two would recover.

They swung. She ducked. Throwing her knees forward, she slid under their weapons, catching their legs with her own. The staff knocked each man to the ground, hard.

Calista cried out as her knees struck the floor, momentarily stunned. The other officers finally found the gap in the counter and were coming up behind her, ordering her to stop.

She didn't. With a stab of pain in her leg, she stood again and lunged for the entrance. Thirty feet. Twenty. Ten.

The cool night air brushed her face as she shoved through the doors. Without thinking, she bolted to the right as the final lamp shattered. She dodged the few pedestrians still out and about this late as she fled down the sidewalk. She was free!

Chapter 24

The Alley Excitation
Or Knees, Thighs, and Jewels

A SHOUT FROM behind Calista told her she wasn't in the clear yet. Two coppers had followed her, pursuing a few dozen feet behind her. Her tall form stood out clearly in the illumination of the street's gas lamps. *I have to get out of the light!*

Unfamiliar with the neighbourhood, she veered right into a darkened alley. No trace of radiance shone from the buildings it passed between, leaving only the glow from the streets at both ends to guide her. A few loose cobblestones caught her foot, causing her to stumble, but she quickly recovered and sprinted out the other side.

Giving only a glance about, she raced across the street, barely avoiding a carriage as it rolled by, a steady clip-clop of hooves marking its passing. Calista dodged around a berkis couple, eliciting a cry of surprise from the female. She cringed. *Quiet you biddy! They'll hear you!*

Spotting a member of the watch patrol turning toward her at the sound, she retreated up the street, searching for another alley. One soon presented itself and she ducked inside, but not before a shout of "There she is!" split the night. *Bloody!*

A faint skittering echoed in the shadows, but she didn't have time to worry about it. Narrower and darker, this passage wreaked of rot, as if a deceased animal — or person — lay decomposing in the gloom. Her foot slipped in something soft and moist, nearly sending her into one of the imposing walls. Panic swelled in her chest, but she continued on until she emerged into the next street.

Calista repeated the tactic a few more times, utilising the alleys between parallel streets to avoid pedestrians, then began doubling back.

She soon lost both her pursuit and all sense of direction. Panting, she leaned against the wall of one of the cleaner alleyways to get her bearings.

"I have never seen anyone run in a dress before."

The faroko pushed herself upright and pivoted, swinging her staff around to confront the shadowed figure who had spoken. "Careful, missy!" the voice protested, stepping forward. "We lost our friends in blue."

Calista sagged in relief. It was Truitt, unwinded, with an obnoxious smirk plastered on his face. "What happened?" she asked, returning to her position against the wall, resting on the worn cobblestones, and setting her staff beside her.

"Fire. By an amazing coincidence, the lamps lighting their fine institution began bursting, leaving the place in blackness. One, however, committed its final act over a desk of papers. All the bobbies dashed back to prevent it spreading. I dare say they will write us off as a loss."

"What is with you and fire?" She stared at him, pressing the rear of her head into the cool stone behind her. Enough light from the outer street reached them for her to study him again. Sitting as she was — posterior on cobblestones, her knees bent — they were nearly on the same eye level, with him standing only a few inches taller. This was a very different berkis from the night she rescued him and the morning romp in his bedroom. He appeared confident, even cocky, but not from arrogance like before. She saw no sign of the sullen individual she'd first encountered. He knew what he was doing — the breaking in, the attack, the flight — and obviously done the same or something similar before. It brought him joy.

He waved the question aside. "I cannot be held accountable for what serves to further our escapes. Perhaps next time, it will involve a more benign entity. Like a top hat. Or an apple."

"Next time?" she asked, cocking an eyebrow. "There will be no next time. They were preparing to take me to Brassmont and execute me! You said I would be in no danger. You said they would let me go! You said — "

Truitt's hand blocked her mouth. "Hush! The bobbies might be back in their den, but that doesn't mean one couldn't come looking in the off chance we stuck around. Understand?"

Calista nodded, and he released her. His fingers barely covered her lips, but it wasn't their strength which had quieted her. It was their tenderness. For the first time since they had met, she'd received a soft gesture from him. To her surprise, she felt her breathing both calm and intensify at the same time. "Shouldn't we move, then?"

"No," he replied. "We should remain here a while longer. Quietly. I doubt they will believe we are still in the area. Are you hurt?"

"Just my knee. I hit it pretty hard during our escape. Running about didn't help."

"Let me have a look at it. Which one?"

"Left." She hiked her dress up to her thighs as he walked around her bent leg to stand between her knees. Her face reddened at his intimate placement and her exposed anatomy, but he seemed wholly focused on the damaged joint. *Should I feel offended?* "Ouch!"

Truitt relaxed the pressure from his probing touch. "It appears bruised, but I doubt there is any major damage. As you said, you've been running, so your movements aren't impaired."

"Can you check the other, too? Please?"

He shrugged and turned to her right leg, gently trailing his fingers around the ball joint. "This one is uninjured," he concluded after a few experimental squeezes failed to elicit a protest from her.

"Are you sure?" What he caused was wholly different from pain, and she wanted more. *He has such a light touch. I should expect that in a thief!* "I may have struck my thigh during the escape."

With only a slight hesitation, he ran his hand down the outside of her leg, pressing into it a few times. Again, no reaction from her, at least not one he noticed. *How far will he go?* "I meant on the inside."

This time, he looked at her. "You hit your inner thigh when running?"

"Yes." She flourished the edge of her skirt, sending ripples around the berkis. "I don't normally run in a dress." From his questioning gaze, she knew he hadn't bought the nonsensical excuse, but she didn't care.

Apparently, he didn't either, as he smoothly repositioned his hand, never breaking contact as his fingertips caressed her skin. A few gentle squeezes sent a shiver through her body. *I'm sure he noticed that. I did!* "Why did you come back for me?"

"You think me heartless?" he asked in return, his voice dropping in volume and tenor. His hand continued its slow journey along her limb.

"No." *Keep going!* "But you might have been caught. Then we would both be in cells."

"I don't get caught." The cocky grin returned as he stepped closer, his right hand taking up a similar position to his left on her other leg.

Gods yes! Heat radiated through her body from a place beneath her belly, despite the cool night air. His face hovered so close to hers. His warm, slow breathing caused hers to become more rapid. Even in the low light, his blue eyes danced before her own. "But why?"

Those piercing azure points glided over her curly black hair, her pink cheeks, and her crimson lips before returning their gaze to her own deep brown pools. The smug grin softened. "I told you before. Such beauty should never be locked away."

Calista threw her arms around the berkis, yanking him into her chest, his head beside hers. She squeezed, letting all her fear and tension drain in the embrace. Her eyes dampened. The highly independent faroko hadn't realised how much she desired the connection. The caring. The touch. *I need this!*

Truitt's arms, shifting from her thighs to her shoulders, told her the feelings weren't one-sided. His nose nuzzled her ear, and she reciprocated the gesture, adding a nibble to his lobe. He shifted further into her embrace, pressing his hips against her stomach. A curved protrusion pushed further into her flesh.

Calista pulled back to meet his eyes, but their lips found each other's instead. This time, he was the aggressor, teasing her tongue playfully. His left hand entwined in her hair and guided her head forward, while the fingers of his right drew a line down the side of her corset.

Touch them! her mind called out. The heat coursing through her raged into passion. She wanted to consume him. No. She *needed* to consume him, to make him her own. Her hands slid into new positions. One against his back, forcing him against her body, the other cupping his rear. A rough squeeze sent a jolt through his body, and she impulsively wrapped her legs around him. *He won't escape again!*

Between his searching mouth and roaming fingers, it became apparent that wasn't his plan. At some point, he had kicked off his shoes, as his socked feet were brushing against her inner thigh and groyne. *Is he trying to excite me or climb me? I'll help!* Her right hand shifted, slipping between his legs from behind and lifting him a few inches off the ground.

He yelped softly and bit her lip as his stiff truncheon brushed against the curve of her corset. Calista grinned, meeting his gaze. "Is this an interrogation, or a search?" she whispered.

"My dear, this is a negotiation," he murmured, caressing her cheek. "We are working out the details."

She tilted her head against his fingers. "As in what article of clothing is removed first?"

"As in, what is your threshold? Without screaming, which would draw too much attention to our...business."

Calista squeezed him again. "Far beyond that spanking you gave me. Maybe it is finally time I return the favour."

"You can surely try, madam. But first, your name."

"What about it?"

"I wish to know it. If these..negotiations...are to proceed, I think it only proper."

Oh! "Calista. Calista Temira."

"Very nice to meet you, Miss Calista Temira. It is Miss, is it not?"

"Considering the personal positions your hands," — she began, sliding her hand along his rear — "and feet are, it certainly better be nothing other than that."

"Most true," he replied, running a toe down her thigh until it met her moist nether region, causing her to shiver again. "And I am Truitt Williams, though I believe you already knew that."

"Mmmhmm," she purred. "Now, how about continuing our talks? I'm eager to learn the details." Calista tightened her legs, forcing him closer. *Are we really doing this in an alley? After the past few days, it makes as much sense as anything else.* "All this fuss over a tiny, silly jewel."

His body stiffened, and not in the pleasure-promising way. "The Dragon Eye Gem is not some *silly jewel*," he growled, pushing against her shoulder to put a few inches between them. "It is quite important to... people."

There was his dodge again. "Not to me. Why do you need it? That was the word you used. Need."

"I cannot tell you."

She ducked her head to meet his gaze. "I went to gaol because of you and it. I could have told them who stole it."

He softened. "And I am grateful for that."

"But that hasn't earned your trust?"

"In this, no."

Calista's cheeks reddened as if she'd been slapped. In a way, she had. "So, what? I'm good for saving your arse and a bit of groping, but not to actually be trusted." She released her grip on him and uncoiled her legs. "They were going to execute me!"

The berkis took a step back. "And you'd rather it was me?"

This again! How dare he! "At least it would be the person who did the crime. They think either you or I is the Grey Shadow."

"I don't care for the opinions of a pack of useless pigs," he spat. All traces of the gentle, caring Truitt vanished in a flash.

Calista noticed the change as her own anger rose. "What about what I think?"

"Not particularly."

The nerve! "Well, I'm going to tell you, anyway." She struggled to her feet, rearranging her dress and corset as she stood. "You are an inconsiderate, arrogant, manipulative, lying popinjay. I should have turned you in."

"Then why didn't you?" Truitt demanded, snatching his shoes up. "Everything I hear out of your mouth is what about you. Will I get paid? Will they think I stole the gem? Will they execute me?"

"But that's all your fault!"

"Is it?" he countered, slipping his footwear on. "I didn't ask you to do any of it."

"That's another lie," she snapped, fists clenched. "You literally told me not to reveal you!"

"That was part of a deal."

"Which you broke!"

Truitt finished tying his shoes and stood. "Then you won't be surprised when I break off these negotiations as well. A proper deal could never have been reached, it seems."

"What do you mean by that?"

A shadow fell on them as a figure appeared at the end of the alley, blocking the lamp light. "Here now. What's all the ruckus?" called the gruff voice of an orv. "Do you have any notion of what time it is?"

Calista recognised the long coat and slouch hat of a night watchman. Their shouting had attracted someone, after all. "My apologies. That is your job, isn't it?"

"It is," he replied, ignoring her jab. "And so I know it is late. Perhaps you should be off home."

The faroko nodded, thankful he wasn't too curious about their activities. Or a copper. "We will. Thank you."

He stared at her another moment, as if considering if he should ask, then doffed his hat with a thick hand and resumed his patrol.

"You heard him," Calista said, turning back to Truitt. "We need to..."

He was gone. "That miscreant!" she cursed. She thought briefly about trying to follow him, but given the turn of their conversation, she wasn't sure she wanted to locate him. His words still stung her ears as she picked up her staff. *I've been a fool. And now I'll have to find my own way home. With any luck, I won't encounter that infuriating jackanape again!*

Chapter 25

The Negotiation Reconsideration
Or Naughty Thoughts And Regrets

T HE EXCHANGED WORDS didn't sit well with Truitt, either.

His mission to liberate Calista hadn't gone the way he planned, but it succeeded, nonetheless. The interaction afterwards — the first part, at least — came as a pleasant surprise. He hadn't intended to get intimate in any fashion with her. Her inclusion put all his plans in jeopardy.

Tonight was a mistake, he scolded himself as he navigated the streets and narrow alleys back to his neighbourhood. *All of it. You should have got her out of there, then left. No questions, no talking, and for the love of all things horny, no touching. She lured you in with her knee, and you lost all sense. It was an attractive knee, though. As was the other. And all those warm, fleshy parts in between. I could just —*

Stop it! She's a distraction, nothing more. If you'd been nabbed, everything would be ruined. Everything. Years, you've waited, years, to finally have the chance, and you risk it all for some long-legged bit o' raspberry.

He caught a flicker of something out of his right eye. It moved differently enough from the straggle of citizens to draw his attention. Truitt ducked into a shop doorway, pressing himself against the stone facade. *Who could be following me? Not those bumbling blue bottles, surely. Is it her?* His heart thumped faster as he considered the possibility. *She wants to continue our negotiations!*

But when he peered around the doorway, his hesitant hope fell away. No Calista. No police were present either, but disappointment overshadowed the relief. *You're pathetic,* he chided himself. *You've completely fallen for that nug, when all she's done is cause you grief.*

He stepped back onto the sidewalk, resuming his walk home. *The gem will probably be guarded again tonight by some other hired lackey. I got by the last one. I'm sure I will have the stealth to bypass the next.*

Truitt grinned to himself as he recalled the trick. When Calista had rushed to the doorway at the sound, he'd followed and ducked under her dress. She had assumed he left, so while she searched the rooms, he dodged and weaved around her search until the opportunity presented itself. A quick hand in the box nabbed him the gem, and he was out the window and away!

Tonight wasn't my first time between those thighs! And I am certain she's never aided a thief in quite that manner. If only I could have stayed there a tad longer, I might have —

Knock it off! She's gone. You won't ever see her again, and good riddance! She wouldn't understand what I do. His steps lightened as he saw his flat ahead. He'd get some sleep, put in an appearance at the Right Hand later, and then prepare himself to steal the Dragon Eye Gem a second time. He only had to put Calista behind him.

Besides, it is too dangerous. There can be no more deaths. Not after Persephone.

Truitt reached for the railing of the stone staircase when the hefty fist of an orv struck his neck. He fell forward, stunned, as a thick cloth enveloped him. Everything went black. Strong arms hoisted the sack, and he tumbled to the bottom. Right before he passed out, Truitt heard a voice he recognised.

"We've got him now, Maurice!"

Chapter 26

The Invitation Contemplation
Or You Believed In Me

"**S**O, YOU'RE A fugitive now?"

Calista perched on a stool in the pub, wolfing down another leftover mutton pie and washing it down with a glass of brandy. The alcohol was a rarity. Though she didn't normally partake of it, after recent events, she felt she needed something to relax her.

She had crept in well after midnight, having taken over an hour to find her way back, and slept until late morning. As she consumed her cold breakfast, she had filled Armend in on the happenings of the past few days. The last part — where she and Truitt had been feeling each other up in the alley — she left out, though. And the activities in his flat. She omitted the kiss at the police station, too. No longer sure how she felt about those incidents, she preferred not to have someone else commenting on them.

"I hadn't considered that," she said in response to Armend's question. "Bloody, that's going to make taking new assignments difficult!" She shoved another spoonful of pie into her mouth.

"Not as difficult as sitting within the walls of the prison." The skember tapped the bartop meaningfully. "Or facing the hangman's noose."

Calista jabbed her utensil at him. "Are you defending that shag-bag Truitt? It is because of his unsavoury activities that I'm in this wretched predicament. Now I have to pay for that. Or rather, not get paid."

"Not defend. Merely reminding you that your circumstances could be decidedly graver. You are not in a manor house as we discussed, nor are you locked away in a prison cell. The pendulum of fate has returned you to a position almost identical to where you began."

"Emphasis on *almost*. How am I to accept tasks if the coppers have a watch out for me? How can I do anything? No assignments. No training." Her eyes grew wide. "No baths!"

"Gadzooks!" Armend held up his hands in mock horror. "Calista will have to forego soaking for a spell. A fate more dire than hanging!"

"I'm serious," the woman protested with a laugh. "I do not wish to stink up *your* pub."

"I do not partake of the bathhouse's comforts daily. Are you insinuating *I* have a foul smell?"

Calista hastily swallowed the mouthful of mutton and nearly choked as the meat and pastry combination scraped her throat. "That isn't the same. But after the night at Lady Celeste's and my too-long stint in prison, I am absolutely reeking, I assure you." She set down her plate and reached for the glass of brandy.

Armend scratched his chin in amusement. "Then wash up like the rest of us. Employ a sponge, washbasin, and a pitcher of water. Your room already has these items, does it not?"

"It does. But I cannot immerse myself in that, letting it permeate my skin and ease my sore muscles."

"Then, on your next foray into thievery, perhaps you could procure a bathtub for our humble establishment. Nothing too extravagant, mind you. We wouldn't want people getting the wrong impression of the Happy Swallow."

Calista sighed. "I may have to resort to a life of crime if I can't show my face otherwise." She took a swig of the amber alcohol. "At the very least, if I were to be apprehended, it would be a just consequence of my actions.

"Is there something the matter with your face?" a female voice called from behind her. "Why can't you show it? You told me you were unhurt!"

The faroko swivelled in her seat to see Peg standing in the pub doorway, a large package of brown paper and string held tightly in her tiny hands. "I am, at least from your mad contraption. Come." She waved a hand toward the bar. "You may as well hear the tale. It will spare me a trip to the gymnasium, which, it turns out, I can't do, anyway."

Peg trotted in, her footsteps making little sound as she crossed the floor. This was one of the rare occasions she didn't have a belt full of tools around her waist, jangling with her every move. "What's the trouble?" She tossed the package onto a stool, then climbed up next to Calista, her hooves slipping only once on the polished wood. Skembers were excellent jumpers, but climbing proved more difficult for their hard feet. She might have mounted the seat with a single leap, but such an action would be impolite. One does not jump on furniture. "Did you encounter the Grey Shadow?" she asked, once properly seated.

I honestly do not know. I might have been firkytoodling the Shadow. How many women can say that? "No. But the bobbies believe I *am* the Grey Shadow. They pinched me and tossed me in the stir. I managed to escape last night, with a bit of assistance."

Peg's mouth dropped open. "Great gears and cogs! What business did they have accusing you of that? Tell her, Armend! They had no right to do that to her!"

"Good morning, Miss Pumper," the bartender greeted her, having missed the chance when she first entered. "I cannot, as they did. News must have reached you of the Dragon Eye Gem being stolen two nights ago. Calista's assignment was to prevent that very eventuality from occurring."

"It was? I had no clue. I'm not much for gossip. Do they know who nicked it?"

"I do," Calista told her. "I retrieved the jewel and returned it promptly to its rightful owner."

Peg's hand went to her mouth as she gasped. "Then you *did* tangle with the Grey Shadow!"

"Nah. Just a light-fingered berkis." *Very light-fingered,* she thought, remembering his caresses in the alleyway. "The same one I rescued a few nights ago from kidnappers."

"Bolts! Your story's twistier than a wonky cog! So they believed you nicked it?"

Armend's gaze shifted to the door where a young skember had entered, clutching a folded wad of paper. "Pardon me, ladies. One of my runners has arrived."

Calista glanced at the entrance. The lad looked to be no older than Lavina, though only half her size. "Go ahead. I'll try to give Peg the short version."

As Armend climbed down a narrow set of steps behind the bar, she turned back to Peg. "Two nights ago, I took a gig to guard the gem. While I was doing that, the berkis, Truitt — I told you about him — snuck in through the window. I thought I'd stopped him from taking the gem, but he lifted it from under my nose. I still have no idea how. Anyway, in the morning, Lady Celeste — the owner of the gem — threatened to have me arrested when I said I believed I could retrieve it."

"But it wasn't your fault!" the mechanician protested, completely enthralled by the tale.

Calista had made a nearly identical claim to Truitt. But as she told it now, she realised even if he had lied, she should have been able to prevent him from making off with the jewel. Despite her skills, she hadn't been prepared. *Why did I think I would be a match for the Grey Shadow?* "When I took the job, it became my responsibility. And I persuaded Truitt to give me back the gem, which I promptly returned. But she had me arrested, anyway."

The female skember nodded knowingly at this. "Never trust the well-heeled. Honesty ain't in their bones. If it was, they wouldn't be loaded."

While the logic of that claim eluded her, it reminded Calista of similar comments from Truitt. "So they threw me in a cell, thinking I must be the Shadow. The Duke didn't believe that, though."

"The Duke? You mean Lord Patrick Cameron? The Shadow Hunter?" Peg grabbed the bartop to keep from falling off her stool. "You met the Duke?

"I did." Calista pictured the handsome man in his velvet suit. The one true ray of hope in her misadventures. "He thinks I am the Shadow's partner-in-crime. He wanted me to tell him who the Shadow was."

"But that's not something you know." She paused. "Is it?"

I'm not sure. "I was to be taken to Brassmont and put on trial. If found guilty, I was to be executed."

"Clangers!" Peg slapped the bar. "What for? Helping steal some bauble?"

"Murder." Calista shivered at the word. *Was the Shadow truly that ruthless?* "Did you know the Shadow killed someone? A female faroko, like me."

The mechanician's jaw fell open again. "No!"

Armend hadn't either. Why is this not known along with all the other stories about him? "That night, Truitt busted me out, and I fled here. That's why I can't be seen. Likely every copper in Gravenmore has my description now."

"Hmmm. Which is a pity." Armend's head reappeared behind the bartop, and his body quickly followed as he climbed back to his shelf. "And I'm not referring to your bathing restrictions. You have a request."

Calista frowned. Of all the times for an assignment! "For what?"

"Guarding a precious item. There is no description of what it is. The peculiar part is the request itself." The bartender waved the bit of parchment at her. "This asks specifically for you. Calista Temira."

Peg's eyes widened. "You didn't give the police your name, did you?"

Her mind went back to the evening and the horrible ride to the station with the lewd officers. "Bloody! Yes. I did. I wasn't considering an escape at the time. Told the Duke as well."

Armend tapped his finger against the message. "He is the sender. Duke Patrick Cameron is requesting your services for the night."

"It's a trap!" Peg shouted. "It must be! You go and he'll have you behind bars again."

But the faroko remained unconvinced of any ill intentions. The man she met seemed genuinely concerned for her welfare. Would he truly put her back in that position? "I'll take the task."

"You can't!"

Calista placed a hand on her friend's shoulder. "I believe I can. The Duke was the only one who believed I was innocent. He told me about the Shadow. This might be his way of protecting me, or at the least, offering me another chance to reveal the Shadow's identity."

"But you don't know! This Truitt filched the gem, not the Shadow!" Peg abruptly dropped her voice. "You going to turn him in?"

"I don't know," Calista admitted.

"Why did you not reveal him at the start?" Armend leaned against the bar, seeming to match Peg's conspiratorial stance. "It seems this entire mess could have been avoided if you named the true thief."

The faroko had been asking herself the same question ever since she let Truitt leave Amberlux Manor unhindered. "I don't know."

"And what if this *is* a trap?" Peg pressed. "How'll you extricate yourself a second time?"

Calista sighed. *When did my life get so complicated? Two days ago, I stopped some youngsters from stealing bread, and now I'm wanted by the coppers and meeting with Dukes.* "I don't know."

Peg's lips twisted into a scowl as she ran an agitated hand over her horns. "Well, I won't let you go empty-handed."

"I never am," Calista replied, then realised at the moment she lacked any armaments. Her staff rested against the wall in her room, and the flail sat on her bedside table.

"I mean, I came by to deliver the new blouse I commissioned for you," Peg explained, reaching out a tiny hand to tap the package, "to replace the one my Vibrator shredded."

Armend's eyebrows shot up at the statement. "Pardon me?"

Calista stared at the wrapped item. "Already? You had a custom shirt made that quickly?"

Peg nodded, a grin spreading over her face. "I've got connections. You aren't the only one who gets her clothes ripped by those devices. I've lost sleeves, trouser legs, even a whole posterior once. Mister Lightfoot particularly enjoys reminding me of that last incident. That's when I started exploring different designs."

"What do you mean? What designs?"

"Reinforced shoulders and elbows. Can't be torn or pulled apart. And a few other tweaks." She grabbed the bundle and deposited it on the polished bartop. Her fingers moved to the knotted string. "Let me show you."

Armend cleared his throat. "You are overlooking a vital detail, I'm afraid: how to reach the Duke's house. It lies on the far edge of the Sunside. Your height makes you conspicuous, no matter what kind of shirt our friend Miss Pumper has for you."

"Then allow her to borrow some of my clothes." The trio turned as Silas entered through one of the rear doorways.

"What do you mean?" Calista asked.

"Precisely what I said, Ma'am." He plucked the pair of spectacles from atop his horn and casually rubbed them on his apron. "We differ by a few inches but are about the same build. I am positive there are some items in my wardrobe which could be suitable for you." The orv glanced at the glasses, then, satisfied with the cleaning, returned them to his face. "They don't need to be perfect, just enough to disguise you for your trek across the city."

Calista didn't like the idea that her figure, which she worked to keep in shape, despite her appetite, matched the assistant's barrel-shaped form. But she couldn't deny his clothes would likely fit her, albeit a bit shorter. It would only be until she arrived at her destination.

With no other barrier to the plan, she reached for the plate of cold mutton pie again. "Then that solves it. Send word to the Duke. I accept his request."

Chapter 27

The Manor Convocation
Or Take Those Clothes Off

CALISTA ARRIVED AT the proper address by late afternoon. Ornate iron fencing lined the side of an expansive street, shrubs and hedges hugging their bars with fruitless greenery. The pavement here remained largely undamaged and the cobblestone walkways even and unbroken. Not a scrap of paper or pile of dung marred her path as she reached an imposing gate. While similar to the barrier protecting Amberlux Manor, this entryway stood somehow grander and more formidable. A large brass panel engraved with the property's name, White Cliffs Estate, hung from the centre of one door.

She didn't know who owned the property, but understood it did not belong to the Duke. Whenever the Shadow moved to a new city, so did his hunter, taking up residence in a local's mansion for the duration. The arrangement confused Calista, as she never heard of the Duke actually participating in the physical pursuit of the thief. *I should ask him about it tonight.*

Before advancing another step toward the house, she checked over the street for any vehicle which could be employed to transport law enforcement individuals. She got captured at Amberlux Manor for failing to notice one before and refused to make the same mistake a second time.

The only carriages present were travelling leisurely along the roadway, transporting their well-to-do occupants to places of business, establishments of pleasure, or their own fine homes. None remained parked in her vicinity.

Calista's trip across the city proved uneventful, to her relief. She had scrubbed herself the best she could with sponge and basin, then changed into her tight pants, corset, and Pegs's new blouse. Over that, she'd added a pair of Silas's trousers and shirt, then left the Happy Swallow late afternoon.

As her curves were very different from the orv's bulk, the latter pulled taught across her chest while flapping loosely around her stomach. The pant legs were a few inches too short, but she hoped her own high boots would mask the difference.

The shirt sleeves were the wrong length too, which she tried to hide by keeping one hand in her pocket. Her other remained exposed, however, as it carried her staff. She refused to attend the Duke unarmed, especially if she needed to take a defensive position. The possibility existed that the police had added the weapon to her description, so on the advice of Peg, she'd wrapped it in grease-stained cloth, so it appeared as a steam carriage horizontal rear axle. At least, according to the mechanician.

As a final touch to her disguise, she had tucked her black curls under a dark bowler. The orv assistant owned several of them and loaned her his largest. The whole outfit felt bizarre to the woman, especially the hat, and she looked forward to getting inside so she could remove it.

Suspicion kept her frozen to the spot, however. *What if this truly is a trap? The Duke may be waiting for my arrival, then hand me over to the police. I doubt I could fight my way free. His house is more formidable than the station. I can't expect any assistance from Truitt this time, either. He doesn't even know where I am, and after our exchange last night, he wouldn't show up anyway.* Despite their words, she still found herself wishing for a bit of his arrogant confidence at the moment. An extra weapon would be appreciated, too.

But he was the problem, and she needed to put him behind her. Nothing good could come from that relationship.

With that thought, she slipped through the iron gate and began the trek up the gravel driveway. The manor perched upon a small hill, sitting higher than even the other buildings of the Sunside. It required no such elevation to draw attention, though.

Amberlux Manor showcased a masterful marriage of architecture and elegance. The mansion before her made it look like servants' quarters. The sight of four stories of stonework, numerous balconies guarded by intricate ironwork, and a dozen chimneys reaching for the sky like the arms of earthbound angels took Calista's breath away as she walked. Steep, pink-shingled roofs glowed in the afternoon light, while a covered walkway surrounded most of the lower level, with wide stone steps leading down to a well-tended lawn and garden.

"Yous there!"

Calista spotted an enormous orv marching across the porch. Bulging arms swung from broad shoulders, a fist clenched at the end of each. His muscular chest strained against a waistcoat pulled so tight its brass buttons stretched their threads. He wore no shirt under it, leaving his thick, grey skin exposed. Azure pants, in the same near-bursting state, clad his lower body.

His anger was unmistakable. If the forceful thuds of his heavy footsteps on the stone porch floor didn't make this clear, his puffing cheeks, violently taking in and expelling air to cool his flushed face, made it apparent to even a blind hedgehog.

Apprehension constricted Calista's throat. Her knuckles whitened as the grip on her staff tightened. She hadn't yet reached the front door before facing a fight.

Then she saw his shoes.

Low-cut and wide to house his enormous feet, the leather Franklin shoes sported a two-inch heel, making the orv taller than his already intimidating stature, and a garish brass buckle three times larger than it needed to be.

What caught her attention, however, was the colour. Whether the footwear had been unavailable in black for someone of his build — which given the abundance of cordwainers in Gravenmore seemed unlikely — or some accident rendered them permanently discoloured, she couldn't guess. Whatever the reason, the fearsome figure stomping her way did so in a pair of deep yellow half-boots.

Calista bit her tongue, struggling to contain an outright laugh as he halted his march at the top of the stairs. He stood with his arms at his side, fists clenched, as if trying to intimidate her with his size. "Yous trespassing," he grunted. "No gawkers."

But the faroko employed a similar tactic before in the course of her own line of work and remained uncowed. That, and she found it impossible to take him seriously with his bright shoes reflecting the afternoon sunlight. "I am not. I was invited here. By the Duke." She pulled the bowler off and let her curls cascade down. "My name is Calista Temira. He is expecting me."

The orv closed a single eye and stared at her, fists clenching and unclenching. Obviously ready for a fight, he seemed unwilling to accept there wouldn't be one. "Yous female."

All his brains must have turned to muscle. Thick all the way through. "You are correct," she said, holding her arms out to the side. "I am wearing male clothes as a disguise."

That appeared to clear up the conflict in his head, as he grunted and relaxed his glare. "Alright. Come." He rotated stiffly and began stomping toward a pair of decorative doors.

She climbed the stone stairs to follow when he abruptly stopped and whirled back to her. This close, she could see he stood even taller than her by a few inches. His breathing grew rapid again. "What this?" Fat fingers attached to a thick hand reached for the wrapped staff.

But Calista smoothly shifted it beyond his reach. "It's a steam carriage horizontal rear axle," she explained, hoping she remembered the description correctly.

"What for?"

"Holds the wheels on," she said with a shrug.

The orv grunted, began to turn, stopped, and stared at her. "Name?"

Calista couldn't hold back a sigh of frustration. "I already told you. Calista Temira. The Duke invited me."

Another grunt parted his lips as he looked her over once more, then turned again to the house. Once at the doors, he slipped one open and stepped inside.

He guided her into a cloakroom nearly as big as her quarters in the pub, then into a larger hall. Through a doorway on the left, she saw a library, but the huge orv took her the other way, into an extravagant parlour, three times the size of Lady Celeste's sitting room.

While the manor exterior displayed all rock and iron, the interior showcased a marvel of wood, glass, and polished stone. Rich carpeting adorned the gleaming redwood floors while equally elaborate frescoes decorated the canary-yellow ceilings. Chestnut panelling covered every inch of the walls in between, flowing around a pair of stained-glass windows and a marble fireplace. Delicate oil lanterns set in sconces and an intricate chandelier, though as yet unlit, provided the final bit of utilitarian pieces to the room. Enormous paintings and refined sculptures gave it the grace of the artistic eye.

"It can certainly be overwhelming the first time you enter," said a voice from behind Calista as she openly gawked at the chamber's lavish structure and contents. "Although I have taken up residency in even grander mansions than White Cliffs Estate."

She spun around, nearly stumbling as she turned. Her gaze dropped under the scrutiny of his coal-black eyes, reminding her of his visit in the gaol cell. While free now, she couldn't help but feel like he continued to judge her guilt. "Your Grace! I did not hear you enter. I beg your pardon!"

The Duke held up a hand to halt her protests. While yesterday he had been adorned in a shade of purple, today his attire consisted almost entirely of black. A dark cravat circled his neck, a waistcoat hugged his chest covered by a frock coat, and slim trousers flowed down to polished leather boots, all of it the colour of charcoal. Only a white dress shirt, wide brass belt buckle, and a beige trim along the coat sleeves and wrist offset the bleak ensemble. His slicked-back blonde hair sported a single wave in the front, set between his tall, well-combed ears. "My butler, Ned, informed me of your arrival."

She glanced around and realised the oversized orv had vanished. *How long have I been staring like a cub?*

When she looked at the gentleman, she saw a look of disdain crossing his features as he examined her outfit. "What are you wearing?"

Calista stared down at her ensemble. She had thought it a clever disguise, but under his scrutiny surrounded by the finery of the parlour, she felt ashamed. "Clothes I borrowed from a friend."

His head lifted at the explanation. "Our mutual friend?"

"No," she told him, irritation creeping into her voice. "And I'm afraid if your purpose for inviting me here was to ascertain that person's identity, you will be sorely disappointed."

The Duke's expression softened into a smile, his tone regaining its usual charm. "Fair lady, that was not my intent at all. You made your conviction clear as crystal on our last encounter. I would not dream of inquiring further."

Calista relaxed too. "Thank you. What is the assignment you requested me for? Something about guarding an item?"

"That can wait. First, we must find you an outfit more appropriate to wear. Those clothes might suit a stable boy, but they have no place here."

Her embarrassment returned. "My apologies. I didn't mean to offend you. I needed a disguise, as the police are likely searching for me."

The Duke raised a hand again. "You did not offend. I understand your caution and admire your ingenuity. It is doubtful, however, that the gentlemen of the constabulary are actively seeking your location. They are not paid well enough for that. Still, I insist on a change of clothes."

"I have my own under these." Calista's fingers went to the shirt as she began to work the buttons. "You will see..."

His expression suggested she had handed him something cold and dead. "We have rooms where you can do that. Please do not undress in the entry hall. It is unseemly, even if it is to only remove a top layer." He clapped his hands twice, and another orv, this one of a normal build and attire, glided into the chamber. "Joseph, accompany Miss Temira to the lesser foyer. Once she is ready, bring her to the dining room."

"Yes, sir." He turned his gaze to Calista and held out a hand. "This way, madam."

She allowed him to escort her out of the parlour and through the doorway she saw earlier into a much smaller but still elegant chamber. Decorated only slightly less opulently than the previous room, with another fireplace against one wall, she found it difficult to believe that anyone would describe it as 'lesser'. At the other end, a grand staircase rose to a landing, then doubled back to the second floor. She guessed it would lead all the way to the top.

The orv closed the door behind them and adopted a stance beside the fireplace, facing the wall. Confused by the strange etiquette, Calista quickly removed the outfit she had borrowed from Silas, folded them, and placed them on a plush chair, the bowler topping the pile. She similarly undressed her staff, leaving the dirty rags with the clothing.

Once she finished, the faroko paused a moment to enjoy being solely in her own clothes again. *Now I'm properly ready to take on a job.*

The orv led her through the other door to a long dining room. A finely detailed mahogany table dominated most of the chamber, with enough cushioned chairs lining it to seat a part of ten. Near Calista stood a thick stand adorned with a single multi-candle candelabra. An ornate sideboard took up most of the opposite wall, with varying-sized drawers and a broad mirror behind it. A fireplace set into the far wall hosted shelves above it, supporting elegant vases of different sizes, materials, and colours. Twin windows overlooking the front walkway buttressed it. Panelled wood made up the rest of the space, with more shelves and decorative trinkets. An immense crystal chandelier hung over the table's centre.

At its head sat the Duke, who quickly rose when she entered. "Much better! More daring than last night, but it suits you."

"Thank you." She scrambled to remember any scrap of etiquette she had picked up as his dark gaze inspected her body, but the only tidbit which came to mind related to fork sizes. Still, she managed a partial curtsey, miming holding the ends of a dress she did not wear.

The man's eyes were on the freshly revealed staff, though. "Interesting choice of weapon, as well. Most choose guns or knives, which any fool can wield. I assume you are competent in its usage."

Calista straightened, a bit of her confidence returning as they waded into a familiar topic. "More than competent. Are you?"

"I am adept with several weapons," he told her, his expression turning proud. "Swords are my preferred weapons. Perhaps later I can demonstrate my thrusting techniques. Years of practice have made me quite proficient at penetrating any opponent."

Is he flirting with me? Let's see. "I'd like that. And I can show you how I handle a well-crafted staff."

"Indeed." Her response didn't lessen his smug countenance. If anything, it bolstered it, as he took a more meaningful glance up and down her body.

She sensed something else: a need to ask what so many others have before. "I am six feet, two inches, Your Grace. My parents are of normal height. It is only me who is the freak."

The Duke gave an almost imperceptible shake of his head. "That question had not even entered my mind. Not precisely. I was attempting to assess if there might be a finer selection of outfits in my wardrobe for a woman of your stature."

His suggestion startled Calista. "You keep female clothing in your wardrobe?"

"Not in *my* wardrobe," he clarified. "In the attire collection of the manor. For such occasions when I must attend a public function and require a companion. I prefer to retain several matching combinations for both sexes so that I do not outshine my guest."

"And so they don't outshine you?"

He chuckled. "You will come to understand that likelihood is impossible. Although, given the appropriate attire, proper hair styling, and some training in etiquette, you might approach my own brilliance."

If that is an attempt at flattery, he needs practice. Perhaps on one of those many guests he dresses up. "That is most kind of you to say, Your Grace, but it has been tried before. My manners are as inappropriate as my height."

"Perhaps you are correct," he told her. "And perhaps we will find another reason to get you out of those clothes later this evening. " He abruptly stepped toward her and pulled out the chair to the left of his. "For now, please indulge me and join me for an early dinner. Then we can progress with our mutual tasks."

Without waiting for an answer, he gently took the staff from her fingers and set it against the wall before tucking her into the table. Once she settled, he moved the weapon to a farther corner.

His action surprised her, and she wondered if it intimidated him like it did so many other men. *It didn't seem to intimidate Truitt, though.*

The Duke retook his seat, picked up a tiny bell at the edge of the table, and rang it. He barely replaced it before twin doors on the opposite wall of where she entered swung open. In strode another male orv bearing a silver tray with a single platter of oysters. The faint aroma of seawater drifted through the room, a smell Calista had only encountered once as a child.

A second orv followed close behind, and the pair moved to a sideboard. "I took the liberty of having my cook prepare a light supper for us," the Duke explained, taking the napkin from beside his plate and neatly laying it across his lap. "I trust you don't mind."

I'm in a mansion on the outskirts of town, surrounded by orvs, and have been relieved of my weapon. Why do I feel the lamb accepting an invitation from the wolf to sit down for dinner? But Calista fought down her instinct to run and fumbled with her own napkin. "Not at all. I am sure we will enjoy each other's company."

Chapter 28

The Dinner Interlude
Or Are These Still Alive

THEIR DINNER BEGAN with a delicate offering of fresh, raw oysters on the half-shell with lemon wedges, arranged on a silver tray, which the first orv set down before the Duke. The second attendant busily moved between the farokos, filling in the plates, silverware, napkins, and crystal goblets of their settings.

Calista had heard how elegant such servants were, barely noticed by their employers as they performed their duties. The two neatly dressed orvs did not fit those descriptions. The first tilted the oyster platter as he plopped it down, sending the shelled delicacies sliding to the side, softly clicking as they collided with each other. The other dropped his various cutlery into a rough approximation of where etiquette deemed it proper rather than setting them daintily. One goblet nearly went tumbling when he failed to ensure its base connected with the table before pulling his hand away.

I wonder if Lady Aetherborne would allow herself to be served in this manner, Calista thought as the pair retreated, stumbling back out the doors.

A glance at the Duke's face, his lips stretched tight in a masterful display of self-control, showed he disapproved as well. Once they were gone, his shoulders relaxed. "May I serve you?" he asked, holding a hand out for her plate.

That too, she thought, should be a task left for attendants. *Perhaps he is afraid they would spill the food onto our laps.* She picked up her dish, pausing a moment to marvel at the gold trim and intricately painted centre, and passed it to him. Once he placed three of the shellfish on it, she took it back and set it before her.

At that point, knowledge and experience failed her. The aim was to consume the ocean delicacies, but the longer she stared at the pale, lumpy flesh in their once-protective shells, the more she felt her stomach retreat. "Are these alive?"

"Is there another way to eat them?" the Duke responded, lifting one from his plate and sniffing it. "Fresh as we can get them. Far better than anything you will find from a lowly street vendor." Seeing her tight lips and upturned nose, he lowered the mollusc. "Have you not eaten oysters before?"

"Not since I was a child," she told him. It was a lie, meant to cover her lack of experience. Her parents had tried serving the shellfish to her on a few occasions, but the young faroko always protested, and they eventually stopped trying.

"Then let me provide you with a quick refresher." He raised the shelled delicacy again to his face. "First, garnish it with a squirt of lemon." The Duke took one of the fruit slices and pinched it, releasing a slight spray of juice over the oyster. "Then, place the shell to your lips, open wide, and toss it back." With a swift motion, he flipped the flesh into his mouth, savoured it for a moment, then swallowed.

He replaced the empty casing on the platter and patted his lips with an embroidered cloth napkin. "You then cleanse your palette with a sip of wine." But when he reached for his glass, he saw those instructions were not yet possible. His face twisted in a scowl. "Tobias!" he shouted, causing Calista to jump in her seat. "Wine!"

Several seconds passed before one door swung inward, allowing the orv who set the table to rush in with a tall green-tinted bottle held in his hands. The Duke glowered at him with piercing coal-black eyes as the servant hastily opened the vessel and began pouring into his glass. When the goblet filled to three-quarters, Tobias nervously skittered around to do the same with Calista's. He then promptly placed the container down and retreated from the dining room, closing the door behind him.

"As I was saying — a sip of wine." The Duke brought his goblet to his lips and drew in considerably more than a sip before setting it down again. "Now, you."

Calista dipped her head slightly, looking down at her dish. Three fleshy lumps seemed to stare back at her. She could feel her host's eyes on her. *He might be offended if I decline, and I already suggested I've eaten them before.* Knowing no way to avoid it, she reached for the closest and raised it a few inches from her plate. The salty aroma hit her again, and she quickly snatched up a lemon slice to counter it. A larger squirt than the Duke had given struck the pale flesh. *Maybe I can kill any taste with fruit. Bloody! Did it just move?*

Prepared to drop the mollusc and admit she could not stand the popular delicacy, Calista instead closed her eyes and tossed the oyster into her mouth, almost sending the shell down with it. Barely holding back a gag, she swallowed immediately, not daring to let it linger on her tongue long enough to taste. She wasn't sure it wouldn't latch on in a final defiant act to save its own life. But it slid down easily, without complaint, and she sighed.

She opened her eyes to see the Duke still watching her, but the scowl from before had been replaced by a look of bemusement. "Gallantly done," he told her, motioning for her to lower the empty shell back to her plate, which she did with a blush. "I believe I have never seen anyone so disliking of oysters yet managing to stomach one. You are not required to eat another."

"My apologies, Your Grace." Calista bowed her head, fearing she had offended him after all. "I possess a healthy appetite, but I've never been able to eat oysters. I'm not normally squeamish, but they unsettle me. Same with trotters. I mean no disrespect."

However, the Duke remained far from angry. "You did me no disrespect," he said, his deep laugh echoing about the room. "Indeed, I am honoured to be the first to witness your achievement. And please, no titles. Call me Patrick."

He shouted again, and despite his words, Calista felt her stomach flip. *Or is that the oyster? Sweet bitter pies! What if it tries to come back up?* The thought alone almost caused her to revisit the downed mollusc without any effort on its part, and she hastily covered her mouth with a napkin to hide her gag.

Fortunately, the Duke remained engaged with Tobias, who had promptly returned at the faroko's call with a second attendant, to notice her discomfort. The orv had carried in another platter, this one holding a tureen and two bowls, all as richly decorated as the plates, which the other servant quickly removed.

Once the soup had been distributed to the diners — a rich Mulligatawny broth of spices, chicken, chopped vegetables, and lentils — Calista's stomach had settled. She eagerly sipped at her stew, enjoying this course much more than the first. *And if I eat enough, I can drown that thing in my belly!*

As she told Armend, she could use manners when needed and didn't consume her food in an overtly impolite fashion. While not a lady, she didn't slurp her soup, or spill it on her lap.

Another shout later and the bowls were replaced by dishes of haddock. Calista admired the delicately poached flesh, flakes falling away at the touch of her fork, dropping into the thick sauce pooled around it. *This is definitely dead,* she reassured herself, letting the tantalising aroma tickle her nose.

When they'd finished, the Duke turned toward the doors to bellow again, but she held up a hand to stop him. "Pardon me, Your Grace. Patrick. May I ask how many courses there are? I have the appetite, but isn't this a bit much?"

"Only seven," he told her. "I kept it to the basics, so as not to inhibit you on your task tonight."

Calista struggled to keep her jaw from dropping open. "Seven? How many do you consider normal?"

"Fourteen. For a proper dinner. On special occasions, more. Your arrival here would have heralded at least eighteen, but the business nature of your visit suggests we should curtail such a meal. Are you prepared for the next course? I am certain you will find it enjoyable."

She barely managed a nod before he ordered the food to be brought in. When an orv entered with a platter, the female faroko could only stare.

"Roast pheasant!" the Duke announced proudly. "I know it might be a tad extravagant for this evening, but how could I resist? Winston, you may slice it."

Calista sat in awe as the servant proceeded to carve into the browned meat with a wide knife. Her stomach rumbled as the earthy, sweet smell reached her, sounding as if it hadn't put away two and a half courses already. She had only ever dreamed of the succulent dish before her, and now it was being served to her from a literal silver platter!

Once she and Patrick had eaten their fill of the bird and accompanying seasoned potatoes — though she felt confident that, given a short break, she could find room for more in her stomach — a servant brought in the next course. Both sipped their wine before partaking of the less exciting garden salad. While tasty, Calista found the fresh greens smothered in a vinaigrette wholly dull. "How do you afford such a lifestyle?" she asked, looking for a distraction.

He paused his eating and fixed her with one of his stares. "That is not a question for polite conversation."

She quickly bowed her head. "Please forgive me. I am not accustomed to these surroundings."

Her admission seemed to break his tension, as he stabbed a leafy stalk in his bowl. "I should not have been so abrupt. I am a Duke. The Duke of Pendleton, to be precise. Though it is a hereditary title, my family holds a substantial estate of land. We also keep our fingers on the pulse of several significant holdings."

"So you've always been around... finery?"

Patrick raised an eyebrow. "That is a delicate way of asking if I lived a life of luxury. Well, do not let appearances deceive you. I have had my share of hardships and struggles."

"I see. Again, please forgive my questions." *What does it matter if he's well-off? Some people are rich, some are poor. Drop it!*

"Questions are how we learn, but I would prefer we cease this line of inquiry." He lay his fork down, leaving half his salad untouched. "And I think we've done our penance with this soaked grass. Let us indulge in some dessert!"

The suggestion pleased Calista, and she became giddy to see the greens replaced by a plate of decadent fruit tarts while the conversation changed to a discussion on the various tastes of the pastries.

Finally, Tobias brought out a tray containing a shapely pot of coffee, a pair of china cups and mugs, a bowl of sugar cubes, and a small pitcher of cream. Alongside the beverage accessories sat an elongated plate of chocolates, each with a different shape and filling.

By now, Calista's feelings of distrust had subsided. If the Duke intended on having her arrested, he certainly would not have treated her to the finest meal she had ever partaken in. As she sipped the hot drink from the delicate mug, considering which chocolate to try next, her gaze went to her host.

Patrick appeared similarly contemplative, though not on the sweets. When she prompted him for his thoughts, he smiled, letting the warmth back into his eyes. "One small matter I am curious about, if I may ask. How did you manage to escape that prison cell?"

In an instant, her tension returned. *Why does he want to know that?* "Did they not tell you?"

"Only that you had escaped and started a fire."

That pyromaniac Truitt! "That was unintentional. I was merely trying to hide my retreat."

"Indeed." The Duke gave a curt nod before taking a sip of his coffee.

His attitude surprised Calista. Weren't the coppers aiding him? "You don't trust the police to catch the Shadow, do you?"

"I have the utmost confidence in our men in blue. It is what they are trained for."

"Is it? I always got the impression their purpose was to hassle the poor folks, petty crooks, and drunks." She set her cup down and straightened her posture. She hadn't found the trio who arrested her particularly well-trained. "I can't see them as up to snuff in dealing with a world-class criminal like the Shadow."

Patrick noticed her agitation and paused before answering. "Artist. The Grey Shadow is more of an artist than a mere criminal. I've doggedly pursued him for years and come to appreciate the finesse with which he works."

Calista frowned, remembering the man's own words when they first met. "You think murdering a young woman is artistic?"

Now his face darkened to match. "No. Indeed not. Nor do I find harbouring such a fiend an admiral trait."

She stiffened. "You said you admired my loyalty."

"Not when it is misplaced."

"Then perhaps you found the wrong person for your job."

The pair glared at each other, their coffee and chocolates forgotten. Anger held Calista rigid, but she was unsure why. *Who am I upset with? Truitt for forcing me to lie, or the Duke for reminding me I am? One is trying to catch a murderer, the other might be the murderer. Which side should I be on?*

Finally, the man lowered his gaze and picked up his beverage again. "Please. My apologies. I told you I would not press you on your partner, and I will hold to that. Indeed, I find the entire subject inconsequential now."

His retreat surprised her, and she took it as a sign to continue her questions. "But that is why you move to each city where the Shadow is spotted, innit? So you can personally oversee the investigation."

The Duke took a last sip, emptying his cup, then set it aside. "It is. Finish your coffee. If you still wish to undertake the task I have for you, then I want you to see something. It may change your entire perspective on the Grey Shadow."

Chapter 29

The Trophies Presentation
Or Put On A Pedestal

NOT DONE ENJOYING the chocolates but curious about the Duke's suggestion, Calista dropped one more sweet into her mouth, savouring the creamy richness as it melted on her tongue. She washed it down with a last sip of coffee before announcing her readiness.

The pair of orvs appeared at a command to clean up the remainders of their supper while the Duke gestured to the door she entered through before. As he led back to the room she had changed in, she ducked aside and snatched up her staff from the corner.

If the move upset her host, he didn't show it as they proceeded to the staircase and up to the next floor. Calista only got a glance around from the landing at a sitting area beneath a pair of tall windows before they continued to the third level.

Wood panelling covered everything, breaking the walls into rectangular indentations. Calista guessed it must have taken an entire forest just to decorate the mansion. Not that she had any idea of the size of a forest. Back in Cinderbury, the most growths they encountered were a few scattered groves.

"This manor is truly amazing!" she gushed, brushing her fingers along the railing. The polished oak felt smooth to the touch. "I can only assume a considerable fortune must have gone into its construction."

"Several, by all accounts," the Duke replied as they climbed.

"Where is the owner now?"

"Lord Emberstone had some business in Brassmont and kindly loaned it to me."

I wouldn't mind borrowing such a home for a time. "That's fortunate. Or is it?"

"Apprehending the Grey Shadow is in the best interest of everyone. Such evil must not be allowed to remain free."

Evil? That is not a term I would use for that lying berkis. Could I be wrong about him?

They reached the third floor and though the stairs continued on from there, the Duke left the landing and proceeded down a short hall, with the female faroko matching his steps.

"You have no doubt heard of the riches the Shadow must have amassed." Patrick strode to a heavy set of doors held shut by a thick bolt. He withdrew a brass key from his pocket and inserted it into the lock. "Whatever tales reached your ears, I promise you, the truth pales in comparison." With a turn of the wrist and a solid click, the doors unlocked, and he swung them inward. "Enter."

After such a dramatic speech and flourish, the female faroko felt uneasy about obeying him. But again, she considered him unlikely to be putting her in harm's way after everything of the last hour. Hesitantly, staff gripped tightly, she stepped inside. The lamps within were already lit, and she caught her breath at the sight.

While as elegant as any of the rooms she had seen, the shock came from its added contents. Normally a game room, it had been transformed into a storage chamber for the finest treasures in Leverhelm. Multiple decorative tables bore statues — a few she recognised from rumours — each one likely worth more than the entire mansion. They shared the space with vases and chalices outshining anything she had witnessed in the manor thus far. Around the wide mouths of several were necklaces of silver and glass, studded with jewels which glistened in the light.

Larger statues were sitting on the carpet, and a few bronze pedestals showcased items she couldn't identify. One supported a marble bust of a female skember's head, the lines of her curled horns carved in breathtaking detail. On another perched a rat sculpture, made entirely of metal and gears. Near it lay a pistol which reminded Calista of the contraption Mr Ambrose used to obliterate a rhododendron bush, only more compact with a thicker barrel. A platform a few feet from that held a mask of a distorted face which appeared to be shaped from ivory.

The walls were similarly enriched by multiple paintings hung with little space between them, obviously prioritising numbers over artistic view. With their gilded frames and obscure subject matter, Calista guessed they were priceless.

One with a female berkis torso she recognised as *Moaning Elisa* from Truitt's flat. He claimed it was a copy, as the original had been taken by the Grey Shadow. *This must be too.*

"Fakes. All of them," the Duke explained, confirming her suspicion. "Copies of the treasures the Grey Shadow has stolen over the years, and a reminder of all the times I failed to stop him." He strolled past her to stand beside an orange vase with a thin neck extending upward several inches. An artistic depiction of a mountain range circled the base, etched in gold leaf. "This he took from Lord Stellarspire in Nimbusburg five years ago. One of his first acquisitions." Patrick raised his hand to indicate a painting hanging on the wall above it. "This is 'Steamfire Nocturne', which he stole from Lady Silverthorn in Aetherfall. Worth tens of thousands." He moved to the marble bust. "And this is a perfect replica of Cordillio's 'Head of Lotheria', which he obtained in Seraphim's Landing, despite my best efforts to thwart him. The litany goes on. Do you understand now why stopping the Shadow is of the utmost importance?

Calista stared at the items he described, then let her attention travel over the others again. "Honestly, Your Grace, I don't. I see works of art which I am sure are worth a lot to men such as yourself. How this affects everyone else, though, eludes me. Whether some Lord or Lady possesses such a treasure or some mysterious thief, my life is unaffected."

Patrick stiffened at her assessment. "That is an understandable view of the situation, but naïve. You have been directly affected by his actions. Were you not imprisoned for his deeds?"

"I was tossed in the quod because of the crusade to stop him, not his direct actions."

"His indirect, then," he pressed. "You must accept, therefore, that his actions take their toll on society."

"I guess." *Why is he so insistent? If the police didn't pursue the Shadow, what would happen? A few items most people never see would change hands. Why does it matter to him?* "So you bring these copies with you each time you relocate to a new city and move into some Lord's manor?"

"I do. It is my motivation. My inspiration."

Rather a cushy motivator. Along with the closets of clothes for guests, attendance at fancy outings, and a collection of weapons. Probably his own staff as well. I bet he's only pursuing the Shadow for all the trimmings that come with it. Despite her conclusion, she nodded like the fascinated female she felt he expected her to be. "It is a noble undertaking, even with the hardships it puts upon you. Do you ever get the opportunity to spend time with your family?"

The Duke waved his hand dismissively. "I have no family. My parents died when I was a boy, and I am without siblings."

So the sole heir to a fortune in land and business, and he spends it pursuing some thief? "What about a wife? Surely, a man of your handsome features and handsomer dowry would attract a dozen females eager to warm his bed."

"Far more than a dozen," he corrected, with barely a hint of arrogance at the claim. "And a dowry is for women."

"Forgive me. My knowledge of marriage customs is limited to fancy dresses, rice, and a jolly good spread."

"Indeed." A flash of disdain crossed his face, replaced in an instant by his usual charming smile. "Now that you know why I am relentless in my goal to bring the Grey Shadow to justice, we can move along to your assignment for the evening."

Finally! "I would like that. I need to repay the kindness, and dinner, you have gifted me."

He gave a curt bow, then turned toward the doorway. "Follow." From there, he led her out from the game room, past the staircase, and around a corner into a meagre bedroom. The size, however, remained relative, as small here meant only twice the dimensions of her quarters in the Happy Swallow. It came complete with an immense bed big enough for three, an oak wardrobe, a few sturdy commodes, a dressing table, a trio of overstuffed chairs, and a door leading out onto a balcony facing the rear of the house. On the opposite wall from there, double doors opened into a deep closet. Lastly, a thick door with triple deadbolts at varying heights, all locked, sat in the far wall.

"These are your accommodations for the night," the Duke explained. "The item you are to be guarding is in the room beyond this door. Do not attempt to enter the chamber, as it is bolted. You must ensure it remains that way. When I leave, I will lock you inside, so that no one may enter from there." He paused, as if waiting for a protest. When none came, he asked, "Are my instructions clear?"

"Yes, Your Grace," she replied. "What about the balcony, though?"

"We are on the third floor. No one will be entering that way. But on the off chance some foolish individual makes the attempt, you will be here to stop them."

She nodded. *This is it? Guard a room, when he surely has his servants to do that?* She recalled Lady Aetherborne saying her staff could not guard the gem at night. Perhaps the same situation applied here. "I won't let you down."

"No, you will not. If you've no further questions, I shall take my leave, as other affairs demand my attention."

Other affairs? Is he planning to hunt the Shadow tonight? But she kept her curiosity to herself. "No more questions. The task could not be clearer."

The Duke nodded again. "Then I bid you goodnight. I, or one of my servants, will release you in the morning. Be on your guard."

Calista did not appreciate the confinement, but Lady Aetherborne had insisted on the same. "Goodnight. And thank you."

She watched the man leave and heard the click of a key in the lock. She drew in a deep breath and let it out slowly, trying to calm a sudden knot in her stomach. *I have to stop spending my nights behind locked doors!*

Chapter 30

The Assignment Violation
Or What's Behind Door Number Two

ONCE HE LEFT, Calista lay her staff against the bed and drifted around the chamber. The sun had only begun to set, so she figured no one would attempt to gain entry yet. She had a moment to relax.

But she couldn't. Despite the Duke's kindness, she found it impossible to shake the idea that something felt amiss. *Maybe because the last time someone locked me in a room and told me to guard a valuable item, I got accused of stealing it and tossed in the jug.* She ran her hand idly over the dressing table, letting the etched wood tickle her fingers. *Could this be an attempt to frame me? If they were unable to convict me on one charge, perhaps the Duke is setting up another. In the morning, that door will unlock and a dozen police officers will be waiting on the other side, ready to take me to Brassmont. No trial. Just a public hanging.*

Panic rose in her chest, and she instinctively crossed to the balcony door and threw it open. The cool night air caressed her cheeks, easing her fear. She wasn't completely trapped. She glanced over the iron railing to the outside of the mansion. Despite the Duke's assurance, the stone facade didn't appear too difficult to scale. *If I see any sign of deception, that is my route to freedom.*

Somewhat relieved, she lifted her gaze to the well-manicured grounds. A lush lawn sprawled away from the building, with a few elm trees strategically planted to provide shade. To the left, protected by a line of low hedges, lay a flower garden of geraniums and petunias. On her right sat an oval pond, complete with lily pads and a short dock extending into it. Further afar, she spotted a gazebo, its circular frame casting long shadows over a pair of iron chairs. *If I must escape that way, I will be easy to spot from the house. Outrunning burly Ned in his yellow shoes should be no trouble, but what about the others? What if the police bring horses?*

She felt her fear rising again and drew in a deep breath. *Stop thinking like that! If the Duke wanted me arrested, I would have been slapped in cuffs the moment I entered the manor. He wouldn't have treated me to dinner, invited me to change clothes, and showed me his collection of fakes!*

And what a collection! I don't know how the genuine items could look any finer than those. How would you tell them apart? And if you can't, what does it matter?

Calista shook her head slowly, letting out a chuckle. *Truitt was right. Rich people are odd. To make such a fuss over wall decorations and flower holders is pointless. Meanwhile, children must steal bread to survive.*

But is Truitt any different, with his fine furnishings and art copies? Add to that he wanted the Dragon Eye Gem, a tiny jewel with no real value, and he's just another elitist. He only plays at being poor.

She stared at the colours of the setting sun as they played upon the yard. The vibrant yellow and demure pink reflected clearly on the pond's surface. A slight breeze brushed across the water, sending the hues into a dance of ripples. *That's my life. Every time I think I've found some calm, someone drifts in, unsettling everything.*

But as she considered the idea, she discovered she wasn't entirely upset by the disturbance named Truitt. He was neither intimidated by her nor licking her boots, knocking her off-kilter in ways no one else ever had. He was deceitful, manipulative, and a rogue. If not for him, she might have those promised fifty pounds. So why did she wish for his presence now?

And if I had earned the money, what then? Would I have set myself up the same as these other rich snobs, buying a house and pretending pretty pictures and baubles were more valuable than a life? She remembered her anger at Lady Aetherborne's suggestion such a lifestyle was not for her. Why? Did she secretly wish to be like them?

The notion unsettled her, and she shivered, as much from that as the evening air blowing across her skin. Seeing the sun dipping below the horizon, she moved to return inside.

With a start, she noticed two entrances back into the manor. On her right, the open glass and oak door leading into her dim room. On her left, a nearly identical door stood, closed tight. From its placement, she knew the second must lead into the chamber she was meant to be guarding. Had the Duke forgotten about it? Even if it remained similarly bolted shut, any would-be thief might easily shatter the pane and gain entry. So why leave so easy an entryway?

Dread began knocking at the back of Calista's mind. The Duke may not be planning to frame her, but nothing of the situation made sense. He must know she failed the first time guarding the Dragon Eye Gem, so why put her in the same position again?

Enough! I took the assignment, and I'll complete it! With more ferocity than she intended, she stalked back into her room, nearly slamming the balcony door shut. She dropped into one of the chairs and threw her arm over its side. *No more games. Once this is over, I can return to the pub and put all of this Shadow nonsense behind me.*

She stared through the balcony door as the sun continued to sink. The silhouettes of furniture grew, creeping across the carpeted floor, while the room itself became ever darker. It fit Calista's mood. *I won't be able to get back to my life. The police will still be hunting me, and if I remain in Gravenmore, they will eventually find me. I'll have to leave the city and move to another. Maybe someplace like Seraphim's Landing. According to the Duke, the Shadow's already been there. And if the law tracks me to there, I might steal aboard a ship. It is unlikely they'll pursue me beyond Prettanika.*

In the dark, she drew in a deep breath and let it out slowly. Was she truly contemplating leaving her friends and her life here to become a fugitive? Sitting in the gloom, with only faint outlines of light marking the borders of the room, such an outcome seemed possible.

But to never see Armend again? Or Fenton? Or Peg? Or Truitt? Could she do that? She would be completely alone.

What about the Duke? He knows I am not the Shadow. Perhaps he would use his influence to convince the police I'm innocent! Her heart skipped at the idea. She only needed to complete tonight's task, and he would owe her. They never discussed payment, so she could claim that as her reward!

She sat in the gloom for a good hour, replaying her options over and over again in her mind, trying to work out the positives and negatives of each decision, as she stared out the balcony door.

When she found herself completely lost for what action to take, a dull thud reached her, as of something in the distance striking wood, and she sat up straight. *Blast it. My job is to guard the room, and instead, I've been wallowing in self-pity!* Without making so much as a whisper, she slunk to her staff and pulled it soundlessly from its resting place. Her long ears strained to find any trace of the sound, but nothing moved in the darkness.

It must have come from outside. Tail twitching in anticipation, Calista crept to the balcony door and peered through the glass. The moon had not yet risen, leaving the space beyond nearly as dark as the room. She could see only blackness.

If an intruder was coming up the side of the building, she would have to stop him before he reached her level. No longer caring for stealth, she wrenched the doorknob and stepped outside. She saw no one on the elevated platform. Stepping up to the railing, she scanned the yard beyond, then the facade below her. If anyone lurked there, they remained hidden in shadows.

The Grey Shadow! It has to be him! A jolt of excitement shot up her spine. *The Duke must have planned this! Locked up an item of great value so the thief would come here, and I would have a chance to catch him and redeem myself! I'm saved!*

Another thud from behind her, softer than before, took her attention back to the building. No one had entered her room while she sat in it. That left only one other possible location for the noise to be coming from.

The Shadow had already infiltrated the chamber she had sworn to protect.

Bloody! I've botched it! The only chance I have now is to prevent him from escaping! Her knuckles whitened as she clutched the staff tighter and stepped up to the other door. Heart pounding in her chest, she gripped the knob and yanked it open.

Nothing. No surprised villain rushed past her in a panic to flee capture. No shout of surprise from a startled thief. Not a sound.

She deftly transferred her weapon between her hands as she slid inside, tugging the door shut behind her. Her eyes strained to see any movement in the gloom while her ears perked up for any noise. Even her nose stood on high alert, sniffing for any scent that would be out of place in a mansion's chamber. Like the citrus smell of an orange.

Calista remained there for what seemed hours, every muscle tense. If she messed this up, her life in Gravenmore would be over. It was the Shadow or her, now.

Thump!

She nearly cried out at the abrupt noise. It came from somewhere near the centre of the room. The faroko was definitely not alone!

Her mind flashed to what the Duke had told her. The last female to interfere with the Shadow's heists met a brutal end with a snapped neck. *Well, I'm armed and know he is here. Let him try to attack!*

As her eyes adjusted, she began to make out more details of the chamber. It appeared to be another bedroom, only less furnished than her own. A bed sat against the far wall, an arm-chair on the left, and a chest of drawers with a lantern on the right. In the centre, where she had detected the banging sound, stood a raised cupboard with curving sides, four tall legs, and a pair of doors.

Where is he? If he only appears as a bit of smoke, then I'll never see him in this light. He must have struck that cabinet by accident. Or to distract me!

Fearing an attack from the side as she stared at the wooden artifice, she swung her staff in a sweeping arc to her left. When it met no resistance, she quickly did the same to her right. *Perhaps he really is smoke!*

Thump!

The sound didn't surprise her this time, only its location. *Whatever is doing that is in the cabinet.* She extended her hand slowly toward one of the handles, then drew it back. Instead, she moved to the lantern and lit it, keeping her gaze locked on the troubling furniture. *A little light should banish any Shadow,* she told herself, hoping it to be true.

With the room now bathed in low radiance, she took up her staff again, inhaled slowly, and threw the cabinet doors open.

Inside lay a figure, just over half her height, bound and gagged. His body recoiled at the sudden illumination, and he tried to heave himself away. He must have been trapped for hours, though, draining his strength, as all his efforts produced were more of the thuds Calista had heard before.

Despite his rumpled clothes and dishevelled appearance, she recognised the prisoner instantly.

"Truitt!"

Chapter 31

The Amorous Debriefing
Or No Further Negotiations

CALISTA CAREFULLY LOWERED the berkis to the floor. Though trussed up and gagged, he tried to wriggle free, but his sluggish attempts betrayed his grogginess. *How long has he been in here with so little air?*

She kneeled before him and yanked the gag off, then gently turned him on his side against the rug as she worked to undo the knot. "Sweet blushing peaches! What are you doing here?" she demanded. "And how did you get yourself bound up in this?"

He sputtered, trying to clear his head. "You think I did this to myself? I was kidnapped. Again. Presumably by the same ruffians who took me before."

The faroko couldn't believe her ears. "That's absurd. What would the Duke want with you?"

Truitt flinched as if she had slapped him and his eye grew wide. "Are you referring to Duke Patrick Cameron? This is his abode?"

She finished untying the knot. "Well, the one he is borrowing while in Gravenmore, yes."

His lips tightened as his body tensed, her answer driving the lethargy from it. With care, he climbed to his feet. "That confirms it, then. I suspected it might be him."

"You aren't making any sense. Did you bump your head?" Calista stared at him with fresh concern. "Wait, did you try to steal from the Duke? Did they catch you and toss you in here?"

Anger crept into her voice. "I knew you were bold, but I didn't think you were a noddle."

Truitt rubbed a palm over his waistcoat in a vain attempt to smooth it. Calista noticed he wore the same outfit as the night he broke her out of gaol. "No, I did not *try* to steal from here," he told her. "I *do* steal, remember? No try. But not from him." He probed his head as if checking for a bump as she suggested. "My last recollection is of my flat entrance. I was prepared to enter when I was jumped. Then I awoke here, trussed up like a goose for the table." When he discovered no abrasion, he dropped his hand and examined their surroundings in the lamplight. "So this is the Duke's house."

She shrugged, following his gaze. With the illumination, she observed more details of the room. Though similar to her own in style, the furnishing possessed a more feminine touch she found appealing. "Like I said, not really his. It's on loan from Lord Emberstone while the Shadow is in the city."

Truitt abruptly turned his attention to her. "What is *your* purpose here?"

"Rescuing you, again, it seems."

Her flippant reply didn't satisfy the berkis, however. "You could not have known I was here." He squinted as if examining her for some telltale sign. "Are you working for him?"

"Tonight, yes. He had an assignment for me to guard..." Her voice dropped away as she shuddered. *He had me guarding Truitt! That means he did kidnap him! But why?*

"Guard me?" he asked, completing her thought. "Is that what you were about to say? I should have known." Truitt's tone turned cold, his expression dull. "Well, lass, your deception was complete. I was taken in by your feminine wiles. Congratulations." He took a step back. "So what does your master have in store for me next? Am I to be dropped in the river, rocks tied around my legs? Or perhaps he'll snap my neck, like poor Persephone?"

A knot of dread formed in her stomach. It crept up her spine and constricted her chest. *How did he know about her,* unless... "You *are* the Grey Shadow! How could you murder that young woman?"

"I did nothing of the kind! That was the work of your master, the highty-tighty Duke."

"But he told me the Shadow killed her!"

Truitt slapped his head. "Have you not put the pieces of the madman's puzzle together yet? The Duke *is* the Grey Shadow!"

"That's impossible!" But the claim lined up with her own doubts, like why the Duke needed to travel to each city. *And all those trophies. They weren't replicas. They were the genuine items!* "But why kidnap you?"

"Perhaps he is afraid of the formidable competition," came the response, devoid of sarcasm or modesty.

"And me?"

"Well, you aren't without your assets. Did the Duke offer to undress you, or demonstrate his technique?"

"In swords! Patrick offered to show me his..." Her voice trailed off again as she remembered the exchange. *And I showed interest!*

"I advise you to leave these premises immediately, while your freedom is unimpeded," Truitt said, his tone softening. "I intend to see that his is, for a very long time."

Calista hesitated, unsure if she heard him correctly. "You plan to catch him?"

"The current situation appears to make that feat a more challenging one to attempt, but that has always been my purpose. I intended to steal the Dragon Eye Gem and use it as bait to lure the mysterious Shadow to a location and time of my choosing."

Her face reddened. "I suppose I am to blame for hampering that plan."

"Indeed. But now that I know his true identity, I can devise a new scheme." Truitt glanced about the room again. "Once we are free of this palace."

"So *that* is what you couldn't tell me?" Calista asked, finally understanding his avoidances and lies. "That you needed the gem to trap the biggest thief in Leverhelm?"

He nodded. "I could not risk my plan being revealed. Nor the possibility that you would become entangled in the whole nefarious affair." He looked at her, a flash of regret on his face. "It seemed in the latter I failed most profoundly."

So while I thought the Duke was after Truitt, it was the other way around! "What about Persephone? How do you know about her?"

Truitt's shoulders slumped, and his defiant expression crumbled. "Persephone Brassington was my cousin's wife. The sweetest of lasses. Married less than a year when she ran afoul of the Duke. Unexpectedly working late when he performed a heist. She must have startled him." He paused, the admission momentarily draining him. "Her death devastated my cousin and sent shockwaves through my entire family. I vowed if I ever had the chance to avenge her, I would take it, no matter the risk to my own life."

Calista felt her heart melt at the story and his promised retribution. "That is incredibly noble of you."

"Hush. I haven't achieved it yet."

"It proves you possess immense kindness, after all." She reached out a comforting hand, placing it gently on a shoulder.

He accepted it gracefully, and they stayed like that for a few seconds, each recognising that what separated them — the lies and the danger — had fallen away. She knew the truth, and they were both in peril.

Despite the threat, a sly grin crept onto Truitt's lips. He looked up at her, a twinkle appearing in his watering eyes. "That's not the only part of me that's immense."

His smile spread to Calista's face. "I know. And as you've said, I'm not without assets myself." She tugged him closer, all trepidations gone. Now that she knew he wasn't the Shadow and all his lies — well, most — had been attempts to protect her from his mission to avenge a family member, she wanted to finish what they started in the alley.

"Not to quell your ardour, but this is neither the time nor the place for such exploration." Despite his words, her potential partner traced his fingers over one of her breasts, feeling its warmth through her blouse.

"Neither was the alleyway," she purred, similarly running a hand down his body, letting it linger longer in certain spots.

Truitt looked hungrily up at her. "Are you suggesting we resume our negotiations?"

The faroko leaned in until their noses were almost touching, the warm air from their rapid breathing intermingling. She stared into his ocean-blue eyes, finally knowing what she wanted. "I am proposing we cut straight through to the merger."

Without waiting for an answer, her hand clutched his arse and pulled him into her embrace. Their mouths collided, eagerly mashing together in desire. Her other hand gripped the back of his head, not letting him escape the kiss until she was satisfied.

But Truitt seemed in no hurry to part. His own hands worked to increase their pleasure, with one gripping her shoulder for balance while the other teased the breast it had sampled before.

When she finally loosened her grip enough for him to breathe, he drew his head back only slightly. "My dear, this truly is not the place for such an undertaking," he whispered, keeping his lips near hers.

Calista chuckled. "Agreed." She didn't release him, though. Instead, her grasp tightened as she rocked to her feet, hefting the berkis in her arms. He let out a slight yelp as she took a few long strides and deposited him on the bedspread. "Better?"

Truitt couldn't help but laugh himself. "I meant, we are prey in the lion's den, so to speak. Heroes in the villain's lair. Flies in the spider's web."

"And here I thought we were lovers in bed." She lowered herself to the mattress and began crawling over it, the prone berkis her target. He lay entranced as she straddled him, knees on each side, hands above his head, supporting her. It was the same position they had taken in his apartment during their first 'interrogation', and she hoped he appreciated the reference. Only this time, the only jewels she sought were his own.

Calista dropped, leaving her face hovering above his. Their lips met again, a light caress which quickly became an eager search. She brought a hand up to his cheek, then moved it down his neck to his chest, running her hands along his rumpled waistcoat. Before going further, though, she reluctantly broke off their kiss.

"I am sorry," she told him as he stared puzzled up at her. "My mouth is dry. I'm a better kisser than this."

"You heard no complaints from me," he said. She could feel his heart pounding against her chest as they pressed tightly together. A grunt of pleasure escaped his lips as he slid his hand between them and into a pocket. "However, if it would make you happy, I have some hard candy." He tugged the black pouch out so she could see it.

Calista eased off him, letting him use both hands to open it. "In that tiny thing? You carry around a single piece?"

"That would indeed be foolish," Truitt agreed, pulling a white and pink sweet from the fabric. "But like my slingshot, it is more versatile than it appears."

"The magic pouch! Lavinia told me about it. She said you have coins and candy in it."

"Which she enjoys often enough. Take it. Like the slingshot, it doesn't run out."

The faroko took the piece from his fingers and brought it to her mouth. "Pear drops!" Her lips parted in a smile as she popped it inside. The sweet and fruity flavour jump-started her saliva as she rolled it around her tongue. "These are my favourites! How did you know?"

"It is merely a coincidence," he began, tucking the pouch away again. "I also enjoy — "

She was back on him before he could finish, pressing her lips to his. The rest of her torso crushed against him, shoving him down into the thick mattress. Her hands played down the side of his body until they found his waist. *Forget the shirt. I want his pants off now!*

The physical onslaught excited her partner, and Truitt returned the kiss with equal passion. Their tongues wrestled, fighting for the pear drop as it slipped wildly between them. His hands reached for her breasts but switched to her head when they couldn't find space between their two bodies.

Calista had his pants unbuttoned and begun to pull them down when his fingers caressed her ears. His touch in such a sensitive area sent a wave of pleasure down her spine, and she let out a moan. *Gods yes!* The moan became a predatory growl as she yanked his trousers down, his slingshot tumbling to the side. Seconds later, his drawers joined them, leaving his full erection pointing to the ceiling.

She pounced, her fingers wrapping around the stiff member like she would her staff. Truitt's body arched in pleasure at the move, and she grinned. "It appears this is in good working order. But we'd better be sure."

Still holding tight, she brought her other hand up and began unbuttoning the rest of his clothes. Before long, her fingers traced through the dense hair on his bared chest, feeling the heat coming off his body. Just as her ears were sensitive to stimulation, the furry patch above the stomach of a berkis was highly sensual. Truitt's eyes rolled back in his head from the dual stimulus.

She brought her face close to his again. "Tell me how you stole the gem that night," she purred, the scent of pear tickling his nose.

"What?" He tried to rise, but between her palm pressing him down and her grip on his member clouding his conscience, he was fortunate enough to manage basic speech. "Now?"

"Why not? We have the time."

"We truly do not. We must — "

She cut him off again with a squeeze of her hand, sending a fresh wave of pleasure through his slight frame. "We must know how you got by me that night. I never saw you take the gem, so how did you do it if you aren't the Grey Shadow?"

"Stealth!" he blurted out when she began stroking his chest. "I can move quickly and quietly when I need to."

"So can I. There was more. Out with it." Calista punctuated each sentence with a stroke of his erection, evoking slight spasms from his groyne.

"Alright! I hid under your dress. When you crossed to the doorway, I darted beneath your skirt. Satisfied?"

The smirk on her face said she was. "Did you like what you found there?" she teased.

"I do not know what you are referring to. I was doing a job."

Calista tucked the candy in her mouth into one cheek. "No girl likes to hear it described as that. You were between *these*, and they didn't tempt you?" She withdrew her hand from his member long enough to slap her thigh. "I think I should be offended."

"My focus was on more important matters than your supple limbs."

"Then let me reintroduce them to you." Calista slid off the mattress, releasing him momentarily. Just as easily as she had removed his trousers, she shoved her pants and drawers to the floor, letting the fabric pool around her feet. With practised grace, she stepped out of the fabrics and climbed back onto the bed and resumed a position on top of the berkis. Her thighs stretched on either side of his shoulders and head as her wiry madge, damp from their previous foreplay, tangled with his chest hair. She felt the tip of his erection tap her now bare arse. "At least part of you likes them. How about the rest?"

"They are quite... long. And muscular. And if you are under the delusion that I will apologise to either of them, then..." He gave a flick of his fingers.

She thought he intended some kind of obscene gesture when she felt a slap on her left buttock. It wasn't the first time. "What was that?"

"You wanted to know. That's how I distracted you." He lifted his hand toward her face. "This ring allows me to strike anything I focus on. Nothing damaging, but enough to be noticed."

"More magic."

"Indeed. And you don't approve."

"I didn't say that. I was thinking about how you just confessed to focusing on my arse."

"Something of its size makes it an easy target. Hard to miss."

"It's not too late to squash you into marmalade." She wiggled her hips threateningly, eliciting a grunt from him. "But I have other plans before you go all squishy." She lifted herself off his chest and began to angle herself backwards. *I've played too often with his staff in my hands. I want it somewhere else.*

From his wincing expression, she could tell he recognised what she planned and was preparing himself for the merger. *I threatened to snap it once. He probably thinks I will now.*

Calista changed her mind and position, grabbing him under the arms and performing a rolling flip. She wouldn't have tried it without her fighting experience or a larger partner, and in a few seconds she lay on her back, the naked berkis held above her.

He stared wide-eyed at her, shocked by her move and strength, and she couldn't control her giggle. She always let the male have the dominant position. Now, she wanted Truitt on top. *Dominate me!*

She slowly lowered him to her, letting his chest press against hers. One hand went to his rear, the other to his head as she pulled him tight. Their mouths met again, and soon the pear drop was back in action. It was merely a pawn in their passion, though. They hungered for something more.

They kissed for several minutes, then Truitt shifted his lips to her chin and down her neck. Her fingernails traced patterns on his buttock as his fingers tugged first the corset, then her shirt, free of their fasteners.

With a burst of enthusiasm, he yanked them open and continued his oral ministrations on her exposed breasts. Calista shuddered and grabbed his head again when his teeth clenched gently on a nipple. She guided his lips down to her belly, feeling their soft press against her bare flesh. Every move he made spurred on a growing lust in her until she thought she would cry out.

"I need you..." she moaned, but didn't complete her sentence. Instead, she gripped his hips with both hands and lifted him a few inches. All she needed to do was reposition his eager truncheon, which had been thumping against her lower belly, and she could take him into her. They would be merged, all negotiations done.

He would be hers. At that moment, she wanted nothing more.

Then her ears twitched. Someone cleared their throat, coughing softly in the darkness. Calista strained her neck to meet Truitt's face, thinking to tell him this wasn't the time or place for it. She growled, preparing to scold him for his timing. *How can he think of talking in this position?*

Her eyes caught movement beyond the bed. Someone — multiple someones — were standing near the door. Two were orvs, their burly silhouettes unmistakable.

The third figure's tail swished softly as it moved forward. Duke Patrick Cameron made a show of looking over the couple, now frozen in shock. A sneer twisted his lip.

"Don't let us stop you."

Chapter 32

The Identity Exposition
Or The Shade Of Shadows

THE PAIR TURNED their attention to the door, now wide open. Just inside its frame stood Duke Patrick Cameron, attired in his all-black ensemble. He clutched a strange gun, decorated with coils of wire, metal, and a glass, bell-shaped tube. Beside him were two male orvs, whom Calista recognised immediately. One was Joseph, who first led her to the small foyer. The other, still donning his frock coat, despite being indoors, was Bertram, whom she had fought to rescue Truitt from a few nights ago.

"I hope we are not intruding." The Duke lowered his hand until the weapon aimed directly at the couple. "Only I distinctly remember ordering you not to open this chamber."

Truitt scrambled out from under Calista as she hastily drew her arm up to cover her chest. "Don't you know it's impolite to enter a room without knocking?" she scolded.

"Don't you know it is impolite to fornicate on your host's furniture without first obtaining permission? As for knocking, that action would have been futile in light of the way the pair of you were so thoroughly engaged in amorous congress. You failed to even hear us enter."

"Anyone could miss the sound of a small key turning," Truitt said, tugging his drawers.

"There are three deadbolts," Patrick corrected. "All with large keys."

"You're the Grey Shadow!" Calista shouted, abruptly re-membering their larger situation as she pulled on her own pants. *Why didn't we leave?*

"On occasion. At the moment, I am an aggrieved noble who has caught two thieves in his home. The law would be unlikely to interfere if I were to execute them on the spot." He paused as Calista and Truitt sloppily finished dressing, their expressions a mix of agitation at being interrupted and con-cern over the strange gun he held. "Now, if you have replaced your attire properly, we may proceed to a more suitable loca-tion for discussion."

The orvs stepped forward. Joseph took Calista's wrist into a tight grip and began carefully patting her down for weapons. "My apologies, madam," he told her as his hand brushed her stomach. His fingers darted into the pockets but didn't linger, as they only encountered a few coins. When he found the small iron flail, the butler examined it momentarily, then tucked it away in his own clothes.

"That's stealing!" Calista protested.

Bertram similarly frisked Truitt, though a bit less gently. His meaty hands jabbed the berkis several times as they probed his smaller body. "That's for the rocks," he growled, ap-parently not forgetting the multiple hits he and Maurice took from his slingshot during their first encounter. He found the weapon, but when he failed to locate any of the pebbles it used, he left it untouched.

"The rocks were for you kidnapping me," Truitt retorted. "Seems I didn't hit you hard enough."

Bertram's scowl deepened, and he drew back a hand as if to strike. Under the watchful eye of the Duke, however, he quickly dropped it. "I wanna be the one who puts your lights out," he muttered before straightening and turning to his mas-ter. "All clear, boss."

Patrick nodded. "Then grab her staff and bring them both to the game room. What more fitting place to decide their fate than surrounded by the greatest treasures of Leverhelm?"

The orvs did as ordered, half leading, half dragging the captives out through the other bedroom, down the corridor, and into the chamber holding the Shadow's ill-got gains. The Duke walked behind them, his arm resting the gun against his chest, as if ready to spring into action at any sign of resistance.

Once in the grand hall, faroko and berkis were set before the stolen items, not far from where Calista had been admiring them only a few hours before. She sensed this gesture aimed to demonstrate that they, too, were prizes for the master thief.

Bertram took up a position near her, casually gripping her staff. Patrick moved to a spot several feet in front of her. Joseph flanked him on the left while Maurice, in his bowler, stood on the right. Behind the trio, Ned towered above everyone. Calista noticed him still puffing like a steam engine and wondered if that was his natural disposition.

She glanced down at Truitt. Considering their position, she expected him to be more enraged than he appeared. He remained calm, almost serene, at her side, though. She knew he had wanted a confrontation with the Shadow, but probably not defenceless against an armed opponent with accomplices. *We should have left when we could, instead of playing 'Find the Truncheon'!*

Calista turned her attention back to the Duke. A smug grin plastered his face as he tapped the gun against his shoulder, unnecessarily reminding her of their predicament. "Didn't you say you didn't like guns?" she inquired with a touch of sarcasm. "That any fool could use one?"

"Indeed," he agreed. "But I would be more foolish to confront you with anything less."

"You need to work on your flattery. Just like I don't need any fancy clothes or hairstyle to equal your brilliance. And my manners will never match yours."

"Given what I found you two doing — and in Lady Emberstone's bedroom, of all places — not to mention your table etiquette, I have no doubt. I imagine you were raised among the sows on a farm where all in attendance never spoke in words longer than one syllable."

"Toast your blooming eyebrows, you lily-livered gasser!" Truitt shouted, suddenly breaking his composure.

"And behold! The white knight rushes to your defence." Patrick waved his free hand at the berkis. "How droll. I did not realise you were so defenceless."

"I am not." Calista kept her own voice calm even as the heat of anger rose in her chest. "But Truitt is right. You are a gutless scoundrel, kidnapping him like you did. What do you want with him?"

"The only item I wish from him is his absence. Yours as well, now." Patrick's lips twisted into a sneer. "From the way you two were basket-making, am I to assume he is our mutual friend who filched the Dragon Eye Gem and got you sent to prison?"

"You betcha it was me who stole it." Truitt met the Duke's glare with his own. "You aren't the only prig in this city, you foppish chuckle-head."

"He also rescued me from gaol," Calista added, the feeling in her chest mixing with pride. "And you knew I was innocent, but would have let me hang!"

"Tut-tut. It would never have come to that. I merely upped the penalty to flush your accomplice out." Patrick brandished the gun, aiming first at one of them, then the other. "And it worked. Now I have you both."

"*You* increased the punishment?"

"I said they wouldn't hold you," Truitt told her, still glowering at the man. "Not until this mollycoddle gollumpus changed the rules."

"Indeed, they would not have. You have some knowledge of the justice system. Most likely spent some time on the inside." The Duke's tone grew darker, along with his expression. "And if you insult me again, I will have Ned here hang you upside-down by your ankles while the Hedgecock brothers practise their knife skills on you. It would be most entertaining."

Calista gasped at the name. "The three bloodthirsty skembers? They work for you?"

"For now. But of course, you met them before. When Lady Aetherborne sent out word she needed someone to guard the gem, I saw it as the perfect opportunity to stack the odds in my favour. Had they received the assignment, I could have waltzed in and taken it like a waif in a chocolate shop."

Truitt's lips curled with an expression of contempt, nearly matching their captor's. "What did I tell you? The infamous Grey Shadow, greatest cracksman in all Leverhelm, can't pinch so much as a trinket without assistance. I bet even his smoky form is just another trick. You get yourself a magical bauble, lets you go all see-through?"

"You insolent clack box! A word from me and Barnaby and his brothers will have you skewered."

Despite their peril, Calista couldn't help but admire the berkis's courage. Before she had questioned whether his bluster was that or stupidity. Now, she understood his provocations were designed to keep the Duke talking. "He has a point, though. How do you become the Grey Shadow?"

"With this." The male faroko raised his left arm and tugged back a well-tailored sleeve to reveal a thick silver and brass bracelet. "A little bauble — as you would call it — I commissioned from a Spellsmith. She could not manage full invisibility, but insisted I would be nearly impossible to see in darkness. And so I became the Silver Phantom."

"The who?"

"The Silver Phantom?" Truitt openly laughed this time. "More like the Spoony Poltroon. What an idiotic name. Silver is shiny. If you were shiny, you wouldn't be much of a Phantom."

The Duke did not rise to the insult. "But my appearance is not grey, either. Neither are shadows. They are black."

"Not all," Calista chimed in, puzzled by the direction the discussion had turned, but determined to keep it going, whatever path it took. Their lives might depend on it. "If you stand beside a gas lamp in the late afternoon, it casts a grey shadow."

"And none of them dispense oranges, you dandy dullard," Truitt said. "Perhaps you should have called yourself the Fruit Phantom."

A pained expression crossed Patrick's face. "When I began, that *was* the moniker attached to me. I didn't even realise any such items were appearing until I heard that title. Only after being spotted for the first time — by a guard in a jeweller's shop I was not aware of — was the name 'Grey Shadow' made public. I suspect the spell was faulty, but I could not return to the Spellsmith who infused it."

"Why not?" Spellsmiths were uncommon, and she didn't know of any in Gravenmore. For the average person with enough money and a desire for extra flair, such an individual could infuse an object with a bit of magic. Normally, they did little more than simple tricks, such as glowing on command or temporarily appearing as a flower or other decorative item. A casting which could cause someone to become transparent would have cost a small fortune.

"Because his Lordship here is a snuffler," Truitt answered first. "Undoubtedly did in the poor chum foolish enough to aid a blackguard. He'd likely shaft his own mother if she got his pease porridge too hot."

The Duke straightened to his full height, running a palm down the front of his coat. "We never ate that peasant food in my household. But we are getting away from the matter at hand."

"Which is?"

"What is to be done with you both. The lass here entirely failed to keep guard, even disobeying a direct order not to enter the chamber which held you."

"Hang about." Calista assumed a defiant stance, placing her hands firmly on her hips. "You ordered me not to try. And I didn't. I entered quite successfully."

For the first time since they had come to the game room, Truitt shifted his eyes to her. "So that excuse is acceptable when *you* employ it?"

She shrugged. "You can spank me later."

"Ahem. Gun here." Patrick waved the odd pistol, drawing their attention back to him. "Neither of you appears to grasp how dire your predicament is. I cannot let either of you leave here alive, now that you know my secret. Since I have the gem at last, I may dispose of you at my leisure."

Chapter 33

The Interference Confusion
Or I Would Have Gotten Away With It

TRUITT WAS THE first to regain his voice after the Duke's forthright declaration. "You can't kill us."

"My little device here says otherwise," the male faroko told him, tapping the odd gun with his finger. "But yours will not be a wasted death. It will provide a worthwhile distraction."

His callousness enraged Calista. "You are a sick bastard. I cannot believe I accepted dinner with you!"

"You've eaten? I've been locked in a cabinet, with no food and only the occasional trip, blindfolded, to the privy." Truitt fixed his gaze on Patrick again, his eyes piercing with a steely intensity. "One of your ruffians, incidentally, possesses roaming hands and a filthy mind. Once I figure out the identity of the scoundrel, I shall skewer his liver."

"He had a meal served that included raw oysters." Calista's face contorted disdainfully as the recollection of the still-alive blob of flesh descending her gullet resurfaced.

"With lemon slices?"

"Yes."

"That illegitimate scrub."

The Duke tapped his weapon. "Again. I have a gun."

"That tot's toy? With the glass and wires? What will you do? Make a pair of spectacles from it?"

But Calista didn't join Truitt's mockery. "Careful. I've seen something like it before. Setting fire to bushes."

"Indeed. Barnaby told me of Mr Ambrose's experiment." Patrick lowered the gun, momentarily admiring its construction. Though diminutive compared to the police's standard revolver pistols and closer in size to a derringer, its barrel appeared too narrow to accommodate conventional ammunition. A slender trigger linked to a cluster of wires ascending the glass tube, and where the hammer would traditionally rest, a stubby brass cylinder protruded. The entirety of the object managed to present itself as both menacing and comical. "This is a smaller prototype of his work. While it will not set you alight, it contains enough power to give you a nasty jolt. I have it turned to maximum voltage, which I believe to be sufficient to stop a man's heart. Or a woman's. So unless you wish me to test it, I suggest you listen."

Calista looked at Truitt. He opened his mouth as if to spew forth another series of insults, but apparently thought better, and quickly clamped it shut.

"Very wise," the Duke said, acknowledging their restraint. "With both of you secured this evening, I was able to retrieve the Dragon Eye Gem from its resting place in Amberlux Manor. It will now become part of my permanent collection." He voiced the last with a generous flourish of his arm to the priceless items around them.

"What have we to do with that?" Calista asked.

"What have you to do...?" The man's countenance assumed an expression of utter astonishment that swiftly transformed into ire. "The pair of you interfered numerous times in my attempts to obtain it. Never have I had such a problem in any other heist!"

"But we haven't done anything."

"Haven't you? When I first approached Lady Aetherborne's residency to get the layout of the grounds, I found you" — he idly shifted the gun to point at Truitt — "skulking around, apparently with the same intent. I followed you afterwards to the den of iniquity, then had Maurice and Bertram here lock you away. That's when it seems you" — the weapon swung in Calista's direction —

"released him, setting the neighbourhood ablaze in the process. With the city alerted by the fire, I dared not attempt the theft."

Recognition flashed on the berkis's face. "You were the beggar! And to think I considered slipping you a pence."

The Duke ignored his outburst. "When I learned of Lady Aetherborne's seeking protection for it, I sent the Hedgecock brothers to secure the position. I feared I or this clod had been spotted. When Barnaby failed to win the assignment, I chose to bide my time a little longer."

Calista's jaw dropped open. "So I might have actually faced the Grey Shadow that night!"

"Indeed," Truitt said. "If he had not copped a fright."

That earned him a dirty glance from Patrick. "When I was informed a thief had been caught trying to steal the gem, I rushed to the police station, expecting to find you" — the gun moved back to point at the berkis — "but only found you" — and then to Calista. "So I spun a story, hoping you might reveal his whereabouts, as he had not returned to his usual hole. I did not expect him to come to your rescue."

Truitt straightened. "A gentleman does not allow a lady to languish behind bars."

"You two are neither. Fortunately, I had my men searching for you. So when you made your appearance, it was a simple matter of following you home and securing your capture. And once I viewed your flat — you really should keep it secured — I realised you could be more useful to me than I expected. So you were brought here."

The berkis's bluster fell. "Why?"

"To give our trusty men in blue what they desire. The Grey Shadow, or at least the appearance. The Hedgecock boys bring you into their quarters with an item I've stolen — something of far lesser value than the Dragon Eye Gem, but still significant — and behold! The most feared thief of Leverhelm is apprehended at last!"

"Do it! I will tell them the truth! That their beloved Duke is the true culprit!"

"But would they believe you? I think not. Especially when you are dead. They will search your flat and find all those lovely stolen works of art."

"Those are just copies. They wouldn't fall for that." But Truitt visibly shuddered, his confidence broken.

"Wouldn't they? You imagine any of those simpletons could tell an original from a forgery?" Patrick pointed to the collection behind the pair. "I've brought my treasures to each city, and not one person ever questioned my word about them. If they cannot see these are the originals, they will never determine that yours are not."

A glance at Truitt told Calista he was lost for words as he stared at the criminal before them. "What about me?" she asked. "Why include me in your caper?"

"Why, you are the icing on the proverbial cake. After your escape, I queried around. An abnormally tall faroko is an uncommon sight, and one of your former clients — a Miss Zusa Lolly — was more than happy to pass along how to reach you. I put out word that you were for hire, and you arrived on my doorstep, none the wiser." The Duke's smile widened, obviously pleased with himself. "The police already believe you are the Shadow, or at the least, in league with him. When you are presented with your accomplice here, there will be no doubt as to the veracity of the claims. Both of you will be out of my way, and I shall be free.

"Then I had you guarding him while I nipped out to steal the gem," he continued, his long fingers fishing the jewel from a pocket and holding it up in the light of the oil lamps. "Quite ironic, don't you think?"

Truitt looked at Calista, the sight of the precious stone reviving his tongue. "The Duke thinks himself clever, but you and I kept him from nicking it before without trying. Even then, he needs magic. A true master thief would not have required help or interference. I retrieved it from under your nose with sheer cunning and grace."

The female faroko knew that wasn't wholly the truth. *You used your ring to distract me, you crafty dodger.* She kept quiet, though, hoping the provocation might still provide them with an opportunity to escape.

However, Patrick seemed to understand the purpose, too. "Your attempts at goading me are as futile as your situation. I have the gem now, and you do not."

"I had it first."

"Then proceeded to return it. Hardly the move of a master thief."

He risked losing his chance at capturing this monster to protect me! "He only did it for me."

The Duke emitted a malevolent snicker, a sound full of unpleasantness and malice. "True love, indeed. You two will have plenty of time to explore that. From the gallows."

Truitt ignored the threat. "I planned to use it to lure you out to a location of my choosing."

The Duke laughed again. "You believe I could be so easily manipulated? I would simply have the police step in and arrest you. Even if I were to have shown up alone, what would you have done? You are no match for me, physically or intellectually."

"I would have killed you." Truitt stated his intent with such stark directness that a shiver coursed down Calista's spine.

The target of his vengeance remained unfazed. "Would you really? For stepping into your stomping grounds. The petty thief jealous of the master?"

"For what you did to Persephone."

Patrick's eyebrows rose in a derisive arch. "That featherhead? She nearly ruined my heist of that priceless dragon and lotus vase." He nodded toward a porcelain gold-trimmed vessel, decorated by illustrations of an elongated lizard and flowers.

"You killed her for a bit of pottery!" Truitt bellowed, the frigid tone replaced by a seething rage.

The Duke shrugged. "Did you not hear what I said? Priceless."

Calista saw Truitt clenching his fists. Her eyes strayed to the bulge of his slingshot in his back pocket. *Not defenceless af-*

ter all. He had had enough of this, and so had she. Time to make a change. "Calm down, Truitt. You know you get hot-headed and can't think straight. Like when I rescued you."

"You didn't rescue me," he snapped, shifting his glare to her.

"No, of course not. But you were too stupid to run when you released yourself from the chair." She turned to the Duke. "Not that your orv friends are much smarter. Is Ned as dim-witted as Bertram and Maurice here?"

The Duke's expression suggested the change in topic was not entirely unacceptable. "They are not blessed with great intellect, I confess. Nor grace, as you experienced at dinner."

Pompous popinjay! "Truitt is the same. This dunderhead not only got himself kidnapped — twice, mind you — he can't help but set places ablaze." She shot the berkis a derisive look. "Remember how you started the fire at the Bedevilled?"

He returned her gaze with a glower. "Indeed I do."

"Enough. It is time to bring this conversation to an end. Along with the pair of you. Corpses will be as convincing to the police and without this incessant chattering." Patrick snapped his fingers. "Maurice. Joseph. Take them downstairs. We can despatch them there, then deliver their bodies to the constabulary. I will find some lesser trinket to plant on them and notify the Hedgecock brothers."

But Calista and Truitt's eyes remained locked. *Please forgive me!* she willed. "Would you be stupid enough to do that again?"

Truitt followed her gaze to his back pocket and his expression abruptly brightened. He shifted his attention past her to Bertram, who held her staff a few feet away. Off to the side, he saw the two named orvs moving toward them. He looked up at Calista once more and flashed a smile.

"Looks like I'm just a dolt." He whipped out the slingshot, drawing it back lightning fast as a pebble materialised in its loop. With a sudden release, he propelled the rock hurtling at Bertram. "Ptow!"

It smacked the orv's fingers, and he shouted, yanking his hand away. No longer supported, the staff fell forward.

Calista snatched it up and snapped it into Bertram's face, while Truitt pivoted, sending another pebble into Maurice's nose. The orv tumbled backwards, covering his horn and howling.

The Duke's calm veneer crumbled. "He has a weapon! Why didn't you take his weapon?"

Joseph stared at the berkis, seemingly even more surprised than his boss. "We found no stones on him, so it didn't seem to matter."

"Well, he has them now. Get him!"

"I've got more stones than all of you put together. Ptow!" Truitt flung a third stone at the Duke. The faroko's reflexes were better than those of his orv servants, however, and he stumbled out of the way.

Two orvs persisted in their agonised protests, while the remaining pair, Ned and Joseph, began their advance. The Duke, having regained his balance from the dodge, joined them, gun raised.

Truitt looked up, locking eyes with Calista. Their postures echoed the night of their initial encounter, facing similar adversaries. However, the stakes had been markedly escalated.

"I now accept it would have been more advantageous to flee when the opportunity presented itself," he told her.

"Your revelation comes a little too late." She let out a huff as the trio of foes approached — the Duke with a snide smile, Joseph with a hostile but polite expression, and Ned huffing himself crimson. "I can't believe I'm about to die because of your big... heart."

"Don't forget your sizable... assets."

"That cuts it." Calista flexed her fingers around her staff, finding courage in its solidness. "If we survive this, you are so getting that spanking."

"Square enough." Truitt gripped the much smaller slingshot in his hand. "Then I look forward to my future backside tanning."

Chapter 34

The Clockwork Intervention
Or If Not For That Meddling Rat

T
HE PAIR DIDN'T have time to reflect on the decisions
that brought them to this point. With the orvs Joseph and
Ned advancing on them and the armed Duke regaining his
balance, they needed to focus on escaping the manor alive.

Patrick was the first to act, though, squeezing the trigger of
his gun. The weapon hummed loudly, then a surge of vibrant,
crackling electricity shot forward, tracing a direct path toward
Truitt. The berkis yelped and leaped aside, the charge barely
missing his shoulder.

Bertram, one hand still protecting his injured face, made a
grab at Calista as the Duke let off another shot. She jumped backwards to sidestep the lunge, knocking over a brass pedestal
while Truitt managed to avoid the second blast of energy, tumbling to the floor with a grunt.

He landed next to the stand's former occupant — the odd,
thick-barrel gun. Quickly scrambling to his feet, he snatched the
weapon in his free hand and discharged it toward Patrick.

Instead of electricity, a square expanse of netting flew outward, propelled by four iron balls at its corners. Despite the lack
of aim, the mesh connected with the Duke, temporarily entan-
gling his head, chest, and arms in the fine rope strands.

Still gripping the Dragon Eye Gem in one hand and the gun
in the other, the male faroko struggled to release himself from
the fibrous grip. In frustration, he discharged the weapon again.

"Truitt! Watch out!" Calista cried.

The surge flew wild, coming within inches of Joseph's nose and stopping him in his tracks before striking the contents of another pedestal. This one held the mechanical rat. Rather than being blasted off, energy flowed into its slight form.

Calista had thought it merely a sculpture, but when red light filled its eyes and it raised its whirring clockwork body to a sitting position, she realised it was only dormant.

The unexpected animation of the item startled the room's other occupants, and for a moment their focus shifted to the rat as it leaped off its stand as nimbly as any living creature.

Seeing an opportunity, Truitt invoked his ring.

The ethereal slap knocked the gem from Patrick's clutched hand, sending it bouncing along the plush carpeting. Sparkling red in the lamplight, the tiny jewel drew both the Duke's and Truitt's eyes. Both men had sought the prize for days, and each possessed it for a time. Even while embroiled in a fight, the pair couldn't resist its allure.

Nor could the rat. Bounding on miniature legs, the artificial rodent dashed across the floor. Its mechanical jaw closed around the shiny orb with a faint 'clink' before it darted from the room and into the hallway beyond.

Truitt followed it immediately, only taking a moment to relinquish the now empty net gun and glance at his opponent. The Duke was too busy struggling to free himself from the mesh, though, to give chase or even release another energy bolt.

The electricity seemed to have supercharged the artificial creature as it scurried over the floor almost faster than Truitt could follow, its wiry, jointed tail bobbing along behind it. It never paused or altered its route, seeming to know exactly where it was going as it ran into a dimly lit chamber at the other end of the hall.

I've got you now! The berkis sprinted through the open double doors and quickly scanned the room. While furnished as a bedroom, complete with a tall mirror, several stands and racks had been added, all holding a variety of swords. While no expert on the weapons, Truitt's early life among those who collected them allowed him to identify a few. Most were sabres and court blades, as would be worn for formal functions, but he also noticed multiple cutlasses and a half dozen rapiers.

The sound of scraping drew his attention to the wall on his right. He spotted the rat's tail just as it disappeared behind an enormous oak and brass desk littered with the trappings a Victorian gentleman would use for correspondences. Truitt raced to the spot, but the space the clockwork squeezed through proved far too narrow for him to even slip an arm into.

Now that he knew the identity of the Grey Shadow, he no longer needed to draw the thief out with the jewel. But the Duke still wanted it, and that meant it could be used as leverage if Calista failed to defeat the orv henchmen. There was also an ability the gem was rumoured to possess he wished to test.

A loud hum alerted the berkis in time to leap aside as a blast of energy sparked through the air and struck the wall, leaving a black mark and the smell of charred wood. He spun to see Patrick standing in the doorway, a menacing sneer twisting his lips.

"Give me the gem now, and I may reconsider the condition in which you and your lover are relinquished to the police." The Duke brandished the gun before him, a faint trace of smoke drifting from its tip. "Refuse, and my little toy here will charcoal your tallywags."

"I believe you have misread the situation." Truitt straightened and slowly reached for the slingshot in his pocket. "It is you who will be taking the long walk to the stone jug. Calista and I kept you from stealing the gem without even trying. Together, we'll make sure you never steal or murder again."

"With your little pebble shooter and her hunk of wood against my gun and henchmen? That seems highly unlikely, wouldn't you agree? I am a famous noble and the most feared thief in the country. Neither of those titles was earned by letting street rats like you interfere in my affairs." He shifted the weapon to his other hand, then aimed it at Truitt. "Now, give me the Dragon Eye Gem."

The berkis knew he was right. His slingshot magically reloaded with pebbles when he needed it, but could that defeat something that hurled lightning? And while Calista proved herself a decent fighter, could she overcome four of the orv brutes? *I need to level the playing field!* He glanced around the room again, looking for anything he might use. All he saw were bedroom furniture and swords. *He must have some kind of phallic obsession. There's even one on the desk. Maybe...*

Truitt reached up and grabbed the hilt of a rapier atop the writing table. "I challenge you to a duel," he announced, brandishing the thin blade. "Winner takes all."

He intended the action to be intimidating, but it only drew a laugh from Patrick. "If that is how you wish to die, so be it. I will skewer you like a pig." He whipped aside his coat and slipped the gun into a holster on his waist before snatching up another rapier from a nearby rack. Unlike the others, it sported a small brass box attached to the guard, with a copper wire extending up the blade. When the Duke flicked a protruding switch, sparks flew from the weapon's tip.

"How skilled are you?" he asked, taking a step toward the berkis.

"I know a little," Truitt lied, trying to cover his fear. The gamble didn't quite balance the chances for the opponents, but he had no choice but to continue.

"I hope you know more than that, or this will be a most unsatisfactory victory. Look around you. These are not mere playthings of the rich. I am proficient in the use of every single one." Patrick made a quick slash with the rapier, sending more sparks into the air. "So prepare yourself!"

Truitt gulped, staring up at the faroko nearly twice his height. He was outmatched, and he knew it. But he had desired a confrontation with the man who killed his cousin's wife for years. There was no backing out now. He drew in a quick breath and lunged.

Patrick easily knocked the clumsy attack aside, energy crackling as the blades clashed. "Poor opening move," he clucked disapprovingly. "I expected more."

Truitt shrugged his shoulder to loosen it up. His days spent holding cards in the Right Hand had left him unprepared for a physical fight. "I'm a tad rusty, I confess. But it's coming back to me."

Patrick nodded, then abruptly leapt forward and swung, slashing Truitt's arm and sending a jolt through his body. The berkis yelped and retreated. "Bad form! Allow me one of those devices to ensure this is a fair dual."

"Why would I want that when I'm winning?" the Duke chuckled.

Truitt gritted his teeth. "I wouldn't be so sure."

"Oh, but I am. Here, let me help convince you." The faroko stepped forward and vanished, weapon and all. An orange appeared in the space he had been, roughly three feet above the ground, and dropped with a thud.

Before Truitt could react, a slash from the now-invisible Grey Shadow sliced into his other arm. The pain of the blow and electricity nearly forced him to drop his rapier as he ran left, hoping to evade his opponent. He swung wildly at the air, but another stroke from the blade cut through his pants and opened a gash in his leg.

With a cry, he stumbled to the floor, his rapier flying from his hand and landing a few feet away. He rolled onto his back, scanning the room frantically for his foe. At last, he made out the wispy traces of grey shimmering in the air as they approached.

"That served as a minor amusement, but the time for games has passed." The Duke's confidant voice rang out from the space, amplifying Truitt's fear into a panic. "Now I will end this equally insignificant annoyance."

Chapter 35

The Faroko Obstruction
Or Taking The Rap

C ALISTA WATCHED THE Dragon Eye Gem fall to the carpeting, only to be immediately snatched up by the mechanical rat which had inexplicably come to life. Seconds later, it had skittered from the room, with Truitt in close pursuit.

She tried to prevent the Duke, still caught in the netting, from freeing himself and following them, but Maurice stepped between her and him. "Your hairy friend is going to pay for that," he menaced, reaching for the slasher at his hip.

"I rather doubt that," she told him, looking for a path around the brute. "He's a terrible miser with money." Calista didn't want to fight the brutes. Now that she and Truitt knew the truth, they could work on proving it to the law. She only needed to collect the berkis and get clear of the manor.

"Stop nattering and grab her," Patrick shouted as Joseph helped him pull the last of the netting off him. "Forget that. Kill her. Just leave her face intact for the police to identify."

Calista's heart began racing as she watched the Duke storm out of the room. *Oh my giddy aunt! I'm out of options. Fight it is.* With that resolved, she flicked her staff, and the end struck Maurice's side, barely missing his fingers as he reached for the iron-hooked whip. "Let's leave the slashers alone for now. You wouldn't want to damage any of these fine items, would you?"

Instead of answering, he swung at her, hand balled into a fist. It was a clumsy attack, which she dodged without thinking. The staff came up again, striking his knee. He yelled a curse. "Hit her, Bertram!"

She had forgotten the orv behind her and quickly spun. His reflexes were faster this time, however, landing a partial blow to her head. It would have been a harder punch, but his fist skidded across her shoulder. Her opponent hadn't adjusted his swing for someone four inches taller than himself.

"I got her, Maurice!" the gleeful thug shouted. "Did you see — "

His next words were cut off when Calista's staff returned the hit. Her strike was perfectly placed. Bertram stumbled to the side as she turned back to face the others before they could launch a similar ambush.

"Striking a lady is the act of pigeon-livered flapdoodles," she said, remembering Truitt's insult. "And attacking from behind shows you have the spine of a jellyfish."

An irate Maurice, still nursing his knee, looked to the remaining orvs in the room. "Joseph! Ned! Do something!"

"She is correct," the well-mannered Joseph told him. "Even if the master ordered us to. And I am unarmed."

"Perhaps there is a true gentleman among you, after all." Calista nodded to him, then shifted her gaze to Ned. The hulking, horned individual looked on with seeming anticipation — his cheeks puffing away in a somehow calmer manner — but made no indication he would get involved. At least not yet.

A loud crack sounded behind her. She recognised the sound of a whip and tried stepping aside to avoid it. The sharp iron tip struck her shoulder, though, and she cried out. The reinforced cloth remained undamaged, but it hurt nonetheless. In response, she danced into Bertram, hitting him in the side with her staff.

This time, he didn't back away, instead yanking the slasher toward her. She blocked it with her weapon, letting the whip coil around it, as she did in their first encounter.

He had learned from that, however. Calista felt herself pulled toward him as he yanked both weapons to him. Before she realised his tactic, he held the staff tightly in one hand as he uncoiled his slasher with the other. "I got her, Maurice!"

While not quite true, the faroko knew if she let go, they would have little trouble subduing a weaponless target. She saw Maurice approaching out of the corner of her eye, a menacing smile on his face. Calista possessed strength, but there was no way she could fight him one-handed, even if his partner didn't use his whip again.

"Hold tight, Bertram!" the nearing orv shouted.

"Yes, Bertram," she repeated. "Hold tight."

Before he could puzzle out her purpose, Calista gave her end of the staff a sharp twist, then pulled. The wooden rod split abruptly in the middle, and she whirled her half around, catching Maurice in the stomach.

As he hunched over, moaning, she brought the three-foot shaft back, slamming Bertram's fingers. He yelled and dropped the other half, which she easily caught. *Now it's a fair fight!*

"I told you — " a second strike smashed his nose — "it is not nice" — the other section slammed his ribs — "to hit a lady!" She spun and inflicted the same two-hand attack on Maurice. "Or a reasonable stand-in for one."

"I believe they grasp that concept, madam." Joseph stared at the pair crouched on the floor in obvious pain. Orvs were the toughest of the races in Gravenmore, but not impervious to the well-placed blows of a trained fighter.

"Perhaps," Calista began, watching Maurice placing a hand on the ground to balance himself as he struggled to rise. She didn't give him the opportunity. A few more hits to his leg and back sent him sprawling on the lushly carpeted floor. "Yet these two appear particularly obtuse."

"We do have orders to despatch you," Joseph reminded her, gesturing to the imposing figure of Ned behind him. "Impolite as it may be."

Gentleman or not, I still end up feeding the worms. "You don't have to obey those. You can just let me walk out of here."

But the butler shook his head, honest regret showing in his expression. "Should you depart these premises and divulge your knowledge to the constabulary, our master would undoubtedly face arrest and the grim fate of the gallows, with us no doubt following suit. Therefore, though I harbour no desire for your physical suffering, I perceive no alternative but to employ force to ensure your silence."

Calista flexed the rods in her hands. A glance confirmed Maurice and Bertram remained immobile before she responded. "Then while I appreciate your candour as well as your manners, I must insist on rendering you senseless through physical means. When you are ready."

Joseph gave a curt nod, then adopted a boxing stance, fists in front of him. With rapid movements of his feet, he shuffled forward and to the side, staring at her from behind a raised hand. "I should warn you, I've spent a considerable number of hours in the Stalwart Fisting Society of Nimbusburg."

"That only matters if you got in some fight training, too." Calista stepped around the prone Maurice, staying out of his reach. "I prefer a sturdy shaft in my hands."

"Then prepare for defeat, as my fists will beat your staff." Just as he finished his challenge, Joseph darted forward with a quick right jab toward her. It missed, and he instantly retracted his hand and danced away.

"Not bad. A few feet off the mark, but still a good start."

"Merely warming up, madam. You will feel my next thrust, I assure you."

What is it with these men and their thrusting? "What happened to not hitting a lady?"

"Faced with the gallows, I must regrettably set my manners aside. Ready."

Though his punch had not come close to reaching her, she recognised from his moves that he did indeed have some training.

But it wouldn't suffice against an opponent with a long reach and even longer weapons. "I wish you luck, Joseph. I truly do. But I am going to lay you out now." Calista stepped toward him, making no attempt to duck as his fists came at her. One struck her jaw, the other her shoulder. She didn't flinch, however, instead delivering a steady string of strikes to his stomach, side, fingers, and head. He dropped to the floor, unconscious.

A fierce roar sounded behind her, and she spun to see Ned bearing down on her. Still slightly stunned by Joseph's blows, she barely had a chance to hit the oversized orv before he grabbed her by the shoulder. Thick fingers dug into her muscle, but she suppressed a yell as she pummelled the staff halves against his stomach. They had as much effect on him as the first two strikes, however.

Then he latched onto her other shoulder and squeezed. This time, she cried out as his meaty grip applied pressure on both sides and hoisted her off the ground. Her fingers lost their strength, letting the staff pieces drop soundlessly to the carpet.

She panicked. "Ned! Let's talk. You don't really want to hurt me, do you?"

The brute looked up at her face, now several inches higher than his, as her feet dangled above the floor. Puffing cheeks blew hot breath into her grimacing expression. He shut one eye as if to focus better on the question. "Yes."

Lovely! "Before you do," she said through clenched teeth, "I wanted to tell you how wonderful your shoes are!"

His grip relaxed a hair. "Huh?"

Calista concentrated on her tail, sending its tip down to the unconscious orv below her. With it, she felt around his tight jacket. *He put it somewhere!* "Your delightfully cheerful footwear. I have never seen a pair that particular shade."

Still confused, Ned lowered her slightly as he bent his neck downward. The extra inches allowed Calista's tail to extend a little further. It glided over a distinct bump. *There! Just a bit more...* "Don't tell me no one has ever complimented your taste in shoes. Such a delightful hue of yellow with a fancy red bow."

"Huh?" he asked again. "No bow." Without thinking, he lowered her a bit more as he leaned forward to see what she was talking about.

Her tail slipped into the pocket and found the flail. After a slight shift, it slid into the opening. The latch snapped into place, securing the iron ball to the tip. *Got it!*

But his change in position allowed her brawny opponent to spot her lie. "No bow!" he repeated more emphatically, resuming his pressure on her.

Calista's eyes bulged with the pain, but she did her best to keep her focus on her tail. She raised the weighty end behind her, bringing it up to her shoulder. Taking as deep a breath as she could, the female faroko spread her legs, extending them to each side. She grunted against the strain as the orv pulled her closer to him. "No bow!"

She lashed her tail down and under. The iron orb cleared her opened legs easily, striking their target with the force of a hefty kick: Ned's nuts.

He went cross-eyed as a single 'eep' escaped his lips. His hands released Calista as they shifted to his nether region, and she dropped the last few inches to the floor as he tumbled over sideways. His cheeks resumed their rapid puffing, but now it was in pain instead of anger.

Calista massaged her throat, easing where he had gripped her. *That's a new attack I hope I never have to repeat!*

The faroko moved around the multiple bodies on the carpet, each in their own little world of hurt, retrieving the halves of her staff. Once sure none of them were about to follow, she ran toward the door. *I have to find Truitt and the Duke!*

But apparently, her fight wasn't over. The pair of orvs who served them dinner, Winston and Tobias, came running up the last few steps of the staircase toward her. She didn't know if they had heard the commotion or had standing orders to aid their master at this time, but the reason was of little consequence. Their hostile expressions and clenched fists were explanation enough.

Neither carried any weapons, which made Calista's task easier, and she quickly dispatched the first one, Winston, with a half dozen blows. Tobias, however, caught her off guard with an unexpected jab to the face. His movements revealed a level of fighting skill she hadn't anticipated, and as he struck her again in the stomach, he wrenched the rods from her grasp.

The blow positioned her perfectly, though, granting her tail the freedom to arc over her back. In a seamless motion, it directed the flail forcefully into his face. He fell to the floor, stunned.

Before she could retrieve her weapons, she heard more footsteps coming up the stairs. She rushed to the railing and peered over. The Hedgecock brothers were bounding upward as fast as they could, the larger steps slowing down their progress. "There she is, boys!" yelled Barnaby from the front, spotting her dark curls above them. "Draw your swords!"

The command was ill-timed, as the other two skembers attempted to do just that. Once they held the bare blades, they could not continue their ascent without poking themselves and each other. After a few tries and one yelp, the swords were put away, and they resumed their climb.

I don't have time to fight all three of them, not with those weapons! Then she remembered Peg's explanation of the shirt. The reinforced elbow and shoulders were defensive, but it also possessed an offensive component. Her fingers went to the top button, and she ripped it off with a sharp tug. Following the mechanician's instructions, she scraped it along her shoulder. The fastener began hissing, and she quickly tossed it toward the trio.

It bounced off a few steps, then exploded with a force which caused the brothers to stop. The button landed too far ahead to do more than startle them, though. Peg explained they needed to be in close proximity to her target to truly hurt, so Calista plucked off another and sent it flying.

This one fell neatly at Barnaby's feet, and the resulting percussion knocked him backwards into his brothers. With much cursing and clattering, the trio got back up, with the youngest, Brisco, shaking a fist up at the faroko. His anger quickly changed to alarm as he watched her toss another at them, and he scrambled to get out of its path.

Down they tumbled as the third button exploded, its concussion causing a shockwave through the skembers. She needed to reach inside her corset for a fourth, but the dispatching of that seemed to convince the brothers she wasn't worth the effort, and they retreated to the bottom floor.

Calista glanced around. Seeing everyone she fought remained disabled, she ran to the nearest door in search of Truitt and the Duke. *I have to find them before he does something stupid. Either of them!*

Chapter 36

The Circuit Completion
Or What A Shock!

TRUITT LAY ON his back, staring at the shadowy form before him. His heart pounded so fiercely it sounded like striking hammers to his ears. Though the cuts on his arms and leg throbbed with pain, his foremost concern centred on the murderous villain standing before him.

"This is a coward's victory!" he shouted, expecting a final stab through his chest or a slice of his throat to follow any second. "Look at what you've become! A mere shadow of a man."

"Says the berkis grovelling on the floor," boomed the Duke's voice. "I am more than ten men. When I look in the mirror..." The smokey form halted its advance as it passed the full-length looking glass. It shifted slightly, as a breeze might twist a whiff of smoke. Was Patrick admiring himself? "Curious. Now that I see it, I do seem more grey than silver."

"Truitt?" Calista's tall figure appeared in the doorway, panting heavily. "Are you alright?"

"Ah. The young lady wishes to share your fate." The disembodied voice chuckled. "Very well. I can frame dead bodies just as easily as living."

"Calista, watch out!" Heart pounding, Truitt scrambled painfully to his feet. His leg buckled under the weight, but he found his rapier nearby and closed his fingers around the cold iron. *He's not going to hurt anyone else!*

266 | *The Dragon Eye Gem Affair*

The gash in his arm surged with pain as he brought the foil up and thrust it blindly into the smoky presence. He knew he couldn't defeat the Duke, but he might slow him down long enough for Calista to escape.

However, the blade completely missed the limbs of the invisible faroko, instead piercing the holster at his hip. The point of the rapier drove straight up the wireframe barrel of the gun, completing a circuit that sent a surge down the weapon. Truitt yelled as it burned his hand, and he released the grip.

The metal he forcefully introduced to the electric rapier did more than shock the berkis. Sparks of energy erupted from the gun and an arc of electricity like lightning in a storm bridged the gap between it, the blade, and the bracelet on the Duke's wrist.

The air exploded with sharp snaps and crackles, while the once-grey smoke transformed into a darker, more furious mass. A brilliant flash of light pierced the tumultuous scene. Truitt instinctively shielded his eyes, yet amidst the blinding brilliance, the unmistakable outline of a skeleton emerged, vividly etched in his vision.

Then it was over, and the now fully visible and thoroughly unconscious Patrick collapsed to the ground. The scourge of Leverhelm was finally defeated.

"Truitt!"

Calista raced to the berkis as he sagged to the floor. Though not in as bad condition as the stunned Duke, the duel and his wounds had exhausted him.

"You did it!" she told him, dropping to her knees. She supported his back as she examined him. He was bleeding and sore, but alive. "You defeated the Grey Shadow!"

Truitt nodded. "Was there any doubt I would?" he mumbled. Despite his flippancy, in the final seconds of the fight, he wasn't sure wholly what was happening. "Is he dead?"

"I do not believe so," she told him, glancing at the prone body. Wispy smoke drifted off the finely tailored suit and his wavy blonde hair had adopted blotches of brown, but she could see his chest steadily rising and falling.

"Then we will need to prove he is the Shadow. What of the orvs?"

"Hurting. I managed to subdue them — and the Hedgecock brothers, with some help from my shirt — but I don't know for how long. We must get moving."

"Your shirt?" Truitt's gaze went to the white blouse Peg had gifted her. The missing buttons created a plunging neckline deep into her corset, revealing a pleasant amount of plump cleavage which temporarily mesmerised the berkis.

"I see you will survive just fine," Calista noted wryly, seeing his transfixed expression. "You can admire them later, once we are done with this place."

"Right." He wrenched his stare away from her chest, taking the opportunity to look about the room. There was no sign of the clockwork animal. "We need to retrieve the Dragon Eye Gem. That rat thing took it behind that desk."

"Hasn't that jewel caused us enough trouble? Let's leave it for the police to find."

"No." Truitt struggled to sit upright, lifting himself off her caressing hand. He had learned to trust its touch, but there was another purpose for it at the moment. "I have a use for it. Please, fetch it."

It was the first time he had used the polite request before in a non-condescending way, and she rose to fulfil his wish. The desk loomed immense, boasting a row of tall drawers on each side, a thick oak surface, and a series of shelves and nooks at the top rear. After examining it for a moment, the towering faroko female found a secure corner to grip, and she moved it without much strain.

On the carpet behind it lay the mechanical rodent, once again defunct, but still clenching the red jewel in its jaw. Calista scooped it up and returned it to Truitt, who remained on the floor.

"Interesting piece of work," he remarked, looking over the rat. "I've heard about such constructs before, but never seen one. Might be valuable."

Calista gave him a disdainful glance. "Do you view everything by its value?"

"Naturally. Everyone does. How else do you determine how much interaction you have with it? If you don't see it as something worthy of your time, you move on. I just happen to tend to the more monetary aspect of determination."

He pried the jewel loose, then set the rat aside. With Calista's help, he rose to a standing position. While the cuts on his arm and legs were surface only and had already stopped bleeding, he still found it painful to use them. "There is a property of the gem I wish to test," he told her, cupping it gently in his palm.

"Here? Now?"

"If the rumours are true, this is the perfect situation. Take my hand."

She did as he asked, slipping her fingers into his and giving it a squeeze.

Truitt smiled up at her. "Hold tight, my dear." He stroked the precious stone with his thumb, then abruptly tossed it high. "Cleanse!"

As he shouted the word, the gem exploded into what appeared to be a thousand tiny shards, forming a large cloud above them. Truitt and Calista ducked, but just as quickly as they burst outward, the pieces contracted, reforming into what looked like an oversized crimson flying insect. In mere seconds, they needed to reevaluate that view, as it expanded to the size of a sparrow. Now they could make out small, bat-like wings, an elongated neck, and a flailing tail. The perfect miniature replica of a dragon.

But it didn't remain little for long. It zipped toward the door, wings humming, continuing its growth spurt. It had grown to rabbit-size when it flew from the room and vanished from their sight.

"Did you know it was going to do that?" Calista asked, stretching to her full height.

"Kinda." Truitt rose with her, still clutching her hand.

"Now what?"

A cry of panic answered her question. After that, a deafening roar shook the walls, accompanied by half a dozen more shouts. Distant thumps followed of something, or someone, hitting a wall, then more yells.

A smile crept onto Truitt's face. "We wait until it's done. It should clear out his henchmen and anyone else in the house."

Calista's long ears perked up at the commotion echoing from around the manor. It sounded as if the magical dragon was seeking out every orv in the building and sending them packing. "Will it hurt them?"

"I honestly don't know," he admitted. "After what they did to us, I don't care."

The faroko nodded in agreement as another roar echoed from somewhere below them. "But this much ruckus will most likely alert the police. We should leave before they arrive."

"*I* am not a fugitive from the law," Truitt teased her. He knew if his own adventures into the world of crime were ever discovered, that position would change. "But we can't depart until that thing is finished. It won't injure me, as I am the one who invoked it. It shouldn't hurt you, as long as we are holding hands."

Calista let out an exasperated gasp. "Shouldn't? You don't know?" She nearly released his hand in anger before gripping it tighter.

"I have had to glean every morsel of knowledge regarding it from whispers and stories." He affected an injured tone. "I am content that this portion, at the very least, has proven true. Perhaps, in the future, we may find occasion to employ it again."

"No! We can't take the gem. It has to be here for the police to discover."

"Why? We cannot leave behind a jewel this valuable."

"Because it is the *only* way to clear my name." Calista's tail twitched angrily as she brought her free hand up, fingers bent inward, as if to throttle the berkis. "We have been over this before. They need to pin *your* theft of it on someone. That means they must find the gem here with him." She kicked the still-unconscious Patrick, releasing some of her frustration.

"What's wrong with being a fugitive?" Truitt asked innocently. "Just stay away from the bluebottles and you'll be fine."

"Truitt!" Her hand moved closer to his neck. "I refuse to live the rest of my life in fear of being arrested for a crime I didn't commit."

He shrugged. "Then relocate to another city. Perhaps Ravenedge or Steamstead. Your identity will be unknown there. I will need to relinquish my flat, though. Raffles and the lot might feel my absence. They would definitely miss my money. My uncle, however, would find solace in my departure. Nevertheless, it is an endeavour we could manage."

Calista dropped gracefully into a low crouch, her gaze fixed in disbelief at the berkis. Their eyes met and held each other, unwaveringly. "You would abandon everything you have here to be with me?" she asked in a hushed tone.

Truitt paused, then tore himself away from her penetrating stare. "What an idiotic question," he blustered. "I said I would, didn't I?"

"Oh, Truitt!" She threw her free arm around him, tugging him in a tight embrace. He groaned at the pressure against his wounds, but didn't pull from her grasp. After a long moment, she released all but his hand. "But that is an idiotic suggestion! The gem stays here. Understand?"

"Alight!" The berkis glowered at her, but a trace of a smile parted his lips. "I will leave the gem with Patrick."

"Promise. And a real one this time. No more lying."

Truitt paused, then nodded. "No more lies. The gem stays."

She pulled him in again, more tenderly than before, as her lips sought his. They kissed, not the frantic kiss of passion, but the patient, drawn-out kiss of lovers enjoying a moment of affection. Despite their tumultuous interactions over the past few days, their relationship had finally reached a balance.

Their touching embrace only lasted a minute before his hand, now free of the gem, slipped into her open neckline. Prodding fingers slid eagerly between the flesh of her cleavage.

The exploration was mutual as her own hand dropped from his back and found fresh purchase on his left buttock. With a mischievous moan, she squeezed.

Truitt jumped, and their lips parted. "It is not a proper time for that," he chastised her.

"Nor was it when we played 'Find the Truncheon' in Lady Emberstone's bed." She glanced toward her neckline. "And your argument would bear more weight if your fingers were not currently sampling my wares."

The berkis quickly, if a tad reluctantly, withdrew his hand. The residual warmth faded as a breeze of air struck the pair. Both turned to see an enormous crimson head sticking through the doorway, the scent of smoke wafting off its elongated snout.

"It appears your conjuring has finished," Calista noted, rising to her full height as the crystalline dragon flapped gingerly into the room. While larger than a horse, it moved with an unexpected grace. "We best be going."

Truitt eyed the beast. "Agreed. Uhm..."

She heard the hesitation in his voice. "What? Don't tell me you don't know how to turn it back into a gem."

"I'm trying to remember! Hush woman." As before, he raised his free hand high. "Shrink!" he commanded. Nothing happened. The dragon merely stared back at him. "Be a gem!" Truitt called out again. Still nothing. He frowned, not daring to look at Calista's scowl. *Think! It was an easy word. Something about the jewel.* "Wait... Shine!"

The crystal creature shattered, a thousand cracks appearing over its reptilian body. Like before, it briefly exploded into tiny shards before condensing back into the gem, which dropped neatly into Truitt's hand. "See?" he said, finally meeting his partner's gaze. "I told you I knew."

Calista offered him a sceptical eye-roll. "How could I have ever doubted you?"

"Don't get cheeky!" he scolded. "Go now! Depart at once! I shall ensure that the authorities find their way to our friend."

She grinned, then bent down to kiss his cheek. "Take care and be quick!"

"You do the same."

Calista grabbed up the defunct rat and sprinted to the door. She gave the berkis a last glance before creeping into the hall. There was no need for stealth, she soon realised. Most of the area lay empty except for a few orv guards on the floor. Her fingers went to the leathery throat of one. He was alive, the dragon having inflicted no other damage than a faint-inducing bout of panic.

With a chuckle, she stood, wishing she could have seen their expressions when the artificial reptile burst forth from the manor bedroom. After a moment of searching, she found the two halves of her staff, still gripped in the hands of another henchman. Once she pried them out, she returned to the game room. Joseph and Ned lay unconscious, but the others had vanished, undoubtedly driven out by the dragon.

As she descended the stairs, she kept watch for any further guards. She stumbled upon a few more comatose orvs, but saw no signs of any attackers. Even the Hedgecock brothers had enough sense to flee.

Once on the bottom level, Calista recovered Silas's clothes and made her way to the front door. The tweeting of whistles, numerous shouts, and a swarm of police officers appearing under the gas lamps at the estate's outer gate changed her mind, though, and she decided to find another exit.

However, there was still time for a quick detour through the kitchen.

Truitt sighed once the faroko had left the bedroom, then stared at the gem in his palm. *Someday you will be mine again.* He caressed it lovingly, wishing Calista's logic hadn't been so solid. But he knew that until the Dragon Eye Gem was back with its owner and the Duke shown to be the true thief, her name would never be cleared.

He walked to where Patrick remained prone on the floor. Both rapiers lay nearby, and he picked up the one he had wielded, feeling the weight again in his hand. He swung it once, then brought the point toward the chest of his fallen opponent. *You declared you would skewer me like a pig. You deserve that fate more than I.*

But he didn't follow through, instead tossing the weapon aside. Just as he couldn't take the jewel with him, he could not kill the Duke. The only way out of their situation was for the law to find him, the gem, and the stolen items.

A grin split his face. He had nearly forgotten the Shadow's treasure haul. Nimble hands pulled back the Duke's waistcoat and deftly placed the jewel into an inner pocket. He reached for the bracelet, then reconsidered. The discharge which knocked the faroko unconscious also left an unsightly scorch mark around his wrist. Even if the item still functioned, he knew it too needed to remain behind to prove the police had captured the right man. *Engaging in virtuous endeavours certainly hinders the pursuit of other people's wealth.*

His eyes shifted to the orange on the carpet, all but forgotten in the chaos. Nothing about the fruit had ever made the news, so he assumed it was entirely mundane, except for its materialisation. His ring had never produced produce, nor his pouch. Still, he picked it up gingerly and examined it. *Where did you come from? Spain? Morocco? Some poor street vendor in Brassmont?* The image of a fruit seller puzzling over how his stock kept vanishing appeared in his head, and he chuckled. It would have to stay here, of course, with the other items as further proof of the Duke's double life.

With the evidence laid out and Calista gone, Truitt sauntered from the bedroom, around the prone orv bodies, and into the game hall. His heart began pounding as he took in the sight. The finest works of art, jewels, and priceless oddities, assembled in one room. The opportunity had not been afforded him to admire it before, when led into the chamber at gun-point. Now, he could revel in their beauty and, more importantly, their infinite value, with nothing to interrupt him.

Except the whistles and shouts, notifying him the police had arrived. *Confound it! I need more time!* He scanned the room, looking for one object of wealth, one trinket he could take which wouldn't be missed. But thanks to the Duke's work in tracking the Shadow's escapades, every stolen good was no doubt documented with the officials in Brassmont. If a single item were to go missing, it might tip off the authorities that someone else had been involved.

Then his eyes fell upon the Moaning Elisa. The titular female seemed even more ecstatic in the presence of so many other works. Truitt felt a similar surge in his loins when he realised his opportunity.

He gave the treasure trove one more longing glance, silently promising he would meet them all again, then hopped out of the room and down the stairs. While he had been brought into the manor covered by a sack, it took him only a short time to find his way to the same rear exit Calista had used. Soon, he was racing past the flower garden in the backyard to safety.

As he crossed into the neighbouring noble's yard in the low moonlight — the rich apparently not concerned with trespassers from other affluent households — he felt a surge of euphoria. *I succeeded! I have avenged sweet Persephone and defeated the Grey Shadow. Greatest thief in all of Leverhelm? Bah! Greatest blowhard is all.*

The jewelled dragon had roused the wealthy neighbourhood enough to draw law enforcement to the scene. For once, Truitt hoped they were up to the task. *And may the hand of providence lead the fair Calista to a sanctuary. That exquisite lady has, once more, come to my rescue.*

Chapter 37

The Resolution Explanation
Or That Is Utter Tommyrot

"**I** TRULY CANNOT believe it. The Duke was the Grey Shadow all along!"

Truitt forced back a smile as he approached the table in the Right Hand Casino. Faye, of course, had already learned of the previous night's exploits and eagerly repeated the information to all within earshot. Between the commotion at the manor and the police wagon's clanging, he expected most of Gravenmore to have heard something of the affair by now.

Raffles nodded as he looked over his hand. As always, the trio sat entrenched in a game of cards. "I said it was 'im, didn't I?"

"Taradiddler! You said no such thing. *You* said the Shadow started the fire."

"To cover 'is thieving. Seems obvious to me. You can never trust them bloated aristocrats. Rotten to the core, every one of them." Raffles gave a curt nod when he spotted the fourth member of their circle. "Evening, Truitt."

The berkis tossed his hat to the back of the chair he usually occupied before climbing up the half-dozen rungs and scooting onto the worn wooden seat. His muscles ached and his shoulder remained sore from lying bound and gagged in the cabinet for so long at the manor. The other cuts he sustained at the Duke's hand still stung, but he had cleaned them up the best he could. Despite his fatigue and pain, the victory had energised him far more than any sleep could. Right now, he longed for the familiar. "Is that why you call me 'lordship'?"

He had made his way home to change outfits and pick up an item. Then, he nipped back to the manor to watch from among a throng of onlookers as the police brought out first the Duke in handcuffs, then his remaining henchmen. While Joseph prattled on in an attempt to extricate himself from the situation, Ned huffed with evident displeasure. Once they were secured in a van, a contingent of policemen had been appointed to stand guard over the house. The treasures inside required attention until their rightful owners could be duly notified.

"Didya hear?" Faye nearly leapt from her seat at the opportunity to share her gossip with the new arrival. Her regular maroon felt top hat, lensless goggles, and collection of trinkets had been replaced by a shorter headpiece with lace and an upturned brim. Beneath it, her long ears twitched with anticipation. "The coppers finally nabbed the Shadow last night. And mark this... it was none other than the Duke!"

"Did they now?" Truitt didn't meet her gaze, instead turning his head and nodding a greeting to Hugh, who smiled in return. After the punishment he received over the past few days, he felt relieved to see an orv not intent on kidnapping or murdering him. "When I last sat at this table, you informed me it was a person of the fairer sex."

"Pffft. That's old news. She busted out that evenin'. They caught the real crook this time."

"Bumbling buffoons," Raffles muttered. "I wager they nicked the wrong personage again."

Faye slapped the table and leaned toward the older skember. "You just said you said it were him! Now you sayin' it ain't him?"

A single eyebrow arched as he stroked one of his horns. "I am merely making a commentary on the abilities — or lack thereof — assigned to the folks whose supposed to be protecting us."

"He makes a fair point," Truitt said, turning to face the pair again. "How can they be sure they have the right man?" He knew what he and Calista planted for proof, but that didn't ensure the police made the proper connections.

"Cause they found the Dragon Eye Gem on him! And..." She dropped her cards to the table and inclined forward, as though sharing her innermost confidences, rather than mere street gossip. "He had a room full of gold and money and stuffs."

Raffles clucked his tongue. "Gold is money, sweet gabble-monger."

"Shut it. They uncovered all the items he's nicked over the years."

"That would make Kettlebelly 'appy, according to 'is lordship."

Truitt smiled. He had managed to impart some knowledge to the old gambler. "It would indeed. I wouldn't say no to a bit of spare gold and money and stuffs myself."

"You won't get any of that playing cards with us." Raffles cast a pointed stare in the faroko's direction. "*When* we play cards."

Her face twisted in frustration as her tail twitched. "Aren't you listenin'? They caught the Shadow! Leverhelm's greatest thief! Here in Gravenmore!"

"Greatest thief?" Truitt asked, feigning an innocent tone. As the most excitable among the quartet, Faye often became the target of their amusement by provoking her frantic reactions. "Is that not our own Raffles 'Sticky' Oliver?"

"Only if he's stealin' our joy," she grumbled.

"It is doubtful anyone could steal your joy, Faye." He lay a hand on the table near hers. "Please, tell me more about this dastardly villain."

She drew in a deep breath, then exhaled slowly. Even her tail relaxed, its tip descending to the floor again. "Duke Patrick Cameron, the man who's been leadin' the hunt for the Grey Shadow for years, is the Grey Shadow. The whole shebang was a ruse. He moved from city to city, stealin', while suckin' up accolades. Isn't that wild?"

"Extremely." *And I ended his charade.* He wanted to tell her, tell all of them, the truth. That it was he who stole the Dragon Eye Gem. He who worked out the Duke's plan. He who finally defeated the blackguard. But they would either think he was lying or, worse, start asking more questions. They might even discover his true identity and his simple life among them would be brought to a definitive end. Nonetheless, he couldn't resist hearing how the apprehension of the Duke by both him and Calista had been construed. He had given up the gem and countless riches for it, after all. "What enabled the men in blue to capture him in our meagre city?"

Faye's eyes sparkled at the question. "A dragon!"

Truitt covered his mouth in astonishment, masking an emerging grin. "Kettlebelly? Here? I saw no buildings coated in dragon faeces."

"No, muttonhead. Some folks reported ferocious roars coming from his abode, and gawkers claimed to have witnessed the silhouette of a giant reptile through the windows."

The berkis dropped his hand, adopting a scowl. The more he professed disbelief in the tale, the less likely the others would be to connect him to it. "That is utter tommyrot. A dragon indoors?"

Raffles let out a low chuckle. "I said the same. Someone was soused. Who gets the reward?"

Faye abruptly calmed, easing back into her seat. "I forgot about that. No one's said nothin' about that. Maybe the coppers?"

Truitt hadn't forgotten, though. Once he realised the truth about the whole affair, he understood it would never be claimed. The blow would have stung more if his pursuit of the footpad had been for the money. "I rather doubt any reward will be given. If the Duke and the Shadow are one and the same, then the offering of compensation undoubtedly served as a diversion. Has anyone ascertained how he was able to become incorporeal?"

The faroko across from him slouched, obviously not happy with the conclusion. "A bit of jewellery is the word. A necklace or bracelet. Or a ring, perhaps, like you've gots."

He held up his left hand, fingers splayed, to show off the azure band of metal. "I assure you, my adornment does nothing so spectacular as rendering me translucent. It is as plain as the ring Raffles pilfered."

"I wasn't suggestin' otherwise."

Raffles stared at the pair over his cards and cleared his throat loudly. "So the Shadow is nabbed. Might that mean we may knuckle down? I came 'ere for the sport of fortune, not the rum doings."

"Excellent suggestion!" Truitt realised he had barely eaten or drunk in nearly two days and turned toward the bar, raising a hand. "I am in dire need of an alcoholic quaff. Kate!"

The skember closed his eyes and let out a frustrated sigh. "I wasn't meaning that."

Kate approached the table, her heeled boots tapping against the hardwood floor. "What can I do for you?"

"One scotch, neat, if you would be so kind. And some of those little sandwiches. Roast beef or sardines would be nice. Oh, do you have any of those pastries still? The sponge cakes?"

"His lordship plannin' to dine like royalty today, is he?" Faye teased.

Truitt only nodded. "To celebrate the Shadow's capture, of course. Kate, change that. Roast beef *and* sardines on those sandwiches."

"Sure thing." The server smiled at the seated orv across from her. "Hello, Hugh. Can you believe it was the Duke?"

Hugh blushed, as usual, and raised his cards a little higher to cover his face. After a moment, he reconsidered and lowered them to the table, allowing him a clear view of the shapely faroko.

"Quite extraordinary," Truitt agreed. "If Faye has her facts right."

Kate's tail swished nervously around her shoulder. "I confess, I almost suspected you might secretly be the Shadow."

His heart skipped at her words, then began beating faster. "Oh? What drew you to that conclusion?"

"Just a fancy, really. You've frequently been absent since he arrived in town. So it struck me you could be the thief, or trying to capture him." She nonchalantly shrugged before casting an unabashed smile in Hugh's direction, eliciting a blush from him. "Seems I was wrong on both accounts."

Her admission rekindled Faye's enthusiasm for the topic. "What a hoot! Our Truitt, the Shadow? He's about as stealthy as a dancin' elephant wearing bells. He would be as good at stealin' as a fish at climbin' a tree. Why, he's so..."

"Thank you, Faye." Truitt motioned for her to settle down. Once again, he longed to reveal the truth, if just to wipe that condescending smirk off her face. "Your point is made. My apologies for being unworthy of your considerations. My time away from this table did not involve thievery. If it were, I would no doubt have more to show for it." To emphasise his claim, he ran a hand down his ragged waistcoat and faded shirt.

"What were you doin', then?" she pressed.

"My affairs are my own. As are yours." He might have admonished her more harshly, as none of them ever pried into the private lives of the others. One sometimes offered a bit of insight voluntarily. Raffles occasionally mentioned his wife, who was, by his accounts, a nagging shrew who never had a kind word for anyone. Faye apparently had an older brother in Brassmont who did well enough for himself. Hugh liked Yorkshire pudding, though that was observable when he ordered it.

Faye continued ignoring the unspoken rule, however. "Affairs, eh? Was she pretty?"

All eyes fell on him now, even the usually indifferent Raffles, and Truitt found himself scrambling for a deflection. "If you are suggesting my time was spent in the company of a lady, then you are up the pole without your pants." After a beat, he added, "Or, as you are normally absent of pants, without your bloomers."

The faroko tapped the side of her nose with a grin. "I never said a lady."

Raffles looked at her with surprise. "You think 'e's got a Greek lover?"

Kate's eyebrows went up at his interpretation. "She means he is joining giblets with a woman of lesser breeding. Like me."

Truitt tutted. "Kate, you are always a lady in my eyes, without the affliction of actually being one."

"Thank you. I think."

"It's that towerin' tootsie!" Faye burst out gleefully. "She's got you beggin' for her bubbies."

That brought forth a snicker from Raffles. "What would Stilts see in 'is lordship? Nothing but a stub in comparison. Stilts and Stubs."

"Precisely!" Truitt's agreement may have been too enthusiastic, but he needed to move off the topic as quickly as possible. Not only did Calista now belong to the private life he wished to keep separate, he feared they might make a connection between her, the female arrested, and his sudden departure that night. "It would be the height of absurdity — pardon the pun — to believe such a woman would have anything to do with the likes of me. So, if Kate will kindly fulfil my request, perhaps we can get on with the business at hand. Gambling."

Chapter 38

The Pheasant Revisitation
Or Exposed

P EG PULLED A string of flesh from the roast pheasant
and popped it into her mouth. Her lips spread into a
smile as she chewed the sweet meat, then swallowed.
"I cannot believe this constituted only one course!"

The skember mechanician sat at the bar of the Happy Swallow, her usual suspenders, black trousers, and tool belt replaced by a corset and dress. It marked the first time Calista, seated next to her, had seen her in anything resembling a feminine outfit and thought it suited her.

Behind the bar, Armend, also dressed in formal attire, stood on his platform while Silas, who always wore fashionable clothing, sat on a thicker stool built for his girth. Between them all, laid out on a cutting board, rested the remains of the pheasant from the Duke's dinner the night before for each of them to enjoy.

"It's true." Calista waved a half-eaten drumstick enthusiastically. "There were six others, though I'd rather not remember the first. Raw oysters!"

"What is wrong with them? I have had them a few times. Quite a delicacy."

"But they are alive when you eat them!" the faroko protested. Just talking about them started her stomach flopping. Part of her imagined the one she had eaten was still in there, dining on the meat she sent its way.

Peg rocked on her stool. "So fresh and briny! Delicious."

"There are some who believe raw oysters have aphrodisiac qualities," Armend added, picking off another piece of fowl. "Could be quite helpful in an amorous situation."

"Ooh! I definitely must have oysters more often!" Peg laughed. "What about pheasant? Any toe-curling effects from eating it?"

Calista couldn't tell if Armend meant the comment for her. The bartender frequently showed insight, grasping a broader perspective with minimal evidence. *Did he know about Truitt?* "You have someone in mind you wish to test it with?"

Peg blushed, her cheeks turning a light shade of pink. "Not immediately, but I believe it is good to be knowledgeable of these things. Just in case.

Silas swallowed a bit of meat. "So it's over? The Grey Shadow's reign is at an end?"

"It appears so. My sources confirm it." Armend nodded to where he kept his ledger of jobs along with documentation of other information his Listeners brought him. "The police raided White Cliffs Estate last night, arresting the Duke and what was left of his minions, as Calista related."

She had recounted much of the story to them, leaving out her interlude with Truitt and minimising his part in it. She told herself she needed to protect his identity. In truth, she still revelled in the relationship and wasn't ready to share him yet.

Once clear of the rich neighbourhood, she had taken her time to cross back along various roads. Until the police were convinced they caught the true criminal, she didn't want to risk getting stopped. With her height, her staff, the bundle of clothes under her arm, and the large hunk of bird meat wrapped in paper clutched to her chest, she made an obvious spectacle.

"You were fortunate his gun only injured him when it backfired. Electricity can be highly unpredictable." Peg took another piece of pheasant. "Did you notice how it was generated? Like a Phlogiston Reservoir or a Tesla coil? Did it have a crystal or a crank?"

Calista stared at her blankly, not understanding a word of her question. "I honestly could not tell you. I was too concerned with it being pointed at us."

Armend's finger grazed his chin. "Hmmm. That is a remarkable coincidence that the same individual you rescued a few nights ago was also a prisoner of the Duke. Do you know his place in this affair?"

He must suspect something! "Not really. It was the Duke's men who grabbed him the first time, perhaps thinking him some sort of threat." She shifted on her stool, eager to change the subject. "I want to express my gratitude once more for your readiness to come to my aid in case I didn't return by this morning. Having the support of friends means a lot." Her lips, shining with rich roast pheasant residue, parted in a smile. "I also enjoy seeing each of you in your finest attire."

Silas tapped the rim of his spectacles. "It is the only way to storm a manor, Ma'am."

"I did not realise there were rules to such an undertaking," she teased before turning her attention to the mechanician. "Peg, what do you know about mechanical animals?"

"As in iron horses?"

"As in rats made of gears."

Peg fixed her with a puzzled stare. "Why? Do you want one?"

Calista shook her head. "I have one. There was an artificial rat at the Duke's manor. It worked briefly, then stopped."

"Clangers! That sounds brilliant. Mind if I have a look at it? I might be able to repair it."

"I hoped you would. I can bring it around to your workshop in the gymnasium this afternoon, now that I am no longer pursued by the police."

"So you have been pardoned?" Silas asked.

Calista's expression darkened. "Well, no. Not officially. But it would be hard for them to arrest me as the Shadow when they've already caught the real one."

"And I imagine they would prefer to put the entire ordeal behind them," Armend added. "They will have the praise of Brassmont and every other city who fell victim to his thievery, and hopefully not want to advertise the false confinement. Or escape."

Hopefully. "Now I can resume my normal assignment-taking. Well, tomorrow. After a good night's sleep. Peg, tell Fenton it may be a few days before I return for training, however. I got enough of a workout last night to hold me for a week!"

The mechanician nodded as she gouged out another strip of bird flesh. "I will convey that message, along with a portion of this pheasant. I will also talk to my seamstress about replacing those buttons. While I am glad they came in handy, no woman with your assets should be seen in public with that deep a neckline."

Calista looked down at herself and saw her chest from neck to corset top laid bare. After Truitt thrust his hands into the plush cleavage, she had forgotten how much remained exposed. "Certainly not in public," she agreed, then blushed, realising she had been leaning on her stool the whole time, eating pheasant with the two men. A greasy hand hastily moved to cover the area. "My apologies. I didn't mean to offend anyone."

"A woman's beauty can never offend a gentleman," Armend said, as if reciting another quote. "Her aroma may, however. I suggest you visit your favourite bathhouse and change into something more modest."

"Are you suggesting *I* have a foul smell?" Her hands went to her hips as she looked first at him, then at Silas, who promptly averted his gaze. "Dagnabit!" she swore, quickly covering her exposed chest again.

"Not foul," Armend corrected, ignoring the impromptu flashing. "Merely one ripe with personality."

Calista twisted her head and sniffed her shoulder. She winced as a repugnant odour pricked her nose. "Perhaps you are right. I will retrieve a fresh set of clothes from my room and take myself to Get Wet immediately." The faroko turned on the stool, then swung herself back, remembering the bit of money she still carried in her pockets wouldn't be enough for the service. "May I borrow a few coins?"

Chapter 39

The Partnership Proposition
Or Admiring The Plumbing

TRUITT DRAPED THE collar of his robe over a hook on the wall and shoved his drawers to the floor, leaving himself fully naked, except for the ring. He remained exposed only for a moment, as he lowered himself into the steaming bath he had just drawn. The hot water covered him up to his shoulders, turning his skin pink and soaking his excessive body hair. His cuts stung at first, but the heat soothed them as well.

Tubs like his were uncommon, at least for the lower classes. He had deliberately sought a larger, clawfoot version, regardless of the prohibitive cost. Similar to the water heater, he desired a certain degree of luxury, despite taking on the guise of an underprivileged worker. However, he wasn't so wealthy as to afford the most expensive and had to settle for a copper bath instead of cast iron. Of course, weight also needed to be considered, being on the second level of an older townhouse. But he told himself that if he possessed the funds, he would have found a way to overcome that limitation as well.

Truitt stayed at the Right Hand until early evening, then took his leave, claiming business elsewhere. Faye asked if he intended to rendezvous with his clandestine lover, and he provided an honest response: he had squandered all his money gambling with the trio and lacked the means to place any further bets.

He still kept enough to give Lavinia a few coins and pick up a light supper on his way home, and once that was gone, he decided he needed a soaking. The adrenaline from last night's escapades had left his body hours ago, leaving behind the aches and stink of his time in captivity.

On what activity to pursue after that, he remained undecided. His muscles were putting up a good argument for calling it a night and crawling into bed. Most of his brain echoed the sentiment, having received enough stimulus recently to last a month. The section of his mind that controlled his avarice and need for adventure — nearly double the size of the other parts — strongly advocated for an evening on the town. With the Grey Shadow firmly behind bars, the affluent of Gravenmore would be breathing a collective sigh as they let their guard down. The timing couldn't be better.

Soft footsteps beyond the room interrupted his planning. *Some bounder is in my flat, and coming this way!* He tensed, unsure whether to leap from the tub and grab his robe, or simply face his opponent in the altogether.

When he finally decided to remain in the bath and splash anyone who came near, the knob turned, and the door swung inward. He cupped his hand, ready to send water flying, when a curly-haired head appeared in the opening.

"Oh, it's you," Truitt said, letting his body relax again.

"Such a warm welcome," Calista noted. "Who did you think it was?"

"Considering I've been abducted twice this week, I feared it might be a third attempt. A rude individual broke my lock, you see, and I haven't found the time to get it repaired."

"Do I look like an orv?" she asked, stepping into the room and closing the door behind her. As she approached him, her eyes wandered to the depths of the tub.

"Not with those ears and that chest cleft. The posterior, however..."

"...is magnificent and blessed," she finished for him. "Those were your words."

"Voiced under duress." He sighed but made no attempt to hide from her gaze. "You again have me at a disadvantage, as I entered this bath only moments ago and do not intend to exit it until the stink of the last few days has been washed away. If you wish to stay, you will have to endure my upper nakedness."

"I think I can handle it." The towering faroko crouched, settling into a short chair. It creaked under her weight, but remained intact. Her gaze drifted over the copper vessel to the heater bubbling quietly in the corner. "It's quite lovely to have your own private tub. I have to rely on the communal bathhouse."

The berkis saw the chair, built for someone half the woman's size, nearly vanish beneath her. Arousal stirred under the water. "Surely you did not make the journey here to discuss my plumbing."

She returned her attention to him. "Not only. I came with a proposal."

Truitt stiffened, and not in the way he preferred. "I believe you are skipping over some of the finer points of courtship." A glistening, soaked hand broke through the surface of the bath as he began ticking them off his fingers. "Correspondence, where we send saccharine-laced letters to each other from afar detailing our feelings. Formal visits where I would invite you into my home, though you have made that superfluous. Exchanges of gifts and tokens of affection, so when the other is absent, one may fondle an object as a replacement. Attending social gatherings where we can interact under supervision and be socially accepted. Then the proper inquiry into a more permanent arrangement, by the man. Not the woman."

Calista stared at him a moment, her expression unreadable, before correcting him. "A business proposal. A little fun in a rich man's house before defeating a deadly enemy and conjuring a mystical dragon does not a marriage make."

The hand vanished under the water again. "I've known worse. What is your offer?"

She drew in a breath. "When I took the job for Lady Aetherborne to guard the gem, I dreamed of getting my own manor with the pay. I've been scrounging since I moved to Gravenmore and imagined money would be the solution to being happy."

Many do. Born into wealth, Truitt understood that possessing money didn't guarantee happiness, but he allowed her to proceed without interruption.

"When I saw all those expensive items the Duke had stolen and recognised the importance some place upon them, I realised that wasn't a path to contentment. Not for me."

Perhaps we aren't so dissimilar. Except she didn't become a thief. Not yet.

Calista paused to glance at the ceiling, as if sounding the words in her head before speaking them. "I want to help people. Do something with my life that brings peace, if not happiness, to others, rather than seeking only my own interests." She drew in another breath. "And I can't get the orphans out of my mind."

Truitt frowned. He had understood her confession until now. "What orphans?"

"The job I took before the one where I re... where I met you involved catching the thieves plaguing a bakery. They turned out to be a trio of orphans, stealing because they were starving. The owner had them arrested, and they were sent to Etheridge."

He nodded, his mind going to Lavinia. While not an orphan, he tried to help the young orv and her mother when he could to prevent her from facing such a fate. "You wish you could do more to assist them."

"Exactly." Her expression brightened a little. "I let them down. I don't want to let anyone down again."

Like Persephone. "Then you will be forever poor. Those in need do not possess the means to reward you. That is why they are in need."

Calista's lips tightened. "Armend said something similar."

A wave of heat not caused by the steaming water rose in the berkis's face. "Who is that? A lover?"

"Hardly," she laughed. "He is my friend who owns the Happy Swallow, the pub where I live."

"You envy my little flat when you reside in a house of drink? Perhaps I have made a mistake in choosing my location."

"It isn't like that. Armend won the place in a card game, and the original owners tried to renege on the deal. They sent me to convince him not to pursue the claim. Instead, I convinced them to honour their bet."

Truitt gave another knowing nod. "Now he keeps you on as an enforcer, to do his bidding. Very shrewd."

The tiny chair creaked as Calista sat back. "Do you always look for the worst in everyone?"

She is still so naïve. "Not everyone, my dear. But it is usually what I find."

"Then you need to change that view. Armend was one of the first people I truly helped. I made a difference in his life, and he in mine. I like that feeling."

"That is a rarity," he told her. "You are fortunate."

"Don't hand me that guff." She jabbed a finger in his direction. "You risked your neck to find justice for Persephone. Now that you succeeded, don't you feel some satisfaction? Some happiness in doing what is right?"

"I find solace in knowing that fiend will spend the remainder of his days within prison walls before finally meeting a decisive conclusion by the end of the hangman's noose."

"Only solace?"

Truitt considered the joy of last night and excitement this morning. The capture of the Shadow indeed pleased him, far more than he expected. Almost as much as stealing. "Very well. It felt euphoric. More restorative than any rest or food."

Calista slapped her knee. "I knew it! That is why I have been trying to change which jobs I select. I want to make a difference in other people's lives."

"You definitely made a difference in the Duke's."

"With your help." Her expression grew contemplative. "We could be partners. In something other than sex, I mean."

Truitt's countenance became thoughtful as he pondered the proposal. *It had felt good. And it would give me more time around her, which is not too bad of a bargain. Except...* "I lack your fighting abilities."

"And I can't break into rich people's houses with your finesse. See? We complement each other."

"I am unsure if that is a compliment. How often would we be entering such places, invited or otherwise? You could simply force your way in."

She leaned forward, looking him directly in the eyes. "You are being difficult. We work well as a team, and I believe we could do a lot of good."

He had seen that, too. "Perhaps."

"But we'll need to establish some rules," she continued. "We got caught by the Duke when we messed around. While enjoyable, we can't get distracted by each other's assets, however tempting." Her gaze wandered down his wet, bare chest, momentarily seeking what lay in the depths of the bath.

Truitt felt what she sought stirring, sending a ripple to the surface. The memory of their last intimate encounter brought it to full attention, and his brain struggled to stay on topic. "We would have to smooth out a few details," he told her, willing his voice not to crack.

"Such as?"

"Finances. Living arrangements."

Calista's eyebrows jumped. "You want to live together?"

"That is something which needs to be discussed. My quarters here are quite satisfactory, but I am not opposed to spending at least part of my time in a pub."

She grinned. "We will need a name as well. For our services. Like 'The Protectors'."

Truitt brought his hands from under the surface and grabbed the sides of the tub, splashing a bit of water on the floor. "That has the connotations of a street gang. Or bodyguards, and I have no intention of protecting anyone's body except my own. And yours, on occasion."

"How noble of you. What's your last name, again?"

Truitt tensed. "Williams," he lied. "Why?"

Calista tapped her chin. "Temira and Williams. How's that?"

"That has all the hallmarks of a law firm, complete with the promise of overcharging and underserving," he said, his face twisting into a scowl. "Besides, why does your name have top billing?"

"Because 'Williams and Temira' sounds like a clothing shop."

"Agreed. Let's find something less business-sounding." The earlier words of his skember associate suddenly popped into his head. "Raffles referred to us as 'Stilts and Stubs'."

"You told him about us?" she asked.

"Tarnation, no! Your name never even arose in the conversation. They have no idea of my involvement in any of this, and I intend to maintain that status. Faye, however, is a hopeless gossip and romantic. She thinks I've been away so much because of you."

"She isn't wholly wrong in that conclusion." Despite Calista's intent to head to the bathhouse, when she returned to her room in the pub to retrieve a fresh change of clothes, she had stretched out for a few minutes on her bed and quickly fell asleep. She awoke shortly before sunset and changed her plans. "Then let's not prove her a liar. I didn't come here just with the proposal." She stood, the chair giving a creak of relief. "Like you, I am also in need of a soaking." Her fingers moved to her corset, and she began unhitching the clasps. "And we have other unfinished... business."

Truitt watched, eyes wide and mouth open, as she stripped, dropping each item gingerly on the floor, until she stood towering over the tub, devoid of all covering. He continued staring as she elegantly lifted a lengthy leg over the tub's edge and let it extend to the bottom. When she did the same with the other, he found himself looking almost straight up at her divine form from knee level.

While not an academic, he had studied some of the classics. She possessed all the qualities he imagined an ancient goddess might embody. Except she was real, and in his flat.

And had a tail, which lashed around and splashed bath water into his face. "You don't mind, do you?" she asked.

Truitt regained enough of his composure and breath to respond. "I will not protest. But this tub is not designed to hold more than a single occupant."

Calista crouched in the water, placing a hand on either side of the tub as she leaned toward him. His arousal spiked, and he felt himself getting hard as her breasts hung a mere few inches from his face. "Then we will have to get real cosy," she whispered.

He gulped.

Chapter 40

The Bathing Reciprocation
Or Getting Wet

T HE FAROKO'S SMILE widened at his discomfort. She shifted forward slightly, letting her cleavage stroke his cheeks. After another moment, she lowered her torso until their faces met.

Her lips found his. The kiss brought a blissful interlude of tenderness, and the tension drained from Truitt. He moved a hand up to caress her, but to his disappointment, she pulled back. "Not yet," she murmured as their eyes locked again. "We have some cleaning up to do."

He watched her snatch the washcloth from its place beside the tub and plunge it into the water. She rubbed it briefly against his chest, eliciting a slight moan from him. When it reappeared above the surface, saturated with the warm liquid, she pushed it toward him.

"Seeing as how I am a guest in your fine tub, I will let you do the honour," she told him, the grin returning. "Wash me."

Truitt couldn't believe her request. When they first met, he wondered what it might be like to get his hands on her 'coker-nuts', as he crudely described them. In that same basin, he had considered how he could examine them without a stepping stool. Now, they were being shoved into his face, with orders to not just look at them, but to polish them clean.

He restrained his enthusiasm, however, taking the washcloth carefully from her. "I shall do as you ask. Though only out of proper etiquette."

"I'm sure," she said, arching her back to present a broader workspace.

He brought the wet fabric up gingerly, giving her protruding right breast a gentle brush. When Calista clicked her tongue in frustration, he applied a little more pressure while widening his stroke. Hearing a slight moan from the female, he increased his efforts.

Soon, he had scrubbed every supple inch of it, even granting the stiffening nipple a detailed going over. He refreshed the washcloth in warm water before vigorously attacking the left breast. After the admonishment she had given him for not paying enough consideration to both arse cheeks two days before, he didn't want her to think him neglectful now. As an extra precaution, he used his free hand to keep the freshly cleaned breast occupied.

All this attention brought Calista slowly to arousal. When she demanded he wash her, she hadn't expected him to do so thorough a job or for it to be so stimulating! Needing to participate more, she ducked her head down and caught his mouth in a kiss.

She anticipated he would slow his ministrations, but his kneading grew more intense. So did his kissing and her desire. While one hand held the side of the tub, her other snaked into the water and slid around his waist, lifting him slightly from the bottom. In response, he brought the washcloth up to her shoulder, then her neck, caressing her skin more than washing. Far too gradual for her liking, he glided it along her cheek, then upwards toward her ear.

"Lower," she ordered, breaking off their kiss momentarily to purr the command. In the manor, they had been in a rush, fearful of being discovered. Now, she wanted to draw out their passion as long as she could.

As their lips joined again, Truitt did his best to obey, sliding the wet cloth back down over her chest, then continuing on to her belly. In their position — mouths engaged and him still fondling her breast — he couldn't reach very far. His erect member, bobbing beneath the water and her taut stomach, was more likely to touch the region than him.

Realising the limitation, Calista moved her hand down to his. She caressed his fingers before gently taking the washcloth from his clutch. After breaking their kiss again and pulling her head back, she began to stroke his face with the fabric. Her powerful digits brushed along his cheek and chin before moving to his ear. With their heads only a handspan apart, all that filled their vision was the other person's eyes — his blue a sky to her earthy brown.

Both grew still, lost in the secret world which formed between them. His hand paused its fondling, and her's its stroking. Even the regular in-and-out of their breathing slowed to almost stillness, as if not daring to disturb the moment.

Then their mouths met again, their tongues entangled in a way their bodies had not yet. It hadn't been a conscious choice, but neither acted based on thought now. Desire set their movements on automatic.

Truitt renewed his kneading with relish, employing both hands in the hefty undertaking. Calista dropped the washcloth at his hip as she ran her fingers over his belly. Then her attention shifted lower, and she grabbed the eager erection, letting its thick firmness fill her grip.

The action sent a surge through the berkis. He involuntarily pushed himself upward, breaking their kiss and planting his rear firmly on the tub's bottom.

Calista giggled. "Oops. Too much coal in your furnace?" she teased. She hadn't let go, however, and when she saw him struggling to answer, she laughed again. "Let's swap positions."

She released him as she dropped her posterior onto the other end of the copper vessel. Truitt bent his legs and tucked in his feet just in time to avoid having them squashed. "I do not believe there is sufficient space for this," he began when his voice returned. "We should — "

He hastily stood when her lower torso jutted toward him. The tub lay only a little longer than the berkis, which more than sufficed for him. It would serve Calista if she only sat in it and let her legs stretch the length. The Amazonian faroko, however, liked to recline during her soaking time. That meant her limbs needed to reside elsewhere now.

Fortunately for Truitt, she chose to extend them over the sides, letting her calves rest along the top on either side of him. In this position, Calista's arms lay along the copper sides at the opposite end, with her shoulders, head, and neck exposed. The water level threatened to overflow the container with her extra mass, but it covered just over half of her body, with her posterior sitting in the middle. Her expressive tail pressed against her back, its tip emerging behind flowing curls.

From the berkis's point of view, that left him hemmed in by sturdy thigh leading down to a mesh of black hair before rising again to her twin orbs peeking above the surface. She couldn't have been more inviting if she'd wrapped a red bow around her waist and sent him an engraved invitation.

As he often did when confronted by excessive amounts of her naked flesh, Truitt struggled to find the right reaction. Part of him wanted to scold her sternly for disrupting his bath. The other part — currently controlled by his hardened penis as it hung perpendicular to his body — longed to slide down her thigh and lose himself in her submerged cave of wonders.

"Well?" she asked when she saw him staring into the water. Again, she hadn't planned to have him serving as her personal attendant, but if he wished to get his hands on her as much as she desired to explore every hairy scrap of his body, she figured he'd enjoy it. Even if his face showed confusion, the bit of his anatomy that controlled his brain the most appeared fit to burst at the chance. That was for later, though.

Besides, he did such a fine job of it. "You haven't yet taken care of my lower torso. I suggest you start with my toes and work your way up." Her smirk widened. "Or down."

That brought him out of his stupor, or at least clarified what his next move should be. He stared down near his own legs until he spotted the sunken washcloth. Picking it up, however, proved more difficult, as he needed to reach around his aroused member when it refused to bend with him. He ignored Calista's snicker at his predicament, turning instead to her left foot. She wiggled her toes invitingly, drawing a slight smile from his lips, and soon he was working the soaked fabric over the digits.

He approached the task with the same diligence he had with her breasts; before long, both sets of toes, their attached feet, and the span of muscular limb up to her knees were scrubbed to a healthy pink. When it came time to move on to her thighs, he glanced at her for confirmation. The expression of pleasure she wore — head reclined, eyes closed, lips curled — made it clear she wanted him to proceed.

He did. The horny berkis remained acutely aware of how much each stroke along her outer leg brought him closer to the posterior he regarded as magnificent. How every time he ran the washcloth down her inner thigh, he neared her crotch. He'd once wished to trot down that Petticoat Lane, and he had come close a few times. Now that he not only received permission but knew she expected him to engage with it, he found himself uncommonly nervous.

Still, he scrubbed away at her lengthy limbs until the only section left untouched below her waist was her muff. Calista stayed quiet, though her breathing had grown rapid. The steady rise and fall of her chest sent slight ripples across the surface of the water.

Taking a deep breath of his own, Truitt gripped the washcloth in both hands and dropped to his knees. At this level, the liquid rose over his chest. He tensed, then reached out to one thigh. It seemed wrong to breach the sensitive nether region without some warning. He dragged his fingers leisurely down the thick flesh until he came to her middle.

Calista gasped as she felt his digits trace the edge of her sex. They probed hesitantly, then plunged. Her head snapped up at the sudden thrust and a moan escaped her lips. She gripped the sides of the tub tightly as the berkis continued his examination. Despite his small fingers, they seemed to find all the most sensitive spots. The desire she'd experienced before with their kissing rushed back tenfold, spreading outward from his searching touch.

All thoughts of cleaning fled Truitt's mind. His new task — his new pleasure — was seeing how far he could push the female faroko. He only peripherally noticed her intensifying moans and whimpers, along with the trembling of her arms on either side of him.

He wanted to hear her scream.

One set of fingers didn't seem adequate, however, and he moved his second in to help, the washcloth abandoned. He found the particular bit inside he required, but it still wasn't enough. Like her, he hadn't planned for this scenario, but now, in the thick of it, he needed to go deeper.

Calista cried out when he thrust in his entire right hand. The surprise and arousal caused her to buck her hips upward, increasing the sensation. After another loud gasp, her rear slammed back to the bottom, and she instinctively lunged forward.

Her reaching hands took hold of Truitt's head, the only part of him still above water as he strained to pleasure her. She shoved him under in a reactive attempt to have him repeat the gesture.

It produced the opposite effect. As his face was pushed into her belly, he hastily extracted his hands and thrust them against her hips, desperately trying to reach the surface again and breathe.

"Oh, my!" Calista's senses abruptly returned, and she realised she was drowning him in her passion. His head popped back up when she let it go. "I'm so sorry!" she told him as he sputtered and shook the water from his hair. "I didn't mean to dunk you!"

Truitt took in a few lungfuls of air before answering. "It seems you believe in reciprocity, though I did attempt to warn you."

Her expression crinkled in confusion. "I don't understand."

"You made me wet after I did the same to you."

Calista laughed, some of the guilt easing from her mind. She moved her grip to under his shoulder and pulled him forward. His drenched form slid easily over her slick belly until they were eye to eye again. "Then let me make it up to you," she said gently. Her right hand slipped over his backside to hold him in place while her left recovered the washcloth from between her legs. "It was quite rude of me to interrupt your bath time. And since you did such a fine job washing me, I believe I should return the favour."

Finding himself just inches from her delicate face again, Truitt offered no reason to deter her from the task. He found himself smitten anew as his gaze swept over her plump lips, strong nose, and chocolate eyes. Having his chest buoyed by her firm breasts and her palm pleasantly cupping his arse cheek only added to his enjoyment of their positions. Even his stiff member nestled comfortably in the curve of her belly. "Reciprocation is an excellent policy," he agreed.

She smiled, knowing he wouldn't disagree. Her hand guided the damp cloth over his back, moving it in long, gentle strokes. Again, his fitness surprised her as she probed the muscles along his shoulders. "I never realised being a thief would build up such strength," she half-teased as her fingers squeezed his arm.

"I never realised being a fighter would build up such curves," he replied, bringing a hand up to caress her right breast. "The safest means of entering an abode not your own is usually through an upper floor. Reaching that level requires a certain fitness."

"I can imagine," she cooed, running her fingers down to his spine, then quickly tracing it over his bottom before stroking his thigh. "Sturdy legs, too."

Truitt wasn't sure how he felt about her assessing his various parts. He hadn't thought anything wrong when he observed the enormity of her posterior or the plumpness of her breasts. While he appreciated the attention, he couldn't help but think she was mocking him. "All the better for climbing, my dear."

"I would like to see that." She continued her ministrations to his legs, swapping the washcloth — and buttock — between her hands so she could tend to his other side. Truitt accepted the shift with a small grunt, momentarily thrusting into her stomach. "Be patient," she whispered with a smile. "We'll take care of that bit of anatomy shortly."

The berkis opened his mouth to speak, but her lips interjected. Both Calista's palms gripped his rear as she slid him further up her body, allowing for a deeper kiss. His protest forgotten, Truitt gave into the buss.

After several blissful seconds, however, he pulled away. When she searched his expression for a reason, he shook his head. "As much as I am enjoying our respective positions," — he ran his fingers down her side — "the water is growing cold. While you may enjoy the occasional frigid plunge, I prefer the comfort of a warmer environment."

Calista noticed the liquid had cooled significantly, too, though she wasn't prepared to end their engagement. "Would a drier setting, such as a bed, perhaps be more to your liking?" she asked, hoping his suggestion implied a change, not a termination.

It was. "I believe that would be a suitable option, yes," he told her. Despite their agreement, neither moved. Instead, their eyes shifted down the length of the other's naked form. Truitt's fingers reached for one of the breasts he lay upon while Calista slid a hand between her belly and his waist, seeking the part of his anatomy as yet unhandled.

Then abruptly, the faroko changed her mind. "We aren't done here, though. I still need my backside scrubbed. Considering how well you and it get along, I am sure you won't be opposed to one more cleansing."

Before he could say no, she gently lifted him off her, sliding him leisurely down her again until could stand on his own. He backed the rest of the way up as she sat up and brought her legs in. For the second time that evening, he found himself staring up at her nude form as she stood. Glistening drops of water flowed down her skin before rejoining the bath below. The level dropped significantly to almost half with her absence.

The view proved fleeting, however, as she turned in place and lowered into a crouch. Her tail flicked about briefly before resting its tip on the tub's bottom. She gripped the sides to steady herself, then looked over her shoulder at the stunned berkis behind her. "I'm ready."

Truitt felt his member spring up. He faced a strong but sexy back, taller and wider than himself, that flowed down into the broad posterior he admired so much. She was right in that observation, and now he had the chance to revisit it in a less oppressive setting. He could enjoy it without the rest of her body pressing down on him. After he retrieved the washcloth — once again tricky with his excited truncheon — he applied it to her waist.

While not as stimulating as him stroking her chest or thighs, Calista giggled as he alternated between scrubbing her back and fondling her arse cheeks. He was a paradox of playing the thoughtful gentleman, seeking permission for access to her body one moment, and the next, eagerly putting his fingers on every bit of her anatomy he could reach. After everything they had been through in the past week, she appreciated the first but wanted the second.

The water had turned cold, though, and if he wished to play, she would accommodate him. "Watch yourself!" she called as she abruptly stood up. The arse cheek Truitt had been reaching for suddenly rose above his line of sight. Just as quickly, she spun again, and now he faced her muff. Like when they first met, it acted as a stark reminder of their difference in height.

And as when they met, he found it wholly seductive.

The heady perfume of her arousal struck his nose. He wasn't the only one turned on by their situation. What lay at the bottom of the tub before now hovered just inches from his face, and he longed to continue his exploration.

Calista had other plans, though, as she crouched, bringing them nearly eye level. She wrapped her arms around him and tugged him close into a crushing hug.

"Bath time's over," she told him, then rose again, lifting him with her. The wet skin, which acted like a slippery slope in the water, now formed a seal between them. Their body heat intermingled as she stepped out of the tub and onto the floor of his lavatory. She giggled when she saw the look of awe on his face. "Time to dry off. I hope you have more towels."

He knew her strength, but found himself repeatedly awed whenever she displayed it. Still, he tried to ignore the deep line of cleavage caused by her breasts pressing against his chest, the oversized hand which shifted to his arse, and the three-foot drop beneath his dangling feet. "The rack behind the door," he instructed her. "Though I have none matching your stature."

"No one does," she beamed. For the first time, the fact brought her pride, not shame. Compared to the berkis in her arms, her height seemed even more imposing. But while he made the occasional comment about the expansiveness of her posterior, it didn't appear to bother him. On the contrary, by the feel of his erect penis against her stomach, he enjoyed it.

She bent at the hips and lowered Truitt to the floor before moving to the described location and retrieving two more towels. He had already grabbed the one he'd set out before and wrapped it around himself, though his member jutted out in front.

Calista rubbed the cloth vigorously along her elongated ears and through her tresses, sending droplets of water everywhere. Her natural curls always took a while to dry, so she didn't spend a lot of time on them now. She looked instead to the soaked berkis.

With a considerable amount of their body covered in one-inch long hair, his kind needed to work harder than hers to dry off. When she first saw him nude, she hadn't considered how much time he might have spent patting himself down before her arrival. She wondered if all the towels in the flat would be enough to remove the moisture from his slight form.

She immediately dropped to one knee and wrapped her other towel around him. After a few minutes of energetic rubbing, Calista felt he could move comfortably without dripping too much about the quarters.

Truitt, however, didn't want her to stop. He hadn't thought they could be more intimate than their earlier embraces and found himself aroused on a whole other level. Her hands had gone everywhere, probing and massaging his body in ways he had never been touched. Even his throbbing truncheon enjoyed her attention, though briefly. He had been hard since she entered the room, and he believed she was trying to keep him that way, without release, until she said so.

"That's the best I can do for now," she told him, pulling the towel away and leaving him exposed. He had dropped his own when it became apparent she would be handling the drying. From the look on his face during the process, she knew she was rubbing in all the right spots. He looked nearly orgasmic when she stroked his chest hair. "My turn."

The huge female stood and began tackling the water still clinging to her body with one cloth. She dropped the other onto his head. "I'll take care of the top. You get the bottom."

Chapter 41

The Final Consolidation
Or Taking It All In

TRUITT PULLED THE towel off his head, preparing a retort to what he thought was her teasing him again. He quickly realised from her actions to wipe down only her upper torso that it was more an order than a jest and got to work.

The same legs, feet, and toes he had scrubbed in the water now required an equally thorough but gentler going over. He found it involved much more stretching and bending with Calista extended to her full height. Never one to back down from a challenge, though, he soon had every drop of moisture from her thighs to her soles patted dry.

Above him, the faroko finished wiping herself down, too. When she saw him eyeing her groyne again, she spun around. "I'll take care of that, for now. You tend to my magnificent and blessed posterior."

Truitt blushed. She was never going to stop reminding him of his words. The change in venue wasn't too disappointing, though. He ran his fingers tentatively over the right cheek to better gauge the task. While Calista could cup one of his easily in a single hand, he needed both palms just to cover the expanse. Had it grown since the spanking a few days ago? His mind boggled at the idea.

Seeing her arm come down on her front to dry the other side, the berkis brought his towel into play. After a few blissful minutes of rubbing — accompanied by a few furtive squeezes — he dropped his hands and admired his work.

Calista had to bite her tongue while he attended to her backside, his gentleness now the complete opposite of when he spanked it. Despite his combative nature, he could show great tenderness when he needed to. And did he just kiss her buttock?

She took a step and turned halfway to look down at him. "As this is the first time I have partaken of your bathing services, I must say it has been thoroughly enjoyable."

Truitt knew it had been far more than that for both, but only nodded his head. "We do our best to pleasure our clients. I mean *please*." His eyes followed her tail as it swayed near her naked thigh, the light fur adorning it still dark with moisture. "If I may, you there is one last item which needs my attention."

Seeing him reach for the appendage, Calista turned again so he could access its entire length. A slight purr escaped her lips as his delicate fingers traced along it, applying just enough pressure to squeeze out the remaining water. No one had ever handled her tail before, and she hadn't realised how starved for attention it was.

Suddenly, his grip changed as he gave it a tug. She turned her head to see him stepping toward the bedroom, her tail clasped between his fingers. His pull didn't hurt, but she shifted sideways to give it more play, anyway. "Where are you taking that?" she asked through smiling lips.

He didn't answer. Apparently, Truitt was accepting her offer to move their antics to the bed and not giving her the option to decide differently. The berkis who appeared unsure of her joining his bath now had no qualms about her joining him in the drier accommodations.

So she walked backwards, letting him lead her through the doorway into the larger bedroom. He continued tugging her along as he scrambled onto the cushioned sleeping platform. Only when her calves came up against its edge, forcing her to stop, did he release her tail.

When she turned, she saw Truitt standing in the middle of the bed, hands on his hips, a grin on his face. His member had relaxed in the short march between chambers, but began to stiffen again as she fixed him with her own smile. "Proud of yourself? You dragged me to your secret lair I would have never found on my own," she teased.

"I have returned you to the scene of the crime," he corrected, waving a hand to indicate the surrounding room. "You might no longer be wanted by the police, but you must still answer for your assault on my personage that morning."

Calista adopted a similarly serious pose, crossing her arms over her chest and jutting her hip to one side. "Is that a very long-winded way of saying I am wanted by *you*?" she asked, raising an eyebrow in mock skepticism. "And here I was, thinking you wished to demonstrate your climbing skills."

"Bah. This bed is no challenge to get upon."

"I meant me." She dropped her arms and straightened. "How high do you think you'd get? There are a few well-placed handholds, but the surface is a bit slick."

Truitt's mouth fell open, her suggestion again rendering him dumbfounded. Calista laughed, then lunged forward, taking the opportunity to snatch him up. The berkis yelped as she spun him and herself, then grunted when she dropped into a sitting position and he landed on her lap. He reached out instinctively for something to steady himself, wrapping his fingers around the tip of her left breast.

"Look at that!" Calista cried out. "He found one of the spots already! He doesn't seem to be climbing, though part of him is getting a rise." When Truitt shifted the errant hand to cover the growing member she referred to, she moved her own hand to block it. "That staff of yours has been searching for a place to nest all night. Let's see if we can make it comfortable."

"Wait." He struggled to stand, but after some assistance from the faroko, he faced her properly. Her legs extended to each side, as they had in the alley, with his feet a few inches from her madge. He did his best to ignore both temptations as he looked down into her eyes. "While this evening has been one of the most pleasurable for me in a longer time than I care to admit, there appears to be some confusion I wish to clear up."

Calista's smile faded. Had she misread their relationship? Everything pointed to him enjoying their playful romp and sexual interludes, especially the bit of anatomy currently pointing at her. While their association had started as more of a battle, she thought they had established a lasting peace treaty. His tone and words, however, said something different.

Her heart ached. She entered his flat that evening, hoping she had found a partner in both business and love. Had she pushed things too soon? "I am listening," she told him, though in truth she fought the urge to shut her ears to whatever admonishment he had for her.

"Contrary to appearances, I am *not* your sex toy. Nor am I your servant. If we are to proceed forward in any capacity, it must be understood we are equal partners, despite any anatomical differences."

He still wanted a partnership! She realised what he had meant about their having to work out the details. Well, she had a few requirements of her own. "While we are on that point, then, I am not *your* sex toy. My cleavage is not open to your random groping, nor is my backside a target for your slaps. You will request my permission from now on before any such engagement."

She thought Truitt's shoulders sagged a bit at the reply. "Agreed. May I approach?"

He couldn't get much closer than they already were, but she nodded. "You may."

The berkis shuffled forward, his feet creating slight wrinkles in the coverlet. He stopped when their faces were nearly touching. His heart pounded in his chest at their proximity. She was breathtakingly beautiful to his eyes, but it wasn't merely her outward appearance that excited him. The faroko possessed a playfulness, an adventurous nature, and a passion that reached deep into his soul and wrenched it from its shell.

He had settled into his simple life, supplementing his time gambling in the Right Hand with the occasional larcenous outing. He had grown comfortable, complacent — almost forgetting the thrill of his thefts. The challenge had faded.

Some of that passion returned when the Grey Shadow arrived in Gravenmore. He found a purpose in that, with his chance to avenge his cousin-in-law and get justice for his family.

Then *she* came along, upsetting his world and rekindling his love for the challenging. She *was* a challenge for him on every level — physically, mentally, and most important of all, emotionally.

He'd had sexual partners before, and while his time with those females had been entertaining, there had never been enough of a connection with them to stay in the relationship. Now, though, he found one with the beautiful, daunting, aggravating, and mischievous woman before him.

Truitt reached out, laid a hand on her shoulder, and kissed her.

Calista threw her arms around him, returning the gesture as she pulled him in close. They had kissed multiple times before now, but this one was different. Their hands didn't stray, instead straining to hold the other even tighter. At the moment, all they wanted — all they needed — was that.

When they pulled away, the couple shared the same tender smile between them. Forehead pressed against forehead, fingers entwined.

A giggle from Calista finally broke the silence, and she looked down. She couldn't help herself. Their embrace had jammed the berkis's seemingly ever-alert truncheon tightly between her cleavage from below. "Someone found a resting place, after all."

He laughed, too, seeing its placement. "Please forgive him for not asking permission before his engagement."

"As long as you don't fault them for taking hold without first obtaining consent."

"Perish the thought." He lifted his gaze again and ran his fingers through her dark curls. "However, I had hoped it might have access to a more southernly abode."

She raised her own head, then planted a brief kiss on his chin. "Oh, that can be arranged. On a purely professional level, though. We wouldn't want to be seen as playing with toys."

Calista gripped his sides firmly again and lifted him slightly as she lay back on the bed. Once her head rested on the mattress, she lowered him to her stomach.

His erection fell a few inches shy of the mesh of hair covering her groyne, but Truitt quickly scrambled to reposition himself. The berkis planted his face just below the woman's breasts, making it hard for her to hear his next words, but she imagined, given how polite he had been during most of the evening, it was a request to enter.

While gentlemanly, she found it wholly in conflict with what she wanted. "Yes!" she yelled. "Yes, yes, yes!"

He heard. The engorged truncheon slid inside, its girth tickling the passage and eliciting a squeal from her. She grabbed his buttocks, her fingers clenching the pliable flesh, and pulled him into her as far as she could, moaning with the exertion.

His own hands slapped about until they took hold of her breasts. He used them as leverage to lift his head long enough to inhale deeply. Then his grip shifted to her hips, and he pushed his backside upwards.

Calista felt the retreat and eased up, letting the shaft slide partially back out. Then, in sync, he thrust, and she pulled, plunging it deep inside again. She let out a whimper, and the pair repeated the move. Up and down, in and out.

As they sped up, she bent her knees and shoved her feet into the bed. Her body rocked upward each time she yanked him forward. Some part of her mind went back to Peg's steam engine, driving its piston, pumping away relentlessly, and found herself matching its mental rhythm.

Pressure built inside her. She'd wanted him like this all night, their bodies locked together in the most physically intimate way possible. She felt him hanging onto her, his fingers jammed against her sides and tightening with each plunge. He was in her, their merger finally complete.

Truitt was hers!

The realisation drove her over the edge as he released inside her, and she screamed. Fingernails dug into his cheeks as she bucked one more time, a wave of blissful ecstasy coursing through her naked form. She moaned again, trying desperately to hold on to the feeling.

Then she relaxed. She felt Truitt's body go limp as well, and she placed her hands on his back. After another few moments, he found the energy to push himself out of her one last time. His member, thoroughly drenched and drooping, flopped happily against her leg.

She didn't know how long she lay there, but at some point, it registered the berkis was pulling himself up along her torso. After all that, he still had the strength to climb her! Calista gripped his shoulder and tugged him the rest of the way until their eyes met again.

They kissed. She shifted her arm and slid him down to the bed, where he flipped onto his back. Her legs closed, and she turned on her side, resting her head on his chest.

"You truly live in a pub?" he asked her after a few minutes. "I don't know why I hadn't considered such a residency before."

"It wasn't a pub when Armend got it," she replied, twirling a few strands of his belly hair between her fingers. "The Plump Pillows Hotel wasn't the sort of business he wanted to run, though."

"Perhaps a merger of the two would have been interesting," Truitt mused. "When an individual finds himself too drunk — or his companions do for him — he simply nips off to a comfy bed to sleep it off."

"This bed is plenty comfy," she replied, stretching her legs until her toes hung off the end, "if a little on the small side. But I find I'm liking things a little on the small side."

"And I've found a new appreciation for plump pillows," he said, tickling one of her nipples. "But not all of me is small, you know."

"Oh, I know," she giggled, then sighed, doubt still scratching away in the back of her mind. She needed to find out where they stood. "Are we good, Truitt Williams?"

"Sweet Calista Temira," he whispered, bringing his hand up to her chin and lifting it to meet his gaze. "We are splendid!"

She exhaled again, this time in relief. The pair, fighter and thief, lay there quietly for a while, basking in the afterglow, not just of their joining, but in finding someone to share themselves with.

"While I consider our merger complete," Truitt began after a bit, "I would not be opposed to exploring different forms of integration."

Calista ran her finger down his belly, then along the length of his staff, which showed signs of recovering. "I can see the possibilities," she agreed, "With one provision."

"Which is?"

She kissed his chest before looking up at him. "I want to be on top this time." When she saw his eyes widen, she laughed. "Don't worry. I promise not to squash you into marmalade."

As the pair restarted their lovemaking, their positions reversed, a recently obtained painting settled into its new surroundings. Anyone familiar with Truitt's flat — the number of which could be counted on a single hand — would not have noticed the fresh acquisition. It replaced an identical version which, until early this morning, had hung in its place. Well, nearly identical.

The Moaning Elisa, with her eternally crossed eyes, protruding tongue, and reddened cheeks, watched her new owner trapped beneath thick thighs on the bed below as he formed an expression very like her own. He had earned it, and the painting.

While the berkis thief feared removing any of the priceless treasures from the Duke's stolen collection, he didn't think anyone would notice a swap. As he said himself, none of them could tell an original from a forgery.

If someone examined the painting at that moment, though, they couldn't miss the titular female blinking. They might even have heard her sigh. "Not again."

Epilogue

CALISTA ENTERED THE Happy Swallow mid-morning the next day. She and Truitt had taken the evening to hammer out a few details of their partnership and explore their possibilities, as well as each other.

Armend's ledger lay open on the bar, with the skember jotting something onto one of its pages. He looked up as she approached. "Good morning! I was just wondering what assignment you might like. Stimulating while earning a high reward, is that correct?" His eyes returned to the book as he scanned the entries. "I have a few in mind, though none as well paying as Lady Aetherborne's, but I believe that was a blue moon occurrence."

The faroko hopped onto a stool. "Definitely. But that isn't the kind of job I want anymore."

"Alright," he said, still focused on the numerous scribblings. "Perhaps something more altruistic? I don't have any opportunities to recover kidnap victims at the moment, but I can send out feelers. Perhaps my network can discover a similar job."

"Not that either." She paused, considering his reaction. "You don't seem surprised I came through the front door instead of down the stairs."

"While wearing the same clothes as yesterday, yet somehow smelling fresher." He met her gaze now. "And something else. It is not my place to track your whereabouts at every hour."

Calista looked down and blushed. She still hadn't replaced the buttons and hastily placed a hand over her chest. After her night with Truitt, she got her bath, but little after that could be considered clean. A few debts were collected, and she ensured the berkis would have a sore arse for hours. It turned out to be quite a productive interlude. Now she needed to take steps to make sure it proceeded.

"I am unsure if you possess a listing for what I am looking for," she told Armend, remembering what she and Truitt discussed. "I want to be of help to others still, but the really troubled. Not the rich needing to protect their precious items or shopkeepers having trouble with pilferers. I want the dirty jobs. The ones which will truly make a difference. Ones that will allow me to go to bed each night, perhaps not richer in money, but knowing that my day was spent making someone else's life better." She finished with a sigh, surprised at her own speech. "I don't suppose you have anything like that."

The skember bartender stroked a horn, then shook his head. "Those are some lofty requirements, noble as they are. I am afraid to say there is nothing in this ledger that you would find suitable." He moved his hand to the book's side and closed it softly.

Calista felt her stomach fall. "I understand. My partner and I will search for another source of information."

"Is this partner the reason you entered through the front door instead of coming down the stairs, wearing the same outfit as yesterday with the odour of something else?"

He does know! she thought, her cheeks flushing. "It is."

"Then I must say it is about time. Let me find a proper mission." His fingers coiled around the edges of the black journal and lifted it from the bar.

She looked at him curiously. "You said you had nothing like that."

"Not in this ledger, no." With a deft motion, he slid the book under the wooden top. When his hands reemerged, they were gripping another ledger, red and three times thicker than the other. He dropped it onto the bar with a thud and proceeded to flick it open.

"This one, however, should keep you and your partner quite busy."

The End

Races

Faroko - Faroko are graceful humanoids with tall, rounded ears similar to a donkey's. A long, semi-prehensile tail extends from their lower back, often swaying with their movements. The average female faroko stands between 4'10" and 5'4", while their male counterparts are slightly taller, ranging from 5'4" to 5'6". Their slender build makes them agile.

Berkis - Berkis are short humanoids with flat noses and bodies are covered with coarse hair. Females are petite, standing between 2'6" and 3'0", while males are a little taller, ranging from 2'10" to 3'8".

Skember - Skember are the smallest of the races, with goat-like back legs, similar to fauns. They have curved horns adorning their heads and short, pointed ears beneath them. Female skembers typically stand between 1'4" and 1'8", with males ranging from 1'6" to 2'4". They are excellent jumpers and sprinters.

Orv - Orv are towering, powerfully built humanoids with a rugged physique, thick fingers, and a head like a rhinoceros, complete with prominent horns. Their tough skin and strength makes them the perfect candidates for tough tasks. Female orvs average between 5'2" and 5'8" in height, while males are slightly taller, ranging from 5'6" to 5'10".

Characters

Truitt William Hobart - Male berkis. Lives in the Mids but dresses poorly and frequents the Ward to gamble

Calista Temira - Overly tall female faroko. Uses her height and fighting skills to hire herself out for odd jobs

Armend Quinn - Male skember. Owns the Happy Swallow Pub and collects information about tasks for Calista

Silas - Male orv. Very polite, spectacle-wearing assistant to Armend

Raffles "Sticky" Oliver - Male skember. Gambler and card playing associate of Truitt

Faye Runaway - Female faroko. Gossip and card playing associate of Truitt

Hugh - Male orv. Rarely speaking card playing associate of Truitt

Kate - Female faroko. Server at the Right Hand Casino

Lavinia - Young female orv. Lives in the Ward with her mother. Friends with Truitt

Fenton Lightfoot - Male berkis. Fighting trainer to Calista in the Harden Up Gymnasium

Peg Pumper - Female skember. Mechanician who maintains the exercise machines in the Harden Up Gymnasium

The Grey Shadow - Infamous thief who has been moving from one city to the next, stealing each city's most valuable treasures

Duke Patrick Cameron - Male faroko. Nobleman hunting the Grey Shadow

Maurice - Male orv. Henchman for hire

Bertram - Male orv. Henchman for hire and slightly dumber companion to Maurice

Lady Aetherborne - Female faroko. Noblewoman and owner of the Dragon Eye Gem

Beatrice - Female berkis. Servant of Lady Aetherborne

Mattigan Chambers - Male berkis. Attendant at Get Wet Bathhouse

Madeline - Portable steam motor Peg uses to soup up exercise equipment

Zusa Lolly - Female faroko. Owner of Great Buns Bakery

Ned - Huge male orv. Henchman of Duke Patrick Cameron

Joseph - Male orv. Henchman of Duke Patrick Cameron

Winston - Male orv. Henchman of Duke Patrick Cameron who serves food

Tobias - Male orv. Henchman of Duke Patrick Cameron

who forgets the wine

Hedgecock brothers - Male skembers. Barnaby, Buford, and Brisco. Henchmen for hire.

Rowland Stephen Ambrose - Male faroko. Scientist wielding an experimental electric gun

Archie Tinker & Laura Kipps - Male orv and female berkis. Fighters for hire wielding whips and guns

Lucius Thorne - Male faroko. Police officer

Percival Whitlock - Male skember. Police officer

Reginald Hightower - Male orv. Police sergeant

Victor - Male Skember. Childhood friend of Calista's

Gravenmore locations

The city of Gravenmore sits in the Leverhelm region of the Imperialist Kingdom of Prettanika. The Lampwick river flows through it, though the smoke-belching factories on its shore no longer required the flowing water to power their engines.

Gravenmore is divided unofficially into four sections.

Sunside - Western side of the city, full of nobles, rich, and very well off

Mids - The middle class and major part of the city, sitting between the Sunside and the Ward

Ward - Poorer part of the city, once similar to the Mids, but largely abandoned when the factories took hold in the Rookery

Rookery - Poorest part of the city on the eastern side. Where the factories sit and its workers live

YOU'LL FIND A few locations in these sections that are mentioned or significant to the story.

The Right Hand - Casino in the Ward, frequented by those who have too much time on their hands or too little will to escape its temptations

The Happy Swallow Pub - Converted pub from an old hotel in the Mids. Armend won it in a card game, and believes the previous owners might try to take it back

Get Wet Bathhouse - Elegant Bathhouse in the Mids, frequently visited by Calista, much to the annoyance of the men who also attend it

Harden Up Gymnasium - Gymnasium in the Mids. Hosts specialised exercise machines which never work quite as well as expected

Great Buns Bakery - Bakery in the Mids. Owned by Zusa Lolly, who would send orphans to prison — and does

Amberlux Manor - In the Sunside. House of Lord and Lady Celeste, who owns the Dragon Eye Gem

White Cliffs Estate - Fine mansion in the Sunside. Owned by Lord Emberstone. Temporarily used by Duke Patrick Cameron

Bedeviled - A line of five abandoned houses in the Ward thought to be haunted. Children should not go near it. Nor should anyone else.

Truitt's place - Flat on the second floor of a converted townhouse in the Mids. Has some expensive additions which would make any bath loving faroko jealous

Ironstaff Station - Police station in the Mids. Converted from a bank. Not a good place for orphans or unfairly charged females

Just A Cigar - Tobacconist in the Mids that stocks a variety of cigars that Armend enjoys. He has Calista pick up a box at times when the pub keeps him too busy. She gets her Pear Drops there

Keep It Trim - Barber-shop in the Mids which Calista visits sometimes, but not often, as she prefers a longer hairstyle

Terms & Slang

Adam and Eve's togs - naked

addled - unable to think

arse - ass

barking at a knot - doing something that is a waste of time

basket-making - love making

beadle - a minor parish official

beggar poor - very poor

biddy - a woman

bit o' raspberry - an attractive woman

blackguard - a scoundrel

bloody - an exclamation of anger

bluebottle - a police officer

bobby - a police officer

bobtail - a lewd woman or prostitute

bolts - an exclamation

bounder - a morally reprehensible person

bricky - brave or fearless

bubbies - breasts

buck - a handsome man

bugger it - a curse

bumbailiff - a bailiff who makes arrests

buttocks - arse cheeks

chavy - a child

cheeky - impudent

chirky - cheerful; an expression of joy

chuckaboo - a good friend

chuckle-head - a stupid person

church bell - a talkative woman

clack box - a talkative person

clangers - an exclamation

codswallop - foolish or untrue

coker-nuts - breasts

collie shangie - a quarrel or fight

copped a fright - become scared

copper - a police officer

copper's cage - a prison cell

copper's shanty - a police station

cracksman - a burglar

crafty dodger - a person skilled in deception

dagnabit - a curse

damn and blast - a curse

dandy - a man overly concerned with how he looks

devil-dodger - a priest

dollymop - an amateur prostitute

dolt - an idiot

don't sell me a dog - don't lie to me

dowager - An elderly lady of dignified demeanour; a rich widow

draw the long bow - lie or exaggerate

dullard - a stupid person

duller than ditchwater - boring

dunderhead - a stupid person

fancy bits - lady bits

featherhead - a foolish person

fiddlesticks - a curse

filcher - a thief

firkytoodling - kissing, cuddling

flapdoodle - a sexually incompetent man

flummadiddle - foolish or worthless

footpad - thief

foozler - one who does things clumsily

foppish - a man who is overly concerned about his clothes and appearance

gabble-monger - a person who talks a lot and gossips

gadzooks - an exclamation of surprise or annoyance

gaol - jail

gas-pipes - tight pants

gasser -a person who talks a lot

gentlemen in blue - police

gibfaced - ugly

gigglemug - a person who is constantly smiling; foolishly happy

gollumpus - a large, clumsy, loutish fellow

Greek lover - gay partner

groyne - groin

hang it all - a curse

harlot - a prostitute

have the morbs - temporary melancholy

haybag - a woman

hen - a female

hightail it - run away

hoary - grey or white from age

in the altogether - naked

jackanape - a conceited, impertinent person

jammiest bit of jams - attractive young females

jewels - man bits

jobber knot - a tall, stupid fellow

join giblets - have sex

kettledrums - breasts

kneebiter - an annoying person

leg it - run

lily-livered - a coward

long walk to the stone jug - go to prison

mad as hops - excitable

madder than a box of frogs - crazy

madge - lady bits

meater - a coward

mechanician - a person skilled in constructing or repairing machines

men in blue - police

miscreant - a person who behaves badly

mollycoddle - a pampered man

Mrs Jones - a room with a toilet; privy

muff - lady bits

muttonhead - a slow-witted person

my giddy aunt - an exclamation of surprise or shock

nattering - talking idly

nick - jail; to steal

nicking - stealing

noddle - empty headed

nug - a loved one

nut - a head

pease porridge - a type of porridge made from yellow split peas

petticoat lane - lady bits

pie hole - a mouth

pigeon-livered - cowardly

poltroon - a wretched coward

pompatic - pompous

popinjay - a pretentious person

prig - a thief

pulpit-pusher - a priest

push off - go away

quod - prison

ratbag - a general insult

rookery - poorest part of a city

rum doings - strange or suspicious activities or events

rumbled - found out the truth

sauce-box - a mouth

shabbaroon - an ill-dressed, shabby person

shaft - stab

shag-bag - a poor, sneaking fellow

shebang - situation or affair

skedaddle - run away

skilamalink - someone who cheats or swindles

sky pilot - a chaplain

sniffy - having a haughty attitude

sniffys - snobs

snuffed it - died

snuffler - a murderer

soused - drunk

spoony - a silly or foolish person

square enough - fair

starkers - naked

stone jug - prison

take the egg - to win

tallywags - testicles

taradiddler - liar

tarnation - damnation

third leg - male member

tip the velvet - cunnilingus

toast your blooming eyebrows - a polite way of telling someone to go to hell

toff - a stereotypical aristocrat

toffness - a stereotypical aristocrat

tommy-rot - nonsense

toplofter - an arrogant person

topper - a hat

tot - a child

tot-hunting - prowling for women

trollop - a sexually promiscuous woman

truncheon - male member

unlicked cub - a lout who has never been taught manners

up the pole without your pants - confused

water closet - room with a toilet

well-heeled - well-off, rich

well-to-do - has money

what the deuce - a curse

About the Author

A. D. RIDER was born in the wrong century, so now he explores other times through writing. He specialises in gaslamp romance fantasy adventures. Blending elements of Victorian-era intrigue, magic, and heartfelt romance, he crafts stories that transport readers to enchanting worlds filled with daring escapades and passionate encounters. When he isn't penning his next adventure, he can be found spending time with his dogs and enjoying nature as they drag him along.

If you enjoyed this book, please leave a review!

To keep up with A. D. Rider along with special deals and new releases, please join his newsletter, *Hot Air.*

https://www.authoradrider.com/subscribe